THE DEEPER I FALL

ERIKA KELLY

CW01496986

THE DEEPER I FALL

Erika Kelly

Cover design and Formatting by Serendipity Formatting

Cover image by Letizia Haessig IG @lety_

Edits by Theresa Walsh and Honey Palomino

Praise for The Calamity Falls series

KEEP ON LOVING YOU

"I adored this book! It is exactly what I love in a second-chance romance. The characters are so vibrant and real, I was rooting for them with every page." —*USA Today* Bestseller Devney Perry

"*KEEP ON LOVING YOU* is such a fun and sexy second-chance romance that I didn't want it to end. Their connection is a swoony blend of tender first love and sizzling heat, and Erika Kelly delivers a highly entertaining and sigh-worthy romance that shouldn't be missed."
—Mary Dube, USA Today

WE BELONG TOGETHER

"I loved every sweet, heart-wrenching, crazy, mixed-up minute of this book. It was an emotional journey from the first chapter to the last. This is Erika Kelly at her best, and this is a not-to-be-missed book!" —Sharon Slick Reads, Guilty Pleasures Book Reviews

"Erika Kelly damn near pulled my heart from my chest with Delilah and Will's story. It's so well-written that you feel everything. My heart got tugged so hard! I honestly cried at a few moments in the book. I fell all the way in love with "Wooby." It's hard not to, really." —Ree Cee's Books

THE VERY THOUGHT OF YOU

"Wow, THE VERY THOUGHT OF YOU was simply OUTSTANDING! This second chance, friends to lovers romance is enchanting and entertaining." —Spellbound Stories

"I just finished this story, and I want to start all over again. Or maybe at the start of series. To once again feel the events, the emotions, that brought these amazing characters together. To hear the banter and the arguments, the sorrow, the loss and the happiness that brought a family together and closer." —Nerdy, Dirty, and Flirty

JUST THE WAY YOU ARE

"An alpha cowboy and a smart, sassy princess collide in JUST THE WAY YOU ARE in Erika Kelly's latest, and it was fabulous! I was cheering for Brodie and Rosalina with every page. If you love stories with heart, steam, and plenty of swoon, don't miss this one!" —USA Today Bestselling Author J.H. Croix

"With the Calamity Falls series, Kelly doesn't shy away from charming. She captivates with delectable characters that wrap themselves around a heart. From the first hello to the final goodbye, Rosalina and Brodie are a match made out of the unpredictable, but the sweetest kind of heaven. JUST THE WAY YOU ARE is the perfect example of why I am hooked on this series. SWOONWORTHY READ!" —Hopeless Romantic Book Reviews

IT WAS ALWAYS YOU

"This book was full of every emotion you could ever feel. Gigi and Cassian proved you can conquer anything with true love." —Cat's Guilty Pleasure

"I could not put this book down! Erika Kelly always delivers a great love story and never disappoints! I recommend this book for romance lovers looking to get lost in a great love story." —Reading in Pajamas

CAN'T HELP FALLING IN LOVE

"I love everything about this emotional and sexy, second chance story. Erika Kelly writes a story that makes me feel like I'm right there with the two main characters, Beckett and Coco. It is a slow burn, passionate story with lots of underlying tension. I not only enjoyed this story, but I found it impossible to put down." —Cocktails and Books

"I loved everything about this book. I loved all the characters, from Beckett, 'I don't believe in love,' to single mom, small business-owning, closed-off Coco, to a fairy-believing five-year-old who will steal your heart! I cannot gush enough about how spectacular I thought this book was." – Bookcase and Coffee

WHOLE LOTTA LOVE

"BRILLIANT! This book was incredible, I could not put this book down, that is how good Lu and Xander's story was. I fell in love with these two characters instantly." – Harlequin Junkie

"Whole Lotta Love was absolutely perfect! You will instantly love this couple and their journey to find happiness!" – Just Love Books

YOU'RE STILL THE ONE

"Griffin and Stella really are soulmates. They bring out the best of each other, and when they're together, everything is better. Their world is better with the love they feel for each other. And I think they made my world better a bit, too." – Jersey Girl's Bookshelf

"WOW! WOW! WOW! Welcome to all the feels! I ADORED Stella and Griffin's story. I was completely lost in this book and didn't want to put it down. I FELT everything, and I can't tell you how much I loved it." – Books According to Abby

Titles by Erika Kelly

The Calamity Falls series:
KEEP ON LOVING YOU
WE BELONG TOGETHER
THE VERY THOUGHT OF YOU
JUST THE WAY YOU ARE
IT WAS ALWAYS YOU
CAN'T HELP FALING IN LOVE
COME AWAY WITH ME
WHOLE LOTTA LOVE
YOU'RE STILL THE ONE
THE DEEPER I FALL
LOVE ME LIKE YOU DO

Have you read the Rock Star Romance series? Come meet the sexy rockers of Blue Fire:

YOU REALLY GOT ME
I WANT YOU TO WANT ME
TAKE ME HOME TONIGHT
MORE THAN A FEELING

Sign up for my newsletter to read the EXCLUSIVE novella for my readers only! You'll get two chapters a month of this super sexy, fun romance! #rockstarromance #teenidolturnedboyfriend Also, get PLANES, TRAINS, AND HEAD OVER HEELS for FREE! I hope you'll come hang out with me on Facebook, Twitter, Instagram, Goodreads, and Pinterest or in my private reader group.

This book is dedicated to Sharon for always, always being there.

Acknowledgments

- Dear Superman, we have walked through the fire and never stopped holding hands. I love you.
- Thank you to Sharon for being the best friend in the world.
- Thank you to Erica for being a friend in this crazy business.
- Thank you to Melissa for always straightening my crown.
- Thank you to Theresa for landing in my life at the exact moment I needed you.
- Thank you to Honey for stepping in at the last minute and doing such a great job!
- Thank you to Olivia for being my partner in all things romance, cooking competitions, dessert, and Sunday brunch.
- And thank you to the readers, bloggers, reviewers, and all my author friends who make this job so richly rewarding and worthwhile.

Prologue

Tonight, Seraphina Maud Crutchley was a superstar.

She didn't feel like one very often. Rarely, in fact. But in this moment, with the spotlight trained on her as she stood in the middle of the ballroom surrounded by every single luminary in London's elite, she felt a wild mix of emotion: pride, certainly, but also the teensiest sense of imposter syndrome.

Honestly, she didn't know what to do with all the attention, so she smiled and kept her focus on the stage.

"The Lumley Foundation has hosted this ball for over a century." The CEO, in his black tailcoat and white bow tie, addressed the crowd of glittering donors. "Thanks to the addition of Phinny to our team, we've seen our donations quadruple. With her sparkling personality and boundless compassion, she is most certainly a bright star among us. Thank you, Phinny, for putting together such a spectacular array of auction items." He gave her a nod, and the audience broke into applause.

Her stepfather squeezed her shoulder, and her mum whispered in her ear, "I'm so proud of you, darling."

It was the most glorious moment of her life. Thanks to the blinding light in her eyes, she couldn't see the audience, so she just waved her appreciation. When the applause didn't die down, she began to wonder what was going on. The acknowledgement was lovely, but surely, she hadn't done anything *that* exceptional.

She supposed scoring a reclusive billionaire's superyacht for a week was quite a coup, but still…

This response is a bit much.

It was only when the spotlight turned away from her that she discovered the reason for the crowd's enthusiasm. Cameron Lumley had taken the stage. Shaking the CEO's hand, he grabbed the microphone. Then, her elegant, handsome boyfriend flashed his movie star smile. "Good evening."

Even though his family ran the foundation, he had no reason to be on stage right then. He might not run events, but he sure was an impressive sight. His custom-made suit hugged his broad shoulders and muscular thighs while his commanding presence captured the attention of everyone in the room. "On behalf of my family, I'd like to thank you all for your support this evening. As you know, the charity is my life's work, so it's only fitting that the woman who owns my heart now plays such a central role in it."

Surprise jolted her.

I own his heart?

They'd been together a while, but they hardly had some grand love affair. Not even close.

What's he going on about?

Her parents moved to stand on either side of her, enormous smiles stretching across their faces.

Cameron extended a hand. "Darling, please come up here."

She almost shouted *Why?* She didn't need to get up on stage. The band should start playing, and the patrons should go back to dancing. That was the order of events.

Her mum took the champagne flute out of her hand. "Don't just stand there."

With all eyes on her, what choice did Phinny have? But while her brain sent the signal to her legs, they refused to cooperate. A wave of nausea hit, and she went hot all over.

Her stepfather set his hand on the small of her back and gave her a nudge. "Go on now. Don't embarrass us."

That got her moving. As the crowd parted, she made her way to the steps. On some level, she knew what was happening, but her mind was racing, and she couldn't think clearly.

Please don't do this.

We're nowhere near ready for this. They'd grown up together but had only begun dating during their last year at university.

Casually dating.

Cameron stood center stage, while the CEO reached for her hand and helped her up the stairs. It was hard enough to move in her ball gown and shapewear bodysuit, but with her legs shaking, she moved like a newborn foal.

Which was fitting since her heart was positively *galloping*.

"Darling…" Cameron reached for her hand, kissing her palm.

And then, he dropped to a knee.

In the middle of the grandest charity event of the year, her boyfriend—emphasis on *friend*—was about to propose. "I have loved you my entire life, but it was only when I saw you coming out of Trinity Hall that I knew it was time to start our future together. Every day has gotten better, and I can't wait to spend my life with you. Seraphina, will you do me the honor of becoming my wife?"

With the audience's collective gasp, the air was sucked out of the room.

She couldn't breathe. Blood roared in her ears, and her vision blurred around the edges.

In the silence, she had the strangest sensation of floating. She could picture herself grabbing a handful of helium balloons and drifting off the stage, out the window, and sailing over the rooftops of London.

Cameron's smile faltered, and it jerked her back to the moment. She couldn't embarrass him. "Yes. Of course, yes."

Relief washed over his handsome features, and he stood to his full height. He wrapped an arm around her and faced the ballroom, raising their clasped hands as though she were a trophy.

In the middle of the audience, Phinny found her parents. She'd never seen them so happy.

But why? The moment felt surreal. She'd never gushed about him to her parents. Never once talked about marriage or babies or any kind of future with him. They were two people from similar backgrounds who had fun together. *We're just dating.*

Marriage?

Standing on that stage, she felt like a paper doll cut-out.

With a tug, she was led back down the stairs.

Immediately, well-wishers swarmed them. His family, their friends…everyone was gleeful.

And it was all a lie.

Because she couldn't marry him.

Flee. It wasn't a thought so much as an alarm that rang through her body. She wrenched her hand out of his grip and made her way out of the ballroom. When she saw a sign for a powder room, she ducked inside and locked the door.

Oh, God. What is happening?

As she ran cold water over her hands, she looked up into her wild-eyed reflection. Her pulse pounded violently. Why had he proposed publicly? Now, calling it off would create a scandal.

It didn't have to be like this.

A hard rap jerked her attention from the mirror.

"Phinny?" *Cameron.* "Open up."

Angry that he'd put her in a terrible position, she opened the door, grabbed his wrist, and pulled him inside the lavender-scented bathroom. "What was that?"

His eyes flickered with hurt. "What do you mean, what was that? It was a marriage proposal."

"But why? Cameron, we're not ready for that."

"We've been dating three years. When did you think we'd be ready?"

"I don't know." *Never.* "We haven't talked about it."

"What on earth do you think we've been doing all this time?"

"We've been *dating.*"

"Yes, on a course toward marriage. Why else would I be exclusive with someone if not with the intention of marrying her? Why are you acting like this came out of nowhere? You can't pretend you didn't know it was the path we've been on."

She couldn't argue his point, and it flustered her. Because, really, it uncovered a truth that would only hurt his feelings. *I don't love you.* "I can't possibly get married now. I haven't done anything with my life."

His jaw snapped shut, like he was trying to contain his anger. "Whatever you want to do, what better way to do it than as Cameron Lumley's wife?"

Obviously, that made perfect sense. Marrying into one of the wealthiest families in the United Kingdom would afford her any opportunity her heart desired. And it wasn't like Cameron cared what she did. That wouldn't change once they got married. He'd still go off with his mates on trips, and she'd go clubbing with hers. Sometimes, they'd do the holidays together, while other times, they'd be with their own families.

She knew exactly what her life with him would look like because that was the kind of marriage his parents had. And she didn't want to wind up like his mum, spending more time with her wine than her husband.

She pulled off the engagement ring. "I'm sorry, but I'm not ready to get married."

He just stared at her as though waiting for her to laugh and say *Gotcha. Of course, I'll marry you, silly!* "Are you serious?"

"Quite." His presumption that she'd just fall in line with some plan he'd never voiced irked her. "Cameron, come on. Do you even love me?"

"Of course, I do." He seemed calmer, as if they could now settle things. "I like you better than anyone else we know."

Well, there's a ringing endorsement for marriage. "And I like you. But I need more time."

"How much time?"

"I don't know."

"Are we talking a few weeks?"

Weeks? "I'm twenty-four. What's the rush?"

His expression shuttered. "Waiting these three years has cost me nearly two million pounds."

She flinched as if he'd flicked cold water at her face. As soon as he married, he'd tap into his trust fund. With each child he added to his family, the monthly allowance would go up.

Quite the incentive to keep the Lumley line going.

She'd known that. So, why did it sound so ugly to hear him say it out loud?

He must not have liked her crestfallen expression because he reached for her elbows and bent his knees to look her in the eyes. "Darling, there's no one I'd rather spend my life with than you. You make me laugh…you make me happy."

"Well, yes, because I don't require anything of you."

He chuckled. "Most definitely, that's one for the plus column. But it works both ways. We give each other room to live our lives. Trust me, that's a good thing. We'll never grow restless or resentful."

I want more.

And what a bombshell revelation that was. She'd just been going along, having fun, not questioning anything, and she'd given no thought to where she was heading. Now that he'd forced her to think about it, she had to accept she hadn't done a damn thing with her life.

She couldn't say what she wanted to do exactly, but for

the first time, she felt something missing. Something between the phases of parties, clubs, and shopping and getting married and popping out babies. "I need more time."

The smile vanished. He straightened. "No."

Fear sliced through her. She might not be ready to marry him, but she'd never contemplated a life without him. Like her parents, he was a major cog in the machine of her world, and she didn't know how to operate without all of them. "No, you won't wait?"

"I have waited. Three years is more than enough." He softened. "Look, you'd make a smashing stylist. Or you and your mum could open a boutique. Once we're married, you can use a portion of the extra fifty thousand pounds a month to do whatever you want. It doesn't matter to me, but we either get married now or it's done."

"It's done? Or we're done?"

"We're done. If you're not ready to marry me after three years, then I've got no reason to believe you'll be ready by four years or even five."

"I can't imagine my life without you, but I can't marry you because you've run out of patience with me. I'm sorry, Cameron." She took in the proud jut of his chin and the look in his eyes that screamed *Are you seriously going to walk away from me?* She liked him very much. They'd had a lot of fun together. But she didn't love him.

And so, she walked out the door.

Cut from her mooring, she felt adrift…uneasy. She hustled toward the exit as though the manor were on fire. The tight silk liner of her dress and the five-inch stilettos hampered her progress, though, as people rushed toward her, eager to share the happy occasion.

She couldn't talk to anyone right then, so she hurried on. Pulling out her phone, she tried to text her parents' driver, but her trembling fingers kept tapping the wrong pads, making her delete and start over.

"Seraphina?" Her mum glided along the hallway.

"Where are you going?" her stepfather asked. "We've just opened the bubbly to toast your wonderful news. Let's find Cameron. Come along."

The moment her mum reached her, the smile faded. "What's going on?"

Phinny handed over her phone. "Can you please ask Fergus to come 'round?"

Her stepfather snatched it. "We'll do no such thing. All of our friends are here to celebrate with you."

"There's nothing to celebrate." Phinny let out a tight breath. "We're not getting married."

"Of course, you are." Andrew's eyebrows shot up. "Don't be ridiculous."

When she'd met him as a little girl, she'd called him by his first name, but since she couldn't pronounce Andrew, she'd wound up saying Dewzy. For the first time since he'd come into her life, that term of endearment didn't fit. In this moment, when he cared more about his reputation than her feelings, he was purely her stepfather. "I gave the ring back. I'm not marrying him."

"Seraphina." Her mother sounded appalled.

"I told him I needed more time, and he said he wouldn't give me any."

Clasping her wrist, Andrew led them to an alcove. "You've known each other your entire lives. How much more time could you possibly need?"

"There are things I still want to do."

"Like what?" her mum whispered harshly. "You want to shop more? Travel more? Have more spa days? What exactly are you so eager to do?"

Like a can on the road flattened by a tire, Phinny's spirit compressed under the weight of her mum's words. She'd never considered herself frivolous. She'd been living the only life she'd ever known. "I don't know. But I would rather find out than get married to a man I don't love."

Her stepfather had always indulged her, and in return she'd tried very hard to please him. So, to see the tick in his jaw, the color flood his cheeks, truly upset her. "What on earth do you think we've been doing, Seraphina?"

"What do you mean?" A sickening feeling rolled through her.

"You don't have a proper job, you live in an apartment we own, you use a credit card we've given you…why do you think we've been supporting you all this time?"

The great beast of fear loomed over her like a dark, menacing shadow. "I—" Her mind went blank.

"We've supported you because you were going to marry Cameron," her mum said. "And Lumleys do philanthropy, just as I've done. Just as you've been doing. *That* has been our expectation. If we thought for a moment you had no intention of marrying him, you'd have been polishing your CV and applying for jobs your last year at university. You'd have been paying your own bills upon graduation."

"Now, go and find your fiancé," her stepfather said. "And get things back on track. Or the locks to your Knightsbridge apartment will be changed by morning."

"What?" She could barely process his words. He couldn't possibly mean to throw her out onto the streets?

"Darling, please." Her mum patted his arm.

Oh, thank God. Her mum would always take care of her. They were a team. Her parents were upset. She understood that. But they'd never make her marry a man she didn't love.

But then her mum's features hardened. "Let her make some calls, see which of her friends will allow her to sleep on their couch until she gets a job."

Chapter One

TEN MONTHS LATER

"No one liked Kurt Grevers."

In the mountain chapel, the scent of lilies and melting candle wax mixed with perfume and cologne. The heavy weight of loss bore down on Declan Cadell, and he looked away from the eulogist and down at his shiny black dress shoes.

I *liked him.*

"But everyone respected him."

Yes. Declan's head jerked up. *That's exactly right.*

"They respected his work ethic. To this day—ten years after retiring from the sport he gave his heart and soul to —he remains the top goal scorer, assist producer, and point scorer in NHL history." The lawyer's gaze roamed the packed room. "They respected his sportsmanship. You won't find a single player anywhere who'd speak ill of him. But his legacy goes well beyond his athletic achievements. He will forever be remembered for his loyalty, his integrity, and his generosity. He's done a hell of a lot more for this town than anyone knows, since he didn't want the attention."

The man's tone held a challenge, like he was pissed at people for underestimating the hockey legend. But Declan didn't know why. Anyone who knew Kurt thought the world of him. And for those who hadn't seen past his gruff exterior…Kurt hadn't given two fucks about them. He hadn't needed anyone.

Except for us. Declan couldn't help scanning the room. He hadn't wanted to see if the guys had come to the funeral because if they hadn't…well, he didn't think he could get past that.

Kurt had given them everything. It wasn't his fault they'd blown it all to hell.

In the crowd of townspeople, hockey players, and sportscasters, Declan found each of his childhood friends —now grown into men. *Good.*

He was just tuning back into the eulogy when his gaze snagged on a woman he didn't recognize. In a rugged western town like Calamity, Wyoming, she stood out with her sleek blond hair, pouty red lips, and enough bling to be seen from a space station.

"If you got a smile out of Kurt, you felt like you'd won the lottery." The man delivering the eulogy wore a bolo tie over his western dress shirt. "It was rare but genuine. And today, if he's watching from up in heaven, you can bet he's smiling. He'd be touched to see how many people turned out to bid him farewell. Because he might not have wanted to talk on the phone, and nobody left a dinner or a meeting quicker than he did, but that didn't mean he didn't like you. It just meant he wasn't a man for small talk. He got to the heart of the matter and got out. So, on Kurt's behalf, I'd like to thank you for joining us here today, as we lay our teammate, father, neighbor, client, and friend to rest. I hope you'll join us in the community room for a lunch hosted by the Cooters and provided by Harley and Lu Emporium."

The quiet murmur of chatter filled the room as people slowly made their way out of the chapel. Declan wasn't in the mood to talk to anyone, so he moved against the flow toward the side exit. He'd head to the ranch, the only place where he could say a real goodbye to the man who'd meant so much to him.

But he was blocked by a tall, broad-shouldered dude in an expensive suit. With a big grin, Jaime Dupree clapped a hand on his shoulder. "Hey, man. Long time, no see."

"Yep." Not that Declan held a grudge, but Jaime was the reason their friendships had blown up ten years ago. That aside, he didn't feel like talking to anyone. "I'll see you around."

Unaffected, Jaime said, "You'll see me in Harrison's office in fifteen minutes."

Declan's gaze moved to the podium, now vacated. Harrison was Kurt's attorney and the eulogist. "Why?"

"He needs to talk to us about Kurt's will."

"What does his will have to do with us? We're not related to him." But hope flickered in his chest. There were a few things he wanted. Like the potato masher that had been in Kurt's family for generations. It might seem lame, but he associated it with dinner at the ranch.

He'd like pretty much anything from the hutch in the living room. It was stuffed with artifacts from the Grevers family. Kurt would never have thought to give any of it to one of his players, though. Everything would go to family.

Jaime shrugged. "We're about to find out."

With the church only a few blocks outside of town, they walked to the law office. It was a perfect late spring day in Calamity. A small Old West town just outside Grand Teton National Park, it didn't get a lot of days like this when the skies were cloudless and blue, the air warm and breezy. He breathed it in, filling his lungs and taking in the startling background of the mountains jutting out of the earth.

"So, a coach, huh?" Jaime asked as he waved at someone biking past.

"Assistant." Together, they crossed the street. "But yeah."

"You like it? Coaching?"

Declan cut a look to his former friend. Like Kurt, he'd never been much for small talk. And with an elephant in the room so big he could hardly see around it, he was even less inclined to shoot the shit.

But now wasn't the time to talk about what had gone down ten years ago. Not on the same day they'd laid their mentor to rest. "I like it a lot."

"You don't miss playing?"

"Sure, I do." But he still got a lot of ice time, so he didn't mind too much. "Don't you?"

"I miss it every day. Don't know if you heard, but I wound up going to college here and playing on the team. Coached it for a few years until Kurt offered me the job with Mountain West." Jaime hunched a shoulder. "I like coaching, too. But it's not the same as playing."

Nineteen years ago, Kurt had caught four rowdy boys building a dirt bike course on his land. Instead of calling the police, he'd started an elite travel hockey team. Declan and his friends had gone from being reckless kids to driven, high-performing athletes. They'd been inseparable.

And look at us now. All four of us in that chapel, and we didn't even acknowledge each other. He should've said something. He shouldn't have left without shaking their hands.

As they reached the office building, Jaime asked, "How long are you in town?"

"I head back tomorrow." Training camp started mid-September—so in twelve weeks—and the coaches met over the summer to watch tape and pinpoint the weaknesses on the team and to onboard new players.

Jaime laughed. "You haven't changed a bit, man. Gotta get you drunk tonight, then maybe you'll talk." As they reached the building, he stepped ahead and opened the door.

Declan had lived in big cities for a long time now, so everything in Calamity looked squat in comparison. No skyscrapers, no gleaming tinted-window office buildings. Just a lot of green space, boutiques, and cowboy bars and restaurants.

Once inside the air-conditioned office, Jaime headed for the reception desk. "Jaime Dupree and Declan Cadell. Harrison asked to see us."

The elderly receptionist gave them a compassionate smile. "He's expecting you. Go on in."

Declan entered first, coming to a hard stop when he saw the fancy woman from the chapel sitting by herself in a corner of the spacious office. Booker and Cole—the rest of their foursome—sat in chairs facing the desk, scrolling through their phones. Acting like strangers.

Well, that sucked.

The woman had to be Kurt's daughter. It made sense she'd be here. *But why the four of us?*

The attorney glanced up from his paperwork. "Ah, wonderful. Everyone's here." He gestured to the empty chairs.

Declan nodded to the men who'd once been his best friends in the world. Both stood and each brought him in for swift hugs and back thumps. He noticed Booker didn't do the same to Jaime.

Once they all took their seats, Booker said, "All right, so what's up? What are we all doing here?"

"I'm Harrison Goodman, Kurt's attorney, and as the executor of his will, I'll be guiding the estate through the probate process." Gathering a pile of papers, he got up and came around the big desk.

The woman watched him, growing more anxious as he moved down the row of former hockey players, handing out documents. When he reached the last chair, the one closest to her, she lifted her arm, but the lawyer had nothing left and returned to his seat.

It was just a flash. If Declan hadn't been curious about her, he would've missed it. But he caught the deep stab of rejection that pinched her features. In the next moment, her shoulders went back, her chin tilted, and she turned her gaze to the window.

He wanted to dislike the princess who'd cut her dad out of her life, but he'd just caught a glimpse of the fragile, wounded girl beneath the snooty exterior.

Ah, hell.

He wanted to let her know that Harrison was just getting the small stuff out of the way. That the bulk of Kurt's estate would obviously go to her. He had no other family.

But she'd figure it out soon enough.

"Gentlemen, if you'll take a look, you'll see Kurt has given each of you an equal one-quarter ownership of the Wyoming Renegades hockey team."

Energy electrified the room. Booker shifted back in his

chair, Cole jerked, dropping the papers perched on his knee, and Jaime lit up like a box of firecrackers.

"You serious?" Jaime asked.

Harrison nodded. "Now, there are some stipulations. If you choose not to take ownership, the quarter rights cannot be sold or traded. So, if one of you doesn't want the team, ownership goes to the remaining three. If two of you don't want the team, then it's shared by the other two."

"And if no one wants it?" Booker asked.

Harrison cut a look to the woman. "It goes to his daughter. And if she doesn't want it, the team is sold, and the money goes to charity."

The lawyer rolled out a bunch of legalese, but Declan tuned him out because he wasn't sure how he felt about the gift. It was generous, no question. Yet, for some reason, he was disappointed.

He almost laughed out loud when he realized he'd have been happier with a potato masher than an NHL hockey team. But he guessed if he'd gotten anything, he'd have liked it to be personal. A letter, even. Something that acknowledged him personally.

That proved he meant as much to Kurt as Kurt had to him.

But that was ridiculous. The man had mentored all four of them.

He couldn't believe he was thinking about shit like this when Kurt was *dead*. Damn, he couldn't wrap his head around it. He'd only been fifty-two. Healthy as could be.

Or so he'd thought.

So, maybe Declan couldn't focus on an inheritance until he'd processed the tremendous loss. Maybe then, he'd be excited about owning a team.

"I'm in, man." Jaime's voice broke through his thoughts. "Totally."

Cole, the league's hottest player and renowned playboy, reached down to collect the papers. "I can't own a team while I'm playing."

"Can he?" Jaime asked.

"It's something we'll have to look into." The attorney looked to Booker for an answer.

"I'm good, thanks. It's a conflict of interest with my job." He reached for the arm rests, as if about to get up. "Is that it?"

Everyone turned to him, a little surprised that he'd rush out of here. But Declan understood. Thanks to Jaime, Booker's hockey career had crashed and burned before he'd even shown up for training camp.

"Not just yet." Harrison gathered a stack of papers and tapped them on the desk to align them evenly. "I'd like to stress that no one has to make any decisions right now. The stated beneficiaries will receive a copy of the will within thirty days of Kurt's death, so you've got some time to think it over. I only called the meeting because I saw you're all in town for the funeral."

"Pardon?" the woman called in a very posh British accent. "I'm sorry to interrupt, but am I here for a reason? If not…." She gestured to the door.

"Yes, you are. I just need to finish up with them." Harrison held up a finger. "I'd like to read a letter Kurt wrote."

A strange energy passed through the room. It almost felt like the awakening of the old bond between the foursome, a thread of connection pulling taut as they waited to hear from the man who'd meant so much to them.

The lawyer pulled out a sheet of paper and cleared his throat. "Boys—"

"You've got to be joking." Clothing rustled, and the woman stood. "If he wrote them a letter, then he knew he was dying."

The attorney looked chastised. "He had some notice, yes."

"He knew he was dying and didn't think to reach out to his only child? Are you kidding me? Okay." She let out a huff of breath. "Well, I won't intrude on his love letter to his precious hockey boys. I'll wait in the reception room." She strode out, leaving a trail of expensive perfume in her wake.

Declan didn't know her. Only that she'd refused to come out here to see her dad, and eventually the relationship had faded into nothing. He wanted to assume she was a spoiled princess here to grab a hefty inheritance. Instead, he could see her hurt, and it rustled up emotions unfamiliar to him. Tenderness, concern…the need to protect her. "We can do this later," he said. "Why don't you handle her part of the estate? We should be the ones waiting."

"As you might expect from Kurt, there's an order for his will, and I'm following it." Harrison returned to the letter. "Okay, here we go." He paused, drawing in a breath. "Boys, I grew up believing that if I did all the right things —got good grades, showed up on time, and worked hard —I'd earn a life free of hardship. Unfortunately, life doesn't work that way. It never gets easier, and the hits keep on coming. In the end—and that's where I am now, at the end of my life—I'm sure of two things: the only reward for living by a code of honor is peace of mind. And let me tell you—it's a good one. The other is that I'm sitting here in my office on my thousands of acres of land, my bank accounts stuffed with money, and my shelves packed with awards—and none of it matters. Because I will die alone."

Once, a defender had slammed Declan into the boards so hard it had knocked the wind out of him. *That's what this feels like.*

"He didn't have to die alone." Declan got to his feet, paced to the window. *Dammit, Kurt.* "I would have come home." He whipped around. "Why didn't he say anything?"

All eyes were on him, filled with surprise and concern. But no one answered because what could they say? *That's just how Kurt was.*

"Sorry." Declan returned to his seat. "Go on."

The lawyer nodded and turned back to the letter. "It was a shit thing that happened to you ten years ago. Especially you, Booker." Harrison glanced up to catch the man's reaction, but other than a tightening of his jaw, Booker remained impassive. "And I'm going to wager none of you has found the type of camaraderie in all the years since you last saw each other. Now, regardless of where you are in life—and believe me, I know, I've been watching—you need to forgive each other. I bought the Renegades so we could all be together, and it didn't pan out. But now that I'm gone, I want you to use it to mend your friendship. You won't regret it." Harrison stopped reading.

The worst thing about death was the sense of helplessness. It was not being able to see, touch, or hear the person ever again. It was not having the chance to say goodbye.

He hated that Kurt had died alone. He would've... fuck, he'd have given up everything to be here with him.

With each man lost in his own thoughts, the room remained silent.

Until Harrison cleared his throat and continued reading the letter. "I'm proud of all of you. Things didn't go the way you'd expected, but you all made good lives for yourselves. I'd hoped to meet your wives, hold your babies, and sit with you and have a beer when your troubles got too deep. That's not going to happen now, but there's one thing I can do and that's try to bring you together again. Yours, Kurt."

Declan struggled to swallow past the hard knot of pain in his throat.

...meet your wives, hold your babies...have a beer when your troubles got too deep.

He lowered his head, blinking back tears that blurred his vision. He would've liked that. He'd expected that.

"I'm just going to put it out there," Jaime said. "I want everything he talked about, so I'm in. And I hope you guys are, too."

When no one responded, Harrison said, "Well, we won't be signing any documents today. I'll reach out to each of you in thirty days."

As the others got up, Jaime said, "Guys, come to the ranch tomorrow night for a barbecue. We can talk about it then."

"I'm only in town for the funeral," Booker said. "But I don't want the team, so it's cool." He turned to look Jaime right in the eyes.

Tension snapped through the room like a live wire.

If Booker said anything to worsen Jaime's guilt,

Declan would intervene. They'd been eighteen. They'd had a history of doing stupid shit.

Instead, though, Booker said, "We're cool."

Color flooded Jaime's cheeks, and he practically slumped in relief. "Thanks." It came out a gruff whisper.

"I've got a flight tomorrow, too," Cole said. "But I can push it back." He gave Booker a look that said *So can you.*

In the past, Booker had made snap decisions. He'd always been confident, knew his place in the world. But this time, he seemed to waver.

"We'll all be there." Declan glanced at the door. "Now, let's get out of here, so Harrison can talk to Kurt's daughter." He figured every second that passed deepened her sense of rejection. And that just wasn't right. When he started out, the others followed.

"Declan," the lawyer called. "Hang on. I'm going to need you to stay."

"Me?" His pulse pounded. "What for?"

"And please call Seraphina in."

"Shouldn't you talk to her alone?" Declan didn't think she'd want some stranger listening in.

"You're part of it."

"Part of what?"

Harrison tipped his chin to the waiting room. "I need to speak with both of you."

Declan couldn't think of a single thing tying him to Kurt's daughter, but he was curious as hell. So, while his old friends headed out, his attention was fixed on the gorgeous, elegant woman. She was doing her damnedest to maintain her regal demeanor—straight spine, chin tilted—but her eyes—those fucking bright blue eyes that saw and assessed everything as if she were a mouse in a roomful of cats—revealed pain and fear.

She was a fish out of water if he'd ever seen one. "Harrison wants to talk to you."

She rose out of the chair like a queen. "Thank you." Hefting a black leather purse decorated with silver studs, she headed back into the office.

Once they took their seats, the lawyer said, "Declan, this is Seraphina Crutchley, Kurt's daughter. Seraphina, this is Declan Cadell—"

"One of Kurt's hockey boys. Yes, I figured that out."

He didn't like the way she'd diminished the relationship, especially since she was the one who'd refused to come out for her custodial visits. She'd broken Kurt's heart, so why would she be resentful that he'd formed the Mountain West Elite Hockey Club? What did it matter how he'd spent his time?

"What, exactly, do the two of us have in common?" Her eyes went wide. "Oh, don't tell me he's my long-lost half-brother?"

"What?" Declan said. "No."

"No," the lawyer said. "But there's a codicil to the will, and it involves the two of you."

"I merit a codicil?" Underneath that snarky tone, Seraphina's voice broke. "That's better than nothing, right?"

"Yes. Your father"—he cut a look to Declan—"*Kurt* is bequeathing one of you his ranch."

"*One* of us?" She dropped her purse to the floor, and a water bottle rolled out.

Declan didn't think he could stand much more of this. Watching her dodge one hit after another from her own father…what had Kurt been thinking? He'd never known Kurt to be a vengeful man. He'd never held grudges.

"That's correct." It clearly pained the lawyer to say it.

"And who decides which one of us gets it?" she asked.

Exhaling in exasperation, the lawyer squeezed his eyes shut. When he opened them, he said, "It goes to the winner of a trivia contest."

"I'm pitted against a hockey boy in a *contest*? Please help me understand what's happening here." She looked helplessly to Declan.

He was no help. He was just as shocked.

"The competition will be held thirty days from today, on July twelfth in the Music Box. Kurt wrote the questions himself, and I'll be reading them." The lawyer exhaled in defeat. "The event is open to the public."

"Whatever good memories I had of him, this…this has wiped out every single one." She rose out of her chair. "Thank you for your time."

"Where are you going?" Harrison asked.

"I thought he'd already hurt me as badly as a father could." She yanked her purse by a handle. "I'm not going to give him the satisfaction of participating in his cruel game." With a nod, she turned and started out of the room.

"The ranch has been in your family since the eighteen-hundreds."

If the lawyer thought that would catch her interest, he was wrong. "The Grevers are not my family." She reached the door and twisted the knob.

"It's the single largest property in Wyoming and the most profitable ranch in the country."

She gave him a flat look.

"And it's valued at seven-hundred-million-dollars."

Seraphina stopped, her purse dangling from the bend of her arm. "Pardon?"

"And all you have to do is answer more questions correctly than Declan."

"What kind of questions?" She asked quietly. "World affairs? Hollywood trivia?"

"Uh, no." Harrison looked uncomfortable. "Questions about your father."

"Of course. The original narcissist." She blew out a tired breath. "I really wish you'd mailed me this information. I didn't need to fly all the way out here for this."

Declan shot her a look. "You'd have missed your father's funeral?"

"My *father* lives in London. The sperm donor hasn't spoken to me in twenty years. That's how important I was to him."

"I'm sure you understand there are two sides to every story," the lawyer said. "And I believe Mr. Grevers's intention was for you to hear his. To that end, if you choose to participate, he requires both of you to live and work on his property for a month. He believes that will give the two of you an equal opportunity to learn about him."

"Why does *he* need to know my father?" She tipped a chin to Declan. "He's not a blood relative."

"No, but Kurt often referred to Declan as the son he never had."

All the years of living on his own, being fully responsible for himself, melted like shaved ice, exposing the howling child that still waited at the end of the driveway for his parents to come home. Who clung to his grandfather's hand so he could fall asleep at night.

To hear that acknowledgement from Kurt undid him.

And no lie, he wanted the ranch more than anything.

Not for the money or the training center he'd always dreamed of running there, but because the ancestry, the history on that land, had meant everything to Kurt.

But I'm not a Grevers. Seraphina is.

Which meant he had to do the right thing. "The ranch is yours. I have no claim to it, and I wouldn't take away your legacy like that. So, if you'll excuse me, I'll wait to get the will in the mail and figure out what to do about my share of the Renegades."

"Oh, thank God. I'm terribly sorry for the attitude I've been throwing around. It's just all so overwhelming and, frankly, hurtful." Giving him a warm and unbearably sweet smile, she reached for his hand. "I can't thank you enough. You've no idea what this means to me."

Sure, I do.

I'd give my left nut to have a family legacy like yours.

He gave her a nod and headed for the door. He wondered if she'd mind if he went inside the house one last time. He'd like to take one last look around. "Actually, there's one thing I'd like."

"Name it." She flashed her dazzling smile.

"In the kitchen, top drawer next to the stove, there's an old-fashioned potato masher. I'd like it."

"You want a kitchen utensil?" She must've realized how rude she sounded because she waved her hand. "I'm sorry. Of course, you can have it. How about I leave it here with Mr. Goodman?"

With a curt nod, he headed out of the office. Maybe he'd hike the property down to the river where they used to fish. He needed time alone to process Kurt's death. Passing the receptionist, he nodded. "Thank you."

And then, right as he reached the door, he heard Seraphina ask, "Can you give me the name of a good realtor? I'd like to get it on the market as quickly as possible."

Declan stopped in his tracks. Swiveling back around, he barreled into the office. "You're *selling* Kurt's ranch?"

"Of course. I live in London. I…" She looked to Harrison for support, as if he'd side with her.

He didn't. The lawyer gave her a hard, flat look. "As I just said, that land has been in your family for generations."

"Yes, but it's not really my family, and I've no use for a cattle ranch in Wyoming. I'm sure you understand." She gave Declan an earnest look. "I'd be happy to send you a token of my appreciation."

Okay, he'd heard enough. He slapped his palm on Harrison's desk. "I'm in."

"Excuse me?" the woman asked. "You just said you're not entitled to Kurt's land. I'm his only child." Seraphina sounded distraught.

"And if all you're going to do is sell it, then maybe I'm more interested in it than I thought." Declan focused on the attorney. "You said we have to live and work on the ranch?"

"Correct."

"I'll have to take a leave from my job, so don't bother mailing the will to my Pittsburgh address." He snatched the lawyer's card out of a granite holder and shoved it in the back pocket of his jeans. "You know where to find me for the next month."

Chapter Two

THE TAXI HAD LEFT PHINNY IN FRONT OF THE massive wood and iron gate guarding Kurt's property. She should ring the buzzer, ask to be let in, but she didn't want to go into that house yet.

She didn't want to be here at all.

How could he do this to her? What had she ever done to cause him to be so cruel? She'd been six years old when she'd thrown a fit about visiting him. Of course she hadn't wanted to leave her mummy and fly across the world to spend time with a man she barely knew. Why would he punish her for that?

And, really, what effort had he ever made to get to know *her*?

The sun beat down on her head, and cars roared by on the four-lane highway connecting the Tetons to the town she'd just left behind. A cool breeze rustled the sagebrush bushes and carried the scent of wildflowers.

I want to go home.

Of course, she didn't have a home anymore. She had a house she shared with four strangers. She felt very much alone in her little room, but it was nothing like this. She wanted to call her mum, but she couldn't deal with the rant that would surely follow the news about the contest. If she still had friends, she'd call them. Only a few months ago, they would've rallied around her and showered her with advice.

They'd probably tell her to flirt with the hockey boy until he was so besotted, he'd walk away from the competition. Then, she could sell the ranch and get on with it.

Never eat ramen noodles again! Ha ha!

But of course, they didn't know she ate ramen now. They didn't know anything about her life anymore.

And they hadn't met Declan Cadell. Seriously, they didn't make men like that in her world. He was big, tattooed, and rough-looking. If she'd run into him at the Tube station on her way home after a night of clubbing, she'd have been scared.

His dirty blond hair brushed the collar of his white dress shirt, and he'd rolled up the sleeves to his elbows, exposing the tattoos that covered his muscular arms.

He looked mean. He looked hard. He looked…

Delicious.

A shiver tripped down her spine. And just when she'd thought she'd read him all wrong, when he'd been sweet enough to hand over the ranch because it was the right thing to do, she'd talked about selling it and…whoo boy, he'd turned into the kind of man you don't mess with.

And now here I am, stuck in this Cowtown for a month. A *month.*

Pressure built behind her eyes, and she blinked back tears. Battling with more emotions than she could sort through, she wished she hadn't checked out of the motel.

She wanted nothing more than to hide under the covers and eat a packet of biscuits. But she had to stay here because Kurt had given her no choice, and now, she had to see this through.

She had to win, sell the ranch, and gain the kind of financial security that meant she would never again face the terrifying threat of not having enough money to eat or pay for a roof over her head.

Right, so let's get going. Splashing around in fear would lead nowhere. She pressed the intercom button. Hitching her purse higher on her shoulder, she faced the gate, ready to stride on through. But it didn't open. She pushed again, looking up at the security camera. "Hello?"

Nothing. A hawk soared overhead, and a cow mooed somewhere in the distance. All alone in a massive valley filled with hay bales, bison, and sage-covered meadows, she felt like a tiny speck of nothing. She pressed the buzzer again while checking out the area. On one side of the driveway sat a sturdy mailbox. On the other was a farm stand that looked like it hadn't been used in years. With all the traffic on this road, she bet it had once done well.

Above the gate arched a heavy-gauge steel sign. *Gongshow Ranch.* A row of tiny wrought iron cattle meandered across the top.

That's a weird name.

A humming sound drew her attention, and she found the gate slowly swinging open. *Well, here goes.* Grabbing the handle of her carry-on, she started the long trek to the house.

Fear poked at her, little jolts of electricity that made her pulse quicken. In the taxi, she'd quit her job—she'd had no choice. And while she had free room and board here, she still needed income. She'd only brought enough clothing and toiletries for a long weekend.

And what about my house? Did she pay for July or give up her room? She had just enough money in her account to cover rent and her share of utilities.

The biggest issue, though, was the auction. The foundation had already scheduled its first planning meeting, and Mrs. Lumley would be calling any day now, inviting her to run it again. It would just be a formality, though. They assumed she'd take the job—and they'd be correct. Only this year, Phinny needed a salary. *That'll go over well.* But her circumstances had changed, and she had no choice.

She just dreaded Mrs. Lumley's response.

Let's not think about this right now. Jet lag combined with emotional exhaustion was a formidable force. It took every ounce of strength she had to keep walking.

After a bend in the road, the house appeared. Made of stone, wood, and gleaming tinted glass, it was an architectural feat of hip and valley roof and butted windows. A driveway cut through a large patch of emerald-green grass.

Heading up the stone pavers, she didn't remember Kurt's place being so…lush. For some reason, she'd had this image in her head of cactus and dirt, but the ranch was resplendent with healthy landscaping, well-tended outbuildings, and freshly painted barns and stables.

Lowering the handle of her carry-on, she lifted it up the stairs and stood in the shade of the porch. She didn't know why she dreaded knocking so much. It wasn't like Kurt would answer the door.

Oh. Her hand flew to her heart. She hadn't anticipated

that pinch. Over the years, she'd learned to stuff her sorrow and hurt under bravado.

Emotions were messy in the Crutchley house. One didn't revel in them, and so she'd done her best to suppress the hurt and anger. She'd tried very hard not to think about Kurt at all.

But it hadn't worked. Nothing had. All these years, she'd still waited for his call.

It was the real reason she'd stayed with Cameron so long. It had taken her a few months of bawling her eyes out, alone in a strange bedroom in a smelly old house, to come to terms with the truth. She never wanted to yearn for anyone the way she had her biological father. So, she'd stuck with someone she'd liked an awful lot but would never fall so in love with that she'd experience the same sense of anxiety, the hopelessness. That leap of her heart every time her phone rang, the flurry of excitement when the mail was brought in.

Anything from Daddy?

If she were honest, she'd spent more than half her life waiting for Kurt to show up with tears in his eyes, confessing how much he'd missed her.

But he hadn't missed her at all. And nothing drove it home better than making her compete against one of his hockey boys for a piece of land that had been in the Grevers's family for generations—and had nothing whatsoever to do with Declan.

Chin up. She knocked on the door. It was time to put all that useless hope and yearning to rest along with his body. At least she had a roof over her head for the next month—*and it's free.* Exhausted, defeated, she'd had enough. So, when no one answered, she grasped the doorknob, ready to breeze in.

But it was whisked right out of her hand. And Declan Cadell stood there, so tall and imposing he took up the doorway. "Yeah?" That gravelly voice was as thrilling as it was frightening.

She rocked back on her heels. Good lord, the man took her breath away. Blond hair that looked like he'd run his hands through it, deep hazel eyes—more green than brown—and a generous mouth that made a woman think of long, slow kisses. "What're you doing in Kurt's house?"

"I'm staying here." Spoken with the confidence of a man whose size meant he didn't take crap from anyone.

Hold my Dom Perignon. "Nice try, puck chaser. But this is *my* father's house, and *I'm* staying here."

"Oh, *now* he's your father? Well, let's see, you haven't set foot in this house in twenty years, and I always stay here when I'm in town…so, I'd say that gives me priority over you. Besides, I got here first."

Frazzled, dead on her feet, Phinny didn't have the energy to argue with this brute. "According to the terms of the will, I'm supposed to stay here, too." Besides, she had nine hundred pounds in her checking account. Hm, she really needed to give up her room. Even if she left the furniture behind—she'd bought it at a charity shop anyway—at least she'd have money to buy clothes, toiletries, and food whilst here. "You were so nice in the lawyer's office. What crawled under your skirt and bit your ass?"

He cracked a grin. "The princess has teeth." Leaning against the threshold, he folded his arms across his muscular chest. "You know, I didn't get why Kurt involved me in this game. Why he'd put the land that meant everything to him into play. It represents family, roots… his legacy."

"I hope that's the first trivia question because I've got the answer. To hurt me, that's why."

He shook his head. "If you think that, then you don't know him at all."

Of course, I don't know him. How could I?

"I'd have gladly walked away, knowing it's with his daughter, where it belongs, but the minute I heard you ask about a realtor, I knew why he picked me. Kurt knew better than to give this place to a spoiled little rich girl who cut him off because she didn't like to get dirty. And he knew I'd honor his legacy and do right by every single ancestor who gave his blood, sweat, and tears to turn this land into what it's become today. So, you can bet your ass I'll do everything in my power to keep it out of your hands. See you at the Music Box in one month." He shut the door in her face.

Mortification swept through her body like a flash fire. She hadn't been prepared when her parents cut her off. It had taken a long time—okay, she still hadn't adjusted to being flat-out broke.

But people liked her. They always had. Sure, she'd lost her friends along with her credit card and fancy address, but that had to do with her financials not her personality. So, to have this man think so little of her when he didn't even know her…it wasn't fair.

How does it make sense for me to own a cattle ranch in Wyoming?

She knocked again.

He opened quickly, giving her an exasperated expression. "What?"

"The will says I have to live and work here, so step aside, puck chaser. You've got a new roommate." This time, she was ready for him, and she shoved her two-thousand-dollar Valentino Rockstud handbag inside to prevent him from shutting the door. "This place is huge, and there are plenty of bedrooms. Our paths won't even cross."

"You're right. Because we won't be under the same roof. There are plenty of outbuildings. Find somewhere else." He lifted his knee and bumped the purse out of the way.

When she heard the lock slam home, she let out a frustrated growl. "What is the matter with you? You're not his *son*, you asshole." Exhaustion buckled her knees. She could curl up on that porch swing and sleep for days.

From here, she could only see the freshly mowed lawn, the driveway, and the meadowland on either side of the house. *Fine.* Leaving her luggage on the porch, she set off to find guest quarters. On her family's country estate, they had several lovely cottages. She didn't need a house the size of a lodge.

Nor did the puck chaser, so she had no idea why he was hogging it to himself. As she crossed the driveway, she noticed a silver bullet on wheels. She didn't know why it surprised her that Kurt had an RV. It would be perfect for a man who preferred his own company and liked to camp out for weeks all alone.

There it was again. That stab of pain.

She might not remember much, but she would never forget the last phone call her mum had made to him.

She doesn't want to spend her summers on that ranch.
She doesn't like fishing.
For God's sake, Kurt, she's a little girl.
She hates going to visit you.

True, she'd pitched a fit about going, but she hadn't wanted to hurt him. Her mum shouldn't have been so cruel. And as she'd gotten older, she'd always wondered why he hadn't said, *Okay, I'll go there.*

We'll rent a house in the south of France.

I'll take her on a cruise.

We'll go to Disneyland.

He could've done any number of things other than give up on her. After that call, he'd stopped holding her mother to the custodial agreements.

Ugh. Why am I dredging all this up? Striding past the RV, she headed around to the back of the house where she found an impressive barn. Further out, she saw a bunkhouse where the hands lived. Sheds, a stable. A corral. But no guest house anywhere in sight.

Well, I'm not living in a barn. So, the only possibility was the bunkhouse, but surely no one expected her to sleep with a dozen cowboys.

All around her, the ranch was quietly bustling. A truck in the distance kicked up dust as it headed down a lane. Sounds came from the barn, and a couple of workers in jeans and cowboy hats led their horses into the corral, their expressions somber.

There might be plenty of outbuildings, but she couldn't stay in any of them. She stormed back to the house and banged on the door.

This time, when the puck chaser answered, she didn't give him a chance to speak. "You're not the boss of anything. We're on equal footing, so step aside. I'm staying here."

He blocked her way with his big, hard body. "Wrong, Princess. I claimed the house."

"And where do you expect me to live?"

He pointed toward the silver bullet. "Have a nice night. Oh, since you're probably jet lagged, you don't have to report to work until tomorrow morning. But be in the barn at five-thirty."

"Are there even clean sheets in that thing?"

"Look, Princess, nobody's holding my hand here, either, okay? We both got the news about the will at the same time. I got here quicker—"

"Excuse me, but I had to check out of the motel."

He shrugged like he couldn't have cared less. "I got to the ranch manager first. The house is mine, and I found out what work needed to be done and chose what I wanted to do. I suggest you do the same thing."

All the fight drained out of her. *He's right.* She had been expecting everything to be laid out for her. Someone would show her to her room and serve her meals.

Just as she'd lived her life up until ten months ago. "That's fine, but you might want to leave the door unlocked because I'll probably be back for supplies."

"Not gonna happen."

Once again, he shut the door in her face.

What a dick. Grabbing her luggage, she headed back down the steps and over to her new home on wheels. It looked dusty and…sad. Did it even have air conditioning?

What is my life?

There're hundreds of millions of dollars waiting for me on the other side of this nightmare, so buck up. She could do anything for a month.

Used to city living, she filled her lungs with the crisp, clean mountain air, and it calmed her. She'd come here figuring she'd inherit some money. With it, she'd planned on moving into a better flat and having a nest egg. But with this kind of money, she could start a philanthropy of her own. She didn't have many talents or skills, but she had a way with people, of encouraging even the grumpiest old cuss to donate his island or his castle for a week. She put together such great auction items, the patrons fought each other over them.

It's the one thing I'm good at.

Twisting the metal doorknob, she pulled it open and dragged her suitcase up the stairs. The place smelled of must and hot leather, but it wasn't too bad. The kitchen area seemed clean enough. It was small, obviously, but she didn't need much space. She wheeled her carry-on to the back where she found a horseshoe-shaped couch.

Looking around, she didn't see anything more than a kitchen, a table and banquette, and a couch. *No bedroom?*

Okay, whatever. That's fine.

Sunlight streamed through the windows. *There are no curtains.* That might be a problem. But whatever. She'd just have to make the best of it. Exhausted, she dropped her purse on the floor, set her suitcase against the wall, and collapsed on the couch.

Wait. She had to be up at five. She found the energy to plug her phone into the outlet and set the alarm.

Tomorrow was a new day, and she'd kick its ass.

Chapter Three

Phinny's bedroom in Kentish Town sat right on High Street. She was used to honking and drunken laughter, emergency vehicles racing by, and car doors slamming as people got in and out of cabs.

Calamity, Wyoming was eerily silent.

She pried her eyelids open only to be assaulted by sunlight. Rolling onto her back, she came up against something firm. She patted it. Sheets. A blanket. A pillow.

She didn't recall seeing them there when she'd come in yesterday. *Who brought them?*

Still groggy with jet lag, she got up and stumbled into the bathroom. She tried to wash her hands and face, but nothing came out of the faucet. She'd have to fix that. Coming back out, she glanced at her phone. The alarm hadn't gone off yet, so she collapsed onto the couch and closed her eyes.

A deep, masculine voice hurtled her out of a deep sleep. Phinny lurched up.

"Seraphina?" Someone pounded on the door. "Hey, you in there?"

Muffled voices discussing whether they should enter without her consent had her jumping to her feet. "I'm here." Sometime during the night, she'd slipped out of her black dress and put on her traveling clothes. On bare feet, she padded down the short hallway. "I'm coming." She threw open the door to find several people staring at her. "Hello. Hi. I'm up." Groggy, she swayed. "Would you like to come in?"

The man closest to her had an amused look while the guys behind him snickered.

God, she hated being underestimated. It was her Achille's heel. "I'm sorry if I overslept. I don't know why my alarm didn't go off, but I'll take a quick shower and be ready to go in no-time."

The man cocked his head. "You realize this thing isn't hooked up to anything, right? You can't shower, and you don't have electricity."

"What?" She twisted around to take in the RV, the reality of her situation slapping her in the face like a soggy towel. "But Declan told me to stay here. I assumed…how am I supposed to live here for a month?"

He held up both hands. "I'm just the foreman. I've been waiting for two hours for you to get up, but I've got a lot to do for the festival, so I've written up a list of chores you need to get to. Right away, if you don't mind."

"Of course, I don't mind." She blew out a breath, pinching the bridge of her nose. "Sir—"

"Hank. Just call me Hank."

"Hank, I'm going to need you to hook up my new home to make it habitable. I'm more than happy to pitch in around here, but I need the basics like power and water."

"Like I said, I'm just the ranch foreman." He shoved a piece of paper at her. "You'll want to start collecting those eggs. Tigger can only restrain himself for so long."

"Tigger?"

"Right. I could've explained everything to you two hours ago, but I've got a place to run here. I don't know if you know this, but the Gongshow's one of the biggest, most profitable cattle ranches in the country."

His disdain woke her all the way up. Because she hadn't earned it. "Given that I was told to stay here, it never would have occurred to me last night when I tried to charge my phone that my new home wasn't hooked up. Now, I know. It won't happen again." With a nod, she shut the door.

What the hell am I supposed to do? She hadn't showered since yesterday morning—and that was just a quick rinse because her roommates had used all the hot water.

It took a moment for reality to kick in. The puck chaser thought she'd go running back to her luxe life in London. *Ha. Hilarious.* What he didn't realize was that even if she had a fancy life to return to, there wasn't a chance in hell she'd let him win this challenge.

Screw him.

I'm two hours late, so I'll just get caught up on my chores, and then I'll use the bathroom at the main house.

Thinking she'd only be here for a few days, she'd brought a black dress and heels for the funeral, pajamas and flip flops for the downtime in her motel room, and her cashmere wrap in case it got cold on the plane. She glanced down at the skinny jeans and pin-striped boyfriend-style shirt she'd worn for travel.

She couldn't collect eggs in either the heels or the Ferragamo ballet flats she'd brought. Since losing her parents' credit card, she'd taken extremely good care of her belongings, and she couldn't risk a scuff, scratch, or stain since nothing could be replaced.

Honestly, she'd thought for sure the mother who'd dressed her in designer clothes from the moment she came out of the womb would give up on this stupid game. She could've at least passed along her hand-me-downs instead of dropping them at the charity shop.

But, no, her parents remained firm in their commitment to teaching her what life looked like without Cameron Lumley.

Trust me, I get it.

Well, for today, she'd have to wear her flats and jeans and roll up the sleeves of her shirt. Maybe she could find clothing to borrow in the house. Surely, Kurt had a girlfriend who'd left something behind. He wasn't married —obviously—or there'd be no battle for his estate.

Fortunately, she'd brought her portable charger, so she plugged her phone in and headed outside. With the sun already cresting the snow-capped mountain peak, she headed for the barn, reading the list as she walked.

Her steps slowed.

Horse barn:
Muck out the stalls
Feed horses: quart of grain and 2 flakes of hay
Fresh water

Hen house:
Collect the eggs and bring to bunkhouse for cook
Feed and water

Vegetable Garden:
Weed
Collect ripe vegetables

Pig pen:
Feed pigs: scraps from bunkhouse and
feed from bin in barn
Fresh water

She had no idea where to begin. Sure, she'd spent lots of time on her family's estate. An only child, she'd had too much time to herself, so she'd often hung out with the staff. Not that she'd done the work, of course. But she'd paid attention.

I can do all this, no problem. Hearing voices, she headed for the barn. Maybe someone could tell her what to do. She'd need a basket or something to collect eggs, right? But before she reached it, she heard a terrible sound. Shrieking, clucking, and nerve-shattering squawks.

Phinny raced to the chicken coop to find feathers flying and dust billowing. *Oh, God.* It was a modern structure with an oak plywood façade, wooden trusses to support metal walls, and a slanted, corrugated roof that offered shade. Dozens of chickens flapped their wings and strutted in circles, bumping into each other. "What's going on?" She leaped onto a wooden platform—a bridge that joined two identical coops—and headed into the one with a horrible scrabbling sound—nails on wood.

And found a dog chasing a hen.

"Get out. Go. Shoo." It hurried into one of the huts

and gulped down an egg. When it started for another, she swatted at the air. "Oh, no, you don't. Scram."

The wily thing scooted around her and tore out of the coop. She chased after it, making a useless shooing motion.

Winded, she bent over, bracing her hands on her knees, as she fought to catch her breath. As the chickens calmed down, she straightened. "Girls, I overslept. I'm so sorry. It won't happen again."

She didn't have time to find a basket, so she pulled her shirt out of her jeans to make a cradle. She'd collected about a dozen eggs when she realized this method wasn't going to work. There were too many of them.

Okay, hang on. She made a quick assessment, figuring each adjoining coop had about a hundred huts.

Good God, why did Kurt need two hundred chickens?

Carefully, she headed over to the bunkhouse. If she was supposed to deliver the eggs, there must be baskets or something. She couldn't knock, as she needed both hands to hold up the shirt, so she turned sideways and used her elbow to open the door.

And found a bare-assed man changing his clothes.

She closed her eyes. "Sorry, sorry, sorry."

"It's cool. Why are you carrying eggs in your shirt?"

She cracked open an eyelid to find him zipping up his jeans. "I was told to collect them, but there was a *dog* in the chicken coop—"

"Tigger." He pulled on a T-shirt.

"Excuse me?"

"That's Tigger. As long as you give him an egg first thing in the morning, he'll stay out of the coop."

"What kind of dog eats eggs?"

The guy smiled. Young, fit, he was clean-cut and

friendly. "Tigger does." He shrugged. "It's his thing. He'll scarf them down if Tina doesn't give him one."

"Tina?"

His good humor faded. "She's the house manager, but she left right after the funeral. Went to see her sister in North Carolina." He reached for a belt and snaked it through the loops of his jeans. "Anyhow, she keeps baskets in the barn."

"Okay, great. But…why are there so many chickens?"

"Uh, well, it's a self-sustaining ranch. Kurt was really into preserving the land, so we grow everything we eat and use alternative energy. There's a lot of people to feed, so…" He offered an adorable smile. "Lots of chickens."

"Okay. Got it. Thanks for the information."

"I'd help you, but I've got a doctor's appointment. That's why I'm not working right now."

"No worries. I got this." She headed to the barn, thankful for the shade and the familiar scents of horse, hay, and saddle leather. Baskets hung off iron hooks nailed to the wall, so she knocked one down with an elbow and then set the eggs carefully into it. She didn't know where to put it, so she left it on the floor of the office. At least the door would keep Tigger out. Then, she went back to the coop with several baskets to collect more.

An hour later, after delivering the eggs to the cook, she headed to the barn to muck the stalls. She'd certainly watched it enough times but doing it herself…that was another story. She found gloves, a pitchfork, and a wheelbarrow all set out for her, so she got right to work. But only half an hour into it, she had to pull the gloves off to get a look at the blisters covering her pinkened hands. Perspiration ran down her back, plastering the shirt to her.

And she wasn't even halfway done.

She couldn't help wondering what Declan was doing but picturing the insufferable man knee-deep in pig shit made her feel better. In fact, it gave her the inspiration she needed to shove the gloves back on and do an outstanding job. She doubted a hockey boy had any exposure to farm work.

Without instructions, she wasn't sure she was doing it correctly, but she understood the basics, so she'd left each floor bare to dry out and then, when she'd finished mucking, she went back with her pitchfork to spread a new layer of shavings and hay.

Her back ached, and her stomach growled, but she wanted to get the next job done. How long could it take to pull a few weeds from a vegetable patch? Smacking the dirt off her jeans, she headed out of the barn.

But when she got there, she nearly keeled over. *You've got to be kidding me.*

It wasn't a *patch*. No, this garden provided a ranch full of people with fresh, seasonal produce. How on earth was she supposed to do a job like this herself? Curious, she wandered the rows of tomatoes, zucchini, squash, carrots, and kale. If she was into gardening, this place would be a dream. Her stomach clenched painfully at the tease of all this delicious food.

You know what? I haven't eaten in eighteen hours. She'd just have to tackle this job later. Making her way around the house to the kitchen door, she knocked.

It didn't take long for Declan to answer. After a brief scan from her face down to her flats, he gave her a bored look. "What?"

"I need a shower and food."

"Cool. Do you need help getting the Airstream hooked up?"

She took a step back. "So, you knew it didn't have power, and you still sent me there?" She was sweaty, starving, and filthy, and he just stood there, as calm and clean as could be. "That's cruel."

"As I've already said, we've both been dropped into this situation, and we have to figure it out as we go along. I didn't know anything either, but I can help you if you want."

"I would appreciate that."

"Let me get my phone and look it up."

"You don't know how to do it?"

"No. *I* don't own an Airstream." He disappeared into the house and came back a moment later. "While I'm doing this, you can order food from Harley and Lu's Emporium." He tapped away on his phone. "It's the gourmet grocer in town." His gaze flicked over to her. "They deliver."

His assumptions really pissed her off. "I could, but I'd rather hire my own chef. In fact, while I'm at it, I'll get my butler to do my chores." She smiled. "Gosh, while you're putting my Airstream together, I'll just stand here and think of all the ways I can make my stay here more luxurious."

Given the arch of his brow, he wasn't too put-out by her little fit. But she was *shaking*. From hunger, exhaustion, anger…*you name it. Screw him.* "On second thought, I don't want your help with the Airstream. I can do it myself." And when it finally clicked—that he stood there perfectly clean and composed, anger turned to rage. "Wait a minute, why aren't you sweating?"

"Because the house has air conditioning?"

"Are you kidding me? You've been in the house all day while I've been shoveling shit and feeding kitchen scraps to pigs? I had to chase a crazed dog away from the coop, and you're what? Playing video games? Arranging hookups on your dating apps?"

The man was completely unruffled. "At the moment, I'm going to meet some friends for a barbecue, but I spent the day doing office work." He gave her a pointed look. *Are we done?*

"So, that's what you're doing for the month? Filing?"

"Well, it's more accounting, but yeah, that's what I'm doing. I asked what my choices were, and that's what I chose. Now, if you'll excuse me."

"I honestly don't know whether you're trying to punish me for selling Kurt's property, or you're just an asshole."

His features hardened, and his intensity unnerved her. "If the only thing you see here is dirt and rocks and animals, then I don't have anything to say to you."

"Oh, come on. You must know I'd run this place into the ground. Isn't it better to sell it to someone who'll operate it like Kurt did?"

"We're talking hundreds of thousands of prime acres in Jackson Hole. If you sell, it'll most likely be turned into a subdivision or kept as some rich guy's playground. How many people are going to spend seven-hundred-million-dollars to continue his work creating an ecologically sustainable ranch?" He stepped outside. "Did you know that Max Grevers came to the New World in sixteen-thirty-five? And that the five Grevers brothers came to Wyoming in eighteen-sixty-four when free land was offered?"

"No. Is that what you and Kurt sat around talking about?"

"Sometimes, but I got that from reading up on it last night."

Like flicking a switch, anxiety lit her up. While she was wasting time doing chores, he'd gotten the jump on her. He was a cleverer opponent than she'd expected. "Where did you find that kind of information? Because it's incredibly unfair that you get access to his office and library while I'm banished to a couch in an Airstream."

He shook his head as if he couldn't believe her stupidity. "I read it online. Just like you can do. And I'm not going to let you sell the land they worked so hard to hold onto for future generations."

"You're not a Grevers." Why was he being like this? "Why do you care so much?"

"I don't have to be Kurt's son to know how much this land mattered to him. It's your fucking history, and I'm going to keep it going just as Kurt intended." He took a step back into the house and shut the door in her face.

She stood there rattled, shame creeping up her neck. And that just wasn't fair. She banged on the door.

He must not have gotten far because he threw the door open. "What?"

"Put yourself in my shoes. That's all I'm asking. Imagine a relative you didn't know passed away and left you a massive farm in Germany. You're a hockey player. Would you keep it? Live on it? If you had no money, no hopes of earning a real living, wouldn't you sell it?"

"Sure, let's play. Except it's not a 'relative.' It's my dad. And what if he involved *you* for the sole purpose of making sure I didn't sell? What if you knew his values and priorities, would you let me sell it? Or would you fight like hell to make sure the man who was like a father to you didn't lose his life's work?" He held her gaze for so long and with such intensity, she could feel her anger and resolve shriveling.

He had a point.

"Now, I have to go." He gave her a look that said *We good?*

Unsettled, she could only nod. Once he closed the door—this time gently—she crossed the stone patio and pool, breathing in chlorine and fresh mountain air. With a trembling hand, she let herself out of the gate and headed back to the garden.

She hated the puck chaser for humiliating her.

Dropping to her knees, she twisted a plump tomato off the vine and bit into it. *Oh, God.* She'd never tasted anything better. She demolished it in four bites.

I hate that I'm five thousand miles from home and so tired and hungry I can't think clearly.

The carrots were filthy, so she reached for another tomato.

And it's all Kurt's fault. I hate him for putting me in this position.

But none of that rang true. Declan's first inclination had been to give her the ranch. He'd only switched course to follow Kurt's wishes. And she didn't hate her biological father. He'd given her a chance to own this land that meant so much to him. He'd just brought in back-up in case she did the unthinkable. She couldn't fault him for that.

Standing up, she brushed the dirt off her jeans. She'd never hated him. That was just something she told herself to cover the hurt of his rejection. She headed back to the Airstream.

Hurt's such a small word, isn't it? It required a plaster on a skinned knee. It meant a big cry when your friends stopped inviting you to go clubbing with them.

No, her father had destroyed her by giving her up so easily.

He'd blown up her very foundation. At her core, she was a good girl. A nice girl. From the time she'd been born, she'd seen the world through rose-colored lenses. An eternal optimist, she made the best of every situation, turned lemons into lemonade.

But when her father had stopped talking to her…it had shattered her sense of herself as being good, kind…

No. Of being worthy.

And, honestly, that was why she'd struggled so hard when her parents had cut her off so unexpectedly. It wasn't that she'd suddenly had to pay her own bills. *That's fine. I'm a grown woman. I can do that.* It was that they hadn't thought she could amount to anything without a wealthy man to provide for her.

She could admit she'd taken everything for granted. Of course, she had. It had been the only life she'd ever known. But now she had a different perspective. Ten months of waiting tables in a diner in Kentish Town will do that. It had taken a bit, but now she knew how to manage her money, and she'd learned to live within a budget. And, truly, she wanted to see what she could accomplish on her own.

Back in her trailer, she checked her messages for the first time since landing in Salt Lake City.

Mum: **What did he leave you?**

Ugh. She didn't want to get into that conversation just yet. No, it was far more important to research her Airstream issue. It only took a few swipes to discover it was quite simple. She could either fill her tank with fresh water or attach a hose.

Electricity turned out to be a bigger issue. If she didn't

find an outlet close enough, she'd have to buy a generator. After checking which ones would be compatible with her model, she looked up the local hardware store to find it would cost close to a thousand dollars.

Fear jolted her. *I can't possibly do that.* Even if she gave up her room in the house, she still had to buy food and shampoo. She needed underwear and shirts. *What am I going to do?*

Wait, what am I thinking? I'm going home with hundreds of millions of dollars.

She knew exactly what to do. Without considering the time, she called her mum.

"Phinny?" In the background she could hear laughter and silverware clinking against China. "Are you all right, darling? Where are you?"

"You're at dinner?" She settled back on the couch.

"Yes, the Gardeners are having a do tonight. Let me excuse myself and find some privacy."

She could picture her mum in a black taffeta Herrera dress, her Burberry wrap around her shoulders, and glittering with rubies and diamonds. If she closed her eyes, she could even get a whiff of her mum's Caron Poivre perfume.

As she waited, the little girl in her wanted to cry it out with her mummy. *I've been shoveling horse shit, and I've only eaten two tomatoes in eighteen hours. I haven't bathed, and my teeth feel like they're wearing socks.*

But the woman who'd been cut off because she wouldn't marry the son of Andrew's business partner hardened right up.

"All right, dear, I'm on the terrace. Tell me, what have you inherited?"

"His ranch."

Her mother let loose an unseemly laugh. "Well, if that's not a message, I don't know what is. He left you the one place you couldn't stand. What about money? After all those years of playing hockey, he had to be worth something."

"I don't know. But in order to get the ranch, I have to stay here for a month."

"A *month*?" Her mum spat out the word as if it were a grain of sand in her oyster. "Isn't that just like him, making you jump through hoops to get what's rightfully yours?"

Her senses sharpened. "I don't know. Is it? Was my father a game player?" She also couldn't help wondering if the ranch *was* rightfully hers. *He must have cousins, siblings...*

Aren't there any Grevers left?

"Your *father's* the finest man I've ever known. He's a good, decent, honorable man, and I can assure you the entire Crutchley estate will fall into your hands once we've passed. Your *sperm donor*, on the other hand, was a stubborn, hardheaded ass."

Phinny couldn't bear to listen to the familiar character-stripping right then. "Yes, but was Kurt a game player?"

Her mum went quiet. And with every moment that ticked past, Phinny's anxiety sharpened. Because she'd always taken her mum's word for it, hadn't she? She didn't have enough memories with Kurt to form an opinion of her own.

And in this moment, her mum's answer mattered very much.

"No, I can't say I recall that. In fact, he was rather too forthright. But it was so long ago, and I was just a child when we met. What did I really know of him? I was a college girl, away from home for the first time, and he was the star athlete on campus."

Laughter outside the window drew her attention to find Hank and some others unloading the bed of a huge pick-up truck. "Well, I'm staying here, so I'm sure I'll learn all about him."

"That's simply not possible. The planning meeting for the ball is coming up. You must be here, or they might hand the auction duties off to someone else."

"Why would they do that? They love the work I've done."

"Oh, you know everything's political, darling. Who knows what favors might be owed or granted? In any event, if you're not there, they might give the job to someone else."

She hadn't realized she was so easily replaceable. "Well, I can't leave the property, so I'll need your help." Considering it was a volunteer job, she hoped her mum didn't flip out. Well, it had to be done. "I'm going to ask them to hire me."

"That's a wonderful idea."

"Oh, thank God. I thought you'd think I was a cow for asking a philanthropy for money."

"Why would I think that? It's a tremendous amount of work, and they hire publicists and marketers. Why not make you permanent staff?"

"That's exactly what I'm thinking." Relief blew out the exhaustion, strengthening her. "Since I won't be at the planning meeting, do you think you could ask them for me? Or the next time you have dinner with the Lumleys, could you bring it up?"

"Absolutely not. My relationship with Margaret still

hasn't recovered since you rejected her son's marriage proposal."

"Mum, you can't still be going on about that."

"Can't I? We haven't had a dinner invitation since."

"What? You talk about her all the time."

"I see them at parties and events, and we work together with various charities, but we've not gone out to lunch as friends or dinner as couples."

"That's ridiculous. How is it your fault?"

"You're my child, and they believe you misled him. He could have been pursuing other women instead of wasting his time with you."

"I never…you can't believe that. I *dated* him. That's what people do."

"Phinny, you must know you embarrassed their family publicly. In any event, this is something you'll have to do on your own. If I get you a job, how will you ever feel proud of yourself?"

"Right. Of course." *More life lessons for Seraphina.* If only her parents understood they did more harm than good, hacking away at her self-esteem and making her feel inept. "I'll call Mrs. Lumley and explain the situation. But that's not why I called. Do you think you could loan me some money? The ranch is worth seven-hundred-million dollars, so I'm good for it. I just need to get through the next month."

"Good Lord. You've got to be joking. That pile of dirt?"

Out the window, she had a view of rugged mountain peaks glistening with snow, a freshly painted barn, and a corral recently raked. "It's actually breathtaking here. The way you described it I'd imagined a dust bowl with tumble weeds summersaulting across empty highways."

"That's not far off what it looked like twenty-some years ago. Yes, certainly. I'll transfer money into your account the moment we get off the phone."

Oh, thank God. She could buy clothing, shoes, and food. Her spirits soared when she thought of all the skin and hair care products she hadn't been able to use in nearly a year. Her hair had turned to straw from using cheap shampoos.

"Thank you, Mum. I need new bras like you wouldn't believe. And I only brought my flats and my old Christian LaCroix heels."

"It's rather petty of him to make you stay a month to get your inheritance. You wouldn't visit while he was alive, so by God, he'll force you there in his death."

"It's possible. I'll never really know for sure why he's done this. But it's more than that."

"More?"

She's not going to like this. "Well, he didn't actually *give* me the land. I have to win it."

Chapter Four

"Win what?" her mum practically screeched. "Your *inheritance?*"

"Yes." Phinny got up and paced toward the kitchen. "It's between me and one of Kurt's hockey boys. At the end of the month, we face off in a trivia contest. Whoever gets the most correct answers wins the land."

"That's indecent. That's…shameful." Her mum breathed heavily into the receiver. "I will never forgive him for treating his own child this way." Her stepfather must've come onto the terrace because her mum's voice grew muffled as she replayed the news. Phinny could hear Andrew murmuring in a soothing but firm voice.

Since she was the one living it, she really didn't want to deal with her parents' reactions. "Mum? Can you please talk to me?"

But her mum only grew more upset, and her stepfather worked harder to calm her down.

Anxiety tapped a heavy beat on her nerves, fraying them to the breaking point. She just couldn't take it anymore. "Mother!"

"I'm here. I'm just horrified your own father could treat you in such a manner. It's wrong—"

"Stop. I'm the one who has to quit my job and give up my room." It made no sense to keep the house-share now that her parents were loaning her money. "And I'm not there to move out of it. I only brought enough clothes for a long weekend because I had no idea I'd need to stay so long. So, instead of outrage at what your ex-husband did, can you please talk to me?" Emotion she'd fought for days finally bubbled to the surface. "I haven't showered since I left yesterday morning. The only money in my checking account is for July's rent and utilities. I'm living in an RV that has no electricity or running water, and I've spent the entire day shoveling horse shit, feeding pigs rotted kitchen scraps, and chasing a dog out of a chicken coop. I smell, I'm tired, and I'm scared to death."

"Oh, darling, I'm so sorry. Your father says not to worry one bit about the flat. He's going to send Richard there this afternoon to pack up your belongings. We'll take your furniture out to the country."

"Thank you so much. You've no idea what a weight that is off my shoulders. Mum, I'm absolutely knackered. Being here brings up all the old feelings of rejection. I know everything he did wrong to us, but he was still my biological father and…he's gone. Forever. And I guess there was some small hope inside me that one day he'd… want to know me." The words rushed out, easing the crowded space in her mind. "That maybe he couldn't relate to a six-year-old girl, but once I'd grown, he'd want to spend time with me again."

"I felt the same way. After I moved back to London, I thought he'd come after me. I thought he'd miss me, miss *us*, enough to change. I used to fantasize about him showing up and begging us to come home."

"But he never did." Phinny said it flatly because she'd heard the story so many times. But now that she stood on his land and sat on his couch, she wanted more information, more details. She wanted to talk to people who knew him.

"No, of course not. Hockey was more important to him than anything."

Phinny played with the faucet, flicking it on and off. Of course, nothing came out. "Well, I'm going to win that contest and sell the ranch, and then I'll never have to eat another packet of ramen again because I've run out of money for the month."

"I will remind you that's your choice. You don't have to live like this."

"You mean I can still marry Cameron, and you'll give me back my credit card?"

"Oh, for heaven's sake," her mum said. "You never did understand. It's never been about a credit card. It's about your total lack of understanding about how the real world works. Your choice to humiliate Cameron had a social and economic cost to your family. And the cost to you…it's more than I can bear."

Shaky, she sat down on the banquette. "What does that even mean?"

"Seraphina, you work in a *diner*. You live in Kentish Town. For God's sake, you've removed yourself from polite society and as long as you stay there, your future will be with truck drivers and green grocers and not the people who run this country."

She ran her palms on the smooth, yellowed surface of the table. "I didn't love Cameron. I couldn't marry him."

"Then you shouldn't have led him on. Intended or not, you've disrespected him and his family, and that has created a frightening scenario where your father's business might lose its largest and most important client and make us persona non grata among our friends."

"It's been nearly a year. Surely, they've gotten over it."

"The only thing that's happened in that time is *you've* been left behind. Verity's marrying a baron, and Allegra's pregnant with her first child."

Oh. She nearly doubled over with the blow. Not because she wanted to be married and having a baby but because these were once her closest friends, and she hadn't known about any of it.

It *hurt* to talk to her mum. She needed to wrap up the call. "Well, if you wouldn't mind putting some money in my account, I'd appreciate it. I don't need a lot. Just enough so I can eat, buy some clothes and shampoo...well, actually, according to the terms of the will, I have to live and work on the ranch, so I'll need a generator." The Airstream would be fine once it had electricity and running water. "I really don't know how much all that will cost, but if you could loan me ten grand, I'll pay you back in a month."

"I'm afraid we can't do that."

"You..." *What?* "Why not?"

"When I agreed to loan you money, you hadn't mentioned the contest."

Phinny didn't know how much more she could take. "I don't understand. I just told you I'm inheriting hundreds of millions of dollars."

"You *might* be. But since you know so little about Kurt, there's no guarantee you'll win."

"So, you'll tell me everything you know. How hard can it be?"

"Your father left when you were three. You stopped visiting him in America when you were six. And that hockey player you're competing against knew him as an adult. I should think he's got more insights into Kurt than you. I'm sorry, darling, but there's nothing to loan against. I'm sure you understand."

Long after the call ended, Phinny stared out the window. A low current of anxiety ran through her body. She didn't deserve this.

I'm a good person.
I work hard.
I don't lie or cheat or steal.

Had her parents cut her off gradually, it might have been easier. But to punish her for not marrying a man she didn't love, to kick her out of the apartment before she'd had time to save enough for first and last month's rent, had been cruel.

She'd begged them to reconsider, but they hadn't believed she'd take it seriously if they'd given her more time. They were probably right. She'd have been certain they'd forget or change their minds.

Outside, the ranch was a hive of activity. A couple of cowboys worked an unbridled horse in the ring. A truck drove past, its engine knocking and rumbling.

Declan came out of the house, all clean and powerful and broodingly handsome. With his scruff and tattoos, he looked like a brawler, and yet he had an athletic grace about him that spoke of massive discipline. No doubt he worked relentlessly hard to hone those muscles.

He got into the passenger side of a truck, and a moment later, it took off. At the end of the driveway, the taillights blinked red, before turning onto the road that led to the highway.

She looked around the RV, despair creeping in. No loan meant no generator, no underwear…no food. And then she thought about Declan sleeping in a comfortable bed, taking a hot shower, and feasting like a king.

Okay, you know what? Fuck this.

Fuck him. How does he get off doing office work while I break my back weeding?

She quickly packed her suitcase, grabbed her purse, and headed out of the Airstream. Her wheels clattered across the asphalt and rocked over the lawn. When she found the front door locked, she headed around the house to the kitchen. *Locked.*

Phinny eyed the balcony above the terrace. If she climbed onto the counter of the built-in grill, she could reach the uneven stone of the house's façade. Perhaps, if she got her footing, she could heave herself over the banister. *That shouldn't be too hard.*

But wouldn't that sliding door be locked as well?

Only one way to find out. Setting her luggage and purse on a chaise lounge, she hiked herself onto the counter. *Easy enough.* Now, she just had to channel her inner rock climber. She'd never been much for outdoor adventures, but she had to get into that house, and she didn't see another way. *Let's do this.*

Finding a rock that protruded enough to get a grip, she got a foothold after one try. *Victory.* Now, for the next—

"What're you doing?"

Heat sped through her at such an alarming rate, her

palms went clammy, loosening her hold. Looking down, she found a little girl with dusty jeans and riding boots staring at her. "I'm trying to get on the balcony."

"Why?"

"Because the house is locked." Yeah, that wasn't creepy at all. "Hello, I'm Phinny." Her fingers began a slow slide. It was time to get down. "Kurt's daughter. I flew all the way from London to get here, but nobody seems to be home right now to let me in."

Plaid ribbons wrapped around the tips of her pigtails. She couldn't have been older than eight. "Are you the one that made Kurt sad?"

"I…don't think so?"

"I have to go pee pee, and my mommy doesn't want me to go in the bunkhouse, so I can let you in."

"I would love that so much. Thank you." Getting back down was a bit trickier, but she eased her feet to the counter and then jumped to the slate deck.

"Are you playing Spiderman?" the little girl asked.

"It would seem so."

"I don't like to play games like that. I like to ride horses. Kurt was going to teach me to be a barrel rider like my mommy, but now he's dead, so he can't."

It was like a punch to the chest. The air left her lungs, leaving her gasping.

He's dead.

Phinny focused on the mountains in the distance, as waves of grief rolled over her.

I'm never going to know my father.

"Come on." The little girl headed to the door, pulled a key from her pocket, and inserted it. As she walked inside, she pointed to a closed door. "I'm allowed to use this bathroom as long as I don't bother Kurt or anybody." She disappeared inside while Phinny continued into the enormous, clean, and well-equipped kitchen.

The air conditioning immediately dried her skin, the salt leaving it tight. Starving, thirsty, Phinny went right to the refrigerator to find it bursting with food. She peeked inside the pantry to see shelves jammed with boxes and bottles.

Yep. The puck chaser had been living like a king, all right. "That fucking fucker."

"You said a bad word."

Phinny swung around. "I did. I'm so sorry. I'm just really frustrated."

"My mommy says instead of getting angry, get busy." The little girl scratched behind her ear. "I have to go now. Bye."

"Bye. Thank you for letting me in." She watched until the girl left the house. Then, alone, she went back to the refrigerator, grabbed a bottle of chilled white burgundy, and yanked out the cork. She didn't even check the contents of a glass storage container before pulling it out, popping the lid, and picking up chunks of chicken with her fingers. The tang of the vinaigrette made saliva spill into her mouth, and she gorged on cubes of feta, bits of crisp red onion, salty olives, and red peppers. *Delicious*. Once she'd finished, she wanted more. But as hungry as she was, she felt sticky and gross and needed to shower first. Bottle in hand, she rolled the carry-on into the living room.

Whoa. This is not how I remember Kurt's house. Hadn't it been darker? She recalled a more lodge-like décor with wood paneled walls and dark furniture with tartan throw pillows. Or had her mind patched together images from magazine and movies over the years?

I just don't know. Taking a swig of wine, she crossed the spacious, gorgeously decorated room, heading for the stairs. Down the long hall leading toward the back of the house, every door was open except for one. Curious, she turned the knob.

Locked. Huh. She glanced around. *This must be his office.*

Nothing for me there.

Carrying on, she started for the stairs when her gaze snagged on the massive stone hearth. Specifically, the row of framed photographs lining the mantel.

With sudden purpose, she found herself needing to see those pictures. Dropping her purse right there on the floor, she made her way over to get a closer look.

She saw a steely-eyed Kurt in his hockey gear.

Another of Kurt and his teammates hoisting the Stanley Cup.

She picked up a striking shot of cowboys herding cattle. She could feel the movement of the beasts, the energy of the men as they held their lassos high in the air. Setting it back, she skimmed ahead, unable to help herself from searching for a photograph of her.

Her gaze caught on the hockey boys. Four of them. Tall, gangly, laughing, happy teenagers looking like they held the world in the palms of their hands.

The scream of rejection ripped across her body like icy cold storm winds.

This is it. The absolute proof he'd traded her for them. Her mum always said Kurt was all about hockey. He hadn't known what to do with a little girl who wanted to stand on a step stool and make biscuits alongside her nanny. Or have a tea party with her stuffed animals. She'd needed her long hair detangled, and she'd wanted bows and shiny, patent leather Mary Janes.

These boys slammed into each other on the ice. They had cuts and bruises, scrapes and black eyes. Kurt had liked them better.

Even though this picture was taken more than ten years ago, she recognized Declan. With casual stances and easy-going smiles, the other boys had their arms wrapped around each other. Declan stood slightly apart. A shadow crossed his features, but it didn't hide the smile that lit his eyes. He might not be touching them, but he belonged.

She drew a sharp breath. *And I don't.*

I don't belong here.

Any doubt Declan might've planted in her mind about family and legacy got yanked out by the roots.

Of course, I'm going to sell this place.

It means nothing to me.

"Remember our 'Wyoming State Rodeo?'" Jaime said with a big grin. "I thought my dad was going to have a heart attack when he saw us riding that damn hog."

Declan remembered. They used to call him Swagger Pete because he had the biggest balls they'd ever seen on a pig. As he brought a tray of steaks out of Jaime's kitchen, he noticed Cole looked uneasy and Booker…well, he was checked out. It couldn't be clearer he wanted to be anywhere but here. "I remember you laid out on the ground. Couldn't stay on him more than a second."

"But he loved Declan." Cole set his beer bottle on the table. "He'd have carried you to Canada and back if you'd wanted."

"Well, sure, I was the reigning champ." Declan set the platter down and used the tongs to set each steak on the hot grill. "Animals respect the alpha dog."

Jaime's eyes lit up. "Uh huh. You didn't look so alpha after old Bessie knocked you into the mud."

"I was drunk." Declan turned his back on them so they wouldn't see his grin.

"You were twelve," Jaime said. "You were sober as a nun."

Everyone laughed. Well, except Booker. After Kurt had gotten them into hockey, sure, they'd become focused and disciplined, but nothing had tamed their wild natures. Competing against each other riding steers, pigs, and mustangs in their own version of a rodeo was tame compared to the extreme challenges they'd thrown down for each other.

"Whatever happened to Doug?" Cole asked.

A lot of their friends had fallen away over the years. Either their parents didn't let them hang around with such reckless kids or they weren't as good at hockey. Doug had stuck it out until he'd broken his arm.

"He moved to Seattle." Cole tipped back his beer. "He's a forest ranger."

"Not surprised he'd go hide in the woods." Declan flipped a steak. "We scarred him for life."

"How were we supposed to know there was horse shit in there?" Jaime asked.

In the moment of silence, Declan turned to look at the others. All of them but Booker burst out laughing at the same time. To their credit, they'd all jumped out of the second story window of the barn to see if they could fly, too. It wasn't their fault Doug happened to land in manure. How could they have known the hands had shoveled it into the hay pile?

"Never laughed so hard in my life when his head popped up with hay sticking to the shit smeared all over his face," Jaime said.

Even Booker cracked a grin at that one, but he brought the beer to his mouth to cover it.

Jaime reached for the chips in the middle of the table. "Hey, man. You're kicking ass as an agent. How the hell did you get Todd Beckett to sign with you?"

Booker shrugged. "I'm good at what I do." He'd been the golden kid. Blessed with good looks, confidence, family support, and money, he'd sailed through life. Well, until that night, obviously.

"Fuckin' overachiever." Laughing, Jaime shook his head. "I mean, how many kids from Calamity go to *Yale*? Right out of the box, not even six months after graduation, you got Derrell Johnson. You were twenty-two years old."

"He liked my hustle." Booker sounded detached.

Though Declan hated that his old friend had thrown up walls, he couldn't blame him.

"And you, man." Jaime tipped his chin toward Cole. "Livin' the dream. You might be the man to break Kurt's records."

They hadn't seen each other in ten years, not since that terrible night, so Declan suspected reminiscing before having a conversation about what happened wasn't going to work. It would take time to mend the broken relationships.

He didn't know why Jaime wasn't picking up on the mood, though. In the past, when the guys had gotten together it was loud, everyone ragging on each other. Tonight, it was subdued. Polite.

Declan steered the conversation in a different direction. "You've turned this place around." Back when they were kids, the Broken Arrow was a dude ranch. Though they'd barely made ends meet, Jaime's parents had worked their assess off to keep it going.

Which was the whole reason that night had happened in the first place.

"Yeah, it was rough there for a while." Jaime sat back, a pile of chips in his hand. "I tried a lot of things. Obviously, a dude ranch wasn't going to cut it. First, we bought a bunch of tiny houses and tried to rent them out, but the upkeep was too much. Between repairs and all the bullshit from the guests who expected a five-star resort, it took too much time away from our bread and butter."

Declan wished he knew what the other two were thinking. He couldn't read them at all. "What turned it around?"

"You remember my brother was all about the rodeo, right?" Jaime looked at the guys. "Yeah, so, while I was doing all this research, trying to see what other ranches did to make money, Elliott was training on a couple of our broncs. I came across an article about some guy in Montana making big money selling bull semen. Eight grand a straw. Think about it. All we needed to do was sell ten of them and…damn, we'd finally be in the black. All our troubles would go away."

"That's how you turned this place around?" Cole suppressed a laugh. "Bull spooge?" Ten years ago, he'd been the life of every party. With his A-list actor dad gone so much, he'd grown up alone in a mansion, raised by nannies.

Declan had kept up with him over the years—hard not to when he was the hottest hockey player in the NHL. And he was just as wild now as he'd been when they were kids.

Except Declan hadn't seen any of that personality on this visit.

"Go ahead and laugh," Jaime said. "But we're livin' large now. It took a while to get us in a stable position. At first, we didn't have the best stock. But we put almost all the money back into the business until we were able to buy some top-quality sires. Now, we're doing great, and the timing couldn't be better."

"Timing?" Cole asked.

"To own the team."

Cole, the bad boy of hockey, the easiest going one of any of them, hardened. "You realize Kurt's dead, right?"

"Yeah, of course. I just…" Color spilled into Jaime's features, and he glanced down at his hands. He sat there quietly for a moment, and then in a whirl of motion, he pushed the bowl of chips away. "This whole thing is so fucked up. Of course, I'm sad Kurt's gone, but he wanted to do something here, and I…fuck, man, I want it, too." His voice had gone tight, and he stopped talking. Looked like he was tangled up in emotion.

"I don't want my share of the team," Cole said quietly.

"You don't have to decide now." Jaime grew agitated. "We have time."

"Don't need it." Cole hunched a shoulder. "I'm twenty-eight, I'm in the best shape of my life…I'm not giving up hockey to own the Renegades."

"I get that," Jaime said. "I'd feel the same, but you might change your mind a few years from now when you're ready to retire. We can ask Harrison, see if he can find a way to word it so we can hold it open for you guys."

Cole shook his head. "I can't think like that."

Declan understood. He wouldn't want to jinx his future with thoughts of how it might end.

"I don't want it, either." Booker's voice was low, emotionless. "I've got a good gig. I like what I do."

Jaime's knee jackhammered. "Guys, we're talking about an NHL team. Kurt's team. He bought it for *us.*"

Declan wondered how much longer they'd spend ignoring the elephant in the room. Spearing the steaks, he dropped them onto the platter. Well, it wasn't his place to bring it up. "Let's eat." With his boot, he kicked his chair back and fell into it. "Where's your family?" he asked Jaime. "I wanted to say hello to your parents."

Staring at his steak, Jaime looked like he'd lost his mojo. "Maddy's doing study abroad in Paris, so my folks went over there to get her settled in."

Life really had changed for the Dupree family. Used to be, Jaime missed half their practices because he was needed on the ranch.

"And I finally got Elliott to give up his rodeo dreams and go to college."

"Still killing people's dreams, huh?" No, Booker didn't actually say that out loud. But Declan figured that's what the guy was thinking.

Other than the clatter of silverware on plates and the rustle of wind through trees, the patio went quiet. Jaime probably figured he had one shot to reunite the group for Kurt's sake, but Declan didn't see it happening without addressing the issue that had torn them apart. *The only way around is through.* "So, that night." He kicked his leg out under the table, nicking Jaime's boot. His friend shot him a resigned look. "We're going to have to talk about it."

"Yeah." Jaime set his fork down. "I'm sorry, you guys. I…" He had a strangled look, and Declan wanted to step in and save him, but this conversation had to happen. So, he let his friend find his own way. It took a minute to pull himself together, and when he did, Jaime was strong. "I've never forgiven myself for dragging everyone into my pity party that night. The one time I do something selfish…" He took a moment before looking Booker right in the eyes. "I blew up your career, and I'm so damn sorry."

Booker didn't say a word. He sat so still, Declan didn't know if he was breathing.

"It wasn't just you," Cole said. "I was all-in. Hell, it was my idea to take my dad's plane. If we'd stayed on your ranch, nothing would've happened."

With a wry smile, Jaime shook his head. "All these years, I never imagined anyone else was beating himself up over that night. I thought you all hated me. And you had every right to." Jaime pressed his palms onto the table. "I didn't mean to fuck up everyone's lives. I just wanted one more night—"

"Before our lives changed," Cole said quietly.

"And yours didn't." There wasn't even a hint of anger in Booker's tone.

And yet everyone stopped chewing to look at him. If Declan's stomach had twisted, he couldn't imagine what Jaime was experiencing now that their friend had flat-out set the blame on his plate.

But instead of being beaten down, Jaime said, "Yeah, but I was happy for you. I was. I just—"

"Look, I get it," Cole said. "We'd worked our asses off to get to that point, and it was all about to pay off. Any of us would've been crushed if our plans had blown up like that."

"But that's not the point. Booker said no. He was leaving the next day. I should've dropped it." Jaime lowered his head in his hands. "I never should've sent the text in the first place."

They'd all felt like shit the night they'd learned Jaime wasn't going to Canada. His parents had broken the news that the ranch was in the red, and they couldn't afford to keep it. He'd made the choice to stay home and help them save it.

So, instead of playing junior division hockey in Vancouver—given how much hockey he'd missed to pitch in on the dude ranch, Kurt had figured he could benefit from the extra two years of play—he'd stay in Calamity while Declan headed off to University of Michigan, Cole started second string for the Wyoming Renegades, and Booker…man. He'd gotten drafted by the Los Angeles Kings.

He'd been that good.

"I love this ranch," Jaime said. "You know I do. But I wanted to live on my own. I wanted to play hockey."

"I get that." Declan looked at the others. "We all get that."

"You said no." Jaime held his gaze. Then, he looked at Booker. "Both of you said no."

"Not me," Cole said. "And I got drunk at the cabin, too. It wasn't just you."

"Nothing would've happened if I hadn't sent that fucking text. I'd do anything to go back and make a different decision." For a long, tension-filled moment, Jaime looked down at his clasped hands. And then he addressed the three of them. "But I can't. It happened, and here we are. Kurt's giving us a path back to each other."

Grabbing his beer bottle, Booker scraped his chair back. "Anybody need a refill?"

But Jaime held his gaze. "I really hope we can get past it."

Booker's gaze dropped to his once-badly injured legs and stayed there for a tension-filled moment. Since his family had left town and cut contact, no one knew the extent of his injuries or how his recovery had gone. So, right then, Declan was pretty damn sure that was all any of them were thinking about. *What happened to you? Are you okay?*

Finally, without looking at anyone, Booker turned and headed for the house.

"That was a stupid thing to say." Jaime scrubbed his face with both hands. "Hard to get past it when he lives with the damage every day." Drawing in a breath, he gave the remaining two guys an apologetic smile. "I'm sorry. Tonight should've been about Kurt, about remembering him and appreciating everything he did for us." He looked to the kitchen. "I don't know what to do, how to make it right."

"You said your apology, but now we have to hear Booker out. He never got to yell at us." Declan got up.

"Where're you going?" Jaime asked.

"To get Booker back out here so we can finally get it all out." As he crossed the patio, he heard the nicker of horses and distant laughter. Woodsmoke from a bonfire scented the air. He slid the screen door open and headed into the kitchen.

But his friend wasn't there. And while he put in an effort to look around, Declan already knew. So, after checking the driveway for confirmation, he headed back outside. "He's gone."

"He left without saying goodbye?" Jaime sounded surprised.

"Yep."

"Fuck." Jaime let out a breath. "I don't know how to fix this."

"Maybe you can't." And that was something they'd all have to live with.

Chapter Five

"Well, that sucked." Declan sat in the dark of his friend's truck.

The engine idled, and Cole's frame barely fit the driver's seat. He was a big, muscular guy, movie star-handsome like his dad. He'd always been happy and easy-going. Declan had never seen him this...contemplative. "I can't believe Kurt's gone."

"I know. Try living in his house, eating his food, and working in his office." It stirred up an ache—that familiar sense of helplessness that came with grief. He couldn't bring Kurt back, couldn't see him one more time. Would never get to say goodbye.

"That's got to be weird. I feel like shit, though, because I fell out of touch. I..."

"You pulled a runner." Instead of playing for the Renegades, Cole had taken Jaime's spot on the Canadian junior division team.

"I can't believe Jaime blames himself. This is on me. *I* did this." He gazed out the windshield into the darkness. "I just had to take it too far, you know? It wasn't enough to hang out at his place. No, I had to steal my dad's plane."

"Pretty sure we've all got a list of things we shouldn't have done, but we can't go back and do it differently. If Booker hadn't gotten hurt, it would've been a great night. We'd done that kind of shit countless times. That one time, things went sideways. I know it's easy to say, but you've got to let it go. Guilt doesn't make Booker's life better, and it sure as hell isn't improving yours."

Cole cracked a grin. "You always were the smart one."

"Uh, that was Booker. Valedictorian, remember?"

"He was book smart. You're smart here." Cole tapped his temple. "You were always the reasonable one. The rational one. I think you're the only thing that kept us alive."

Eh. He wasn't so sure about that. "We took calculated risks, and we were all athletic and coordinated, but ultimately, I think we got lucky."

"Until we didn't." Cole shifted restlessly. "It's not Jaime's fault. All he did was invite us over. I'm the one who had to turn it into something bigger."

"Let me ask you something. What if my parents hadn't gone on vacation? What if the driver of the car that hit them hadn't had vodka for breakfast that morning? What would you say to me if I told you those thoughts keep me up at night?"

Cole turned to him, a shaft of moonlight cutting across his face. "Do they?"

"No, but you get my point." He made a rolling motion with his hand. *Go with it.*

"I'd say you're spinning your wheels. And that you've got to make peace with what happened and move on."

"And since I can't get my parents back, I can at least

honor them by living a good life. By becoming a son they'd be proud of."

"I know you're right. But you didn't cause the accident. You hear what I'm saying? I *caused* Booker's accident."

"No, man. You didn't. Turbulence did. How many times had we done that jump before? Hundreds. Nothing had ever gone wrong. Cole, listen to me. You've got to let it go. Shit happens. Booker's alive and doing well."

"Yeah, I hear you. Most days, I'm fine. But seeing him tonight…knowing he bailed on us." Cole shook his head.

"This is the first time he's seen us in ten years. First time he's been back here. Add that to Kurt's funeral…it's a lot to take in."

"You're right."

"And maybe Jaime isn't the only one who needs to apologize. Call him up. Write him. Do something to get this off your mind." He reached for the handle. "All right. I guess I'll see you in a month."

"Yeah, maybe. But if I'm not taking my share of the team, there's no point in coming back."

Reluctant to leave his friend alone, Declan asked, "Is your dad in town?"

"Nah. He's filming in Mexico."

"More *Clan Mackintosh*?" His dad's blockbuster franchise about a feud between two clans in Scotland that spanned three-hundred-and-fifty years was equal parts soap opera and historical. Declan had watched the first three but had lost interest after that.

Cole nodded. "There are fifteen books in the series, and each movie outsells the one before it, so it's not going to end any time soon."

Declan hated to think about him all alone in that huge house. "Why don't you stay here tonight?"

"I appreciate it, but I've got a flight out first thing in the morning." Cole's features softened. "Actually…" He almost looked like the kid Declan had once known. "I bought my own place a few years ago. Don't know why since I don't live here."

"I guess you plan on coming back."

"Oh, I don't know about that. I've never lived in it."

"So, it's just sitting there?"

Cole shrugged. "I'm renting it out to a single mom with a pile of kids." He smiled as though he were standing right in the middle of the chaos and loving it. "They're going to destroy the place."

"I'm guessing she's a beauty?"

"Never met her. Probably never will."

"Okay. Well, it was good to see you." Declan opened the door and planted one boot on the driveway. "It's your choice, but I hope you don't reject the team outright. At least hang on and see if Harrison can figure out a way to keep the opportunity open for those of us who can't take it right now." He glanced to the house. "I know we've all moved on, but it might be nice one day to all hang out again."

"Yeah."

"Whatever you do, just…don't let guilt drive your decisions."

"I hear you. I'll think about it."

As Cole drove off, Declan headed toward the house. The lights were off in the Airstream, and he imagined Phinny curled up on the couch. Shame got a good grip on him.

While Kurt's daughter slept in an RV, he'd offered

Cole a bedroom in this huge house. Even reminding himself about her plans to sell the ranch failed to get him fired up.

He might not like her, but he shouldn't have treated her like that. Tomorrow, he'd make sure she had everything she needed. He'd already brought by blankets and sheets, but he'd get her food, a generator, and basic supplies.

The minute he opened the door, he felt an energy, a presence, and he knew he wasn't alone. The kitchen lights were on, and reverb pounded beneath his boots. Kurt made sure the bunkhouse was stocked with everything—video games, big screen TVs, and all the necessities—so if the guys thought they could take advantage of an empty house, they were wrong.

Striding across the living room, he noticed a pair of high heels by the fireplace. What the hell? As he crossed the kitchen, he took in the crusty fork, the dirty plate, and a cake box left open on the counter.

Pissed, he trampled down the basement stairs ready to read the riot act to the hands. It sounded like a party, and he couldn't believe the staff would abuse their boss like this. *The funeral was* yesterday.

Kurt had paid for Alonso's mom's cancer treatments. He'd bought Carrie's kids their back-to-school clothes when their father had taken off for California to hook up with some woman he'd met on the internet.

But when Declan got to the bottom of the stairs, he didn't see a party. He saw a woman.

With her long blond hair spilling down her back, Phinny had a bottle of wine in one hand and a slice of cake in the other. In nothing but her father's jersey, her hips swayed with the beat.

The princess is drunk.

And then it struck him. *Wait, she's in the house. Not the Airstream.*

Declan tried like hell to fight the smile, but it broke through.

Good for her for not taking his shit.

As the Guns N' Roses song ramped up, she bent over and flipped her hair. It was like a shampoo commercial—that glossy mane settling with a bounce.

Now, there was a sight he'd never imagined seeing, the princess head-banging. Little bits of cake flew in every direction, but it was a great song, and he wasn't about to end the show. Not with her toned legs on display and that perfect peach-shaped ass. And that fucking hair. Thick, silky…long enough to wrap around his fist at least twice.

He leaned against the bar and watched her rock out.

Holding the bottle like a microphone, she belted out *Paradise City* along with Axl Rose. "So far away, so fa-ar away—" She jumped onto the coffee table, flipped her hair again, and right as she swung her head up, she caught sight of him and jerked like she'd been Tasered. The bottle of wine slipped from her grasp, and the hand with the slice of cake hit her chest. Reaching for the remote, she shut off the music. "What're you doing here?"

He pushed off the bar. "Looks like you're making yourself right at home." Grabbing the bottle before the wine soaked into the carpet, he was relieved to find it empty. But little bits of chocolate cake crumbs were splattered everywhere. "How'd you get in?"

Wavering, she stepped off the table, holding her arms out to find her balance. "A little girl in riding boots." She grinned. "She was cute. I used to be cute like that."

He glanced up at her. "And now?"

"Now, I'm a hot mess." Her laughter had a bitter edge to it. "Look at me." In a flash, her features crumpled, and tears welled in her eyes.

"Yeah. Well, you've had a few hard hits. It's understandable." He took in the frosting-smeared jersey. *Oh, shit.* "Where did you get this? Did you take it out of the *frame*?"

"There's a whole roomful of his stuff. Can you imagine? Dedicating a room to your hockey sticks and pucks and…and…"

"Trophies? Yeah, *he* didn't put that room together. Tina did. If she'd left it to him, everything would be in boxes or stuffed on shelves. She organized everything."

"He's a narsh—a narshiss…" She looked confused that her tongue wasn't cooperating.

"A narcissist? Nope. Not Kurt."

As though her body were too heavy for her slender legs, she plunked down on the coffee table. Right on what was left of her cake. "I want to go home."

His senses sharpened. "You can do that, you know." That would be the best solution. He didn't think she'd win the contest but knowing the possibility was out there kept him on edge. *I can't let her sell this place.*

"No, I don't have a home anymore."

"Of course, you do. It's back in England."

"My parents changed the locks, and Drewsy moved me out of my room. I have nowhere to go, and I'm just so tired." She gazed up at him with the most startling blues eyes he'd ever seen.

He couldn't stand seeing her so sad, so he sat beside her. "What do you mean they changed the locks?"

"I didn't marry Cameron." She let out a long-suffering sigh. "I don't love him."

He needed to clean up this mess and get to bed, but she was just so fucking lost…he had to ask. "They kicked you out because you didn't marry someone you don't love?"

"You're very handsome. Did you know that? You're scary but handsome."

"How am I scary?" He'd never heard that before. Well, on the ice sure. That was why they'd called him the Intimidator.

"You're mean. And bad. Are you very bad?"

He chuckled. "Very, but only in two places, and since you'll never be there"—*my bed or on the ice*—"you don't have anything to worry about. Come on, let's get you cleaned up." He held out his hand to help her stand.

But she didn't move. "Oh." With a snap of her fingers, she looked around the basement as though seeing it for the first time. "I just remembered why I came down here. Does Kurt have a wine cellar?"

He had one of the best in the state—probably the country—but Declan didn't think now was a good time to tell her. When she sobered up, she might regret chugging a thousand-dollar bottle of Château d'Yquem.

Then again, maybe she brushed her teeth with champagne. He didn't know the first thing about her. "How about we pick some up tomorrow?"

"No, that's okay." She scrunched her nose. "I don't really like booze."

"You liked it tonight."

"I hate-drank."

"You what?"

"I was hot and tired, and I smelled like horse, and then I got inside the house and realized Kurt didn't have a single picture of me anywhere, so I grabbed a bottle and started drinking."

"All right, well, that's a lot to deal with, and I can't help with most of it, but I can apologize for my part in your unhappiness. I've been pretty shitty to you. I'm sorry about that."

"Wait, you're being nice to me now?"

"Mostly because I don't want you to smear any more chocolate cake around."

"Oh, I would never smear cake." She said it so solemnly he had to laugh.

"It's on your ass." He pointed, and she twisted around.

"Oh, no."

She looked so upset, he grabbed a dish towel from the bar. He tried handing it to her, but her motor skills weren't the best. Instead of taking it, she bent over to give him access to her tight little ass. *Just do it fast. A quick swipe and get out.*

"Did you see that pretty blue box of yumminess? I *love* cake. I never get to eat it, though. My mum didn't like sweets in the house, and now that I'm on my own, I can't afford them."

He folded the towel over to wipe away the stubborn frosting. "What do you mean you can't afford *cake*?" Wasn't she a rich girl?

"Hey." She turned to him so quickly, her hair fanned out and feathered over his cheek. "Why does Kurt have so much frozen lemonade?"

"I can't keep up with this conversation. How about we go to bed, and we can talk more in the morning?"

"No. Come here." Reaching for his hand, she towed him into a large closet that held an additional refrigerator and box freezer. She lifted the lid. "Look."

It was stuffed with cans of pink lemonade. "Oh, right."

"What?"

"It's for the Wild West Festival." Maybe it'd be cancelled now that Kurt was gone. He'd have to talk to Mitch about that. He closed the lid. "Another thing we'll handle in the morning. Come on, let's get out of here. I'll walk you back to the RV."

She wagged a finger at him. "Nuh uh uh. I'm not staying there anymore. You thought you could pull one over on me, but I wised up. I'm living here this month, just like you."

"Yeah, okay." It was only fair. He gestured toward the stairs, and she led the way.

"I wasn't asking your permission." As she climbed, she wobbled and grabbed the handrail. "Whoa. It's like being on a yacht in a storm, right?"

"I don't know. I've never been on a yacht."

"Oh, it's fun. Except in a storm because then I get sick. I went whale watching once when I was little, and I threw up about twenty times. Mum was so embarrassed, she said she'd never take me again."

"Your mom's got issues."

At the top of the stairs, she swung around. Cheeks flushed, complexion smooth and creamy, she looked young, innocent, and stunningly beautiful. "What did you say?"

"I said you should go whale watching again if you want to. You might not get seasick the next time you try it."

"Let's do that. Let's go whale watching."

"Ah, okay. Wyoming's landlocked, though, so maybe we could try something else."

"Really? You want to do something with me?" She was about to clap her hands but missed, got disoriented, and reeled.

As she toppled into his arms, his right leg went down a step to brace himself. Her scent filled his senses—underneath the cake and wine, he caught a whiff of soap, coconut shampoo, and something so unbearably sweet and feminine, his skin went hot. With her elbow jabbing into his ribcage, he shifted her, ready to set her upright, but she sank into him. Her body relaxed, and she sighed. Just as her eyelids fluttered closed, he pushed her upright. "Come on."

She blinked in confusion. "I thought we were going to do something."

"We are. We're going to sleep."

"Where's the fun in that?" But she continued up the stairs. "What did you used to do here as a cute little boy?"

"Who said I was cute?"

"Oh, I saw pissures of you. You were all scowly and adorable. I'd have had a terrible crush on you. But you were probably like Kurt, so I wouldn't have liked you."

Under the bright kitchen lights, he could see puffiness under her eyes and little flecks of mascara. In spite of the exhaustion, disappointment, and grief she had to be experiencing, she had an inherent joyfulness that made him feel like an asshole for being so hard on her.

She gave him a knowing look. "I'll bet you had lots of girlfriends. I'll bet you had sex under the bleachers and in the back of cars. You probably made out with girls on Lovers Lane."

"I think you've been watching too many American movies."

"After a touchdown, your cheerleader girlfriend

probably came running onto the field and threw herself into your arms."

Definitely too many movies. "I played hockey. We didn't have cheerleaders." He gave her a little nudge. "Come on. Let's go upstairs."

The moment she turned around, she saw the blue box on the kitchen table. "Oh, look. Cake." She practically skipped across the room. "Want some?"

When he caught up with her, he read the inscription. *Happy birthday, Sarah.*

"What?" She touched the space between his eyes. "Why did you get all crinkly?"

"Because that little girl who let you in here? You just ate her birthday cake."

"I did?" Her eyes went wide, flooding with tears. "Oh, no. What have I done?" With a look of determination, she marched toward the pantry.

"What're you doing?"

"I'm making her a new one."

He followed her into the large, immaculately organized space and watched her scan the containers, cans, bottles, and boxes. "Um." She pulled down a large canister. "Flour, right? What else? Sugar. Cake's got to have sugar."

Christ. "Have you ever made a cake?"

"No, but it can't be that hard. I have to try or that little girl's not going to have a birthday cake."

He pulled the canister out of her arms and set it back on the shelf. "I'll pick one up in the morning. She won't need it until later in the day." He'd noticed the Harley and Lu's Emporium logo on the box, so he was pretty sure he could order another identical one. "Look, I'm going to clean up a little. Are you good on your own?"

"Oh, sure. I'm used to being on my own."

"I meant finding your way upstairs but go ahead and break my heart some more. You chose a bedroom, right?"

"I picked the one furthest from yours. All the way at the end of the hall. I don't want to run into you. You don't make me feel good."

"I'm sorry about that, but I'll repeat it in the morning when you're sober. Now, do you want me to help you up there?"

"No, thank you. I might just take a little nap on the couch."

"Okay, just take off that shirt first."

Even though she didn't move, her spirit seemed to retract like a crab pulling its limbs into its shell. "I showered. Do I still stink?"

"No, you've got chocolate cake…" He motioned to her face and chest.

She looked down. "Oh." She started lifting the shirt. "See? I'm a big, hot mess."

He reached for her wrists. "Hang on, Stripper Barbie. Let's not take it off yet, okay? Let's get you upstairs where you can change into something else. I'll deal with Kurt's jersey later." He took her elbow and guided her across the living room.

"See what I'm saying?" She made a vague gesture toward the mantel. "No pictures of me."

He did a quick scan and realized she was right. "Not there, maybe, but I'm sure he has some."

"No. He never wanted me."

She was killing him. "Now, I know for a fact that's not true."

Grabbing his arm, she stopped, those blue eyes filled with hope. "How do you know?"

"Kurt talked about you all the time."

"He did?"

"Sure." That wasn't exactly truthful. Kurt didn't talk much, but that only meant when he did mention his daughter, Declan had paid attention. She'd mattered to him. He tried to urge her toward the stairs.

"What did he say? Did he say why he stopped talking to me?"

"No. He didn't confide in me about stuff like that. Now, come on, Seraphina. You have to change out of this shirt."

"Nobody calls me Seraphina."

"What do they call you?"

"I'm Phinny. Except when I do something wrong, and then I'm Seraphina." She lowered her voice to imitate a pissed-off snooty man.

When they finally reached the grand staircase, she let out a gigantic sigh. "I'm sad that he's gone."

"Me, too."

"Well, but you *miss* him. I didn't know him. And now he's gone, I never will."

"So, you don't hate him anymore?"

"No, silly. I never hated him. He hurt my feelings. He made me sad." Her voice sounded so delicate, just a wisp.

"Yeah, I can see that." At the end of the hallway, he steered her into the bedroom that held her carry-on and purse. "You didn't bring much."

"Well, I thought I'd only be here for two days. I couldn't afford a motel for any longer."

Didn't seem like she could afford much of anything. "Don't you have a job?"

"Of course, I do." She sounded insulted. "I'm a waitress in a diner. And I'm very, very good at my job."

A waitress? Nothing was adding up. He'd seen her clothes, heard the stories from Kurt. "And your parents don't help you out?"

"Oh, no. They've warsh…warsh…*washed* their hands of me." She face-planted onto the bed.

Which meant the cake was now on the duvet. "Just because you didn't marry some guy?"

She rolled onto her back. "He's not *some guy*. He's from the second wealthiest family in England."

"If you come from a wealthy family, why do you need to marry someone from one?"

"Well." She let out a dramatic sigh. "Our parents are in business together." She crooked a finger at him to come closer.

He set a knee on the bed and got up close to that lush mouth. He wanted to brush the hair out of her eyes and tuck it behind her ear. He wanted to stroke the back of his hand over her cheek to see if it was as soft as it looked.

"He sucked in bed." She said it at full volume, and he jerked back. "Shex. He wasn't good at the shex."

"That's a good enough reason not to marry someone." He started to get up, but she yanked his arm, and he toppled onto her.

"Don't tell anybody, but he doesn't tickle the pickle."

"I don't…are you saying you have a pickle?"

"No, silly."

"Then whose pickle are we talking about?"

"Okay, not a pickle. What do I have?" She hiked up on her elbows. "A button. He doesn't lick my button."

"Ah, okay. Gotcha. He doesn't go down on you."

"Yes. *Exactly*. I've known him my whole life, but we'd only ever been friends, so when he first asked me out on a date, I was so excited. He's very handsome, and he's always been so nice to me, and I thought, yay, we're going to do the shexy things." She cupped a hand over her mouth. "I got another secret. I tickled his pickle in the parking lot of a restaurant."

"You might not want to tell me these things."

"Oh, and we did it in a closet at a party."

"Phinny, I promise you're going to regret this in the morning. I'll tell you what. I'll grab you—"

Eyes bright with mischief, she fisted his shirt and pulled him back down. "I gave him a blow job right in front of our families." Laughing, she shook her head. "They weren't in the bathroom with us, but they were right there, in the dining room. It was his sister's engagement party. But Cameron didn't like doing it in fun places. He only likes shex before he goes to bed." Falling back onto the mattress, she pumped hips. "Unh, uhn, uhn." She screwed up her face and shouted, "*Oh*." When she settled, she gave him a disappointed look. "It wasn't good with him."

"Yeah, that sounds pretty bad."

"Do you tickle your girlfriend's pickle?"

"I'm not seeing anyone, but if I was…hell, yeah, I'd lick her button."

"Wait." She wrapped her hand around his forearm. "Do you *like* doing it?" She looked so serious.

"I love it."

Her eyes went wide.

He placed his palm over her hand. "Phinny, sex isn't fun unless we're both into it."

"What do you mean?"

"Well, if she's just lying there waiting for me to finish…I'd rather tickle my own pickle."

"Your girlfriend's very lucky."

"Well, like I said, I'm not seeing anyone right now."

"You should be. You should totally have a girlfriend. You don't know how many women I know who don't get shatisfied by men."

"So, it's my civic duty? To have a girlfriend?"

Her eyelids drooped. "I'm very tired."

"Hang on. Sera—er, Phinny, you don't want to fall asleep with chocolate cake on your shirt." He tried to gently shake her, but she'd gone limp. "Crap." He should just go, leave her to deal with everything when she woke up. But she was going to be hungover and seeing the mess she'd made would only make her feel worse. "Okay, look." He slid a hand under her and set her upright.

Her head tipped back, hair spilling like a waterfall. "No, no, no. I'm shleeping." She tried but didn't seem to have the strength to lift it on her own.

"Come on. Raise your arms."

She gave a sleepy smile. "Are you going to tickle my pickle?"

"Nope. Not when you're drunk, and not when you're sober. I am *never* going to lick your button."

"You don't like me?"

"You're pretty cute when you're drunk, but you're Kurt's daughter, and my purpose in life right now is to keep you from selling his ranch." He lifted her arm. "Hold it there, okay?" He gave her a shake, so she'd understand the directive.

"My nanny used to put me to bed when I was little." She wore a goofy smile. "I'd always stay up too late. I just wanted to be part of them, you know?"

"Yeah, sure." *Part of whom?*

"They'd have fancy dinner parties, and the house would smell so good. You could hear everyone laughing."

She attempted to mimic the sound. "Oh, my God, there'd be these bursts of it. Talk, talk, talk. So much to say. And candles everywhere. It was all so romantic and lovely. Mummy would catch me sitting behind the curtains in the parlor, and then nanny would carry me up to bed. She'd sit on the toilet and prop me on her lap and brush my teeth. Hmmm." Her head tipped sideways, like she wanted to rest it on his shoulder, but he was trying to get the jersey over her head.

The moment she was topless, he had to look away. Because he didn't think he'd ever seen anything as hot as that sexy scrap of lace that held her full, jiggly tits. He could imagine the weight of them in his hands and picture what they'd look like when he pushed them together. He wanted to watch her features soften with pleasure when he sucked her pretty nipples into his mouth.

He wanted to show her just how good sex could be.

But that would never happen, so he laid her back down and folded the comforter over her. Balling up the jersey, he leapt off the bed. "You are *nothing* like what I thought."

It's going to be a long-ass month if she keeps being this adorable.

Chapter Six

It felt strange to live in Kurt's house without him. Declan kept expecting to enter a room and find him sitting in a chair reading or huddling over his laptop working on receipts.

This morning, after asking Mitch if he could borrow a car, he headed for the kitchen. The aroma of coffee had him half-hoping he'd see Kurt on a stool at the island, mug in one hand, paper in the other.

He'd found nothing but a warming coffee pot. Grabbing the keys, he headed outside. On his way to the garage, he ran into the foreman.

"Oh, hey, how's it going?" Hank asked.

"It's okay. Trying to keep up with everything."

"Yeah, it's a lot. Tina really runs the show. Sorry she wasn't here to show you the ropes."

"I've got Mitch. He's been great. He said she'll be back in time for the festival." Mitch had said they were still hosting the event.

"Yeah, she wouldn't miss it." He kicked the tip of his boot in the dirt. "It's hardest for her, I think. She was the one who took care of Kurt at the end. He wouldn't let anyone else in the house. Can't really blame her for taking off for a few days. It's got to be tough to be in that house without him." Hank's gaze roamed across the meadow. "Kurt was the best. It's weird not to see him driving a tractor or fixing a fence."

"I know. I keep thinking I'll run into him." He probably shouldn't bring it up, but he needed to understand. "Why didn't he tell anybody?" *Well, me, really.*

It hurts that he didn't.

"It all went down pretty fast."

Having lost his parents and his grandfather, Declan knew loss never got easier. Grief was insidious, grabbing hold of your lungs and squeezing. It made a man feel pretty damn helpless. "Mitch said it was an embolism?"

"Yeah. Started as a stroke. Tina noticed he had a slight limp, so she made him go to the doctor. And then a specialist saw the clot. There was nothing they could do." Hank took a few shaky breaths. "They said he could go at any moment." He paused again, then cleared his throat. "Basically, he wanted to get his things in order. He passed a few weeks later."

"He'll be missed." *Stupid words. Meaningless.*

Kurt had turned the land his family had wrestled with for a hundred and fifty years into a model of sustainable ranching. He'd taken a bunch of reckless, wild kids and made them into elite hockey players. He might've been quiet, but his presence was authoritative and profound. He led by example, and when he focused on something, he gave it his all.

"Doesn't seem right to hold the festival without him."

"Kurt wouldn't have had it any other way." Hank

smiled. "You know what he said when Tina suggested canceling it?"

"The loom ladies are already on their annual trek out here? That people have been dreaming about his bison burgers all year? That it keeps the past alive?"

"You knew him well." Hank chuckled. "Yes, to all of that."

"What can I do to help?" He thought of all that lemonade in the freezer. Which, unfortunately, called up an image of slim, toned legs and sexy, long hair. Soft, bouncy breasts cupped in lace. And those eyes.

Through them, he could see all the way to her sweet, feisty, wounded heart.

And he liked the view way too much.

"Just like the ranch, he's got everything covered. I don't know if you remember Glori Van Patten, but she's been running the festival for him since they first started dating. She'll be here tomorrow for a meeting. You can talk to her then."

He did remember her. *Nice lady.* "Sounds good."

Hank shifted uncomfortably. "Rumor has it, his daughter's going to sell the place."

Word spread fast in a small town. "It's too soon to know what she'll do."

"A lot of people have been working here a long time. For most of us, this is more than a job. Kurt…well, he made it more like a family."

"I know that. And I can't speak for her, but I can promise you if I win the contest, nothing will change."

He stuttered out a laugh. "Frankly, I needed to hear that."

"I don't suppose she showed up for work this morning?" He'd been up early getting a handle on the accounting and bookkeeping. Kurt had two offices. His private one was locked, but the business one…well, that was where Declan would be spending his days.

"She sure did. Right on time…to tell me she'd found another job on the ranch."

"Huh." She must've talked to Mitch. "How's that going to work for you? Don't you need someone to do Tina's chores?"

"I do. Though, to be honest, she doesn't muck the stalls. I added that one to the list because it frees up one of the hands, and we've got a lot going on now that we're down one guy." Hank lowered his head. "I'm not sure any of us realized how much work Kurt did around here until he…left." He sighed. "Anyhow, if it's too much for her, I can get someone to cover everything till Tina gets back."

Too much? Or too hungover? "I'll talk to her. I don't see why she can't do her fair share." Last night, he'd spent an hour cleaning up after her just so she wouldn't be embarrassed. Chocolate frosting wasn't easy to get out of carpet fibers. "I'm heading into town. Need anything?"

"I was going to get a generator for the Airstream, but it looks like she moved into the house."

"She did." It was a big house, but between her scent, her big personality, and that smoking hot body, she took up a lot of space. "I'll see you later." Flipping the key ring around his finger, he got into Kurt's old Jeep. He'd always loved this car. No top and no doors meant he got to experience the awesome views and the chill in the air that swooped down from snow-capped mountain peaks.

It was also the same car Kurt drove to pick Declan up from the airport or take him to the training center. Yeah, it held a lot of memories.

Heading out of the driveway, he found it hard not to

notice the empty seat next to him. *Damn. I hope he knew how much I cared about him.*

He'd thought it—he'd just never said it. They just weren't like that. Kurt had always dressed up his invitations to visit as a favor. *Why don't you come out for the winter clinic? I need some help.* Not, *what're you doing for the holidays? You're welcome to spend them here.*

But they'd both known the real reason. They were each other's family. Right then, he sure wished he'd hugged the man and told him…well.

That I loved him.

And he did. He'd loved Kurt. *Fuck. I should have said it.* Regret got him in a chokehold. *He shouldn't have died not knowing how much he meant to me.*

As he neared the end of the driveway, he slowed while the sensors tracked him and opened the gate. Just before he turned left onto 191, he caught a shock of color in his peripheral vision. *What the hell?* Phinny sat at the farm stand in another of Kurt's jerseys. This one was maroon and gold from the University of Minnesota, his alma mater.

He slammed on the brakes, jerked the gearshift into Park, and jumped out of the Jeep. "That shirt you're wearing? It's a collector's item. It's probably worth two-hundred-thousand-dollars."

"Really?" She pulled out the fabric to get a look. "Huh."

He pointed a finger at her. "You're not selling it. Nothing in that house is yours. You realize that, right?" He'd have to talk to the attorney, find out what Kurt had planned for the contents of the house.

Phinny rolled her eyes. "I'm not selling anything. I

borrowed a few of his shirts until I can get into town and go shopping."

"Okay, but you can't go into that room and take his jerseys out of their *frames.*" *Who does that?*

"What? No, I got this out of his closet. He's got a whole stack. I think he messed up his signature on them." With a pained expression, she stood. "And look, I'm really sorry about last night. I swear, I don't usually drink. When I woke up to chocolate cake on my blanket, I went down to the basement to see what damage I'd done there, but I guess it wasn't as bad as I thought?"

She looked to him for an answer, but he didn't give one. *Yeah, it was a shitshow down there* wasn't necessary. And why did she make it so hard to hold onto his anger? She was fierce, but underneath all that attitude was a vulnerability that undid him.

"I don't suppose you could take me into town? I have some errands to run. And…" Her chin dipped in embarrassment. "I need to replace the birthday cake."

"I already ordered it. I'm going to pick it up now."

"You did? Oh, that's so nice of you. Thank you so much."

"I didn't do it for you."

"No, I know. I just meant…"

"I know what you meant." He gestured to the table. "What're you doing out here?"

She lifted a plastic cup. "I'm selling lemonade."

"Why?"

"I've got a splitting headache, and I spent half the night with my head in a toilet bowl. And it just felt like everyone was making fun of me, making me shovel horse poo while you're inside working in Kurt's office." She watched him carefully, as though trying to see if she was correct. "The codicil says I need to live and work on the ranch, but it doesn't specify which job, so…I'm selling lemonade."

He'd thought she was a spoiled princess. He'd thought she was too frivolous to value the lifestyle Kurt had offered her. But now, he knew her family had kicked her out because she wouldn't marry for money and that she'd felt rejected by her biological father.

He didn't pity her. She was too resilient for that. But he did see her in a new light.

"No, that's not what we're doing. Someone has to do that work until Tina gets back. But lay off the lemonade. It's for the festival."

"It's not like I'm actually selling it. Only one person's stopped by all morning."

"Whatever." Every time he closed his eyes, he saw her plump breasts in pink lace. Last night, he'd tried to stop thinking about the fall of her hair and the sway of her hips. He hadn't been able to shut down the way she'd looked on her back, whispering about tickling the pickle.

She eyed him warily. "As long as you and Hank aren't trying to put me in my place, I'll do the chores."

"Good. Now you can stop being paranoid."

"Oh, come on. I see how you all look at me. And I get it. I carry a two-thousand-dollar purse and wear designer clothes. I know I look rich, but I'm not. And no one's bothered to talk to me about anything."

"It's got nothing to do with your clothes. It's the fact that you plan on selling the ranch. But Hank's not an asshole, and he's not going to mess with you. The work needs to be done, and if it's not you, it's going to be someone else."

"No, it's fine. I'll do it. And I'll replace the lemonade and pay for the cake."

"It's already paid for." He started toward the Jeep. "But if you want to come with me, let's go. I'm meeting a friend in town."

"Oh, thank you." With an eagerness that didn't match her sophisticated look, she stuck the pitchers and glasses under the table where they were hidden by a red gingham tablecloth. After setting the sign she'd made under the leg of her chair, she hurried over.

She had a freshness, a sweetness, he found irresistible. "Where do you need me to drop you?"

As she climbed into the passenger seat, she shoved her bag in the footwell. "I mean, don't go out of your way. I can just have a look around town. I only want a few things."

"Like what?" He turned onto the highway.

"If I'm staying a month, I'll need some shorts. I'd love a cute sundress or two, but I suppose that doesn't make sense if I'm mucking stalls. I suppose I'll need trainers, another pair of jeans, and a few shirts."

He didn't think she'd find what she needed downtown. "The stores on Main Street are either touristy or fancy boutiques."

"Oh. Well, I don't suppose you've got an ASDA or something like that?"

"I'm not sure what that is, but we've got some bigger stores just outside of town where you can probably find what you need."

"Ah." She looked down at her lap. "Maybe I should stay here then. I can't afford a taxi or anything."

"I can take you shopping after my meeting."

"You don't mind?"

"Not at all." As he accelerated, the wind lifted her hair, making it stream behind her, and she grinned as though she'd never been in a convertible before.

Nothing could suppress this woman's happiness. Regardless of her shitty situation in life, she glowed from deep within.

As they passed the bison preserve, she gathered her hair and twisted it, somehow tucking the ends into a nest, holding it all in place. The nearer they got to town, the more traffic they encountered. They passed Wild Billy's with its neon sign of a cowboy on a bucking bronco, and she flashed him a grin. "I love it here."

He turned onto Main Street to find families posing in front of the antler arches of the town square, cyclists gathering out front of Calamity Joe's coffee shop, and a few store owners setting up summer kiosks.

Finding a parking spot, he killed the engine. "I'm meeting a friend there"—he pointed to Joe's—"and then I'm picking up the cake from the place next door." He leaned across her to indicate Harley and Lu's Emporium. "I haven't lived here in seven years, so I could be wrong about the shopping. Take a look around, and I'll meet you back here in an hour."

"Just enjoy your coffee and don't worry about me." When she looked at him like that, those blue eyes filled with pure sweetness, her hair tousled as if she'd just rolled out of bed—with a mouth made for kissing—he felt the roar of attraction.

"Yeah, okay." He jumped out of the Jeep and made his way into the coffee shop. *What the fuck's wrong with you?* He didn't like hot messes. Avoided them like the plague. He liked women who had their shit together because successful women with busy lives didn't sit around planning a future with him that would never happen.

But there was something about Phinny, something…

Who cares? She's Kurt's daughter.

It's never going to happen.

Scanning the crowded café, he saw that Jaime had already grabbed a table for them, and he headed over. "Hey."

His friend pushed his chair back and half-stood for a handshake. "You want to order coffee or something?"

"Nah. Still can't stand the stuff."

"Yeah, but you're an adult now." Grinning, Jaime lifted his mug. "Adults drink coffee."

Eyeing a plate of baked goods, Declan dropped into a chair. "What're those?"

"Muffins." Jaime said it like it was obvious. "Scones."

"Since when do you eat shit like that?"

"I don't know." He laughed. "I was being a nice fuckin' host." He shoved the plate toward Declan. "Just be polite and eat it."

"I don't eat that shit." He gave a big, phony smile. "But thank you."

"Asshole." Jaime just shook his head. "So, last night didn't go like I'd pictured."

Guess we're diving right into it. "It's a complicated situation."

"I think I wanted too much too soon."

Yep. "And it's not going to work like that."

"No, I know. But if Booker and Cole walk away from this opportunity…" He sat back in his chair, running a finger along the rim of his mug. "Then, it's over. They're gone for good."

"Nah. Cole bought a place here."

"He did?" Jaime looked hopeful.

He nodded. "Plus, his dad still lives here. He'll be back."

"Booker won't."

"Not likely, no. He doesn't have family here, and he's got pretty bad associations with—"

"Us. Yeah, I know. And that's on me. I apologized. Obviously, that's not enough, but I don't know what else to do."

"We've got a month before anyone has to decide."

"Yeah, but if they're not *here,* then I can't try and convince them. I wanted them to meet the team. I wanted…" He leaned forward. "I wanted us to be friends again."

"Ah, man. I'll be your friend."

Jaime laughed, tossing a balled-up napkin at him. "Fucker."

"Look, I get what you're saying. You think they'll go back to their lives and forget about this opportunity. And they might. But I can only speak for myself when I say there's a lot more going on than the Renegades. Kurt didn't tell any of us he was dying. We're all floored that he's gone. And the idea that he wanted to bring us back together, through the team he bought for us…no one's going to forget about it. I think we all need time to wrap our heads around what happened."

"That's fair. I guess I just can't see us getting anywhere unless we're all in the same room, talking it out." His friend watched him like he was waiting for an answer. A solution that would fix everything.

And Declan couldn't do that. "Look, last night you apologized. There's no better start than that."

"And now what?"

"Take a trip to New York, meet Booker for dinner. Keep the conversation going." He tapped the table. "Just…don't have an agenda. Go because you want to catch up, not because you want him to forgive you."

"Yeah, you're right. I feel like such an asshole, starting out with a trip down memory lane."

Especially when Booker's last memory of them was a ride to the ER.

Jaime glanced up at him. "What about you? Are you going to do this with me?"

He knew he should. It didn't make sense to turn down an opportunity like this, but he liked coaching. "Did you know I asked Kurt to let me start the training center? After Sam died?"

"No. He never said anything."

"He shot me down. 'Why would I do that when you've never finished anything in your life?'"

"Harsh."

"Yeah, it was. But I never finished college, I never played in the NHL, and now I've been an assistant for seven years. If I stick with it, I can be a head coach. I don't want to walk away before I get my shot."

"I get it, but we're talking about *owning* a team."

"Yeah, I hear you. That's why it's a tough decision."

"You know I'm coaching Mountain West, right?"

Declan nodded.

"Some of the Renegades run clinics for me in the summer, and I want you to come meet them."

"I can do that."

"Cool." Jaime grew thoughtful. "I'll tell you what. I've worked with a lot of teams now, and it's only driven it home, that what we had was special."

Declan understood that. "Kurt liked to say he'd never

seen players so in sync as we were, and it's because we grew up doing wild shit together. We'd built not only trust, but a way to communicate without words. We could anticipate what each other was going to do." He tipped his chair back onto two legs. "I miss you guys, and I want to do this with you, but I don't want to give up coaching."

"I'll figure it out. I will. I'm going to make this happen."

"You can't push them. They have to get there on their own."

"No, I know. I'll talk to Booker privately. Cole, too. And I'll make a trip to New York. That's a good idea. After we finish eating these delicious fucking muffins, I'll walk over to Harrison's office and see what he can do to keep the door open longer than a month. It's all legalese anyway. He can word it however we like."

"You'll be a fat cat billionaire by the time I'm ready to own a team. By then, you won't want to want to give up your share."

Jaime's expression faltered. "I've had money for a while now. I've done the big vacations and fancy cars. Don't get me wrong, it's fun. But it's not enough. There's something missing, you know?"

"Nope. I've never had money. Probably never will." He thought about Phinny out there all alone, visiting shops, looking at price tags she couldn't afford. "Listen, I've got to get back to the ranch."

"Not until you tell me about the codicil and Kurt's hot daughter."

"Oh. Yeah." Declan picked up a muffin and examined it. Underneath the cinnamon crumble top, he thought he saw peaches and pecans. "Kurt's pitted us against each other in a cage fight over his ranch."

"What?" He laughed. "Why would he do that?"

"In one month, she and I go head-to-head in a trivia contest. Whoever gets the most answers right, wins the ranch."

"That place is worth millions."

A hell of a lot more than that, but Declan just nodded. "In the meantime, we have to live and work on it for the month."

"Damn. I don't know what he was thinking."

"I'm pretty sure he just needed backup in case his daughter wanted to sell it. For whatever reason, he chose me."

"It's not for 'whatever reason.'" Jaime chuckled. "It's because you two always had a special relationship—"

"He felt sorry for me."

Jaime cocked his head, looking surprised and confused.

"I was the orphan, raised by Sam."

Jaime sat back in his chair. "I can say with absolute certainty no one thought of you like that. You were a total fucking badass. Even as a kid, you were bigger than everybody else. You didn't say much, but when you did, everyone listened. And even with your size, you were better at hockey than all of us combined. Speed, agility, strength…everyone was in awe of you."

Warmth spread through him. He hadn't known they'd thought of him like that. He'd always been a little self-conscious since the guys came from big, happy families, and he'd only had Sam. How many times had Jaime left practice early because his mom wanted him home for a birthday or graduation party? Or couldn't hang out after school because he had to take his sister somewhere, or his brother needed help breaking a mustang?

He'd envied their obligations. Worse, he'd found it embarrassing that he didn't have any. Not that he hadn't loved his grandfather. He had. But it had just been the two of them.

"I can't believe you thought Kurt would give the biggest privately-owned piece of land in Wyoming to someone he felt sorry for."

"Like I said, he wanted back-up in case his daughter tried to sell it."

Jaime nodded. "And he chose you because you're the best of all of us. You're the honorable one, the guy with the best judgement."

"Oh, come on. Booker was the Valedictorian. He was the superstar. He's the only one of us who got drafted out of high school."

"Yeah, he's driven to succeed. But you're driven to do what's right. And that's why Kurt chose you. But also, let's just be honest here for a second. You were drafted, too. You just wanted to go to college first."

"Okay." He'd already been determined to win the contest, but Jaime had just reinforced it. "I've got to get back to work."

"See, that right there. You're honoring the terms of the will. Not everyone would do that. I'll bet the daughter's not doing shit."

He thought about her sitting in the shade and selling lemonade.

But then he thought about her parents, how they'd cut her off for not marrying a rich guy. And how she not only lost her dad, but he was making her fight for her rightful inheritance. "She just lost her father."

Jaime waved a hand dismissively. "She blew him off a

long time ago. Did you see her shed a single tear during that funeral?"

Declan hadn't cried, either, but that's because there was something missing in him. Every day after his parents died, he'd walk to the end of the driveway and wait for them to come home. People tried to explain that they'd never come back, and he'd ignore them, convinced the next car would be their white KIA.

The adults would sit on the porch and discuss him. *Why's he doing this? How do we get through to him? Has he cried yet?*

And he'd never forget his grandfather's response. "That's one determined kid. His will's so strong, I half-expect them to come back myself."

He didn't say any of that to Jaime, though. Instead, he said, "We all process grief differently, and she's got a lot to deal with."

"Come on, she's a gold digger. She's here for the money."

"Hello." *Phinny.*

Her voice sent a shockwave through him.

Holding a cake box, she stood beside the table with a bright smile. She thrust her hand out to Jaime. "I saw you in the lawyer's office yesterday, but we haven't properly met. I'm Seraphina Crutchley, the gold digger."

Chapter Seven

JAIME GOT UP SO FAST, HIS CHAIR SCREECHED ON THE hardwood floor. "Jaime Dupree, local asshole. I'm sorry about that. I don't know the first thing about you."

"You know that I blew Kurt off a long time ago, and you were close to him, so I understand where your loyalties lie. And considering I *do* plan to sell the ranch when I win the contest, I'm quite sure no one here will think highly of me. But it's not a popularity contest, is it?" She turned to Declan. "I just wanted to let you know I picked up the cake. I'll wait outside for you."

With her scent lingering, Declan watched her go, his opinion of her changing with every encounter.

"She's really going to do it." Jaime looked almost fearful. "She's going to sell Kurt's ranch?"

"Not on my watch." He got up. "I'll catch up with you later."

"Come by the rink tomorrow. Meet the guys."

"Will do." Declan headed out into the bright sunlight and found Phinny sitting on a bench right outside Calamity Joe's. A group of backpackers loaded up a van, and several people gathered around Coco's Chocolates' kiosk.

Standing behind her, he looked down at the top of her head. Sunshine gleamed on the naturally blond locks. "You ready to shop?"

"Sure am." She lifted the bakery box. "I had them take it off your credit card, and I paid with mine."

"You didn't have to do that."

She got up and looked across to the town green. "I don't remember it being so busy here."

She was right about that. Calamity had seen explosive growth over the years. Everything was much more upscale. Now, they had a gourmet food store and a charming, European-style chocolate shop.

"My mum always called it a low-end ski town."

"*Low end*? No, it's never been that. Look at those mountains. Calamity's always been a destination for hardcore skiers." Her mom had done a number on her. They got back in the Jeep and headed out of town. "This is some of the most radical terrain you've ever seen."

"You ski?"

"Oh, yeah."

"You do all the dangerous stuff, huh?"

"Used to. Not so much anymore."

"The most dangerous thing I've ever done is ride a horse."

"I thought it was defying your parents?"

She cut him a look, clearly still not sure she could trust him. But when she saw his teasing expression, she relaxed. "You're right about that. I never in a million years thought they'd cut me off from everything."

"It doesn't make a lot of sense. They raised you to be a

certain way. If they wanted to teach you a lesson, why not do it gradually?"

"Because they really, really wanted me to marry Cameron."

"Yeah, but this isn't the eighteen-hundreds. We don't marry for business alliances anymore."

"It's more than an alliance. My stepfather's business hinges on theirs. And I did date Cameron for three years."

"So? People date for longer than that and don't wind up married."

"Everyone had expectations, and when I broke them …" She hunched a shoulder. "I guess I came off looking like a frivolous party girl who'd used and abused the great Cameron Lumley. It's complicated."

"Is it, though? If your kid said she didn't love some guy, would you get all bent out of shape and cut her off?" He slowed for a red light.

"No, I wouldn't." Smiling, she tipped her head back and closed her eyes against the bright sun. "Thank you. I didn't know how much I needed to hear an outsider's perspective on it."

When it turned green, he accelerated. "Look, clearly, Kurt didn't know your financial situation when he wrote up his will. I'm not going to hold you to working on the ranch if you need to get a full-time job."

"Oh, you're good. Wow." She shook her head. "I almost fell for your whole nice-guy schtick. Nicely done, but no thanks. I'm not going to win the contest only to have you call me out for a breach of contract."

"What? I wouldn't do that."

"Right." She patted his arm. "I heard what your friend said. You're the 'honorable' one." Her tone said *We'll see about that.* "It doesn't matter. It could be anyone who called me out. No, I'm going to do my morning chores and then work at the farm stand in the afternoons."

"Selling glasses of frozen lemonade for a buck?"

"That's just a front, silly."

As they neared the town of Jackson, more strip malls popped up on either side of the highway. "What does that mean?"

"Remember I told you I had one customer this morning? She knew Kurt and told me all kinds of stories about him. So, I figured what better way to learn about him than talking to the people who knew him? And I'll replace the lemonade I use, so don't worry about the festival."

"It's none of my business what you do. You're welcome to anything in the house. I've got no rights to any of it."

"And take lemonade out of the mouths of parched festival-goers? Heavens, no. But guess what?"

Her exuberance made him smile. "What?"

"That lady I met this morning? She invited me over. She's got pictures and stories."

Huh. Looks like I'll need to step up my game.

"You look surprised. Did you think I'd spend the month shopping online and painting my nails?"

"Not after our conversation last night."

She tipped her head back and groaned. "A gentleman's not supposed to remind a lady of her embarrassing moments."

"What gave you the idea I was a gentleman?" He pulled into a giant parking lot. "You're in Calamity now. This area was built by outlaws. If you're looking for polite behavior, you're in the wrong place."

"Right. I forgot who I'm dealing with. Rugged

cowboys and badass hockey players." She sat up when she saw the massive store. "This is where I'm buying clothes?"

Had he gotten it wrong? Maybe they had different ideas of being broke. "You're not going to find designer clothes here, but they'll be cheap."

"No, that's fine. It's probably just like an ASDA." As soon as he cut the engine, she got out and met him in front of the car.

"What happens to your diner job if you're here for a month?"

"Oh, I quit already. They're not going to hold that open for me. Besides, I hope to get a salary from the foundation where I work."

"Foundation?"

"I put together auction items for an annual fundraiser. I've always volunteered, but this year, I'm asking them to hire me." Her gaze connected with him, as though she thought he might be judging her. "I'm actually quite good at my job."

"I'm not surprised." Why did she sound defensive? "Are you not supposed to ask for money?" They wove their way through parked cars.

"Oh, God, no. My mum and I have always volunteered at several philanthropies. It's what a Crutchley does. But I need the income, and if they value me as much as they say they do, they'll hire me. All foundations have a staff."

As they entered, Phinny breezed right in. He suspected she wasn't used to shopping in places that had carts, so he grabbed one for her and followed along as she touched every single item in the store. Bath towels, coffee mugs, wreaths, nail polish in every color of the rainbow and...*dear God*. The woman loved candles.

"Mm." She closed her eyes and inhaled. "This one's lovely." She offered it to him.

He held up a hand. It was the thirtieth one she'd tried. "They all smell the same at this point." She laughed, and he felt it in his bones. A softening, a lightening. It was unreal what she did to him. "But if you're not buying any, maybe we should move on."

"No." Reluctantly, she set it back on the shelf. "I can't spend money on them."

"Right, so let's hit the clothing section."

An hour later, she'd tried on every single color and various sizes of T-shirts, shorts, sundresses, and jeans. After she'd finished, she sorted through each piece of clothing she'd piled into the cart and checked the price tags. "Let's see. Three-ninety-nine times three…you know what? I don't need three pairs of shorts. It's just a month, and I can wash everything." She lifted all three pairs out of the cart, deciding which to return. "I really like these. My butt looks good in them, doesn't it?" She actually looked to him for a response.

"Phinny, your ass looks good in anything."

Her cheeks pinkened, and she held the shorts to her chest. "Thank you." She said it breathlessly, and he honestly couldn't believe this gorgeous woman didn't know she was hot.

Her ex is an asshole.

"You know what? They're on sale, so I'll get all three." She picked up a vintage-style T-shirt. "This is cute, right?"

The graphic was for Wild Billy's restaurant and bar. Orange rhinestones outlined the cowboy riding a bucking bronco. His silver hat glittered. "Sure."

"Was Wild Billy's around when I was a kid?"

"Oh, yeah. It's been around for a hundred years."

"I don't remember Kurt taking me there." She tossed the shirt and shorts back into the cart. "Of course, I was only five the last time I was here." She took over pushing the cart.

"You have to remember he was a celebrity. He couldn't go anywhere without people asking for autographs. He never talked about it, but I'll bet he had so little time with you that he wanted you to himself. Either way, Kurt wasn't an asshole. He didn't try to make your visits bad."

"You have a nice way of thinking about it."

His heart wrenched at how wounded she looked.

"If I'd said that same thing to my mum—that Kurt had never taken me there—she would've said, Well, Kurt was an asshole. God forbid anything take him away from his precious ranch. Or something like that."

He didn't know what to say. "I guess she had her own experience with him."

"Maybe that's why he wanted me to stay here for the month."

"Makes sense he'd want you to form your own opinion about him."

"They were just so different, Kurt and my mum." She wore a thoughtful expression. "It's a wonder they got together at all."

"What's she like?"

"Oh, my mum's a force. She's on the go all day long."

"She works?"

"She volunteers quite a bit, but mostly she shops, goes to meetings and luncheons. My parents go out six nights a week."

"Yeah, Kurt wasn't into any of that. He didn't do dinner parties, and he only shopped for what he needed. And his gifts were quiet."

"Quiet?"

"It means if your mom wanted diamond earrings for her birthday, she'd be disappointed. Kurt didn't even own a watch." He caught a flash of bling in his mind's eye. "I take that back." Recently, he'd opened a drawer in his office and found a pile of them. "He had them because of endorsements and gifts, but it wouldn't occur to him to buy one. Not when he was either playing hockey or rounding up the herd."

"Well, there you go. No wonder my mum couldn't stand him. Her love language is gifts." She said it with a laugh in her voice, but she looked more thoughtful than amused. "I remember once Andrew rang to say he was going to pop home because he had something for her. She'd been having trouble with her car—it'd been in and out of the shop for months—and she was bouncing off the walls with excitement because she'd somehow got it in her head that he'd bought her a new one. You should've seen her face when he walked in the door and handed over some documents she needed to sign."

As they passed through the lingerie section, she grabbed a pack of lacy underpants and pajama shorts with a matching tank top. "And honestly, if she doesn't get invited to a dinner party, she thinks she's been snubbed and worries endlessly about what she might've done. And then, she'll throw a revenge one, making sure it's bigger and better." Her hand covered her mouth. "Listen to me going on like that. I'm making her sound awful." She set her hand on his arm and gazed up at him. "She might be all those things, but she's always been very devoted to me. I'm her only child, and we did everything together. Well, until I didn't marry Cameron."

It was just a light touch. Only meant to get his

attention, but her hand was just so…feminine, so delicate…so damn gentle. He wanted her to slide it under his shirt, so he could feel the warmth on his skin.

He got an image of it wrapped around his cock, and his body jerked.

She whipped her hand away. *Shit.* She'd obviously thought he was shrugging her off. He wasn't, but what could he say? *No, don't worry. I just had a filthy thought about you?* "You ready to check out?"

"Yes, definitely." But a pink cowboy hat in the Accessories section caught her attention, and she plopped it on her head. "How do I look?"

Fucking hot. "Fine."

"It's cute, but I don't need it."

"Out here, you wear hats to keep the sun off your face. Get it."

She grabbed a black one and jammed it on his head. "Only if you get this one."

"I don't wear cowboy hats."

"You just said you need them to keep the sun off your face."

"Not much sun in Kurt's office."

"Oh, come on. We're in Calamity. We need cowboy hats." She was so pretty, and she gazed up at him with so much joy, he didn't think his heart could stand it.

He snatched the hat out of her hands. "Fine. Can we go now?"

"Not until I get matching cowboy boots." She pulled on the cart. "Come on. Let's see if they have them."

Right around the corner, they found miles of shoes in every style. She roamed the aisles until she held up a pair of pink boots. "I can't believe it. They have them." Sitting on a bench, she pried off her black shoe and slid her foot inside. "Ugh. I've never worn fake leather before, but it's just for a month, and they're adorable." She shoved it back into the box and dropped it into the cart. "Now, let's get you a pair."

"I don't…" Was there even a point in telling her he didn't wear cowboy boots?

Obviously not, since she'd already forged ahead into the men's section. "Oh, shoot. They don't have them."

"Damn. I'd wanted us to get matching pink ones."

She eyed him over the top of a display case. And then she burst out laughing. "I will accept defeat in this moment, but mark my words, we're getting you a pair of cowboy boots to go with your hat."

"We should get going."

"Okay, but first…" Reaching into the cart, she pulled the hats out, sticking one on his head and the other on hers. "A selfie." She leaned in and held her arm out.

He went to her side, standing there stiffly, at first. But he could see her expression on the screen, the happiness lighting her eyes, and he had no choice but to wrap his arm around her and pull her in close. He didn't smile, but at least he wasn't scowling.

As she took a dozen pictures, the entire world funneled into the scent and warmth and fucking *joy* of Seraphina Crutchley.

The last woman in the world he'd ever be attracted to.

She was way too sweet and innocent for him.

He'd ruin her with his darkness.

She snapped one last picture and then looked at it. "You look like you need Preparation H."

"What?" He grabbed the phone. "I look like I have hemorrhoids?"

"Yes, like you're in pain."

He did look pretty unhappy. He tossed his hat back into the cart. "That's because you're a pain in my ass. We're going now."

"Say what you want, but I'll forever be the woman that got you your first cowboy hat." They got in line, and she started lifting her clothes onto the conveyor. "Thank you, by the way. For making a weird experience enjoyable."

"Buying clothes in a store that isn't Gucci is weird?"

"Yes, actually, it is. Believe it or not, I haven't bought much of anything since The Lock-Out."

"Lock-Out?"

"The day—well, actually, it was the night, because I'd come home at three in the morning to find my key didn't work."

What the fuck? "What did you do?"

"I tried calling my parents but neither answered. I texted my friends, and one of them let me crash on her couch."

"Why would they do something like that?"

"To teach me a lesson."

Your parents are assholes. But he didn't say it. He didn't need to. She knew.

Finished, she turned to him. "What your friend said about me being a gold digger...that hurt." She took his hand. "But you stood up for me, and that was really nice. Most of my friends would've gone along with the backstabber just to be part of the crowd."

"You've got some shitty friends."

"I see that now, but we'd been friends since primary school. They were all I'd ever known, so when they ditched me—"

"They *ditched* you?"

"It's not their fault. It's no fun to go out with someone who can't pay for her own dinner or drinks. What fun is it to go shopping with someone who can't even afford a pair of socks at Harrod's?"

"You're talking about activities. Friendships are based on more than going out."

"Sure, but *how* you socialize is important, and I couldn't keep up with them anymore."

"Do you miss them?"

"I miss being part of them. I miss the text chat, the dressing up to go out. But I don't blame them for not including me. It made them uncomfortable to be around me. I can't even afford a taxi."

"Yeah, I can see that."

"We all grew up with nannies, chefs, drivers, landscapers…all that. Honestly, until I moved out, I never had to lift a finger. I barely had to think for myself."

Somehow, her choice not to marry Cameron seemed pretty damn brave. "What did your friends think about you walking away from your ex?"

"They thought I was mad. And it's not just because of his family. Don't misunderstand. He's a really good guy. Even with our lackluster…" Gripping his arm, she got up on toes and whispered in his ear. "Sex life." When she settled back down, she had a glint in her eyes. "We got on really well. He's a great friend."

Talk about going mad. She had to stop touching him. Stop acting like they'd known each other longer than two days. Jesus, she was just so…appealing. It made him want to violate that sexy, lush mouth. Put a hand on her shoulder and ease her down to her knees. He wanted to see the wicked look in her eyes as she pulled him out of his pants and licked him root to crown.

The conveyor belt moved their items forward, snapping him out of his dirty thoughts. "Did you break his heart?"

She shook her head sadly. "I embarrassed him. I frustrated him. But no, I don't think our hearts were involved. I know mine wasn't."

"Okay, so it's not even been a year. Any chance you'll go back to him?"

"God, no."

"At some point, though, will your parents back off?"

"I don't want them to. I like my freedom. And as weird as it sounds, I like using my hands. It sucks to not have money, but I like figuring things out on my own. Do you know I've never cooked a single meal in my life?"

"I imagine poor little Phinny standing in her kitchen, staring at the refrigerator, trying to figure out how to open it. *How do I get in there? Let me in.*" Pretending to yank on locked handles, he made his voice sound frantic. "Sad Phinny opening the oven and wondering why there isn't a cooked lasagna in there."

"I'm not an idiot." Laughing, she gave him a playful shove. "I share a house with four people who don't wash up after themselves. The kitchen's disgusting. And it's not my fault I don't have any skills." Her eyes sparkled as she gazed up at him. "It's the way I grew up. Do you know, I don't even *drive*? I mean, I have my license, but I never drove after getting it. The only thing I'm good at is putting together auction items. So, if I win the contest, I'll start my own foundation and—" She watched him carefully. "Why do you look like a beetle just flew into your mouth and you swallowed it?"

"What? I don't look like that."

"Yes, you do." Laughing, she reached for him, cupping

his mouth. "You're scowling at me. You think I'm a silly cow, don't you?"

Just the opposite. "You're up." He tipped his chin toward the credit card terminal. "Pay." As she swiped, he said, "I'm not scowling. I'm listening."

"No, I get it. You're horrified that I'm trying to get a charity to pay me for a job meant for volunteers." Phinny took the receipt and rolled the cart out of the store. "Ugh. I know. I'm an awful person."

"If I was scowling—which I wasn't—it was because you said you have no marketable skills." While he put her bags in the backseat, she returned the cart. Once they were both buckled up, he backed out. "You think the worst thing your parents did is cut you off, but I think it's that they didn't tell you enough good things about you." He headed out of the lot. She'd gone quiet, so before turning onto 191, he braked and looked at her. "What's wrong?"

She did it again. She put her hand on his arm. It was such a gentle touch, it made him ache. "Are you serious?"

"Serious about what?

"What you said, that my parents didn't tell me enough good things about me?"

He pulled into the stream of traffic. "Dead serious."

"Says the elite hockey player." But she had a very satisfied expression.

And it made him feel good. Damn, he didn't really like the power this woman had over him. "Some people take a linear path. Like me and my friends. We knew what we wanted, and we worked our asses off to get it. Other people—like you—don't have a clear idea what they want to do, but that doesn't mean they're talentless bums."

"True. But I've been on my own for nearly a year, and I'm still waiting tables."

"You're trying to get a job with a foundation." Why that made her uncomfortable, he had no idea. "Look, what if I told you I've got no marketable skills because I've never played professional hockey. And because of that, I've been coaching for free. If I said I was embarrassed to ask the team to pay me, what would you say?"

"Well, first, I'd say you absolutely have marketable skills. Whether or not you've played in the NHL, you've trained for this sport all your life."

"Exactly. You've never seen me play, but you know without a doubt, I have them. And because of that, you'd tell me I should absolutely be paid for my hard work."

"Yes" She looked chastised. "Point taken."

He nodded. "So, try talking to yourself the same way you'd talk to a friend."

Kicking off her shoes, she lifted her feet to the dashboard, clasping her hands in her lap. "I like that very much." She flashed him a grin so gorgeous, so blinding, he had to look away. "Thank you."

Yeah, he really didn't fucking like the power she had over him.

With her internal clock still messed up, Phinny couldn't sleep. She'd gone downstairs to rummage around the pantry. Now, with a box of crackers in her hands, she set off to wander around the house.

When she'd been little, this place had been filled with antiques. Not that she remembered, but Kurt would send her pictures after she'd gone home. She'd made her mum print a few of them out, and she kept them tucked inside a book on her nightstand.

While she recognized some of the pieces, the décor looked different. Modern accents had been added. She stood before a subtle but powerfully evocative painting of a red-roofed barn set in the middle of a grassy field. Stormy skies lent an edge of threat—*not all is peaceful on this land.*

In town this morning, she'd seen signs for an annual summer art festival. Had he bought it at an event like that? Had she been with him? She'd only visited him in the summer, so maybe he'd bought her an ice cream cone as they'd wandered around. Her mum loved to say that he'd only wanted to fish and camp, the kinds of things a little girl would hate. She called him a narcissist, but Phinny wasn't getting that impression from the people she'd met so far.

When the eulogist had said *No one liked Kurt Grevers,* a rush of justification had come flooding in. *See, it's not just me who thinks he's an ass.* But then he'd gone on to say how everyone respected and admired him, and it had just confused her.

No, that's not what I felt.

She'd been ashamed. Because she was his daughter, and she was the only one in the chapel not moved to tears. And she was just now beginning to see that she didn't know Kurt at all. She knew what her mum had told her about him.

At the farm stand yesterday, she'd met Leddy Champion, a neighbor. She was set to meet her this afternoon, and she found herself eager to hear more stories, learn more about…

My father.

It had been so long since she'd allowed herself to think of Kurt as her dad. And to be perfectly honest, it wasn't being in his home that enabled her to embrace it. It was the distance from her mum.

Not once in her life had she thought or spoken about Kurt without her mum's voice issuing a put-down.

Crossing the expansive living room, she made her way to a wall of built-in bookcases. A Classics major at university, she loved old books with a passion, but what caught her attention were the drawers at the bottom of the shelves. Using her socked toe, she pulled one open to find a neat row of photo albums, spines up. *Ooh.*

Excitement had her setting the cracker box down and opening the next drawer and the one after that. Each was packed with albums. Her pulse quickened. *This is either a photographic treasure trove or something stupid like hockey trading cards.*

On closer look, though, they had dates handwritten on little white cards tucked into plastic windows. They seemed to be lined up by timeline, so she started with the oldest. Pulling it out, she sat on the rug.

The sepia-toned photographs were taken in the late eighteen-hundreds. The first was nothing but barren, rocky land and a stern-faced couple standing in front a log cabin. In the background, she recognized the same thrust of rugged mountains she saw every time she left the house.

A strange sensation crept across her skin.

This is my family.

No matter how she'd tried to convince everyone—including herself—that she had no ties to Kurt, the genetic connection to her ancestors beat in her bloodstream. Spreading the book across her lap, she immersed herself in the past. The men had black hats and bushy mustaches, and the women wore plain, high-collared dresses.

Each image had a handwritten description. Either a name or *???* and a "circa" year. She'd only turned a few pages before she'd moved up in time to the early nineteen-hundreds.

It all felt surreal because for so long she'd viewed herself as a Crutchley—though she shared no DNA with them—and the Pinfields on her mother's side. She'd never had any connection to the Grevers, nor had she ever met any relatives when she'd come to see her father.

Why, though? If this land meant so much, where had everyone gone?

She pulled her phone out of the pocket of her leggings and called the one person in the world who held answers.

"Phinny?" Her mum sounded groggy. "Is everything all right?"

"I'm so sorry, Mummy. I wasn't paying attention to the time. I'll ring you back in the morning."

"Nonsense. I'm up now. Let me leave the room so your father can sleep." A few moments later, her mother came back sounding a bit breathless. "All right, then. What's the matter, darling?"

"I'm looking at Kurt's photo albums, and I don't understand…where are his relatives?"

"I've no idea. They probably left him like everyone does because he was such a stubborn, hard-headed man."

"Mum, stop it. I'm quite serious. I know your opinion of him, and he's no longer a threat. I just want answers."

"A threat? How can a man be a threat when he disappeared completely from our lives?"

She didn't have the patience for this. "Can you just put aside your personal views and talk to me? I'm asking you about the facts of my father's life."

"Your father—"

"No, Mum. Let's not play word games right now. I understand very well who raised me."

"I should hope so. And I've only ever told you the truth about Kurt. I've respected you enough to not paint some false picture of the man. What good would it do to raise your hopes and expectations when he could never meet them?"

Clearly, she wasn't going to get the answers she needed. "I'll let you go back to bed."

"Nonsense. I've been waiting to hear from you all day, and I'm wide awake now." She released an exasperated huff. "All I know is that five brothers headed west in the late eighteen-hundreds to claim land the government was giving away. I'd imagine it was too hard to make a living, so most of the future generations must've left to make better lives for themselves."

"Did he ever talk about aunts, uncles, or cousins? Did you meet his parents?"

"Briefly, yes. They were living on that godforsaken ranch. I don't recall him mentioning other relatives, but of course, he wasn't around much."

Ignoring the jab, Phinny stayed focused. "So, when did his parents die?"

"His father died while we were at university. His mum died shortly after he'd installed me in that house and abandoned us. I had to care for a child and an aging stranger."

"So, you spent time with my grandmother. What was she like?"

"She was…busy. She was old." Her mum grew impatient. "I don't know what you're looking for here."

"I'm looking for details. Something other than 'she

was old.' Was she kind? Did she milk cows? Why is it so difficult to answer the question?"

"Because I was dumped in the middle of nowhere with a woman I barely knew. I had a baby, and I was left alone. I couldn't remember what day of the week it was, let alone what his mum was like."

"Did she cook for you?"

"Yes, of course, she did. Meat and potatoes. Rolls. Pie. There wasn't a meal that didn't have dessert. I must've gained ten pounds the first week."

"It actually sounds lovely." *Homey.*

"Well, it wasn't. She got sick, and then I was caring for a baby and an elderly woman. And where was Kurt?"

"The house is quite grand. What was it like when you lived here?"

"It was old and broken down. And it sat in the middle of nowhere. His parents tried to make a go of a cattle ranch, but they had some very lean years."

"If it was so rustic, why did he move you here? Why didn't you live in Boston where he played?"

"Because he was a controlling bastard." Her mum exhaled into the receiver. "Look, it's impossible to give you an unbiased answer. It was my *life*. I can tell you what he told me, that he wanted to raise his children on his family's land. He wanted me to have the support of his community in Calamity."

Interest awakened in her. "And did you?"

"Yes, actually. After his mum died, they were quite lovely. They brought me food. They plowed the driveway in winter."

"You never told me that."

"Well, it wasn't their help I wanted, now was it? I wanted

Kurt's. I was alone with a toddler in that rotten little house. Winters were unbearable. The cold seeped right through the walls, and we were stuck indoors for days at a time."

"Then, why didn't you move back to Boston?"

"He didn't want us there. He wanted you to go to school in a safe town with good values. Besides, he wasn't around for me there, either. Always traveling or filming commercials. He had time for everything but us."

"Surely, the other wives and girlfriends were in the same boat. You must've had friends through his teammates."

"I don't know why you're attacking me. Those 'friends' weren't going to help me change nappies. It wasn't their job to help me raise my child. It was my *husband's. He* should've been there."

"The other wives must have felt neglected, too. And I'm sure they had children."

"The other wives had *family.* Their mums would come out and stay for weeks when they had a baby. I had no one."

Phinny had never pressed her mum before, and now she knew why. But she did her best to ignore the hostility and self-pity to get some answers. "Except out here. You said you had community here in Calamity."

"The neighbors were *cowboys.* The women wore prairie dresses. You've no idea what a foreign world it was to me."

Ten months ago, before she'd been cut off, she would've gobbled up her mum's words. Used to them fortify the wall she'd built to protect her feelings. If Kurt was a bad man, it was a damn good thing he wasn't in her life.

But tonight, Phinny *heard* them. "You made it sound like you were alone out here. No help, no neighbors, nothing. You told me they rejected you because of your accent. That's what you said. You said you stuck out like a sore thumb, and they treated you like an outsider."

"I *was* an outsider."

If she could talk to one of the hockey wives who'd known her parents back in Boston, she suspected she'd find out that her *mum* had been the difficult one. And now, instead of hurt and anger over Kurt's challenge, she was almost excited. She wanted to learn the truth about him.

"Well, you'd love it here now, Mum. Calamity's got posh shops and fancy restaurants." The bustling Wild West town was charming and lively and far more high-end than she'd expected. "It's even got a gourmet food shop. Not quite as good as Harrod's but close."

"Well, take pictures because I certainly won't be visiting."

She didn't want to talk to her mum anymore. "Right, well, I'll let you get back to sleep. Maybe someone I meet here will know more about Kurt's relatives."

"Darling, I would be careful about stirring that pot. With a property of that value, you don't want long-lost Grevers popping out of the woodwork making a claim."

Disappointment twisted through her. Where Declan's first impulse had been to step away from her inheritance, her mum's inclinations were quite different. "Goodnight."

After they got off the phone, she stared unseeing at the photo album in her lap. Her mum's ugliness left her feeling detached and so alone.

She really wished Declan were awake. She might not know him well, but for some strange reason she liked being with him. She felt safe around him.

It wasn't just his size or his rugged demeanor. It was

his inherent goodness, his strength. In a zombie apocalypse, she'd elect him as the leader.

She wanted to go back up those stairs, tiptoe into his room, and climb into bed. She wanted his strong arms to wrap around her. She wanted—

Awareness rippled across her skin, and her gaze jerked up.

As if she'd conjured him…there he was.

Declan stood at the top of the stairs.

Chapter Eight

TALL, BROAD-SHOULDERED, WITH THE RIPPED physique of an elite athlete, Declan wore nothing but gray sweatpants that hung low on his hips. With all those tattoos, he looked like a biker or a brawler...as far from refined as a man could get.

Slowly, he came down the stairs. "Everything okay?"

Her chest tightened, and all she could do was nod. Fearing he'd pick up on her neediness, she turned back to the photo album. As she waited for him to go into the kitchen or wherever he'd been headed, she forced herself to calm down. But her hyperawareness of him made it impossible to take in anything other than short, shallow breaths.

Sit with me.

Be with me.

I know we barely know each other, and I'm competing against you, but I've missed you in the six hours since dinner, and I want you with me.

Anxiety spiked when a pair of big feet entered her peripheral vision.

"What's that?" His voice matched his tattoos and messy hair—deep, sexy, and with a raspy growl.

She lifted the book to show him. "All those drawers? They're filled with these."

Dropping to a crouch, he pulled out a random album. When he flipped it open, a grin broke through the scruff, turning his rugged features unbearably handsome. "Look at that car. Must be from the Forties." He got up, knees cracking, and moved to the far end of the bookcase. Pulling another one out, he brought it to the leather ottoman and sat down. "Oh, man." Elbows on his knees, he flipped through the pages, shaking his head in wonder. Even curled over like that, he didn't have a poochy belly. The man was all lean muscle.

Needing his comfort, she got up and sat beside him. "Let me see." And, oh, God, she could feel the heat from his bare skin. She wanted him to wrap those strong arms around her and hold her close. She wanted to trace the lines of his ink with her fingertips.

He tilted the book toward her.

"Of course." She laughed. "You would go straight to hockey." She peered closer to get a better look and got hit with the scent of clean cotton, warm skin, and potent masculinity. It hit deep in her gut, stirring a primal reaction of hot, carnal desire. Closing her eyes to breathe him in, an image dropped into her mind. His hands braced on either side of her head, his biceps bulging, that shoulder-length hair spilling forward, as he thrust into her. Hard, rough…holding nothing back.

Lust ignited in her core, the flames licking out and making her burn.

Oh, God. Don't do that. But maybe she'd never had an

orgasm with her past boyfriends because they'd all been so…tidy. So polite. Maybe rough, dirty-mouthed badasses cranked her engine.

Discreetly, she took in the planes and angles of his shoulders and back, the defined ridges on his abdomen. Where Cameron had a lot of dark body hair, Declan's was much lighter, softer-looking. He had a tattoo underneath his belly button that she couldn't make out and a stunning image on his ribcage of four boys playing hockey on a mountain lake in the moonlight. Of their own volition, her fingers moved to touch it. "This is absolutely lovely."

When he didn't answer, she looked up to find him watching her with a smoldering gaze. His skin pebbled underneath her touch, and she boldly traced the outline of the moon. Caught in the magnetic pull of this attraction, she couldn't look away if she tried.

But then his gaze slowly lowered to her finger, and he arched a brow.

The unspoken command had her pulling away. Flustered, she focused on the photographs in the book. *Stupid, stupid girl. As if a guy like him would ever be interested in someone as frivolous as me.*

They'd both been thrust into the same situation, and yet while she'd been tottering around in two-year-old designer heels and chasing after a Border Collie, he'd been cool, collected, and confidently getting shit done. *Whatever. I'm doing the best I can.* And there's nothing wrong with admiring his ink. Looking him right in the eyes, she said, "It's beautiful. Do the guys know it's there?"

"Yeah. We all have it. Got it when we were seniors. Right after Booker got drafted, actually." Unconsciously, he rubbed it.

"I love that. Kurt's not in it?"

He got up so quickly, he knocked the album off his lap. Ignoring it, he headed to a framed photograph on the bookshelf. Before he sat back down, he handed it to her.

She didn't miss the distance he'd put between them. *Yeah, I get it, okay?* Not interested in the hot British mess. *That's fine.* It wasn't like she'd have a relationship with the guy she was competing against.

He tapped the glass. "Kurt took it."

She turned her attention to the stunning photograph. Taken at night, a glowing moon poured molten silver into the lake. Four boys glided across a frozen pond, their sticks cocked back, ready to fire. "You're all represented here. The four of you, plus Kurt. He's always with you, watching you." She smiled. "That's incredibly poetic." He had more depth than she'd imagined. He was still close enough to feel the heat from his body and see the scar at his temple. Another one—longer, deeper—on his jaw snagged her attention. She gently touched it. "Hockey's a brutal sport."

His hand closed over her wrist, holding it in place. "That's not from hockey. It's from dirt biking. I crashed, and my face landed on a rock." His growly voice and intense gaze made her uncomfortable.

Declan Cadell was pure sex.

This man didn't make love. He fucked.

And she'd never been fucked before in her life.

Had never even considered the difference.

She was totally out of her element. And yet…desire surged, making her restless. Making her bold. What if she slid her hand across his thigh, dipped between his legs, and let the back of her hand brush against his cock? She was tired of men being gentle and polite with her. She needed someone who wanted her so much he lost control.

But he clearly wasn't interested, so she picked up the album he'd dropped and looked through the pictures. One in particular drew her attention. "Look at you." The other guys were laughing, easy with each other, but Declan stood apart. He was taller, more muscular. But it wasn't his physique that intrigued her. It was his earnestness.

The guy with the surfer hair exuded confidence, as if he'd had all the advantages in life. "Who's that one?"

"Booker."

"And this one?" The dark-haired guy with blue eyes was gorgeous.

"Cole." He tapped the fourth guy. "And that's Jaime."

"They're all so happy and easy-going, and you…" She didn't want to say the wrong thing.

"I what?"

"You're the handsome guy in school that everyone wants to know, but he has enough friends and he's not looking for anyone new."

He seemed to give it some thought but didn't respond.

"You're self-contained. You don't need anything or anyone." She pointed to the golden boy in the picture. "He's the one I'd have gone for." She said it just to tease him.

"Booker?" But he didn't take the bait. "Figures. Everyone liked him."

See that? Totally unaffected. Not the least bit hurt or jealous. "All that gorgeous blond hair, those dreamy dimples." She made her voice sound all swoony just to rile him up.

"Dreamy dimples?" Declan chuckled. "That guy's an enforcer. If Booker slammed you into the wall, you didn't get up. 'Dreamy.'" He shook his head. "That should've been his nickname."

Oh, my God. The man literally has zero interest in me. "Well, I'm glad I finally get to see the boys he traded me for." She tried to close the book, but he held onto it.

"Why do you say he *traded* you for us? That's a weird way to look at it."

It was hard to concentrate when she was getting hit by all the pheromones wafting off him. "It's not weird at all. After he gave up his custodial rights, he devoted his time to you guys instead."

Declan set it on the floor. "It's not like he came looking for us. He wasn't trying to replace you. You don't know the story, do you?"

She stood up. "It wasn't a complaint. It's just what happened. Look, I didn't like coming out here, so good for him that he found you. Looks like you became the family he didn't have."

He gripped her wrist and pulled. "Before you get all butt-hurt, why don't you listen to someone else's side of the story?"

She was curious enough to sit back down.

"My friends and I used to make dirt bike courses on other people's property. We always looked for remote places, so most of the time, nobody noticed. Well, that all ended with Kurt. We figured his place was hundreds of thousands of acres, so no way would he ever notice if we tore up one little hidden corner."

"He noticed?" Why did she like that about her father?

"Hell, yeah. He was all over his land. We didn't get more than a few days on the best course we'd ever made before he caught us. And, man, he was pissed. Turns out, though, he wasn't pissed about the dirt. It was the fact that we could've gotten hurt, and no one would've been around to help us. Emergency vehicles couldn't get to this location."

"And yet he found you."

"Yeah, and you know what he did? He didn't blow up or yell at us. He didn't call the police. He told us to come for a meeting at his house with our parents."

"Why didn't he call them himself?" *Who would trust little kids?*

"He didn't need to. Your dad was a scary dude. And not because he was a famous hockey player. He was big and powerful, and you knew he didn't fuck around, so when he said something, we listened. He didn't argue, he didn't fight. He dropped a statement and walked away. And you just knew he had the resources to follow up and crush you."

"Was he an enforcer?" She grinned. "See, I know some hockey terms."

"I'm impressed, but no. Believe it or not, he didn't like violence. He liked strategy. That was his thing. Your dad was an intellectual."

The low recessed lights cast a golden glow on his tan skin. Every time he shifted on the ottoman, his biceps rounded, and his pecs and abs flexed. She wanted to run her hands all over him, feel the dips and contours, the heat of his skin, and the power in his muscles.

"So, anyhow, we get to his house. We're all shitting our pants—no idea what to expect. And instead of him going off on us, he tells our parents a story about how he was an only child, how he'd gotten in with the wrong crowd when he was a kid. Our parents were giving us side-eye, wondering what the fuck we'd done, but Kurt just goes on, telling them how his dad never lectured or punished him, how he'd taken him ice skating on their pond. It became a thing they did every day after school. His dad would walk him there, give him some drills to work on, and go back to work. And Kurt became obsessed with it, with getting better."

"With making his dad proud."

A flash of surprise crossed his handsome features. "I never thought about it like that, but yeah, I guess you're right. And then, by the time he got to high school, he realized his dad had been training him to make the team. So that night, he told our parents he wouldn't press charges for the damage done to his property if we learned how to play hockey."

"Can you press charges on kids?"

"Sure, there's a juvenile court, but that wasn't the point. We were these little shits who'd gotten away with skateboarding in town and parkour at the high school because no one could control us. Our parents grounded us, took away our bikes, our allowance…you name it, but we only got more and more reckless." Absently, he touched the scar on his jaw. "And then this guy, the one you'd sometimes see in town or driving down the road, the one people whispered about because he was a fucking legend, made us an offer. He said hockey had worked for him, and he was willing to teach us the game. He told our parents it would channel our energy into the sport, so that we'd become good at one thing instead of being general assholes."

"And it worked. You all became hockey greats." She said it with a teasing tone. "Maybe if I'd played the game, he'd have wanted me around, too."

"Doesn't it get tiring? Repeating the same lines over and over?"

Underneath the sting of embarrassment, the truth rang like a bell. *I'm like my mum.* "Yes." *How awful. The one thing I can't stand about her is the thing I've adopted.*

"So, if you want to hear something different, just ask. Don't play the same refrain."

"That's fine for you to say, but nobody can give me the answers I'm looking for. Kurt's gone, and he can't explain why he gave up on me. He'd fought tooth and nail for that custody arrangement where I came out every summer and spent every other holiday with him. And it just stopped. I made it hard for him when I was *six*, and he backed off. So, I'm sorry if you don't like the woe-is-me thing, but honestly? That's where I am right now."

He touched her arm, looking her in the eyes. "I don't know why he gave up, but I do know he loved you." He glanced down at his hand, looking a little confused. Then, he let her go. "The only story I ever heard was that you didn't want to come out here anymore. It upset you too much, so he stopped forcing you."

"But he could have come to see me. He could've called me or taken me somewhere. For goodness, sake, he could've sent me a birthday card." Alone in this living room with a man who'd inked Kurt's memory onto his body, she just wanted the damn truth.

Why did you give up on me?

"I don't know why he didn't do any of those things. You should ask your mother about that, but I do know your father was a great man."

"Then why did his *lawyer* deliver a eulogy? All the hockey boys were sitting there. Why didn't any of you get up and speak?"

"Like everything else, Kurt planned his funeral. It's what he wanted."

"He wanted it to start with, 'No one liked Kurt Grevers?'"

"Well, I don't know about that. I just know he didn't want a bunch of people giving speeches about him."

"That was a strange way to talk about him. *No one likes Kurt Grevers.*"

"He was talking about his reputation in hockey. Kurt always said he wasn't there to make friends. He was there to help the team win the cup. They gave him shit for not going to baby showers and weddings, but he wasn't a social man. He'd rather be alone in his home than at a party. But I can tell you for sure, they respected the hell out of him."

"Why did you like him so much?" She didn't like exposing her underbelly to this big, bad, hockey player, but she felt safe with him. Like she could let down her guard. For the first time in her life, she could talk about her father's rejection. Sometimes, it felt as though the jealousy that he'd chosen the boys over her would eat her alive.

But Declan wasn't repulsed by her weakness. Just the opposite. His gaze brushed over her like a caress, and it was the first bit of softness she'd seen from him. "I liked him because he cared about me."

"Did you not get along with your family?"

"It was just me and my grandfather, and we got along just fine. But the other guys, they've got siblings, aunts, uncles, grandparents. Kurt and the guys were family to me in a way I wasn't for them."

She glanced at the tattoo on his chest. "You were like the son he never had."

"Not really, no. He treated us all the same."

"And yet you're the one sitting in his living room right now."

A grin cracked his rugged façade, giving her a glimpse of the little boy he'd once been. "I told you why he chose me. I'm the only one who gets what this land means to him."

"You're the only one who *needs* what this land means to him." The others had their own family legacies. "Where does your grandfather live?"

"He died six and a half years ago."

"Oh, I'm so sorry." He really did have no one. Now, she truly understood why he'd gotten so angry about her wanting to sell the ranch.

"In any event, I know he loved you because of the way he talked about you." And just like that, the little boy got swallowed up by the badass hockey player.

Already, she missed him. That little window into his true nature felt like a gift. And she wanted it back.

"I remember this one time, I came into the house and he was sitting at the table"—he gestured toward the kitchen—"drinking coffee and reading something on his laptop. He was smiling, and I asked him what was up, and he said his daughter had won some big equestrian award."

"Are you joking? When was this? I know my mum wasn't feeding him information." Warmth suffused her. How had he known something like that? Had he followed her social media? "Especially something as silly as that award."

"He couldn't have been prouder when you got into Cambridge."

"Oh, well, that's a Crutchley thing."

"Why do you knock yourself down like that? It's weird."

"I've no idea." She laughed to cover her embarrassment. "But that's a very good question. I guess…I didn't grow up playing a sport or an instrument. I studied the Classics at uni. I just don't have any skills." She tipped her head back, gazing up at the wooden beams crossing the ceiling. "As ridiculous as it sounds, I was raised to marry well."

"You won an award for riding horses. And getting into Cambridge's a big one."

"It is…unless you're a Crutchley—" She caught herself. "You're right. It is." But really, now that she was thinking about it, her parents had never encouraged her to have a career. She was raised to follow in her mum's footsteps of hosting parties and attending charity events. "To be honest, there are only two times in my life I've ever felt true pride."

"When?"

"When I pull off a successful auction, everyone looks at me like I'm a superstar. In all the years the event's been held, no one's brought in as much money. It's the one thing I'm good at."

"And the second time?"

"When I got my first paycheck. It wasn't much, but I'd earned it. It sounds silly but paying my bills and not going into debt makes me unbelievably proud of myself."

"Nothing silly about that."

"The truth is…" *Look at me, spilling it all out.* She never spoke badly about her family. It just wasn't done. Her gaze cut over to him, worried she'd find judgment or…disgust. Instead, she found patience and…affection. And it just made her heart swell. "My parents are waiting for me to come crawling back."

"To marry Cameron?"

"That would certainly be ideal, but also, they want me

to experience the real world so I can find out how horrible it is. Then, I'll come back home and wind up marrying the right man."

"What if you don't fail?"

"I wait tables in a diner."

"For now. But what if you get this job at the foundation, and it leads to something bigger? What if you're okay living on your own, just not on their scale? Would that be enough for you? Or do you need what you grew up with?"

"They would feel sorry for me." He scowled, and she instantly regretted speaking badly of her family. "I love my parents. Andrew's a very good man. I came into his life when I was five, and he's always treated me like his own daughter. And all my mum ever wanted was for us to be a proper family. But being part of Andrew's world comes with expectations. There's no higher goal than to mix with the most influential people in England."

"I don't get that. They're making friends based on bank accounts."

"Yes, you're right." She gave him an appreciative smile. "I've never talked about these things with anyone."

"I've got you." He held her gaze, his tone firm.

"I believe you." Affection rushed over her, making her warm and happy. "I've talked more to you today than I ever did with Cameron in three years. Well, I mean, of course we talked."

"But not about things that matter."

"Yes. I never felt anything like this with him." And so he didn't get uncomfortable and think she was interested in anything romantic, she kept the focus on Cameron. "Imagine if I'd married him. How lonely I'd be."

"You don't feel lonely when you're with me? A total stranger?"

"No. Isn't that the strangest thing? I'm so out of place on this ranch, but when I'm with you, I don't feel lonely at all. It's like, now that I'm here, stripped of everything I am in London—a Crutchley, a waitress, a roommate—I find myself craving things I didn't even know I wanted."

"Yeah?" His voice deepened, grew dark and sultry. "Like what?"

I want to kiss you.

I want your hands on my body and your tongue in secret places nobody's ever explored. "I want to feel things I've never felt."

"I'm listening."

"I've never liked kissing before. But I know now it's because I wasn't attracted to Cameron the way I should've been. I've never felt wild abandon. I've never wanted someone so badly I lost my mind."

He sat forward, bringing their faces closer, their mouths a whisper apart. "Never?"

"Not until this moment." The thrill of it set her heart racing.

"So, what're you going to do about it?"

"Well, I'm in the Wild, Wild West, aren't I? I'm going to be an outlaw and kiss you. Right now." In that moment, there was nothing more important than touching her lips to his.

And so, she did. How such a soft, simple gesture could make her heart thunder, she had no idea. She shoved her hands under her thighs to keep from touching that warm skin, the hard muscles. A low current of electricity ran through her, and it all just felt so delicious, so lovely, so perfect.

Had she ever had such a sweet kiss that felt so incredibly hot?

But then, he licked the seam of her mouth, and she burst into flames. His tongue coaxed hers into play, enticing her into a sexy, slow dance. Desperate for more, she wrapped her arms around his neck, shimmying closer until her breasts met his hard chest.

His big hand cupped the back of her head, his possession so exciting she trembled from deep within. His other arm banded around her waist, and she was positive she'd never felt more wanted in her entire life. He kissed like she'd only ever seen in movies, with a passion of a couple deeply, wildly in love. His mouth was hot, indescribably soft, and his tongue tangled with hers.

She lost her mind to the minty taste of him, the clutch of his big hands, as though making sure he got to keep her. When he growled, gripping her ass, and hauling her onto his lap, the kiss turned carnal. Her hands fisted in his hair, and she rubbed against him, all over him, trying to get closer, to relieve the ache throbbing between her legs.

A desperate yearning unlike anything she'd ever experienced had her grinding on his very hard, thick cock.

Toppling her onto the chair, he swung a leg over her hips so he could straddle her, but the ottoman shifted, and her bottom landed on the hardwood floor.

With her legs pitched high, her body bent into a V, she looked ridiculous, and they both burst out laughing. "Oh, my God." Bracing her hands on the leather club chair, she heaved herself up, trying to find her footing without elbowing his balls.

He lifted her onto the chair and collapsed beside her. To see that rugged, serious man laughing…it just undid her.

He was dark, deep, and thoughtful, honorable, and so very kind. And she was helplessly drawn to him.

As their laughter died down, she touched her fingertips to her tingling lips and smiled. "I've never been kissed like that." She stood on wobbly legs. "Thank you for that. I promise it'll never happen again."

Chapter Nine

Damn right it'll never happen again.

Declan dropped the blueberries into the blender. He'd had a shitty night's sleep. And since when did he get all worked up over a *kiss*? Not since ninth grade when Missy Babcock and her friends came to the field after school to watch them ride their dirt bikes.

After everyone had left, she'd pulled him behind a tree and stuck her tongue in his mouth. He hadn't known what to make of the whole experience—he'd never thought of Missy like that. Until she'd showed him her tits. He got it after that.

With Phinny…it was different. It was something about *her.*

After slicing frozen bananas, he poured in almond milk.

Even though he'd showered this morning, he swore her scent still lingered on him. Or maybe it was in the air. Taunting him. Torturing him. Getting him all worked up. It reminded him of her silky hair brushing over his chest and arms.

Blood rushed to his cock.

Nope. Not going there. He'd fantasized about her all night long, imagining sliding between her cool sheets, breathing in that sweet, fresh, expensive scent, getting his hands on all that smooth, soft skin. He'd pictured nuzzling her neck to wake her up, seeing that smile, the happiness in her eyes that lit him up, and her rolling onto her back to welcome him. He could see it so clearly, moving over her, the way she'd shift her thighs open for him. She'd clutch his ass urging him to fuck her harder.

Every time he'd drift off, the imagined sensation of her slick heat on the tip of his cock would send a shock through him, jolting him awake. His favorite fantasy was getting in the shower with her. Gliding his soapy hands up her stomach to cup her breasts. *Fuck.* He could feel her nipples beading in his palms, the restless swish of hips as she reached for his cock and—

"Morning." The back door shut as Phinny came into the kitchen wearing knee-high rubber boots.

Fuck. Shit. He had to burn those images of her soapy body to the ground. Turning back to the blender, he added almond butter to his protein shake. "Did your chores?"

You can't think about her like that.

She's Kurt's daughter.

But that excuse wasn't working anymore. She wasn't just someone's daughter. She was…He glanced up at the early morning light pouring in through the window.

She's sunshine. He didn't know he'd been living in the shadows until she'd shined that bright smile on him. He didn't know how quiet he'd become until he'd heard her full-belly laughter.

He'd never met anyone so willing to show her raw, true self. Her honesty, integrity…

Yeah, he had it bad.

"Yep. Just finished. I have no idea why we have all those chickens, but they're gorgeous." Lifting one leg at a time, she tugged off the boots and set them on the rubber mat. Then, she came right up to him. "I'm sorry for kissing you last night." She said it like an announcement. Like she'd been thinking about it a while and had sorted out what she wanted to say.

She was direct and blunt, and he liked that about her. A hell of a lot. Most people deflected, hinted, or manipulated. Not Phinny. He shrugged a shoulder. "It wasn't a hardship."

When she grinned, it was like a sharp crack of ice in his chest. As warmth trickled out, his skin burned.

"I *meant* that it was impulsive and selfish, and I promise it won't happen again."

"Probably for the best, seeing as we're competing against each other."

"Yeah, about that." She eyed the fancy coffee machine. "I mean, we live together. We're going to look through the same photo albums and files. We've got access to the same information, so we might as well team up."

"I don't have a problem with that because I still think you should get the ranch."

"Declan, you understand I'm selling it when I win, right?"

"I'm positive you underestimate my competitive nature." While he understood the lure of hundreds of millions of dollars, he was getting to know her better, and he wasn't convinced she'd go through with it. He got that owning a cattle ranch in Wyoming wasn't her thing, but he'd seen the way she'd looked at the photographs.

She couldn't hide her feelings if she tried. He could practically read it in a thought cloud over her head. *This is my family. My ancestors.*

If he had a legacy like this, they'd have to pry it out of his cold, dead hands.

But he didn't bother saying it. Only time would tell. He hit the button, and while the blender ground up his frozen fruit, Phinny caressed the professional espresso machine.

She obviously didn't know how to work it, so her fingers skimmed the stainless steel, trailed over the gauges and settings, her frustration growing the longer she examined the levers and control buttons.

When he stopped the blender, he poured his smoothie into a travel mug. "I don't drink coffee, so I have no idea how to use it, but we can look for the instruction manual."

"That's okay. I can live without it."

"You're eyeing it like it's a safety deposit box filled with diamonds."

"Pft. I'm more of a sapphire girl. Hey, I have a question for you. In this entire house, there's only one locked door. It's not Kurt's office, so what is it?"

"Actually, he's got two of them. One's business, that's where Mitch and I work. The other's his private one."

"Is the private one normally locked?"

"Nope." And he didn't know why it was now.

She took in his boots, jeans, and Henley. "Are you going somewhere?"

"Yep. Jaime wants me to meet the Renegades."

"Oh." She sounded disappointed. "So, you'll be taking the Jeep?"

"Yeah, why? What do you need?"

"Well, I'm supposed to meet that woman who stopped by my lemonade stand yesterday, but I can take a cab or something. It's too far to walk."

He knew she couldn't afford a cab, and she'd said she had a license but didn't know how to drive. He didn't see any choice other than driving her himself. "What time are you going to meet her?"

"Not until noon."

"And where is she?"

Phinny pulled a napkin out of the tiny pocket in her leggings.

He read the address. "That's not too far from the rink. How about you come with me, and then we can go to her house together?"

Relief relaxed her gorgeous features. "That sounds great."

"Can you be ready in ten minutes?"

"I can, but if you give me fifteen minutes, I'll be able to shower and put on make-up."

"Fifteen, huh?"

"I can't cook, I can't drive, but I can be camera-ready in no-time."

"And the time starts…" He glanced at the clock on the oven. "Now."

Laughing, she dashed out of the room, giving him a view of that perfect peach of an ass.

He'd held those firm cheeks in his hands last night when they'd kissed. He'd pulled her up hard against him, and she'd squirmed all over his cock. Of course, he hadn't slept.

Not after getting a glimpse of what she'd be like in bed.

Her ex was an asshole not to love her up before fucking her. He'd missed out on all that Phinny goodness. Damn, he got a kick in his gut just thinking about it.

Phinny was passionate. She needed someone who'd get all her cylinders firing at once. He'd like nothing more than to watch her fall apart from his tongue, his hands, his cock.

If her ass hadn't hit the floor, he didn't know what would've happened. He'd been so far gone he wouldn't have stopped on his own. And that was the craziest part. He'd never gotten so absorbed in a woman that he'd lost his sense of time and place.

There was something about Phinny.

Maybe since they were living under the same roof for a month, and they were both obviously attracted to each other…

Nope. Still not fucking her.

To his surprise, Phinny burst out of the house exactly fifteen minutes later. She still had the sleek hair, the make-up and flashy jewelry, but today she wore the cheap shorts, Wild Billy T-shirt, and pink cowboy boots she'd bought yesterday.

And somehow, she rocked it. Not that he cared what she wore. He was just happy to be with her.

Hopping into the passenger seat, she pulled the seatbelt across her chest. "I'm exactly on time."

"I see that." He backed out.

"Yes, but you're already in the car. If I'd taken a minute longer, would you have left without me?"

"Possibly." *Nope.* He headed down the driveway. "Depends how late you were."

"So, you wouldn't have come looking for me? 'Phinny, it's time to go.'" She lowered her voice to sound like him.

"Nah. You knew the deal."

She sputtered out a laugh. "Wow."

"What? You know I have to meet a friend at the rink."

"Oh, my God, you're so much like Kurt. It's hilarious."

"How would you know? The last time you saw him you were five."

She went quiet.

Ah, hell. He hadn't meant to be mean. "Do you have any memories of him?"

"Not really." Her troubled look made him feel like shit for bringing it up. "You know what's sad? I remember my first pair of butter-yellow patent leather Mary Janes, but I barely remember my father."

He braked as the gate slowly swung open. "Well, you were young."

"I wonder if I'd have turned out differently with Kurt in my life." She smoothed her shorts. "If I'd kept coming here, would I have wound up loving it? I can just see my mum's expression when I got off the plane at Heathrow with straw in my hair and a farmer's tan." Her smile faded. "I was on track to become just like her, but if I'd had Kurt to…I don't know, sort of balance out her influence, what sort of person would I have become?"

"I think you turned out just fine. But sure, he'd have had an impact. He would've led by example, though, and left it up to you to follow or not."

"Why did you follow it, do you think?"

As he drove down 191, he could admit the truth. "I wanted to be worthy of his investment."

"What does that mean?"

Yeah, Declan, what do you mean? He gave it some

thought. "He was the best hockey player in the country, and he took time out of his schedule to work with us. I just wanted to, you know, respect his time."

"You didn't want him to give up on you. Lose interest. I can see that."

"Kurt's been retired for ten years, and still, no one's beaten his records. That's how good he was. And the fact that he started a travel team for the four of us…it was a big deal. I wanted it to be worthwhile for him."

"Did the other guys take it as seriously?"

"Absolutely. We all did." *I just really wanted to make him proud.*

"So why is Cole the only one playing professionally?"

Ha. Good question. "Oh, well, you know. Shit happens." Nothing he wanted to talk about. "It's a long story."

"How far's the rink?"

"Not far enough." He fought a grin.

"Hey, I told you my story."

"Yep. You sure did."

She gave him a playful shove. "Oh, come on. How bad can it be?"

"It's pretty bad." Reflexively, his fingers squeezed the steering wheel. "One of the guys almost died."

"Oh. I'm sorry. I had no idea…"

His chest tightened, and his palms went clammy. It didn't happen all that often anymore—ten years was a long time—but when something triggered memories of that night, it all came back to him. And not just the images but the volatile cocktail of emotions.

He'd get that flash of Booker's parachute buckling, and his blood would freeze. "We'd done a lot of extreme shit together, and we'd been lucky."

"I'm guessing your luck ran out?"

"Yep."

"In the lawyer's office the other day, it was clear something had happened, but I couldn't make out what. You were very intense, watching their faces, reading their reactions." She sat up, shifting to face him. "Did my father do something? Is that why he left you the team, so he could make up for something he did to break up your friendships?"

"One day, you'll stop painting Kurt with your mom's brush, and you'll see him through your own eyes. No, what happened that night was all on us. Kurt had nothing to do with it."

"So, if you don't mind my asking, what happened?"

With his heart racing and chest tightening, a weird sensation took hold, like his mind was drifting away from his body. But he wouldn't let anxiety take control. No, he could do this. For her, he would. "It was the summer after senior year. The night before Booker was heading to L.A. to play for the Kings. Cole was going to play for the Renegades, your dad's team. Jaime was heading to Canada to play in the Junior Division."

"And you?"

"I went to University of Michigan."

"Oh, you weren't…" Her jaw snapped shut.

Pretty sure she was going to say *you weren't good enough?* He couldn't help chuckling. He, Booker, and Cole had been all over magazines and newspapers for being the rare trio from a small town in Wyoming to make the big leagues. "No, I could've played. Your dad wanted me on the Renegades, but I wanted a college education."

"So, what happened?" She said it softly, as if she understood how hard this conversation was for him.

"The night before Booker and I left—him for training, me for college—Jaime's parents told him they were selling the dude ranch. They'd been in the red too long, and with him leaving, they just couldn't do it anymore. They couldn't afford to hire someone to replace him. His entire family had given their blood and sweat for that ranch, and he couldn't walk away, so he gave up his spot on the Canadian team to stay and help."

"Wow, that had to be awful for him."

"He said there was no decision to be made. Family first. But, yeah, it sucked, so he asked us to hang out with him one more night. I was already packed, ready for bed. I had to get up at five to make my flight out of Idaho Falls, so I said no. I'd see them over the holidays. Booker said the same thing because we knew, anytime the four of us got together—"

"Shenanigans."

"Yeah. But Cole was down for it, and he told us to meet at the airstrip instead of going to Jaime's house. He'd steal his dad's Piper Cub and fly up to the ridge where they had a cabin."

"Fancy."

Right. She didn't know. "Cole's dad is Trevor Montgomery."

"Shut up." Her feet landed on the floorboard. "You're joking?"

He shook his head.

"Cut it out. Trevor Montgomery, the movie star, is your friend's *dad?*"

"Yeah. He lives in Malibu, but he prefers his place in Calamity. A lot of celebrities move here because they're left alone. No one gives a shit about their portfolio or fame. But anyhow, he built a cabin on top of a mountain.

Coolest place you've ever seen. It literally sits at the edge of the world, overlooking all of Jackson Hole. In any event, they promised it wouldn't be a crazy night, so Booker and I went along."

Her fingers bunched the fabric of her shorts. "Oh, no."

Yeah. "It was fine at first. We had a bonfire. Jaime's the kind of guy who can handle his liquor so you wouldn't even know he was drunk. It was getting late, and I had a big day of travel, so I said we should head out, and that's when Jaime got this wild look on his face, and he announced he was going to BASE jump."

"What is that, exactly?"

As he approached the hot zone of the story, he let out a slow, unsteady breath. "It's when you jump from a fixed object like a bridge or a building—"

"Or a cliff."

"With the right height, yeah."

"Is it like hang gliding?"

"It's a freefall jump, but you've got a parachute. Which you deploy pretty quickly since you're not even two thousand feet up."

"That's…terrifying."

"It's something we did a lot, and there's no better place to do it than that cliff. If the wind's right, it's a perfect landing in the meadow."

"I feel sick right now."

"We told him not to do it, but he was wasted, and he didn't want the night to end."

"Because he knew what was on the other side of it. You'd start new and exciting lives, and he'd be left behind."

All he could do was nod. "And Cole was always down for anything, so the minute Jaime suggested it, Cole was already running into the cabin to get the gear."

Even though he was driving in traffic, he could still smell the pine forest and the smoke from the bonfire, could see Cole and Jaime laughing so hard they practically pissed themselves. The clank of metal, the shush of fabric…Declan was right there, living it all over again. "They were drunk. We couldn't just let them go. If anything happened to them…"

"You couldn't have lived with yourself."

"Right." He shoved his fingers through his hair. "It turned out great. One of the best rides of my life. Jaime landed first, then, Cole, then me. One perfect landing after another."

"Until?"

He heard her voice like she was in another room. Because he was still there. The cool night air, the rush of adrenaline. "It's such a high, jumping off a cliff in the middle of the night. The only lights come from the valley and the moon. You're free-falling until you pull the chute, and it jerks you. Then…you float." *Such a rush.* "I remember feeling this intense relief when I saw them land. And when I hit the ground…" He'd been so damn happy.

"You'd tempted fate, but it had all turned out well."

It wasn't quite like that. He'd never felt like he was defying the odds or pushing his luck. He'd felt… competent. At eighteen, he'd been in the best shape of his life, and all the years of parkour and rappelling and all the shit they'd done had honed his agility. His instincts.

"We were so damn high off a good landing, and we turned around to watch Booker." Tension squeezed the back of his neck, releasing a cold fluid that trickled down his spine. "It's…sometimes there's turbulence." He checked to see if she understood. She didn't. "When air flows over objects close to the ground, it's called turbulence. If you get caught in the flow…" He saw it all over again, felt the abject panic. "It was freak timing, but it got Booker. We watched it happen. Everything was going great, and then the wind collapsed his parachute. He hit the ground and crumpled." Jesus, he could hear the thud of his friend's body, see his legs fold like they were made of wet cardboard.

"Oh, my God. What happened?"

"I ran like I was on fire to get Cole's truck." He would never forget the torturous moments when his hands wouldn't cooperate. They were shaking so badly, he'd struggled to remove his pack. Then, he'd bolted. It was all such a blur—from the time he'd taken off to reaching Colt's house, finding the rack of keys…not knowing which one to take. Time was ticking. His friend could be dying…could be *dead*. He had to get help.

Finally, he'd recognized the stupid hockey stick keychain some girl had given his friend. "We loaded Booker in the back and floored it to the ER." They'd all been deathly quiet. It was like no one could talk over the noise in their heads. Only when they'd entered the ER did Jaime shout, *Help. We need help.* Everyone had turned, wide-eyed, alarmed, not sure what was going on, until Jaime roared *Now*. And then someone rolled a gurney out to the truck, and they wheeled Booker away.

Phinny's hand on his forearm pulled him out of the memory.

He looked at her delicate fingers, the gems in her rings winking in the sunlight. "It was bad. He fractured his femur and broke both ankles. After they wheeled him away…" He let out a tight breath. "I had to call his parents. Woke his dad up. I could hear his mom in the background." *What is it? What's going on?* "We were so fucking lucky his spine was okay, but hockey was over for him. We knew it. It wasn't even a question." Not after seeing his legs crumple like that. "He was in the hospital for a long time, but his parents wouldn't let us see him. And the next thing we knew, they'd moved back east. Didn't even put up a For Sale sign. Nothing. One day, I stopped by to apologize to them and check on Booker— he was one of my best friends—but the house was empty." He would never forget peering through the living room window to find the space cleared of all furniture. His stomach had plummeted. "We never saw him again. Not until the funeral."

"I don't even know what to say. That's just awful. I want to say Jaime's a piece of shit, but—"

"He's not, though. Ever since Cole got his pilot license, we'd been flying up to the ridge. We'd BASE jumped hundreds of times. And all Jaime wanted to do was hang out. It was just going to be a bonfire at his place. Cole took it to the next level by stealing his dad's plane."

"But Jaime's the one who wanted to jump. And it's not like the rest of you had a choice."

"No, we did. It was absolutely my choice to jump with him."

"How were you supposed to get home? Didn't Cole fly you up there?"

"Yeah, it'd have been a ten-hour hike down the mountain in the middle of the night. But to be honest, we weren't thinking about that." It still ate away at him. The what-ifs. What if he'd said no to Jaime that night? What if Booker hadn't hesitated before putting on his chute? It was all in the timing. The gust of wind at the exact moment Booker neared the ground.

"What does everyone do now?"

"Jaime went to college here at the WY—"

"The WY?"

"Sorry, yeah. The University of Western Wyoming. And he coaches the elite travel team your dad started for us. Cole pulled a runner. We only found out he'd taken Jaime's spot in Canada weeks later when hockey season started, and he wasn't on the Renegades' roster. And Booker went to Yale. He's a sports agent."

"And you played hockey at uni, right?"

"I did. For two years."

"I'm sorry for being so pushy. This is obviously none of my business. It's just you're not playing, either."

He'd gotten over the hardest part. Well, sort of. "Right, but that's because Sam got sick."

"Sam?"

"My grandfather."

"Are you telling me you dropped out of college to take care of your grandfather?"

He nodded.

"That's…wow. I guess there was no one else who could help? A friend, a family member?"

"Sure, there were lots of people." In fact, he'd had coaches who promised to provide round-the-clock nursing care in exchange for a contract to play for them. "But he was my grandfather. He raised me, and I didn't want anyone else caring for him. You think I could sleep at night in my dorm bed knowing he was sick? You think I could play hockey like nothing had happened when I knew his days were numbered?"

She gave him a sweet, soft smile. "No, I don't think you could do that." Her head tipped back. "Oh, Declan. You are one dangerous man."

He didn't know what to make of that.

"You look like such a badass, but you're a sweetheart." She gave him a soft smile. "Okay, so you dropped out of college to take care of him. How did you find your way back to hockey?"

"After Sam died, Kurt said I'd always have a place on the Renegades, but I told him I needed to earn a spot on his team. It's not like I'd played or trained in eighteen months. You can't take that much time off and expect to play in the NHL. But I'd stayed in touch with some of the guys on my college team, and one of them played for the Comets. He talked me up to the coach. They brought me out to meet with the team and wound up hiring me."

"Hm, I'm getting the feeling you were kind of a big deal."

He turned off the main highway and headed into a nice neighborhood.

"And you're never going to tell me about your greatness, so I'm going to have to make up a whole story in my head." She sat up when the training center came into view. "Whoa, this place is cool. I'm not sure what I was expecting, but it wasn't this."

"Kurt never did anything half-ass." He parked, and they got out. "I won't be long. Jaime just wants me to meet some of the guys."

She met him on the sidewalk. "Most people would want to own a team by themselves. It would be hard to make decisions with four equal owners, but I guess he wants his friends back more than he wants power and money."

"That sounds about right." Declan wanted that, too. But he wasn't about to get all twisted up over the things he couldn't control. *Like when the people you care about leave...*

"What do you think you'll do?" she asked. "Will you give up coaching?"

"That's a tough one. As much as I want to coach, Kurt gave me this gift." He opened the door for her. Normally, he wouldn't share so much, but this woman pushed him to think, to face his shit. "Turning it down feels like rejecting him."

Maybe it was because of her beauty and her generally happy spirit, but he suspected her parents and her ex didn't really see down to the heart of her. The intelligence, the way she paid attention to details and made thoughtful decisions. The kindness, the sweetness, and the terrible pain of rejection and hurt she lived with. But he saw it. He saw all of it.

And there wasn't anything he didn't like.

So, when she looked at him and smiled, when he saw approval in her eyes, it made him feel like a million bucks.

"But you want to coach, and Kurt had to know that. I'm wondering if he set this all up so you could wind up coaching his team." She made it sound like it was such a simple, obvious thing.

Once inside the rink, she crossed her arms over her chest and rubbed. He'd have to find her a sweatshirt. "Owners don't coach. No, I think Kurt wanted the four of us to make peace with each other. It's nothing more than that."

She gazed up at him with pure kindness. "Well, in any event, you've got three weeks to decide. I'm sure the answer will be clear by then."

As they headed for the ice, he could see the changes right away—a fancier refreshment stand, nicer bleachers, and a lot more advertising signs—but the core of the place was the same. He'd first learned to play hockey with his best friends right here. There was just something about the chill in the air, the shush of skates on ice, that got his blood pumping.

And he knew in his bones he didn't want to watch games from the owner's box. He wanted to be in the middle of the action, to feel the rush of air as players sped past. There was nothing more exciting for his brain and his body than strategizing plays and figuring out a teammate's weakness. And then helping him improve it.

"You can hang out here." He gestured to the bleachers. "You want anything to eat or drink?"

"No, I'm good. Don't worry about me. I'm going to catch up on some emails."

Before he stepped onto the ice, he texted Kelly, the woman who ran the skate desk.

Declan: **Do you have a sweatshirt or something?**

Kelly: **Sure. XL?**

Declan: **No, it's for the pretty woman sitting right behind me.**

Kelly: **Pretty, huh?**

Chuckling, he pocketed his phone and looked around. Clusters of kids worked in different areas of the rink. Among the coaches, it was easy to spot the Renegades— and not just because of their jerseys. They were bigger, fitter, and a hell of a lot more agile.

The moment he stepped onto the ice, he headed over to Jamie and a few pro players. His friend pulled back, welcoming him into the circle. "Hey, man." They shook hands. "Guys, this is Declan Cadell. He's still the all-time point leader in college hockey."

"You're in *college*?" Luc Marchand, a recent trade from Vancouver held out a hand.

"No, I work with the Comets."

"Cool." Luc elbowed the man next to him. "This is Father Tom. He's the keeper of our pipes."

Tom Zegrebsky gave him a chin nod.

"You've got to see his slap shot." Jaime patted Declan's back.

Oh, hell, no. "I haven't played in years." He wasn't going to put on a show for NHL players.

Jaime laughed. "He's full of it. I'd bet the ranch you still scare the shit out of the Comets' goalies."

Declan shook his head but couldn't fight the grin. There was some truth in that.

"Come on, let's give the kids a show," Jaime said.

"I didn't bring my skates."

"Huh. What can we do about that?" His friend made a big show of looking around the rink. "Where could we possibly find you a pair of ice skates?" He cupped a hand over his mouth. "Kelly!"

The woman behind the counter waved.

"Grab me a pair of thirteens."

"You got it." She disappeared down a long aisle. Hockey skates took up one section, and figure skates took up the other.

"Let me grab you a stick." Jaime headed off the ice and into a utility room.

As Declan sat on a bench to put on his skates, he glanced back to find Luc taking control. Stopping drills, he gathered his teammates and sent the kids to the benches in the sin-bin.

Shit like this always got him pumped. He loved playing hockey, loved coaching, loved everything about the sport.

Ready for action, he met Jaime on the blue line.

"Here you go." Jaime handed him a stick.

"You haven't seen me skate in ten years," Declan said.

"Please. I know you." He smacked Declan's biceps. "You're every bit as fit as the pro players. Now, come on. The kids are waiting. Show 'em how it's done."

It had been ten years since he'd skated on this ice, and the squeeze of nostalgia hit him hard. It drove home why Jaime wanted the four of them to own the team together. He missed the camaraderie, the friendship. He'd never had anything like it since.

As he watched, the Renegades' left winger dropped a neat row of pucks along the blue line. His senses sharpened, and he couldn't help casting a glance at Phinny to see if she was watching.

One hand gripped her phone, but her attention was trained on him. When she broke into a smile, it was a direct hit to his solar plexus.

Pleasure streaming through him, he focused on the stick, lining it up with the first puck. He was a peacock, displaying his feathers, and he would not let her down. He channeled his thoughts, his energy on the puck, zoning in on the goalie, on finding that opening. Hockey was so much more than speed and agility. It was the ability to anticipate what a player would do before he moved. It was being so in tune with the play that you were a split-second ahead.

Taking in the goalie's stance, Declan cocked his arm and fired. The man butterflied, but the biscuit sailed right over his shoulder into the net. *Fuck, yeah*. Charged, he moved on to the next one, and even though this time the goalie was more alert now, the puck still tipped his glove and landed inside the pipes. One after another, each one got through. Declan was so in the zone, he barely heard the kids shouting.

Finished, he turned to Phinny. Jaw hanging open, she stared at him in awe. There was a moment there when the world narrowed to just the two of them. Blood roared in his ears, and he wanted her to come running onto the ice and throw herself into his arms.

But then applause broke out, so thunderous the sound hit the high ceiling and rained down on him.

"Didn't I tell you?" Jaime said. "I told you, man. He's a force. He'd have been the best forward hockey's ever seen. Now, who wants to get out there and learn from Declan Cadell? He'll give you a quick lesson right now, and then we'll try to get him to come back while he's in town."

The kids heaved off the bench as one, pouring onto the ice. The other coaches quickly diverted them to their clinics while the forwards gathered around him.

"Hey, guys." But before he began, he got one more look at Phinny to make sure she was doing okay. She fanned herself with a hand and mouthed, "Wow."

And damn if he didn't feel like a fucking king.

Chapter Ten

Still high from coaching, Declan headed out of the parking lot. "Sorry about that." He hadn't meant to make her late.

"No, don't worry. I texted Leddy, and she's totally fine." Phinny gripped the handhold as he wheeled the car around. "That was amazing. I can't believe how good you are. And the way you were with those kids? You're such a good coach." She pulled her hair into a ponytail and twisted it into a bun. "What did Luc say to you at the end when we were leaving?"

As he waited to pull out onto the street, he caught a glimpse of the pale column of her neck. "He asked if I had time to work with one of their second-string players." He hit the accelerator before he did something stupid like reach out to see if her skin felt as smooth as it looked.

"Doesn't the team have coaches that can help him?"

"Sure, but the guy probably wants to kill it during exhibition games, get his shot on the front line. Maybe he wants to surprise the coaches."

"Exhibition games?"

"Before the season starts, we play around eight games. It gives the coaches a chance to see everyone's strengths and weaknesses, figure out who's going to be on the roster."

"So, you're saying if a second-string player does better than, say, Luc, a veteran with an amazing record, he gets to play?"

"If Luc's not hitting the pucks, they'll absolutely put in someone else."

"I don't think I'm built for anything that competitive. I would shrivel under the pressure."

"You've been under a lot of pressure for ten months, and you're doing great."

She gifted him with one of her luminous smiles. "You're right about that." She let out a contented sigh. "Well, watching you was exciting."

Yep. Preening like a peacock.

"We don't have hockey in the UK, so I've never seen it before."

"Even as a kid, you didn't watch your dad's games?"

"No, never. We never even talked about them." She went quiet for a moment, lost in thought. "All this time I've blamed Kurt, but now I'm starting to think about my mum's part in all this. If I were divorced, I feel like I'd encourage my child to know her dad. Wouldn't I put her on the phone with him? All my mum's ever done is badmouth him."

Pretty much what he'd been thinking.

"It's like she did everything she could to turn me against him. I mean, if it were me, no matter how much I hated my ex, I think I'd push for my child to know him. I'd be like *Oh, Daddy's game is on. Let's watch*."

"Makes sense. Why do you think she didn't?"

"I'm going to ask her. I've always assumed he did something terribly wrong that she wouldn't tell me about, like cheating or something, because her reactions have always been so over-the-top."

No way would he let her entertain thoughts like that. "He didn't cheat. Kurt was one of the most honorable men I know. It wasn't in his nature to fuck around."

"You sound quite sure about that."

"I am."

"Honorable. That's the same word Jaime used to describe you. Sounds like Kurt and your grandfather did a good job with you."

He grinned. "Sam and Kurt were nothing alike."

Shifting, she lifted a knee to better face him. "Really? Tell me all about Grandpa Cadell."

"Sam lived hard. He cursed, he drank, he smoked…" He thought of the cigar dangling out of his mouth as he sat with his buddies for his weekly poker game. The big laugh that came from his gut as the guys argued, told jokes, and shared inappropriate stories.

"Oh, no, you don't." She clamped her hand on his arm and gave it a shake. "You don't get lost in memories without sharing them." She leaned over and cupped his mouth. "Say them out loud."

"Okay, okay." Laughing, he gently swatted her hand away. "When Sam walked into a restaurant, people would call out to him. 'Sammy,' 'Sammy, my man.' They got out of their chairs to slap him on the back and talk to him." He could see it so clearly, the sparkle in their eyes, the eagerness. "When they shook his hand, they didn't let go. He was like an energy source, and they needed to get their fill."

"Was he like the mayor or something?"

"Oh, hell, no. He was too opinionated. He was a real character. You either hated him, or you loved him. There's a group in town called the Cooters. If you ever go to the diner at eleven in the morning, you'll see a bunch of seniors taking up tables on the left side. They've got a standing brunch date there, and they range from old cowhands to CEOs and everything in between. Well, that group started because of him. Whenever he walked in, people would pull up chairs and hang out with him. It turned into a daily thing."

"He sounds like a great guy."

"The best." Declan smiled at the memory. "He didn't hold anything back. If he was pissed, he called you out. He drank hard, worked hard, and played hard."

"Our families couldn't be more different. Mine is so proper. They would be mortified to cause a scene of any kind. They have to be invited to the right parties, wear the right clothes. How they behave at home is completely different from how they are in social situations."

"With my grandfather, you got the real deal. He didn't know how to be anything else."

"I would find comfort in that." She gave a wistful smile.

Peering through the windshield, he slowed as they approached Blossom Lane. "I think this is the street."

She glanced at her napkin. "Yes. Number twenty-two fourteen."

"You know what you want to ask?"

"I don't really." She pulled her hair out of the knot and flipped down the visor. "Oh, look at me. I'm such a mess." She dug into her purse and grabbed a tube of lipstick.

Watching her pucker those plump lips, smear on the pale pink that made them shiny and wet, had him nearly driving into the back of pick-up truck. Braking just in time, he jerked the gearshift into Park and cut the engine.

Just as he started to get out, she said, "The thing is, I don't know what kind of questions we'll be asked in the contest. Do I need to know his favorite color? His drink preference? What am I looking for here?"

"I know as much as you do, but I can only assume he wants you to know *him*. To see him through the eyes of people who knew him well."

"Yeah." The simple word came out on a wisp of air. "Well, I suppose I'll just let her guide the conversation. Maybe questions will pop up from that."

"Makes sense. You ready?"

She nodded, reaching for his arm. "Thank you, Declan. You're a good man, and you have the best heart. You could easily have left me on my own and won the ranch, but here you are helping me find out all I can about my…about Kurt."

He looked down at her hand on his arm. How many women had touched him over the years? He'd had women rub the heel of their palm on his dick, grab his ass, and run their hands up his chest with lust in their eyes. None of it had ever made his skin go hot and prickly. He'd never gotten chill bumps.

Why did he react so strongly to *this* woman?

But he couldn't have her, so he had to shut down his reaction. "My interests are with Kurt, so if you still want to sell his place three weeks from now, I can guarantee I'll win."

"Just when I start to warm up to you…"

"Come on. Let's go talk to Leddy Champion." They got out of the Jeep and headed up the walkway. The homes on the street were older, a little worn. With one arm around a squirming, shrieking child, the next-door neighbor hauled several grocery bags up the walkway to her house.

Declan dashed across the lawn and relieved the woman of the bags, walking with her to the front door. After he set them on the doorstep, he started to walk away.

"Thank you," she called.

With a wave, he jogged back over to Leddy's house to find Phinny waiting for him. She gazed up at him with affection. "I see you, Declan Cadell. You come off all mean and badass, but you've got a heart of gold." First, she finger-combed his hair. "There. Now, you look less like a pirate." Then, she smoothed hers and pressed the doorbell.

"A pirate?"

"Yep. You look like a dashing, rugged, naughty rogue." Her eyes were full of mischief.

He didn't know how much longer he could keep from pulling her into his arms and kissing her, drinking in all that sweetness and goodness and joy.

His hand moved of its own volition, brushing the back of hers—nothing more than a tap, a nudge…a subtle invitation. To his great surprise, she responded, turning hers…and they connected, clasped, and just held each other on the doorstep of 2214 Blossom Lane.

He was holding hands with Phinny. And nothing had ever felt so right.

A moment later, the door opened. She gave him a squeeze and let go.

While gestures of affection came easily to her, it wasn't like that for him. Outside of fucking, he didn't touch women. He'd never held hands or wrapped an arm around someone while waiting in line. No one had ever snuggled against him. He didn't invite that kind of thing.

His breath hitched at the realization that he didn't know tenderness.

Not until now.

"Phinny." The older woman stood there with a big smile. "It's so good to see you again. And look, you brought a friend." She gave a quick scan from his face down to his boots. "Hm, judging by the looks of you, I'm going to guess you're one of Kurt's hockey players."

Phinny laughed. "I might've guessed he was a pirate, but I got to watch him skate at the rink, so I can confirm, that yes, he's definitely a hockey player. Ms. Champion, this is Declan Cadell."

"Oh, please. Call me Leddy. Well, come on in." The woman stepped back, allowing them into her foyer. She drew Phinny into her arms. "I didn't get to say this yesterday, but I'm real sorry for your loss, honey." She rubbed her back. "Your dad was one of the finest men I know." She pulled away, holding onto her shoulders. "You look so much like him."

"Do I?" Curiosity sparked in Phinny's eyes.

"You sure do. Come with me into the kitchen. I've got drinks and cookies all ready for you. It's a good thing you brought a friend. I made way more than we could ever eat."

"I should have asked." Phinny followed her across the living. "I'm sorry about that."

"Nonsense. This is Calamity. We don't run on formalities." In the kitchen, she stopped and turned to him, poking him in the chest. "Besides, Sam's boy's always welcome here."

"You knew his grandfather?" Phinny asked.

"Oh, sure. Everyone knew Sam Cadell." Leddy grew

serious. "And just for the record, he never cheated. Not once. Roy was just a sore loser."

Grinning, Phinny whirled around toward him. "Cheated?"

Declan just laughed. "Roy lost a lot money at Sam's poker games."

"That was a known fact." Leddy poured lemonade into tall glasses.

"And I guess his wife kicked him out when he lost the money that was supposed to go to a new truck." Or so Declan had heard.

"One day, Roy stormed into the diner loaded for bear." Leddy put the glasses on a tray. "Turned into a fist fight. He was banned for life." A cat jumped onto the kitchen table, and she swatted the air around it. "Go on now. Don't make me look bad in front of company." She shooed it, but it just collapsed in a pool of sunshine and closed its eyes. "Let's go into the sunroom." She led them into a covered porch and set the tray down on a wicker coffee table.

Once they'd seated themselves on the couch, Leddy said, "Oh, I forgot the darn cookies. I'd forget my teeth if I didn't like to eat so much. Hang on a second." At the threshold, Leddy poked her head out. "I've left a few newspaper articles for you to read. You go and take your time. I'll just be a few minutes."

Phinny picked up the first weathered paper and held it like it was the Magna Carta.

Declan figured Leddy hadn't forgotten anything. She'd just wanted to give Phinny time alone with stories about her dad, so he got up. "Let me help you." Instead of following her into the kitchen, though, he hesitated. For some strange reason, he didn't want to leave Phinny alone.

Not while she looked at the articles like they held a treasure. "You okay?"

She startled but then relaxed into a smile. "I'll be better with a cookie."

Right. Got it. She wanted to be alone. He'd give her that. He figured he'd feel the same way if he got to see articles about his parents for the first time.

"It shouldn't feel this weird, right? It's just a newspaper." She picked up a Calamity Gazette. "It's not like Kurt's going to pop out and go, Gotcha! It's just… living in his house, talking to his friends, and now reading these articles…he's coming to life for me." The stark sadness in her eyes shredded him. "Right when he's gone for good."

"But it's good to learn the truth about him, though, right? You've spent most of your life wondering why he bailed on you, and now maybe you can get some answers."

Sadness dampened her spirit, and she nodded, pretending that everything was all right. "I hope so." She blinked again, furiously this time, still with that brave smile. "I really, really hope so."

A breeze came through the screen, fluttering the edges of the newspapers.

More than anything, Phinny wanted Declan to sit with her, but she wasn't about to become someone he needed to babysit. Smoothing the stack of aged papers, she noticed each one had been folded to a specific page. She skimmed through them for mention of Kurt.

Kurt Grevers is the single largest landowner in Wyoming.

Kurt views himself as a steward of the land.

Innovative tools and breakthroughs...rotational grazing, land that's equipped to sequester carbon, so it's not emitted into the air...no feedlots or chemical fertilizers.

He seeks current technologies to minimize dependence on fossil fuels and chemical fertilizers and pesticides...the higher upfront costs of utilizing green technologies and modern horticulture and animal science are more than offset by ongoing operating costs.

Kurt Grevers defines green.

Engrossed in reading, she barely heard the two return. Declan handed her a plate with two cookies so warm the chips were little pools of glossy chocolate. "Oh, yum. Thank you."

The way he held her gaze...she'd never met anyone who could so clearly communicate with just a look. And right now, he was asking if she was okay. She forced herself to nod, but she couldn't pull off a smile. "These look delicious." It was hard to fake an interest in cookies when all she really wanted was to sit on his lap and bury her face in his neck.

Leddy tipped her chin to the newspapers. "As you can see, Kurt was quite the trailblazer on this sustainability stuff. Don't know if you're aware but people came from all over to talk to him about what he was doing." She drew in a sharp breath, her hand going to her heart. "Ach. He's going be dearly missed."

"Were you close?"

Leddy looked contemplative. "Oh, I don't know about *close*. He kept to himself, and he didn't go out much." She broke into a warm smile. "But when you were with him, he gave you his full attention. He cared very deeply."

"Did he ever remarry?"

The question seemed to take her by surprise, but Leddy was kind enough not to ask why his own daughter wouldn't know something like that. "No, dear. He was a bachelor."

"He must've had a girlfriend?"

"Well, other than Glori Van Patten, I can't say I recall seeing him with anyone else." Her lips pressed together. "I think he was the kind of man who'd rather be alone than spend time with people he didn't feel a connection with."

Declan got out of the wicker rocking chair and sat next to her. He reached for a cookie, but since she knew he didn't eat sweets, she suspected he'd come to give her support.

And she needed it. Because she'd just gotten the answer she'd been looking for. Her father hadn't felt a connection to her. That's why he'd stopped fighting for his custodial rights. She set the plate down, too sick to eat.

She wanted to smile, be pleasant, but she felt like she was stuck in sludge, and her gears were jammed. Nothing worked.

She understood she'd been too young for Kurt to really know her. It wasn't personal, she got that. But he really, truly didn't care. The shock to her system sent her reeling.

Boots stomped on the porch steps, so heavy Phinny felt it through the soles of her new shoes. A large, grizzled old man in overalls and a flannel shirt burst into the room.

Bristling with anger, he took in the trio of them…and then his gaze landed on the plate in the middle of the table, and he broke out into a huge grin. "Cookies."

As he reached for them, Phinny could see bits of dirt on his knees and elbows. He smelled like sunshine-warmed cotton and fresh-mown grass. The old man's paw made a grab, and Leddy yanked it out of his reach. "One, Carl. You may have *one*." She gave Phinny a long-suffering sigh. "The minute I turn my back, there won't be a crumb left."

"True." Carl grinned. "But hey, I've been toiling in the fields all morning."

Leddy rolled her eyes. "He's a beekeeper. He's been checking the hives for all of twenty minutes."

Okay, this is working. Listening to their banter tugged her out of the sludge. "You make your own honey?" But really, this visit was good. She needed the truth. It was the only way to move on…to let go of this constant anxiety over unanswered questions.

"Well, the bees do." As her husband reached out a second time, Leddy shifted the plate. He scowled. "I just collect it."

"His booth at the festival always sells out." Leddy sounded proud.

"Well, sure." The moment his wife let down her guard, his arm whipped out, and he scored a cookie. He gave her a mischievous smile, and Leddy practically melted with affection. "People come from all over to buy it."

They're so cute. "How exciting. Have you always done this?"

"Years ago, someone pointed out that our land is a dense nectar source." Leddy put the plate on the side table. "I had no idea what that meant, but it struck Carl's fancy, and he's been reading up on it and creating all kinds of products with it."

"You mean other than honey?" Phinny asked.

Carl used his boot to pull out a chair and eased himself into it. "First of all, it's a lot more interesting than she makes it out to be. Our property's full of wildflowers in the spring."

"That's my favorite of his honeys." Leddy gave him a loving smile.

"Second, if I wanted to, I could make a load of money off my bees. Did you know you can raise queens and sell them to other farmers? I can sell honeycomb and pollen. It's an industry." Carl arched a brow at his wife.

Phinny laughed. "I'm getting the impression you don't support his hobby."

"Oh, sure I do." She patted his knee. "I'm just waiting to see all this industry."

These two made Phinny smile. "Do you only sell your honey at the festival? You don't have an online shop or anything?" Her parents were nothing like this. They didn't tease or give each other knowing smiles. The only looks they exchanged were quelling ones.

Don't say another word.
Don't tell her that.

Watch what you're saying.

"No," Leddy said at the same time Carl lifted himself out of the chair and walked out the door, letting the screen slam shut behind him.

"Oh, I'm sorry. Was that the wrong thing to say?" Phinny watched him lumber across the lawn.

"Not at all." Leddy smiled. "I hope you have room in your car. Now, I do have a story to share with you." She got up. "I'll be right back."

The moment she left, Declan reached for her hand. "Hey, I think you took what she said the wrong way. About Kurt not hanging out with people he didn't have a connection with? That's got nothing to do with you. You were his daughter. And you were only five the last time he saw you, so it's not that."

In her agitation, she pulled her hand away. "There's not a single photograph of me in his house. After that summer, he never reached out to me. And now? Now, I have to jump through hoops to win land I clearly have no business owning." She couldn't stand the weight or smell of the newspapers, so she dumped them on the coffee table. She never lost it in front of her friends or family. Or if she did, she quickly turned it into a joke. But this time, she couldn't help herself.

"It's humiliating. And I feel…God, I just feel so useless and small."

He got to his feet and surprised the hell out of her when he pulled her into his arms. "I knew him, Phinny. And I swear to you, he would never try to humiliate you. I don't have the answers you're looking for, but I know he didn't hold a grudge against your mom or you. He just wasn't like that."

She knew exactly why she could let herself go around

this man. Because she trusted him. She sank into his embrace, relishing the feel of the strong arms holding her.

"You want to get the door?" Carl carried an orange crate.

She pulled away to let him in. As he set the box down on the table, he pulled out a jar. "You got wildflower honey." He picked up a few others, his thick finger tapping the labels. "Orange blossom. Whipped."

"Whipped?" she asked.

"It's real buttery. You'll try it and see."

Inside the box, she found honeycomb and a honey dipper. "This is for me?"

"Yep."

"Oh, thank you so much."

Carl hunched a shoulder. "Let me know which honey you like best."

Leddy came out with an envelope. "She'll like the wildflower."

Carl scowled at his wife. "I think she can make up her own mind."

"I think she can hear my opinion *and* make up her own mind." Leddy arched a brow. "Women are marvels at multi-tasking."

Carl shot her a hard look. And then he burst into a deep, phlegmy laugh.

Phinny loved them. "You know I'm running the farm stand at the ranch. If you'd like to sell your products, I'd split the profits with you."

"Fifty-fifty, huh?" Carl asked.

"Yep."

He held out his big hand. "You got a deal. Give me ten minutes to put something together for you right now."

"Well, hold on a minute," Leddy said. "Let me tie

some little gingham bows on the honey dippers. And we should probably get ribbon with the name of our apiary. Packaging matters."

"Oh, now we've got an apiary?" Carl teased.

"Yes, Champion Farms."

"Nah." Carl headed out the door again. "We're gonna call it Leddy's Hunny."

"You've been thinking about this for a while now, haven't you?" Leddy called after him.

"I'll meet you at your car," Carl called. "You can start selling tomorrow. In the meantime, we'll get on those labels."

Leddy gave her a warm smile. "You not only look like your father, but you've got his same spirit." She handed over the envelope. "I looked through my old boxes of photographs and picked out the ones with Kurt in them. They're yours now."

Phinny held the envelope against her chest. "This is so kind of you. Thank you."

As she followed Leddy and Declan through the kitchen, she had to accept the fact that Kurt had been a good man. Worse, that Declan might be right. It was possible her father had loved her.

A riot of energy pulsed through her body.

Because if that were true, maybe her mum had lied to her?

And she didn't know how to process that.

Chapter Eleven

With the wind blowing her hair, and the sweetly scented alfalfa fields nothing but a blur, Phinny clung to Declan for dear life. She'd grown up on a country estate, so she'd ridden every kind of vehicle imaginable, but she'd never known anyone who drove an ATV like this man.

Was he *aiming* for the ridges in the soil? Probably, since he accelerated every time they neared one, swerving around it at the last moment. It was the most terrifying and exhilarating experience of her life. A spot of green caught her attention, and she patted his taut belly with one hand and pointed with the other. "There."

He jerked the wheel, flying across the gap between two planting fields and headed toward the road. When he arrived at the green hut, he came to a smooth stop.

She shoved him—*move*—so she could swing her leg off the four-wheeler. "You're an absolute nutter." Feet finally on solid ground, she yanked off her helmet. "Do you know that? You're positively mad."

"Did you have fun?" He took it from her and set it on the handlebar.

"My soul slipped out about five miles back. I think I'll walk home, thank you." She stood in the warm sun and pine-scented air, taking in the small RV park. "The festival must be bigger than I thought if he's cleared a whole section of his property for the artisans."

"It's the biggest event of the year. Most towns have fireworks for the Fourth, but Calamity makes it a three-day event with the annual art festival and Wild West Days." He gestured to the park. "He's had the same people coming out every year for decades. The blacksmith's from Fort Worth, Texas, the weavers come all the way from New Hampshire. It's a big deal." He opened the black cargo container on the back of the ATV and started pulling out rolls of toilet paper.

She grabbed the bag of soaps. As she followed him to the green hut, she couldn't help noticing the site was situated along a dirt road. "Wait. We could've taken a road like normal people?"

"Where's the fun in that?" He set the toilet paper on the shelves.

"If they're traveling in RVs, don't people bring their own supplies?"

"Sure, but Kurt liked to stock the basics in case they run out of anything."

While he tromped back and pulled out a case of water, she lingered inside. Because something struck her. Her mum would've seen a basic hut—the cheap wood, dirty windows, and spider webs in the corners. She wouldn't have seen this place for what it was—an incredible gesture of kindness.

When Declan came back in, she pointed to a framed

sheet of paper hanging on the wall that gave basic instructions for the campground and the Wi-Fi code. "How much of this is Tina's idea and how much is Kurt's?"

"It's all Kurt. Why?"

"Because I'm pretty sure narcissists wouldn't think to provide all these supplies for people who're only here for a few days." Her mum was so wrong about him.

"Yep." He dragged the back of his hand across his forehead. "Before he offered up his ranch, the shuttles would take people out to the lake to watch the fireworks and to the fair grounds for the art festival. That's all it ever was until Kurt came up with the idea to show people what life was like back when his ancestors first populated the land. More recently, the Bowies added a stop at the old ghost town they turned into a living museum. They've got staged shootouts and costumed actors in Owl Hoot. And now they host concerts at the amphitheater there."

"A living museum? That sounds amazing."

"Kurt's got costumed actors here, too. They do demonstrations like butter churning, horseshoes, glass blowing, and cheese-making. Shit like that. He's got a pig race and a petting zoo. It's very cool."

"And the lemonade?" She wasn't embarrassed anymore about that first night, and the grin he gave her was the reason why. This man seemed to like her no matter what she'd done or said.

"He sold bison burgers, fries, and lemonade. Kept it simple. Oh, and he rented an ice cream truck for the day."

"That sounds so much fun. Did he do it back when I used to come here, do you think?"

"Yeah, definitely." He shelved the last of the supplies

and then went to check the electric and water hookups for each parking pad.

"I wish my memories were stronger." She took in the acres of bright green alfalfa set against the dramatic backdrop of the mountain ranges. "I just don't remember it being so beautiful out here." She glanced over to find him watching her. "Nope. I know you want me to feel some connection to this land, but I don't. I love the old photos, but only from a historical perspective. Sorry, but I don't feel ties to the people in them."

Coming up beside her, he set his hands on her shoulders. "In the eighteen-twenties, right over there…" He pointed into the distance. "There was a shack where the fur traders would hang their beaver pelts. You can see a photograph of it in the Reliquary Museum in town."

The whisper of his breath across her cheek sent a shiver down her spine.

He gently guided her shoulders to make a slight turn. "Over there, that's where the original homestead was. The five brothers each got a hundred-and-sixty-acre parcels from the government, and they took turns helping each other build log homes." Letting her go, he folded his arms across that muscular chest. The navy T-shirt hugged his impressive biceps. "Very few people survived the harsh winters and short growing seasons out here, but the Grevers men stuck it out, buying up every plot of land they could get their hands on."

"*How* did they do it, though? What set them apart?"

"I guess Kurt came by his stubbornness honestly." He shrugged. "Maybe they just wanted it more than other people. I know one of them took a job with the forest service. One of the wives worked at the post office, and another was a schoolteacher. You can find all this out in the museum, but one way the settlers tried to make a go of their homesteads was to open their homes to travelers. That's how the dude ranches came about."

"It's interesting, for sure, but I still don't feel like it's my *family*. Do you know what I mean?"

He glanced down at her, the warmth in his eyes cutting right through her confusion. "It will. That's probably why you're here for a month. To give you time. If you want, I'll take you to the museum. It's got a whole room of Grevers history."

She wanted him to stay right there, to keep telling her stories, and it had nothing to do with learning about her family. He made her feel things. Things she never felt around Cameron. Or anyone. "You realize we're in competition, right? This could all be yours."

He pulled away. "You're seeing the cash, but I know what this place meant to Kurt, the amount of time and energy he put into it. I know that he never gave up because his ancestors didn't. Through grizzly attacks, raiding outlaws, long, dark, cold winters with the wind blowing through the cracks in their log cabins, none of them gave up."

"I've never met anyone like you. Who would turn away the chance to have that kind of money?"

"A man who'd give his left nut to have your history."

Phinny sat in the shade of the farm stand admiring her new products. With the right labels, these honey products would fly off the shelves. They were cute, wholesome, and delicious.

As she arranged crackers on a plate, a sleek, black Range Rover pulled off the road and onto the shoulder.

The engine shut off, and the most fabulous pair of ostrich cowboy boots hit the ground. Long, lean, jeans-clad legs appeared, followed by a stunning, black leather Balenciaga bag.

The woman strutted over with her big Gucci sunglasses and Chanel Rouge Allure lipstick—the same red her mum wore. "Well, what do we have here?"

Phinny, in her cheap shorts and T-shirt, stood up. "Good morning. I've got pink lemonade…" Her hand swept across her table. "And delicious, locally-grown honey."

The woman lifted her glasses onto the top of her head, holding back her glossy, dark hair. "The last time Kurt had a working farm stand, he let the Girl Scouts sell cookies. I bought thirty boxes."

"Well, let's hope you're feeling just as generous today. Can I interest you in a treasure trove of honey products?" Phinny made a dramatic sweep of her hand.

The woman grinned. "Well, girl, I sure didn't expect that kind of boldness delivered with a posh British accent." She held her hand out. "I'm Glori Van Patten. Kurt was a good friend of mine for many years." And then the smile faded, and her features softened. "You must be Seraphina."

"That's right." She wanted to ask how she knew but given that Leddy had said she looked like Kurt, this woman must have seen the resemblance, too. "It's lovely to meet you."

The woman swept around the table and drew Phinny into her arms. "Honey, I am so sorry for your loss."

Enveloped in a firm embrace and a cloud of Hermès perfume, Phinny stood a little awkwardly. "Thank you."

The gorgeous woman pulled away. "It was such a shock. He didn't tell a soul. Well, other than Tina. I just want to shake him, you know? For not telling me. For not giving me the chance to say goodbye." She swiped a tear off her cheek. "Listen to me going off on him in front of his daughter."

Surely, Glori knew they'd been estranged. "I'm sure you were closer to him than I was."

"He was the love of my life."

She said it so starkly, so plainly, Phinny was gobsmacked. She could only stare wide-eyed. In a million years, she wouldn't put Kurt with this sophisticated, stylish woman.

"Why do you look so surprised?"

"I'm sorry…I just…well, I thought all he liked to do was hunt, fish, and camp out. You know…" She gestured weakly to the rugged surroundings.

Glori's features pinched in irritation. "Well, yes, we did do all that, but we also went to the theater in Seattle and spent long weekends in New York City." Diggin a calfskin wallet out of her purse, she pulled out a twenty. "We had a favorite restaurant on the boardwalk of Venice Beach." She picked up a jar of honey. "No one is one-dimensional. You know that, right? I've got a meeting about the festival, but if you'd like to come by my house for a visit, we can talk about Kurt's other dimensions. I'll leave my contact information with Mitch." As she sashayed back to her car, she called out over her shoulder, "Keep the change."

The scent of warm bread invaded the office, making Declan's stomach grumble. He checked the time and realized he hadn't had a break in hours. *Time for dinner.*

He filed the last of the receipts and shut down the computer.

As he got up, he caught a spot of metal at the edge of the desk. He smiled when he saw it was the potato masher he'd wanted. Attached to the gingham ribbon wrapped around the wooden handle was a handwritten note.

Might as well take your consolation prize now.

A laugh burst out of him. "Like hell." *Cute, Phinny.* He picked it up, running his fingers along the cool metal. Surprised at the rush of emotion, he closed his eyes, unprepared for the random memory that hit him. It was the Thanksgiving right after Sam had died. Declan had just started working for the Comets, and he'd had no plans to come back to Calamity.

Until Kurt had called. *"Sweet potato casserole or mashed potatoes?"* That was the first thing out of his mouth. Not *How are you?* Or *How's it going?* Not *Hey, what're your plans for the holiday?*

Declan hadn't even hesitated. *"Both."*

"Damn straight. Potato rolls or Hawaiian?"

"Hawaiian."

"There you go. We're on the same page. All right, then. Send me your flight information."

He'd never liked Kurt making the hour and a half drive—well, three hours both ways—when he could easily take a bus. *"You're not picking me up in Idaho Falls."*

Click.

Needless to say, Kurt had picked him up in Idaho Falls.

He missed him, but what he felt was less grief and more…anger? No, frustration.

The thing about loss is that you don't have a say in the matter. You don't get to plead your case in front of a judge. You don't get to negotiate or barter.

You can't turn back the clock and beg your parents not to go on that vacation.

But while Declan hadn't been ready to lose his parents, he'd at least gotten to spend eighteen months making sure Sam knew he was loved and appreciated.

Kurt, though…he'd never said anything. Which meant Declan had never gotten to thank him for giving him a purpose in life, for spending time with him and including him for holidays. *For taking me under his wing.*

He lowered his head into his hands.

Kurt, man, wherever you are, I hope you know how much I appreciated everything you did for me. I know I had Sam, but in so many ways, you felt like my dad.

I hope you know…

I love you.

Tears burned, and a knot formed in his throat.

Okay, this is bullshit. I'm not sitting in his office and crying.

He got up so fast the chair shot back, banging into the bookcase. *Where's my phone?* He found it charging on the credenza and unplugged it, surprised to see a pile of messages. He forgot he'd silenced it so he could concentrate.

When he saw the Comets' General Manager, he

opened that thread first.

Brad: **Coach asked me to get in touch. He's sorry about your loss, but it's been over a week, and he needs you back here ASAP.**

Brad: **This close to exhibition games, we've got some new guys you need to work with.**

Declan hadn't explained the full story, but he supposed he needed to do it now.

Declan: **There's an issue with the will that requires me to stay on the property for a month. If I leave, I lose my inheritance.**

Brad: **WTF?**

Declan: **I know. It's fucked up. Can you send the new guys here? I can get ice time at the Elite West rink.**

Brad: **You know we can't do that. It has to be here so we can onboard them. Besides, we need you with us to go over red flag numbers and tape from last season.**

It wasn't like he didn't know the absurdity of his request, but he couldn't walk away.

Declan: **If I leave, Kurt's ranch will be sold. I've got to live and work here for one month to make sure that doesn't happen.** If it were just a relative, he knew he wouldn't stand a chance. But it was Kurt. That had to mean something to them.

It does to me.

Working in his office, taking care of receipts and orders and payroll had given him a wide view of Kurt's operation. And it was impressive. Kurt worked with several universities and think tanks, allowing studies to be done on his land, all in the name of progress and evolving new technologies. He couldn't let Phinny destroy all that work.

Even if it means losing my coaching job.

Brad: **The property's worth that much?**

Declan: **More than you can imagine.**

Brad: **That Kurt was a crazy mofo. Okay, well, I don't think it's going to fly, but I'll give it a shot. Get back to you soon.**

Declan: **Appreciate it.**

Well, hell. I'm about to lose my job. They wouldn't let him miss a month. Not a chance.

Damn. He loved coaching. If he lost his job, he supposed he could apply for other jobs, ask around…but no. He supposed it made the most sense to take his share of Kurt's team.

The twist in his gut told him what he thought of closing the door on coaching forever.

He opened the next message.

Leslie: **Hey, handsome. I heard you're in town. Want to meet up?**

Declan glanced out the window. He had a few women he hooked up with when he came home. They knew he lived in Pittsburgh and wasn't looking for anything serious, so it worked.

But he wasn't feeling it.

Declan: **Can't. I've got some stuff going on.**

Leslie: **Are you seeing someone?**

Phinny's smiling face popped into his mind. Those toned legs, the smooth skin, the shiny hair.

Declan: **No.**

Leslie: **Oh, come on. I heard you're here for a month! Let's have some fun!**

Normally, he'd go for it. Why not? They were both single. Neither wanted anything serious. So, what had changed?

Phinny filled the screen of his mind. She was on her

back, her lids lowered, tits bouncing as he fucked her slowly, deeply, passion slackening her features.

That's what changed. He'd met Phinny. And she made him feel things he'd never felt before.

There's no going back from that.

He'd only ever known what a hookup felt like. The fun of it. It could be exhilarating—until it was over, and he was left with emptiness. And the dread of wondering how to extract himself from the situation.

With Phinny, he never wanted his time with her to end.

Declan: **Sorry. Not up for it this time.**

Moving on, he saw a text from a number he didn't recognize. It was a Wyoming area code. He opened it.

Heard about you from Luc. I'm a D-man, second line. Having a hard time turning retrievals into breakouts. Think you can give me some time?

Declan: **Who is this?**

Ha ha. This is Maxwell Scott. Left defenseman for the Renegades.

Huh. The Renegades had their own coaches.

Declan: **Assume you're able to come to Calamity? Work at the Elite West rink?**

Absolutely.

Declan: **Happy to help.**

Cool. I'll send you a couple dates, and you can let me know what works.

If he lost the job with the Comets, could he get one with the Renegades? He'd be crazy to give up ownership of an NHL team to be its assistant coach. He knew that, but still. The idea held some appeal. *Yeah, okay. A lot.*

Just as he went to open the next text message, the fire alarm screeched. Racing out of the office, he rounded the corner into the living room to find smoke wafting out from the kitchen.

When he got there, he saw Phinny opening the back door and a cookie sheet in the sink, water running. "Everything okay?" he shouted over the piercing alarm.

As she grabbed another cookie sheet, she held it over her head and waved it underneath the alarm, dispelling the smoke. He opened a few more windows and turned on the fan.

A few moments later, the alarm stopped, but an acrid scent filled the room. Rattled, Phinny headed to the sink to turn off the faucet. "That was my garlic bread."

Before he could say anything, the house phone rang, and Declan crossed the kitchen to answer it. "Hello?"

"This is Mountain Alarm. We got an alert that your alarm went off."

He cut a glance to Phinny who was dumping the soggy bread into the garbage bin. "It was just a kitchen disaster, but we're all good. Thanks for the call."

"No problem. Have a good night."

After hanging up, Declan couldn't help but notice how dejected she was.

She gave him a weak smile. "Sorry about that."

"It's no big deal. As long as we answer the phone, they won't send out fire trucks." He didn't see anything else cooking. "So…just garlic bread?"

"Yeah, well, I couldn't find any ramen packets." She tried again for a smile. "Today, this man stopped at the farm stand and wanted to buy honey, but he didn't have any cash, so he traded me a loaf of bread."

"He happened to have a loaf of bread in his car?"

"Turns out he's a Cooter. He's taken up baking bread in his spare time, and he was bringing some loaves to his friends. I'm not sure how to make French toast, and I didn't want a sandwich, so I thought I'd make garlic bread." She angled away from him but not before he caught her cheeks turning pink.

He didn't like seeing her embarrassed. "You want French toast?"

"Yes. Will you make it for us?"

"Sure. Do you have more bread?"

That energized her. She reached into a tote bag and pulled out a loaf.

"Okay, so this is a ciabatta, and we probably wouldn't want to make French toast out of it. I like brioche for French toast."

"You cook?"

"Well, sure. I'm single, and I like to eat."

"So, what do we do with ciabatta?"

"You said you didn't want a sandwich, but what about a panini?"

She grinned at him. There it was. That weird snap of connection. Other women could offer him no-strings sex. They could be kinky as fuck, but it had nothing on actually *liking* someone. Feeling this…spark.

Was it weird that at twenty-eight, he was only now feeling it? He grabbed a serrated knife from the block and pulled a cutting board out from under the sink.

She came up beside him. "What can I do to help?"

"Depends on what you like in it."

"What do you like?" she asked.

"Ham? Gruyere cheese?"

She crinkled her nose. "I'm not a big fan of ham."

"We could do fresh mozzarella and tomato."

"Oh, my God, yes. I would love a caprese panini."

"Cool." While he plugged in the panini press, she

grabbed the cheese from the refrigerator.

"Do you see any basil?" When she didn't answer, he turned to find her lifting bundles of herbs and sniffing them. He waited, not wanting to make her uncomfortable but pretty sure she didn't know the difference between them.

As she stood there in her cotton shorts, her perfect peach-shaped ass tilted, and his hands itched to grab hold of those cheeks and squeeze. Her hair—normally straight and sleek—looked a little untidy, and he found he liked the more natural version of her.

It made him wonder what she was like in bed. Maybe Cameron had tried, but she just lay there like a limp noodle. But no. He remembered that kiss. The way she'd gotten hot so fast, her hands threading through his hair. The way they'd fisted tight enough to make his scalp sting.

Arousal fired in his dick, as he fell back into the memory of her floral scent and the press of her plump tits on his chest.

"Is this it?" She brought the basil right under his nose.

"Yep." *Shake it off.* He grabbed the knife and cut into the loaf.

"Do we need butter?"

"Yeah, that'll make it crunchy. Or olive oil. Up to you."

"I really have no idea, so just tell me which to get."

When those blue eyes connected with his, it stirred him up. Made him want to get his hands on her waist, lift her onto the counter, and peel off her shirt. "Let's just use olive oil." He wanted to see her plump breasts in that lacy bra more than he wanted to eat. Pretty much more than anything.

She didn't move right away. She stood beside him,

reading his face like a map, tracing connections between his features. And then she pressed her hand on his forearm. "Thank you."

Every cell in his body exploded. His heart…it was like a stalled-out engine suddenly igniting, sparking, roaring to life. "For what?"

"Not making me feel stupid for burning garlic bread. For stepping right in and making dinner."

He hunched a shoulder like he didn't care. But that was a lie. He liked making her happy.

He liked…*fuck*. He had to turn away from her. These feelings were too big. They didn't make sense. He hardly knew her.

And yet…he'd never felt closer to anyone in his life.

"I don't even own butter *or* oil. The refrigerator at my house is stuffed with the weirdest things. Pickled radishes and fermented fish—I mean, nothing I'd ever eat. And it's a mess. I've got four roommates who'd rather play video games than clean up after themselves. Still, I know I should learn the basics."

"Hey." He cupped her chin. "If you grew up with a chef, why would you know how to cook?"

"I've been on my own for almost a year. There are things I should be able to make."

"And you'll learn them. There's no timeline."

"You're absolutely right." She smiled brightly. "I like the way you think. Okay, what's next?"

"We need a tomato."

"Oh." Grabbing one out of the basket, she showed it to him. "Isn't it gorgeous? I pulled it off the vine this morning."

You're *gorgeous. And I want to carry you upstairs and spend the entire night figuring out what makes you moan.*

After washing the fruit, she grabbed a knife and cut thick slices. "I met a woman named Glori today."

As far as he knew, there was only one Glori in town. "Kurt's ex?"

"Yes, you know her?"

"Sure, she came to a lot of our games when they were dating. They'd cook dinner for us." *Well, mostly me.* The other guys usually had to get home.

"She wants me to come over and talk about Kurt."

"That's great. If anyone knew him, it was Glori."

"Oh, good." She brushed the counter with her fingertips. "Hey, listen, if you've got other plans tonight… please don't stay home on my account."

"What? Where did that come from?"

"I don't know. You just seem…preoccupied tonight."

Right. That's because I keep fantasizing about you naked. "Sorry. I heard from the GM of my team. They're probably not going to give me a month off." He brushed olive oil on one side of each of the slices and set two of them on the grill. Then, he layered the cheese, tomato, and basil.

"That's terrible. Don't they understand the situation?"

"They don't care, and I can't say I blame them." He grabbed the sponge to clean up the tomato seeds and juice and rinsed it in the sink.

"Declan, you can't lose your job over a ridiculous trivia contest. If I win, what will you have?"

"I suppose I'll be part owner of a hockey team."

"But that's not what you want."

Out the window, dusk settled over the land, making the snow-capped peaks glow. In the corral, a horse bobbed its head, its tail whipping back and forth. The truth sank like a stone in his gut. "No, it's not."

"Then, you have to fight for it. So many people work remotely these days—"

"Not hockey." He pulled a clean dish towel out of a drawer. "It is what it is. I'll figure it out."

She lingered at his side for a moment, watching him. "I wish there was a compromise."

"What do you mean?"

"That we could split the ranch in half. You'd keep the working parts that matter the most to Kurt, and I could sell off the land that's not as important."

"It's all important. There's not one single acre that—"

"I know, I know." She laughed, touching him again. "I get it. I do. I just meant I wished there was a way for both of us to get what we want."

"Well, I did get the potato masher." Her eyes sparkled with mischief, and her smile tapped into a secret room in his heart, unleashing emotions brand-new to him. "So, thanks for that." He turned away so she wouldn't see the effect she had on him.

"You're welcome. Anything else you want?"

"No. That's really it." Checking the press, he found the bread nicely toasted and the cheese softened, so he served them on plates and handed one to her.

"Glori's not who I'd expect Kurt to date. She's so fancy." She cut her sandwich in fours. "I'm going to see her tomorrow. Would you mind coming with me?"

This woman had him wrapped around his finger. He'd do whatever she asked of him. "Sure."

They were so hungry they wound up eating standing up, his lower back pressed against the counter.

"Mm." She moaned. "This is delicious." Her eyes rolled back in her head, and he had to wonder if she'd look like that when he licked her into an orgasm. "And it's so simple. I can totally make this." All of a sudden, she stopped chewing and her eyes went wide. "Oh, my God." She set the sandwich down and looked around the room. "I just got this memory." She moved to the kitchen table. "Did he get new chairs?"

"Glori did a lot of redecorating over the years, so probably. Why? What're you thinking?"

"It's nothing, really. I just remember my legs swinging in a wooden chair, licking an ice cream cone. It was melting all over my fingers." Her features softened. "Strawberry. Well, there you go. *That's* my earliest memory of being here."

"What was Kurt doing?"

"I don't know. He's not in it." Her forehead creased. "Oh, wait. Wait, wait, wait." She drew in a sharp breath, and everything in her turned soft, sweet. "He was there. He was sitting sideways in his chair, angled toward me, and he had one arm resting on the table. His other hand was in his lap, holding napkins."

"Was he trying to clean you up?"

"Not at all. He was smiling." She looked up to him. "He was happy. To be with me."

The yearning in her eyes did funny things to his chest. "I have no doubt about that." *You make everyone happy*. He washed his plate and hands. "I still can't wrap my head around the fact that he's gone. He held so much power in his body, so much energy. I guess, if you look at it that way, it's not a surprise he died young. They say a heart only has so many beats, and I'm pretty sure Kurt's beat in double time."

When he reached for the dish towel, he found her seated at the table, tears streaming down her cheeks. "Jesus, Phinny, what's wrong?"

Chapter Twelve

DECLAN CLOSED THE DISTANCE BETWEEN THEM BUT stopped short before touching her. He didn't know whether she needed a hug or tissues, so he wound up patting her shoulder.

Like an asshole.

"The way you talk about him...the way everyone talks about him." Phinny pressed her palm flat to her forehead. "It was so much easier when I thought he was a cold-hearted bastard. Not one person has confirmed my mum's stories about the way he abandoned her on this god-forsaken ranch while he went gallivanting about the country playing hockey and filming commercials. And now I'll never know the man I was taught not to love." Her features screwed up, and she cried in earnest.

He'd never felt so helpless. He didn't know what to do, so he crouched in front of her. He'd only meant to be there for her, a quiet support, but she misunderstood his intentions and fell against him. Her body shook, her tears soaked his T-shirt, and he couldn't take it. He just couldn't take this woman's sorrow.

Grabbing under her arms, he lifted her out of the chair and sat her on the counter. She flopped against him, her face tucked into his neck, and she wept. He didn't think anything he had to say would help, so he just held her tightly.

When the tears subsided, she let out a few shuddery breaths. Sitting up, she said, "I'm sorry. I'm getting your shirt wet."

"I don't give a damn about my shirt."

"You're a good man, Declan Cadell. Don't let anyone tell you otherwise." Laughing, she reached for a paper towel and blotted the tears.

"Do you want to go into town and get strawberry ice cream from Bliss?"

She shook her head. "It's fine. I'll be fine. It's all just overwhelming. You'll take me to see Glori tomorrow, though, right? If I start to bawl, I want you to pinch me really hard."

"Won't that make you cry harder?"

"No, I'll be too pissed at you."

He grinned. "Okay, you got it." But she still looked so sad. "How about we raid Kurt's wine cellar?"

"Oh, God, no more wine."

"All right, then name something. Anything. You're killing me here. Let me do one thing to make you happy."

Whatever he'd said, it lit a fire in her eyes. Slowly, she broke into a sexy smile. "Well, there is one thing I want."

"Name it."

"And you'll give it to me, no matter what?"

"Almost anything. I won't walk away from this ranch, and I'm not willing to go into debt for you, so you can forget a shopping expedition to Paris. But anything else… the answer is yes."

Behind her devilish grin was a vulnerability. "I want you." And he really fucking liked the confidence it took to ask for what she wanted.

He arched a brow, giving her attitude to cover the punch of desire that made him go painfully hard.

"One night. Not even a whole night. I want to be with a man who likes giving women pleasure."

Is she serious about this shit? Hell, yeah, he'd give her pleasure. Just the idea of touching her, kissing her, hearing her moans...fuck, he wanted that.

But wait. No. What was he thinking? He couldn't just screw around with this beautiful, perfect woman. *I'm not the right guy for her.* "Hm. There's a flip side to that, you know." Before he spread her thighs to find out if she really wanted him, he had to change the direction of the conversation, turn to humor.

"Is that right?" She played along, but he could see the worry beneath that. She'd exposed herself, and he hadn't handled it well.

But he was in it now. He'd carry the joke along, and then they'd both go their separate ways. He hunched a shoulder. "I'll ruin you for other men. Plus, it'll be addictive. You'll want more. You'll probably want it all the time." He stuffed his shaky hand into his pocket. "And, I mean, I do have other things to do here."

And then he'd spend the rest of the night imagining all the places he'd lick, stroke, and caress her.

"So, what I'm hearing is that you don't have the stamina you once had?"

He chuckled. "Oh, no. No worries there. I'm fit as a fiddle." He lifted both arms and curled his biceps.

But instead of laughing, her eyelids lowered to half-mast, and she got this sultry expression.

Okay, enough of this shit. He needed to tell her the truth. "I think you know I'm attracted to you."

"I don't know anything. You don't show *anything*."

All she had to do was look down to see the tent in his jeans. "Well, I am. But this isn't a good idea." If it were any other woman, he wouldn't even hesitate. But it was this one, the only one he actually felt something for.

"You just said you were attracted to me so, what's the problem?"

"The problem is that we have to live together in this house. If one of us catches feelings, it's going to be awkward."

"By one of us, do you mean me?"

He didn't bother answering.

"Because I'm very aware of the calendar. There's an end-date to whatever we do. You know what? Forget it. If I have to convince you…" She started to walk away.

He never wanted to hurt her, never wanted her to feel rejected. He reached out, but since she'd been in the process of turning, her back landed against his chest. He wrapped an arm around her waist. "There isn't a single moment out of the day when I don't want you. In the car, I want to slide my hand between your thighs. When you laugh, I want to tip you onto your back and fuck the smile right off your face. I want to watch your expression while I lick every inch of your body to figure out where you're sensitive, to find the places that make you moan and the spots that make you shudder."

"So, what's the problem?" Her voice came out a whispered tremble.

"You make me feel things."

"What kind of things?" Her hips swayed, her ass shifting over his hard cock.

Sensation flared and burned a trail down every pathway of his nervous system. "Things I don't want to feel for someone I'm never going to see again."

"Oh." The single syllable dragged out like a sigh. "So, really good things."

"Bad, Phinny. Very fucking bad."

"What else do you want to do with me?"

He lowered his mouth to her ear. "I want you to put that jersey on, so I can bend you over the back of the couch, flip it up, and drive my cock into you."

"That's…that's very graphic." She reached for his hand and pressed it over her breast. He couldn't help the reflexive need to squeeze. "So, if you decide to give me pleasure, it won't be because you feel sorry for me?"

"Nope. It'll be because I've wanted to fuck you since the first night in the basement."

In one fluid move, she spun around his arms, slid her arms up his chest, and scraped her fingernails through the hair at the back of his neck. "I can't catch feelings if I'm asking you for a favor. For the first time in my life, I want to make sex all about me. How can you refuse me?"

That lush pink mouth softened, and her tongue peeked out to moisten her lips.

I can't. Need roared through him, and he kissed her. It was instantaneous, the collision of head and heart. Everything he liked about her—from her smile to her optimism to her inner strength—crashed head-on into the taste of her, the slick heat of her mouth, and the hungry grip of her hands. It overwhelmed him, rendering him nothing but hot, churning, aching need.

His pulse thundered, and he kissed her with a desperation that might've been embarrassing had she not been fisting his hair and trying to climb him like a tree.

He wanted to rip off her leggings and get a grip on that peach-shaped ass, line up his cock with her pussy, and slide into all that wet heat.

But this is about her. What she wants.

Which meant he had to calm down.

Tearing his mouth away felt like disconnecting from a life source, like his lungs would shut down, and his heart would stop beating.

"No, don't stop. Don't treat me with kid gloves." She clasped her hands at the back of his neck. "I want it all, Declan. Give me everything."

"You don't know what you're asking."

"I think I do."

Fuck it. Cupping her ass, he lifted her. Immediately, her legs wrapped around his waist, and he carried her into the living room, dropping her onto the couch.

Dammit, those lust-filled eyes made him crazy, but he knelt in front of her, focused on lifting her oversize T-shirt and tossing it aside. Presented with the plump mounds of her breasts cupped in pale pink lace, he had no choice but to lower his face into her cleavage, filling his senses with her sweet scent and his hands with the heavy, supple weight.

He couldn't believe he got to live his fantasy. That she wanted *him* to do this for her.

All the things he'd imagined doing to her—with her— he didn't even know where to start. He wanted all of it. *Now.*

And he'd nearly walked away.

He pulled down the waistband of her leggings, slowly peeling them off to reveal the smooth, creamy skin of her thighs. She hiked up, and he yanked them off, dropping them onto the floor. With his hands on her knees, he opened her, watching her expression as he ran his tongue up one thigh and down the other.

"*Oh.*" Arching her back, she reached behind and unclasped her bra, letting her gorgeous breasts fall free.

"Jesus, Phinny. Look at you." He cupped them, pushing them together and kissing each nipple. He wanted to swallow her gasps, capture them, so he'd feel the elation of making her this happy for the rest of his life.

Her hips twisted, her hands rounding the back of his head to pull him closer. *She's so fucking responsive.* He closed his lips around her, letting his tongue swirl and suck, just to get those hands fisting in his hair again.

She made a sound of frustration, like it wasn't enough, and his fingers trailed down her belly, dipped between her legs, and slid into her hot, slick core. "Declan."

Pressing kisses along the same path his hand had taken, his pulse spiked when he saw her pretty pink core, all wet and glistening for him.

Just as he leaned in for a taste, she stiffened and pushed him back. "Don't be mad if I don't come right away, okay? Sometimes it takes me a while."

He gathered her hands and kissed each palm. "Phinny?"

"Yeah?"

"Do you trust me?"

She nodded.

"Cameron's an asshole. I'm probably an asshole, too, but not when it comes to wanting you to be happy. Now, can I kiss your pussy or would you rather we do something else?"

She slammed back against the couch, rolling her eyes. "Fine. Go on and give it a shot."

He laughed, and just seeing her smile like that, all the

tension and worry gone, undid him. "You just lay there and think about England."

Her body shook with laughter, but she held his gaze as he slowly licked her from one juicy end to the other, ending with a slow circle around her clit.

Her back arched, thrusting her tits out. "Oh, God."

Yeah. He gave her open-mouthed, licking kisses that had her writhing and her legs falling open. When her hips started pumping, he focused on her sensitive little nub and licked her into a frenzy.

She gripped the back of his head, as if he might get bored and leave. *Don't worry. I'm not going anywhere. Not until you come so hard you scream.* Reaching for her breasts, he plucked at her nipples.

"I'm...oh, God." And then she shouted, "What is happening to me? I can't...." Her hips punched, twisted, and her hands pulled his hair, as she released a long, keening cry. "Don't stop. Don't you dare stop." With one last jerk of her hips, she issued a breathy, lust-saturated, "*Declan.*" And then her ass landed back on the cushion, her fingers relaxed, and she gave him a deeply satisfied smile.

He pulled away, watching her eyelids flutter closed. He got up and sat beside her.

Like a kitten, she curled into him, drawing up her knees, and wrapping an arm across his chest. "That was amazing." She reached under his shirt and idly stroked his chest, completely oblivious to his painful hard-on.

But that was okay because this was about her. He'd take care of himself in a few minutes, after she went to bed.

Her hand caressed in slow circles, gradually making its

way down to his navel. "Would you take your shirt off for me?"

I'd do anything for you. But he didn't know how much more he could take. Sitting forward, he grabbed the material at the back of his neck and yanked it off.

"Mm." Her palm stroked in broad circles. "I've never touched a man built like you." She glanced up at him. "Can I…touch you?"

This night's about her. This night's about her. "Sure." His voice sounded gravelly, and it took all his self-restraint to just stay put and let her take control.

She gripped him through his jeans. "It's so big."

He chuckled through the pain. *Jesus, take the wheel.* That feminine hand stroked him cautiously.

But then, she tightened her grip, peering up at him. "Is this okay?" When she saw his discomfort, she sat up. "I'm sorry. I didn't mean…I'm such an idiot."

He grabbed her hand and put it back on his cock. "Tonight's about you, remember? I'm not sixteen."

"Yeah, but you're obviously in pain."

"The prettiest girl in the world is sitting on my lap naked, touching my dick…I'd say I'm a lucky son of a bitch."

She grinned. "If I promise to make it all better, can I pull it out?"

He laughed. "Yeah, Phinny. You can do whatever you want." As she started to unbutton his jeans, he clamped his hand over hers. "But you have to call it what it is."

"A penis?"

He shook his head.

"A wiener?"

He barked out a laugh. "No. There's only one word I

want coming out of that pretty mouth, and you know exactly what it is."

"Okay, hockey boy." She got up on her knees, her breasts bouncing, and scraped her fingers through his hair. "Can I suck your cock?"

Lust roared through him, and he could only answer by yanking down his jeans and kicking them off.

"Oh. Wow." She gripped him at the base. "I thought they all looked the same."

"How many cocks have you seen?"

"Really only Cameron's. I had sex before him, but I never really saw the guys naked like this." She pumped him a few times. "Yours is making me feel things."

The base of his spine tingled, and desire grew frantic at the edges. He needed to come so badly, the pressure was killing him.

And then she leaned forward, her hair brushing his thighs, her scent wafting up and filling his senses. "Can I taste you?" He grew impossibly harder. "I'll take that as a yes." She licked the tip, a luscious, wet swirl around the head, before taking him slowly into her mouth. Her tongue flicked, and electricity lit up every cell in his body. Her sexy little moan had his hands curling into fists. And then she pulled him out of her mouth. "Hang on. This is an awkward position." She got on her knees, gripped him, and took him even deeper than before. One hand pumped in rhythm with her mouth, while the other caressed his chest.

He held back as long as he could, but he was a man, and it was *Phinny* sucking his cock like she couldn't get enough of it. Of him. He caught a glimpse of her tits bouncing, and it was so fucking hot that his hips punched. "Sorry. Shit." He worried she'd freak out, but instead she worked him harder, faster, her eyes burning with lust. His balls tightened, all the churning tension focused, coalesced, and his orgasm came barreling through him. He pushed on her shoulder, a warning. But she shook her head.

She wanted him to come in her mouth.

Jesus fucking Christ. He couldn't hold back another second. Belting out a harsh cry, his hips jerked, as he came in a scalding, euphoric rush. Burst after burst, the climax didn't end. He rode the waves, one after another, until the tremors subsided. And then, he exhaled with a huff, and she let go. With a satisfied grin, she sat back on her heels.

Body and mind spent, all he could do was reach for her and pull her onto his lap. She molded against him, setting her hand on his biceps and gently stroking. "You're shaking." Cupping his chin, she looked into his eyes, and said, "You're the most amazing man I've ever met." She kissed him, and it just felt so good. He felt…whole in a way he'd never experienced before.

But before he could wrap his arms around her, relax into his first-ever snuggle, she got off him and started picking up her clothes. Holding them against her chest, she said, "Thank you, Declan." At the bottom of the stairs, she turned back with a soft smile. "Best night of my life."

And then he watched her naked ass walk away.

Seconds ticked by. His body cooled. A strange feeling settled over him.

He felt alone. Exposed.

Embarrassed.

And it struck him. His hookups must feel like this when he left them.

Since he made sure they were as satisfied as he was,

he'd always figured he could leave without consequence. But now that Phinny had left him the same way…

He could see it didn't feel good at all.

As Declan drove under the stone archway to enter Wild Wolff Village, Phinny planted her feet on the floor of the Jeep and sat up. "What is this?"

"It's a ski resort." He was still a little off-balance from last night. When they'd met in the kitchen that morning, Phinny had acted like nothing had happened. But she'd rocked his world. She'd unearthed…feelings. It was like she'd taken him to a whole other world, and now he was having a problem with reentry.

Everything felt different today. His smoothie hadn't tasted the same. During his workout, his playlist hadn't sounded the same. And his body…it was like his massive orgasm had altered his cellular structure and now nothing worked quite right.

"Are we still in Calamity?" As the lodge came into view, she stared ahead in awe. "Because I feel like I'm in Switzerland."

"Yep. It used to be a dude ranch, but the Wolff family turned it into a high-end resort. Over the years, they've added shops and restaurants."

"So, Glori doesn't live here? She stays at the lodge when she's in town?"

"No, it's bigger than what you see. It's a club that you buy into at different levels. They've got cabins in the woods, townhomes in the village itself, and then fancy houses in the neighborhoods around it. You can only ski here if you're a guest at the lodge or a member of Wild Wolff Village."

"So, it's like a country club?"

See, he couldn't wrap his head around the fact that she was chatting about Wild Wolff Village when he was still so rattled from last night. Like, why wasn't she touching him? Why wasn't she playing with his hair and rubbing up on him? It was all he could do to keep his hands to himself.

Because she doesn't want you like that. She wanted an orgasm, and you'd made a big deal about how you like to get women off. She just wanted to see what it's like.

And you gave it to her.

Now, it's done now.

"Something like that. There's an initiation fee, and then you pay annual fees that cover concierge and butler services."

"Really? So, you call ahead and say, I'll be flying in tomorrow, please stock the fridge?"

"Exactly. And there are no extra fees. Everyone who works here gets a good salary plus room and board, so the members don't have to constantly reach into their pockets to tip."

"How do you know so much about this place?"

He could feel her watching him, but he was too busy looking for a parking spot. "I worked here in high school." Then again, it was possible he hadn't looked her fully in the eyes since she'd left him on the couch last night.

"Doing what?"

"I worked valet and gave ice skating lessons."

"They have a rink?" Her eyes widened when the village came into sight. "Oh, my God. This place is magical."

"You should see it in winter. It's all lit up, and they have carriage rides and carolers." With its cobblestone streets, chalet-like architecture, the village *was* charming.

Wrought iron lampposts and window boxes bursting with flowers gave it a European feel.

"I can't believe this. My mum would love this."

Nonresidents could take advantage of the shops and restaurants, but they didn't have access to the neighborhoods, so he parked in the lot behind the lodge. They'd have to wait for Glori to pick them up.

"So, I've seen downtown Calamity, the big ranches surrounding it, and now this village. Where did you grow up?"

Getting out of the Jeep, he pocketed his keys. As they headed around the lodge, his hand reached for hers. It was automatic, and it made him go hot with embarrassment. He quickly shoved it into the pocket of his jeans. "Sam's house is a few blocks from the town square."

"Oh, you still own it?"

"I rent it. It'll need some work before I can sell it."

"When did he pass?"

"Six and a half years ago."

She cut him a look but thankfully didn't point out how much he could've gotten done in that time.

"In my defense, I've been living in Pittsburgh, and the hockey season's long."

"Okay, big man. Just say it. It's your last tie to your grandpa." She nudged him. "Say it."

That's when he finally did it, looked right into her eyes, and what the hell was the matter with him? Why did he feel little explosions in his chest? What *was* it about her? The sun on her butter-yellow hair, the glint of mischief in her eyes, and that mouth that had stretched wide around his cock. Desire streaked through him. "That might be part of it, but I really have been busy. Coaches don't just work during the season." Fear stabbed into him at the reminder he might lose his job.

"No, that's not what I want you to say. Say, It's my last tie to my grandpa." A trolley clanged as it approached the stop in front of the lodge. "This place is adorable."

"We can sit here and wait for Glori." He led them to one of the many benches lined up along the village streets. Once they settled, he said, "Yes, that house is the last tie to Sam."

"Nope. Say grandpa."

"I'm not saying that."

She sat so close their shoulders brushed. Neither wore long sleeves, so he got to feel her smooth, warm skin. "Why not?" She bumped him. "Big, bad hockey players don't say it? What did you call him?"

"Sam."

"You called your grandfather by his first name? I thought you were just saying that around me."

"You had to know him."

"Describe him to me."

"I already did. Here. I'll show you a picture." He reached for his wallet, but she placed her hand on his arm.

"No, you told me the basics. Larger than life, played poker, smoked cigars, started the Cooters. But I want to hear how *you* saw him. That's what matters. Not the impression I get from a photograph or his reputation in town."

He looked at her hand on his inked forearm, and it kicked up the lust he was constantly battling. "Uh." He had to get his mind on the conversation, put Sam in the forefront. "Well, he was big, burly, and loud." He thought about his funeral, how many people had come. "He was one of those guys who held onto his friendships."

"Like a collector. I used to be like that."

"Yeah, exactly. In high school, he and his buddies were the guys who smoked between classes, tripped the athletes, and had sex with cheerleaders in supply closets. They rode motorcycles, and when a mom and her kids would cross the street, they'd rev their engines just to scare them."

"And yet you talk about him with such affection."

"Well, he didn't do any of that when I knew him. Remember, he owned the market, so he grew into a responsible citizen. Besides, he took me in. He raised me."

"Did he do a good job? I'm picturing a dirty Declan with no manners and clothes he'd grown out of months ago walking right into neighbor's houses and rooting around their refrigerators for something to eat."

"Ha. No, not at all. Sam took good care of me. You'll be happy to know he made me take a bath every night and brush my teeth twice a day. And he'd whack the back of my head if I didn't say please and thank you." Most of the time, he tried not to think about Sam. The vortex of grief was something he worked hard to avoid. "He was always there for me. In fact, the only time he missed a hockey game was when he skidded his motorcycle out on black ice." At the toot of a horn, Declan glanced up. "After that, he bought a truck. Never missed another game."

A dark blue Aston Martin pulled up in front of them. The passenger side window rolled down, and Glori leaned over. "Hope you two brought your appetites."

"Oh, I'm always hungry." Phinny gestured for him to get into the front seat. "You've got longer legs."

He leaned in, the tip of his nose tickled by her sweetly scented hair. "No, you sit there. You're here to talk to her."

She gazed up at him with the strangest look of

affection. "Declan." With the gentlest touch, she cupped his cheek. "You make it very hard…"

"Hard to what?"

She closed her eyes and broke out in a soft, satisfied grin. As she opened them, she shivered. "Last night…"

What? Say it.

Say something *about it.*

But before she could answer, the driver waiting behind Glori tapped his horn. Phinny gave a dreamy sigh and got into the car.

Chapter Thirteen

WHILE THE TWO WOMEN CHATTED, DECLAN LOOKED over his messages. Nothing from the General Manager but that didn't mean much. They were probably looking for his replacement. If they couldn't find one before exhibition games, he'd be okay. But if they could...

He'd be out of a job. He'd made a name for himself these past seven years. No doubt, he was on track to become a head coach. But what could he do? Phinny was no closer to keeping the ranch than she'd been ten days ago. He had no choice but to hang tight and stay the course.

"Here we are." Pulling into the cool darkness of her organized and spotless garage, Glori parked alongside a mammoth SUV. She led them into the kitchen and dropped her purse on the counter.

"Your house is stunning." Phinny took in the soaring ceilings, the rustic wooden beams, and the modern furnishings. Light spilled in from massive, floor-to-ceiling windows. "I can't believe you live here."

"I love it. When I first moved to Calamity, I had a

lovely Craftsman home not far from town. But when I came back—oh, a decade or so later—I decided I'm here for the long haul and liked the idea of not having to worry about anything home-related. Village Management handles everything."

"May I ask what you do for a living?"

Glori reached for her hand and gave it a squeeze. "What I love about your generation is that you don't assume I got this house in a divorce." Then, she sashayed over to the pantry and made a sweeping gesture to reveal rows and rows of neatly stacked boxes. "I made Extra Bars."

"They're still my favorite," Declan said.

"What do you mean you made them?" Phinny asked.

"I've always eaten well. Salads, whole grains, lean proteins. But some nights I just didn't feel like cooking. I didn't want anything but a bowl of popcorn and a good book, but I figured I should have *something* with protein, so I'd reach for a bar. I was on the eternal quest to find one that not only tasted good but didn't have a lot of sugar. I just couldn't find anything I liked, so I researched ingredients, tried a thousand different recipes, and then I came up with this." She pulled one out of a box. "It's soft as a candy bar, but it has less than a gram of sugar. And the best part is that it's got twenty grams of protein." She shrugged. "It was a cinch to sell it."

"I'm assuming it's popular since they're his favorite." Phinny glanced at Declan

"Very," he said.

"I sold the company three years ago. Come see my latest product." Glori led them across the kitchen. She pried the lid off a storage container and held it out to them.

Phinny took one of the bars and bit into it. "Oh, yum. This is good."

Declan reached in and took one as well. "It looks more like a granola bar."

"You're right. Though it's packed with protein, and the only sugar comes from the chocolate chips, that's exactly how I'd market it. Try it."

He took a bite and chewed. "It's good."

"I love it," Phinny said. "Are you going to sell these?"

"Oh, no, I'm retired now. I still love to tinker in the kitchen, though. And I'm always looking for the perfect snack food. I'm a grazer, so I'd rather eat a granola bar now, a protein bar later, and a handful of nuts before bed."

"Well, wait, what if I sell them at the farm stand?" Phinny asked.

"I'm not sure what the point would be. I'm not going back into business. I'm done with the twenty-four-seven kind of life."

Declan never wanted Phinny to be disappointed, so he said, "Might not hurt to get some reviews on the product. If they're well-received, you could keep it low-key and only sell them at Harley and Lu's Emporium."

"That's not a bad idea. If I could keep production low and not turn it into a worldwide conglomerate…yeah, I'd do that." Glori smiled at them. "Look at us. Just a trio of entrepreneurs hanging out together."

"I'm headed to the rink this afternoon." He had to coach one of the Renegades. "If you've got enough, I could bring a batch to the kids at the hockey clinic."

"If I've got enough." With a gleam in her eye, Glori led them back to the garage. Pulling open the freezer, she showed them stacked containers. "How many do you need?"

Declan laughed. "Good to see you're retired." He pulled several boxes out and set them next to her car.

"Now, come on in, and let's chat." Glori headed back into the house. "Would you like your tea hot or iced?"

"Iced, please," Declan said. "Thank you."

As Glori brought glasses down from the cabinet, she said, "You know, it was your grandfather who got my business started."

"How's that?" Declan asked.

"He was the first vendor to sell my bars." Glori held a glass under the ice dispenser, the cubes clunking together. "He was quite a character. We miss him and his funky little store."

"Is that the market you'd mentioned?" Phinny asked Declan.

"It was *the* market before the population exploded around here." Glori poured the tea.

"Eventually, the big grocery stores took away his business," Declan said. "First, Jackson got one. Then, Calamity. But he stuck it out because he liked hanging out with his friends."

"You called it funky?" Phinny asked.

"He sold the most unusual things." Glori laughed. "Sam had a heart of gold. If someone was hurting financially, he'd let them sell holiday pies or banana bread. Eventually, he had to create a whole section of the store for products made by locals. He had everything in there. Aprons, homemade soaps, candles…"

"Is that why he did that?" Declan asked. "I never put it together."

"That's because he never talked about it. The first time he did it, he set out an order form for holiday pies, and it just happened to show up right after Joanna

Cleary's husband passed quite suddenly, leaving her in a bind."

A sharp pain in his chest had Declan's hand going over his heart. "That was"—he cleared his throat—"nice of him."

"He was a good man." Glori handed out the glasses. "He was also direct, so you either loved him or you hated him."

I loved him.

And he missed him every day. Even when he tried his hardest not to think about it.

"I see you're following in his footsteps," Glori said.

"What do you mean?" Had he offended someone? Some people considered him closed off or gruff, but he didn't think he'd ever been rude.

"I'm on the board of the Sunshine Community, and I know you let them use Sam's place to house homeless mothers and their children. That's a wonderful thing you do."

He could feel Phinny watching him, so he tipped his head back and glugged the sweet tea.

Glori's cool hand settled on top of his. "Sam would be very proud of the man you've become."

No one had ever said that to him before, so he hadn't known how much he'd needed to hear it. But with both women staring at him, he didn't want to sink too deeply into it. He hoped they couldn't see how much it had affected him.

"What happened to his market?" Phinny asked.

How did she do that? He'd perfected the fine art of revealing nothing, so how did she read him so well that he knew to change the subject? "He sold it when he got sick." He'd never been so in sync with someone before. It felt like they were on the same team. "It was just too much for him to handle."

He liked that she didn't try to change him the way so many people over the years had done, trying to get him in touch with his feelings. He was very aware of them *thank you very much*. He just didn't see the point in wallowing.

"That man was a fighter. He had an aggressive form of cancer and was given—what? Three months to live?" Glori asked.

"Three weeks." He would never forget that call. He'd just come off the ice, high off a huge win against Minnesota. In the locker room, they were all celebrating, changing out of their sweaty gear. Someone had just doused him with Gatorade to celebrate his hat trick. The screen of his phone had lit up, and he'd wanted to ignore it, revel in the glory.

But it was a Calamity area code, and he'd gotten a strange prickle at the back of his neck. Right there, amidst the laughter and jostling and shouts, he'd answered. Turned out to be Sam's doctor.

The news had knocked out his knees. He'd had to sit on the hard bench. What he remembered most was the contrast. Everyone laughing, joking, lockers slamming, pads hitting the floor. And inside, Declan had gone perfectly still.

"And yet he held on for another year and a half." Glori patted his shoulder. "And this man dropped out of college and gave up hockey to come home and take care of him."

"That was a wonderful thing to do." Phinny gave him that warm, sweet smile that reduced him to mush.

Declan didn't want to talk about this anymore. "You mind if I use the bathroom?"

Glori pointed. "Powder room's right there." As he

headed for it, he heard her say, "They were very close. Personally, I think Sam fought as hard as he did because he didn't want to leave Declan alone. It was just the two of them."

"What happened to his parents?"

"Oh, it's an awful story. They were so young. They barely had enough money to keep a roof over their heads, but they'd scrimped and saved for their first vacation. There was—"

Declan closed the door a little too hard. *We're supposed to talk about Kurt. Not relive my childhood.* To be honest, he'd only ever known his grandfather. He was six when his parents died, so he didn't have a lot of memories of them beyond the photographs his grandfather had kept.

It was Sam he mourned.

Sam, he missed.

Just for one moment, he let himself remember, but the sinkhole opened at such an alarming rate, he had to shut it down. He washed his hands, splashing cold water on his face.

When he came back out, the women were laughing.

"He did that?" Phinny asked.

Declan found them eating slices of honey cake.

"Well, I'd asked him to be more romantic…" Glori hunched a shoulder. "That was his version of it."

Good. They're talking about Kurt.

"That's really sweet, though." When Declan settled at the counter with them, Phinny touched the back of his hand. "Glori was saying she'd always wanted Kurt to be more romantic, but they had different ideas of what that looked like."

"I wanted flowers. I wanted him to whisk me off to Paris. Instead, he had my oil changed. He once got me a new roof. Can you believe that? I came home to find a truck in my driveway and workers hammering away." Glori gave a sad smile. "But the problem was mine. If I'd been less caught up in my notion of what a relationship should look like and more focused on what I actually had, I would never have questioned Kurt's romantic nature. He didn't do flowers, but every time he saw me, he told me I was beautiful. He asked me about my day and took care of me when I was sick. And let's be honest, I wanted more than he was willing to give. If there's one lesson I've learned in life, it's to listen when people tell you who they are. If you want to get married, don't date a man who says he doesn't. I thought Kurt would fall so in love with me that he'd eventually give in." She held her hand out, looking at her empty ring finger. "He did love me. He just didn't express it the way I wanted it."

"Did you ever get married?" Phinny asked.

"I did. It didn't last. That's why I came back to Calamity." With a wistful expression, she shook her head. "I gave up the only man I've ever loved all for some silly fantasy."

"Did he date anyone after you?" Phinny asked.

"Nope. I put us through hell for no reason."

"But there was a reason." Phinny sounded insistent. "Marriage mattered to you. He could've given you that."

"And by using the same logic, I could've let it go. If I had, I'd have been with him until the very end. I would've been a lot happier without that piece of paper."

"Well, I mean, he was a very stubborn man. Look what he did to my mum, making her live out here all alone with a baby. She begged him to let her stay in Boston with him, but he was single-minded in his idea of raising his family on this god—" Her jaw snapped shut. She went quiet. And then, she said, "On his family's land."

Glori's back straightened. "Is that what your mother told you?"

With an uneasy expression, Phinny nodded. Obviously, trotting out that well-worn narrative in a new environment hadn't landed well.

"That's not the story I heard," Glori said.

"What did you hear?"

"Well, to be clear, Kurt never spoke ill of your mother. And anything he did say was delivered as fact, not as a complaint."

"If you wouldn't mind telling me, I'd love to hear what happened. I want to see him through the eyes of someone other than his ex-wife."

"I didn't know him at that time, of course, so I can only tell you what Kurt told me." Glori sipped her tea. "As for Boston, he said they lived in a nice brownstone, but she was unhappy because the other wives didn't include her. By the time you were three, she'd given him an ultimatum."

"Wait. I was living in Boston when I was *three*?"

"That is my recollection of what Kurt told me."

"I thought he dumped us here after I was born." Phinny glanced at Declan as if he had answers.

He wished he did. "Check with your mom." It was a strange feeling, the way the world seemed to fall away, like the two of them were alone in bed, face to face, heart to heart. He knew she felt it, too, because she didn't look away. In that moment, he was her lifeline.

"I will." She said it softly, intimately, before giving him a little smile. And then she turned her attention back to Glori. "What kind of ultimatum?"

"If he didn't spend more time with her, she was going to leave. He didn't know what to do about that because hockey paid the bills. Your mom had tastes that a high school coach couldn't satisfy. Not to mention, his performance on the ice just kept getting better and better. His career was exploding."

"So, he didn't know what to do with her and shipped her off to Calamity?"

"No. Not at all." Glori set her glass down hard enough to slosh tea over the rim. "He was going to quit hockey for her. He was going to give it all up to coach at the university here. *That's* why they moved back to Calamity. But when they got the offer letter and she saw the salary, she didn't want him to quit."

"Are you serious? I never heard about that." Phinny angled herself away. The color rushing up her neck and spreading across her cheeks made him think her mom's behavior embarrassed her.

"Look, I don't want to badmouth your mother." Glori had to have noticed, too. "But you asked for information, and I'm sharing what I have."

"Did he...I mean, he must've hated her?"

"I never once heard him say he hated her. I know he was hurt and frustrated—"

"*He* was hurt?"

"Oh, yes. Very much so. From his perspective, he'd tried to make her happy, and she still wound up taking his daughter away." Glori reached for Phinny, stroking her hair. "The one thing I know with absolute certainty is that your father loved you very, very much. He talked about you all the time."

She might never get the words she needed from Kurt,

but maybe hearing them from his ex-girlfriend would be enough.

"Then, why did he give up on me?" Tears glittered in her eyes, and she looked desperate.

For the first time, Glori didn't seem so sure of herself. "I think you should talk to your mother about that."

Phinny tensed. "What do you mean? Did she do something?"

Glori looked like she wanted to say something but hesitated.

"Please, tell me what you know. Because after that summer, he never talked to me again. He gave up his custodial rights. I thought…I was sure he'd given up on me."

"Sweetheart, no. It wasn't like that. I know how much Kurt loved you, and I know he was devastated to lose you."

"Then why? He didn't have to lose me. That was his choice."

"That was the summer your mother remarried, right?" Glori asked.

"That's right. Apparently, I pitched a fit about having to visit Kurt while my parents got to go on their honeymoon. I was so upset, they had to cancel their trip. They took me to Disneyland instead."

"That's…" Glori pressed her lips together.

"It's okay," Phinny said. "You can say it. I want to know."

"The way I understood it, your mother offered to take you to Disneyland, but it would have to be the same dates as your scheduled visit with your father. It was the only time your stepfather could take time off from his job."

Maybe if Glori hadn't known specific details, it might

have been easier for Phinny to discount what she said. But her cheeks glistened with tears, and her features pinched. "I must have misunderstood. I was so young." She tried to look dignified, tried to smile...but her bottom lip wobbled—and he just couldn't take it anymore.

Stepping in front of their host, he pulled Phinny into his arms and swallowed her slender body up in his arms. "He loved you. That's the only thing that matters."

Her only response was to burrow her face into his pec and tighten her hold on him.

He swore to God, he would burn the world for this woman.

Phinny couldn't quiet the noises in her head.

With her bedroom at the back of the house, she opened her window, hoping to hear horses nickering or cowboys talking around a campfire. Anything to stop her from thinking.

On one level, she'd always known her mum had wanted Andrew to complete the circle of their family. She'd never wanted the nuisance of Kurt, the disruption to holidays that came with an ex-husband.

But would she have gone so far as to *lie* to her own daughter?

Maybe it was less about lying, though, than wanting something so badly her mum had come to believe it herself.

She wished she could talk to Declan. Ridiculous, she knew that. She'd just met the guy. But that didn't matter because somehow, in such a short time, he'd come to know more about her than anyone else. Sure, it was an extreme situation, but it was also because he cared. She knew he did. She *felt* it.

Knowing he was just down the hall made it a thousand times worse. She was too aware of him. There was just something so solid, so real…so capable about him. She wanted to sleep in the circle of his arms. *God.* Every brush of the sheet or whisper of a breeze made her skin tingle.

I miss him. I want him.

But I can't have him. She hadn't asked directly, but she had the impression he didn't do relationships. He was a loner. But one thing she did know, he was the type of man who went after what he wanted. And if he wanted her, he'd be in her bed right now.

Fucking me. Desire streamed through her, and she rolled onto her side, squeezing her eyes shut. *Go to sleep.* She had to get up early and deal with horses and chickens. She had to find Tigger and give him his egg.

But every time she closed her eyes, she saw Declan's face while she'd given him a blow job, the passion in his eyes as he'd watched his cock slide in and out of her mouth. And when he'd come, his big hand had clamped onto the back of her head and his handsome features had wrenched into a tortured, ecstatic expression.

That was the first time she'd ever seen him really let go. Most of the time, he was alert, watchful. He was extremely in tune with her needs, constantly gauging her feelings. Even when he'd licked her into an orgasm, he'd been all about figuring out her pleasure centers. And she loved that, she really did.

But in that moment, he'd lost control.

God, he was the hottest man she'd ever met. It wasn't just his face or his body or those badass tattoos. It was *him.* Since her visit with Glori had run later than expected, she'd had to accompany him to the rink where he'd coached one of the Renegades' hockey players.

He hadn't been the only guy on the ice, but he was the one who'd captured her attention. His powerful thighs and absolute confidence had been such a turn-on. He was a force to be reckoned with.

Watching him coach a professional hockey player, seeing the man's gratitude…the way he'd broken into a wide grin when he grasped what Declan was saying…it had been exhilarating.

She'd wanted to straddle him in the Jeep, rock her hips over his erection, let him know just how hot he made her. But she didn't, of course. She was careful not to let him see how much she wanted him. She wouldn't dare flirt. *No way.*

She'd asked a favor, and he'd delivered. And that was that.

But she wanted more. She wanted to slide under his covers and feel his arms wrap around her. She wanted him to nuzzle her neck, feel him hard and prodding against her. She'd let him in. *Oh, yeah, I would.* She'd open like a flower bud for him.

Well, wait. He's not hooking up with anyone. She knew that because he spent all his time either working in the office or with her. Tonight, they'd cooked dinner, watched a movie, and gone to bed.

As long as she didn't get clingy or emotional, why couldn't she have another night with him? There wouldn't be real feelings involved because she was leaving in two weeks.

In the meantime…why not?

Chapter Fourteen

THROWING THE COVERS BACK, SHE GOT OUT OF BED and peered down the long hallway. Shafts of moonlight from each bedroom puddled on the gleaming hardwood floor. Since they kept the windows open at night, the house was chilly, and it woke her all the way up.

Even the anxiety of heading to his room made her feel alive. She was stepping out of her comfort zone in a big way, and it was exhilarating.

And terrifying. *What if he's annoyed that I'm waking him up?*

Oh, come on. What man wouldn't like being awakened for sex? And if she was going to do this, she'd better be confident. He wouldn't like a weak, insecure woman. That, she was sure of.

She stopped outside his door. God, what if there was someone in his bed? She would die. But she didn't hear anything. Not a sound.

Had he gone out?

Wouldn't it be hilarious if, every night after she went to sleep, he showered, slapped on some cologne, and trolled the bars for hookups? Here she was thinking they were being all domestic and cozy together while he might be off banging a different woman each night.

Actually, that didn't sound so farfetched. *There's no way a guy like Declan is going to bed at ten o'clock.* That's literally when she and her friends used to head out to the clubs.

Ugh. I'm ridiculous.

If I can't be a sexually confident woman, then I've got no business standing outside Declan Cadell's door. She turned to go but something held her back.

What if she played the favor game again? So far, they'd kissed and had oral sex, but they hadn't had sex. *This could be the last favor I ask.*

Yes, perfect. Knocking lightly, she pressed her ear to the door.

"Yeah?" She heard a rustle of fabric. "Phinny? Come in."

She didn't know how he could sleep with the curtains open like that, but in case he had company, she did a quick scan for panties or high heels.

"There's no one here." He said it with surprise, like how could she think he'd sneak someone in?

Well, she could stand there like an idiot, or she could go after what she wanted. Worst case scenario? He'd tell her to get out. That she was taking the game too far.

And apparently, she'd rather feel the sting of rejection than the bottomless ache of *what if.*

What if I crawl into his bed, and he welcomes me?

What if he feels for me what I feel for him?

Oh, no. No, no, no.

No feelings.

You can have fun with him, but that's it. He doesn't want anything more complicated.

Moving with a confidence she didn't feel, she headed for the bed. "Sorry I woke you." *But I'm feeling frisky.*

Ew, no.

But I ache for you.

Shut up. No.

You know what? Forget it. She wasn't a game player, so she climbed onto his bed and sat up on her knees. "I couldn't sleep."

"Come on." His sleep-roughened voice burned through her like whiskey, igniting a fire in her core. He threw back the covers, and she crawled underneath. Before she had a chance to figure out how close to him she should be, he drew the fluffy down blanket over them.

She breathed in his scent—something clean, like dryer-warmed cotton, and outdoorsy, like hiking on a sunny day. She smiled to put him at ease. *It's just fun here, folks. Nothing more.*

But his serious expression let her know he wasn't buying it. "What's keeping you up?"

Oh, that little whirly thing you do with your tongue. But her stomach churned, and her mind raced, and she just wasn't feeling bold enough to say it out loud.

He cocked his arm and shoved his hand under his head. "Must be weird to hear a whole other perspective on your dad. And live in his house without him." He grinned. "Even weirder to live with a total stranger."

"You're the best part of it." *Oh, dammit.* She wished she could suck the words back in. So, before he could kick her out or give her *the talk*, she said, "I'm scared."

He brushed a lock of hair that had fallen across her cheek and tucked it behind her ear. "Why?"

"Because I'm pretty sure my mum cut Kurt out so she could make a family with me and Andrew."

He didn't look surprised at all. "And if she did…"

"I'm not sure I could forgive her."

"Yeah, I get that." Slowly, gently, he sifted his fingers through her hair. "Would she do that?"

"Yes, I think she would. Looking back, I can see how she changed when she met Andrew, how excited she became. She'd say it all the time, that we're going to do this or that 'as a family.'"

"Kurt was no threat to that. He lived five thousand miles away."

"No, I think he was. He had me for whole summers and every other holiday. That's a big threat." *What does it say about my mum that she could erase Kurt just to have her idea of a family?* The more she thought about it, the faster her pulse revved. Anxiety spun like rotors, practically levitating her out of his bed. *You have to stop thinking about it. That's not why I'm here.* Resting her cheek on his chest, she gave herself a moment to calm down. She had what she wanted—she was in bed with Declan, his strong arm around her, his heart beating powerfully. Stroking his warm skin, she flashed him a smile. "On a happy note, I've now got two products to sell at my farm stand."

"That's pretty cool."

"I was thinking…does Calamity have a store that only sells locally-sourced products?"

"Not that I know of."

"I might talk to Glori about that."

"About her backing you?" Interest flickered in his eyes, and his fingers stilled.

"No, of course not. I'm only here two more weeks."

Whatever had captured his attention died.

"But maybe it's something she'd like to do." It was a winning idea.

"I think she's serious about retirement."

"This is totally different than producing and selling protein bars. For this, locals would come to her. She'd get to hang out in a pretty store with yummy smelling candles and chat with customers. It'd be quite lovely, don't you think?"

"Yes." His fingertip traced the shell of her ear. "Lovely." He went for an English accent.

"Did you just make fun of the way I talk?"

"What? Me? Never."

"Declan." She laughed, getting up and straddling him. *Look who's bold now?* He did that to her, made her feel perfectly at ease. When she braced her hands on either side of his head, his eyes went hot, and he gripped her ass, hauling her over his hard cock. She straddled his cut body, letting her hair fall like a curtain around them. "I'm going to need another favor."

He had a dirty gleam in his eye that made her squirm. "Nope. That's not how it works."

"Really?" She rocked her hips over him, and it got her so worked up she nearly climbed out of her skin. "And how does it work, exactly?"

"I did you a favor. Now, you owe me one."

"Oh, I owe you, do I?" Warmth bloomed in her chest. "All right. Go on and name your favor."

"Anything goes?"

Grinding on him, her blood sizzled, and it felt so good she moaned. "Mm, absolutely."

He brushed the hair off her shoulders. "Show me your tits."

Lust sucker-punched her, and she lifted her tank top over her head and let it fly.

"This is a complicated favor." He cupped her breasts with warm hands. "So, it'll have to be done in steps."

She arched her back, loving the feel of his big hands on her. "Does step two involve getting us naked?"

His fingers squeezed, and his hips lifted, rubbing his cock against her core. "How far do you want to take this?"

She looked him right in the eyes. "All the way."

He reared up, reaching under her arms to lift her onto her knees. "Take off your panties." Slowly, he peeled them down her ass like he was unveiling an erotic treasure. She climbed off the bed, so she could remove them and kick them aside.

With the moonlight spilling through open curtains, his chest gleamed like someone had poured molten silver onto it. She sat on her heels beside him. "Now what?" Her nipples hardened in the cool air.

Kicking off the blankets and baring his naked body, he grabbed his rigid cock. "Now, you ride me."

Holy shit. She liked impolite sex very much. Even more, she loved how Declan took charge. But as she scrambled to get back on his lap, she noticed a vulnerability in his eyes, and it made her wonder if she'd read him wrong. Maybe he felt it, too, and their intimacy scared him. Maybe he wasn't as immune to her as she'd thought.

"Hang on a sec. I want to add a few more steps." Turning around, she got hold of his cock and licked it from root to head.

He went rigid and gripped her ass cheeks. "Good one. Let's never forget it again." He voice came out rough and gravelly.

"And then there's this." Her tongue traveled around the crown before she sucked him into her mouth. Loving the way his hands tightened on her, she flicked and swirled. And then—*oh*—he added a step of his own. His finger slid inside her wet, hot core. Her back arched, her mouth lost its suction, and she lowered her head to his thigh to savor a caress that made her get even slicker.

"You've got the most perfect ass I've ever seen. Makes me lose my mind."

Which only made her tilt it higher…and swish it slightly from side to side. He let out a groan. "Fuck, Phinny. You're so hot."

No one had ever called her that before.

As he continued pumping his fingers and squeezing her ass, she swallowed his cock again, and the pleasure of it all sent her into a frenzy of need. Just when the tingles spread across her body, when she was so close to an orgasm her lips went slack, and she closed her eyes to let it rip her away, he pulled out.

Jackknifing up, he lifted her and flipped her around.

Breathless, she faced him. "I've never been manhandled before, but that's hot." The wild, intense look in his eyes had her pulse pounding out of control.

He opened the nightstand drawer and pulled out a condom. "Ride me." Literally tearing it open it with his teeth, he handed it to her.

Reaching behind her, she grasped him. He was hot, hard, and throbbing, and she was going to lose her mind if she didn't get him inside her. But first, she unrolled the rubber on his stiff length. And then slowly, she eased down on him.

He punched a pillow and lay back down, both hands clasped behind his head like he was a spectator at his niece's soccer game.

"You don't fool me." Swiveling her hips, she flattened her palms on his chest. "I got your number now."

"Yeah?" Tension had his muscles straining, his veins popping, but still, he didn't touch her. He just watched.

"Oh, yeah." Arching her hips, she moved up and down, taking her time, letting him fill her until he was deeper than anyone had ever gone. The slow, slick slide lit her up, making her body vibrate with need and glow with a desire so potent it nearly undid her.

She needed more. She needed all of him. When she sat up, his gaze went to her breasts, flaring with hunger. She needed to feel his desperation and urgency, needed to know he was in this with her, so she braced both hands on his thighs, thrusting her breasts out, and rode him hard.

And then, he broke. With a growl, he reached for her, his big hands cupping her breasts, jamming them together, as he roughly flicked each nipple. "You drive me wild."

"God, Declan." She surged forward, setting her hands on his hard, warm chest, hair spilling all over him, closing out the world until it was just the two of them.

He took control. Grabbing her ass cheeks, he raised her and slammed her down. His masculine scent and powerful thrusts sent her senses into overdrive.

And then he smacked her ass. "Get on your hands and knees."

Even though she'd never liked that position, had always felt it cut off intimacy, she was desperate to have him back inside her, so she clambered off him and tipped her ass in the air. Her back arched, frantic for him to plunge back in and finish them both off.

But instead, he ran his hands up her spine in a slow glide, caressed her stomach and gently cupped her breasts, giving them a squeeze. He took his time to worship her body, and she hissed in a breath, pushing back on him. Her hips swayed until she wedged his cock between her ass cheeks. "If this is another step, I might as well go on and make us some tea."

Chuckling, he swiped a finger through her dripping folds. "Yeah, I don't think so." He rocked against her but didn't push in. At the same time, he pinched her nipple and stroked her clit, and she cried out, her body jerking. "If you can hold off on the tea…" One hand gripped her hip, and anticipation roared through her. Gripping his cock, he lined himself up. "I'm going to fuck you into the mattress now, okay?"

A tremor ran through her, and she barely pushed the word, "Yes," out of her throat.

He slid inside, going deep, one hand clutching her hip. And then, he started to move. Slow, easy strokes, with the other hand caressing her back, rounding her ass cheek, and dipping into her crack. Over and over, he took the same route, making her feverish with need.

He leaned forward, his chest to her back, and he whispered in her ear, "You feel so fucking good." Angling her higher, he reached between her legs and circled her clit.

A bolt of lightning tore through her, and she sizzled.

"You smell good." Voice still at her ear, he thrust into her, faster now, his body heating up. "You taste good." And then he was fucking her so hard, he drove her up the bed with each punishing stroke. She had to flatten her palms against the headboard to keep from slamming into it.

She wished she had a mirror. She wanted to place the grunts and dirty words with his expression. But pure erotic bliss took possession of her mind and body, and she could only concentrate on the tightening, rising sensations, lifting her toward a perfect state of bliss. And then he stroked her into a climax that flung her into a whole other world where she was no longer skin and bones. She soared into a realm of pure ecstasy.

"Oh, fuck. I'm gonna come." Slamming into her, hips punching, he lost his rhythm, lost his finesse, and he shouted with his release. "Fuck, fuck, *fuck*."

Finally, his grip relaxed, and he slowly eased out of her. When he fell to her side, she got to see his sweaty, tired, and deeply satisfied expression. She wanted to curl up in his arms. Wanted to stay with him.

She never wanted this intimacy to end.

But she didn't know his limit. Yes, he was into sex with her. But did he normally hook up with women at their place, so he could be the one to leave? Or did he pat them on the ass, thank them for a good time, and ask them to go?

"Hey." He brushed the air off her face, cupping her cheek. "What's going on?"

She could vomit her insecurities and doubts all over him. *Yeah, that would be fun*. Or she could keep the game going so they'd do it again.

Yes, that one.

So, she smiled. "Just thinking how it's my turn to ask the next favor. And you can bet it's going to be a good one." It took everything she had to swing her legs off the bed and get up. "'Night."

Coffee.

Sliding her feet into shearling flip flops, Phinny headed down the hallway. Seemed ridiculous to hold onto these old things, considering the heel and toes of the footbed had totally worn away. She'd have to get some new slippers. Why did she cling to her old designer clothes anyway?

The closer she got to Declan's room, the more anxious she grew. Last night, she'd told herself he was crossing some kind of line, breaking through an intimacy barrier. But the truth was…she was making it up. She didn't know how he felt because he didn't reveal anything.

I'm the one falling for him.

So hard.

And walking away was going to hurt. But what choice did she have? Even if they fell madly in love with each other, she couldn't stay in Calamity. She supposed she could find a philanthropy that needed help with auctions. Glori could probably help her with that, but she wasn't about to be stranded out here on this godforsaken—

Oh. She'd done it again. Spewed her mum's words when anyone could see this ranch was beautiful, lush, and vibrant. In any event, she couldn't stay here, and he couldn't move to England. *There's no hockey.*

She hoped it wouldn't be awkward this morning, that he wouldn't worry about her becoming clingy. *Ha.*

I want to cling to him like a spider monkey.

Well, she'd just have to keep faking it, pretend she was cool, just like she'd been doing. As she passed his room, she found the door wide open, and the bed made. *Looks like he got an early start today.*

She headed downstairs, mindlessly reaching for the doorknob of Kurt's private office as she passed—only it turned.

What?

This entire time, it had been locked. Declan didn't

have the key. Even Mitch, the ranch manager, didn't have it. She stood there wondering who'd opened it. *Can I go in? I won't touch anything. I just want to take a peek.*

A shadow fell over her, making her shiver. It almost felt like Kurt was in there, and she was a little girl all over again. *Oh. Oh, God.* She remembered.

"Phinny? Is that you?"

The visceral memory hit so hard, she closed her eyes to see it more vividly.

She didn't know how old she'd been, but she'd worn a white eyelet nightgown, her feet bare on the cool, wood floor. She remembered it was dark in the hallway, and she'd been drawn by the golden line of light underneath the door. Her heart had knocked against her ribcage as she'd turned the doorknob and peered in to find her father at his desk, glasses on, reading a computer screen.

He yanked his glasses off with one hand. "What's up, buttercup?"

"Daddy, I can't sleep."

Daddy. Sorrow wrenched her heart. She'd called him daddy. *God.*

As he'd rolled his chair back, he'd crooked a finger, inviting her to come in. She'd rounded the big desk and stood before him, arms held high, waiting for him to pick her up.

He'd lifted her onto his lap. *"Do you want to finish that drawing you were working on this morning?"*

She'd nodded, and he'd swung them around his credenza where he kept art supplies for her. Play-dough, markers, crayons, all kinds of paper—construction, sketch, notepad—and colored pencils. He had a little tub of Elmer's paste. She remembered that the lid had a stick attached to it.

She'd sat on his lap, hunched over the drawing, while he'd gently scratched her back.

Love burst through the dam, spilling into her veins, flooding her very soul.

Daddy.

She hadn't hated him. He'd never been too busy for her.

She'd loved him.

Her hand flew off the doorknob as if it had been burning hot. And then she hurried to the kitchen.

The scent of fresh coffee filled the house, and she was surprised to see a French press on the counter next to two mugs and a cream and sugar set. Declan didn't drink coffee, so someone was here. *Well, this isn't for me.* She'd make her own.

But she was still rattled by the memory, so before coffee, she needed to get outside, breathe in fresh air, and get her chores done. Kicking off her flip flops, she jammed her bare feet into rubber boots, stepped outside into the chilly early morning air, and grabbed the baskets from the barn.

"Good morning, beautiful." The chickens didn't run from her anymore. They didn't cluck and get in a tizzy— probably because she was calm with them now. As she collected the eggs in the comforting darkness of the coop and the soft cooing of the hens, the memory came back to her. Sitting on his lap, his fingertips scratching just as she'd liked, she could recall a feeling of well-being. She'd been comfortable with him. Why had she suppressed those good memories?

Oh, God. She knew.

Of course, she knew.

Phinny set the basket down and headed outside into the sunlight.

Her mum wanted her to be a good girl for Andrew.

She'd wanted her to wear a dress, brush her hair, put in barrettes.

Smile when you look at him, Phinny.

Be nice to him.

Go on, give him the present. Tell him you made it for him.

She could feel the squeeze of her mum's fingers on the back of her neck.

You're not going to Verity's. We're having a family *dinner.*

The first time she'd met Andrew, her mum had gotten her all gussied up, fussed over her hair, and told her quite sternly how to behave. The three of them had gone to Borough Market. She'd wanted a chocolate gelato, but her mum wouldn't let her. She'd acted so weird, jerking Phinny's hand when she pointed to the flavor she'd wanted. Her mom had made her get vanilla so she wouldn't stain her lavender dress.

Once, when she'd cried inconsolably about missing out on a birthday party for a girl at school, her mum had nearly yanked her arm out of its socket because Andrew had just come over.

"He's going to leave if you don't stop. Do you want him to leave? Stop this right now. He doesn't want to be around silly little girls."

Phinny tipped her head back to take in the bright blue sky. She might have been five or six years old, but the message had been very clear. If she wanted to make her mum happy, she needed to be a good girl for her new daddy.

Had Andrew not wanted to get involved with a single mum who still had ties to her baby daddy?

I just don't know.

But I did what mum wanted. I became Andrew's daughter and shut the door on my biological father.

Quickly, she finished collecting the eggs and brought them to the bunkhouse, keeping one for Tigger. When she returned the baskets to the barn and went to grab the gardening gloves and tools, she found the bin empty.

Well, that's odd. "Tigger? Come on, boy." Normally, he'd be at her side, dancing and prancing, waiting for his treat. "Where are you?" She headed over to the garden and found him watching her, alert, but not moving. "Tigger, what are you doing? Look what I've got for you." When she held it up for him, he glanced behind, hesitating, before finally dashing over and gently taking it from her hand. "You're such a good boy."

And then he trotted right back. It was only then that she noticed a red, floppy hat. Someone was hunched over, yanking out weeds. There wasn't much to pull, though, since she took care of it daily. "Hello?"

The older woman startled, clutching her chest. "Oh, you scared me." Pulling out her earbuds, she twisted around, eyes widening when she saw Phinny.

Now the coffee and the unlocked office made sense. "You must be Tina." She marched forward and stuck out her hand.

But the older woman got up, waved it off, and enfolded Phinny in her arms. "Look at you, all grown up."

Phinny pulled back. "Did I know you?"

"Yes, dear. I've worked for your dad for over twenty years." She smoothed the hair off Phinny's damp forehead. "You're a beauty."

"Oh." She'd only just rolled out of bed and brushed her teeth. Her hair was a fright. "I'm sorry. I don't remember you."

The woman had to be in her fifties, but her complexion was smooth. Only the graying hair and bags under her eyes betrayed her age. "You were such a wee little girl. I'm not surprised."

"You're Scottish?"

"Yes. The West Highlands. Your dad hired me because he thought having someone from across the pond would make you more comfortable."

He what? In that moment, after the revelation she'd just had, she felt so fragile, so…breakable. "That's unbearably kind." Tigger nudged her palm, giving it a lick, and she scratched him behind his ears.

"You sound surprised."

"I…" She was touched he'd do something so thoughtful. "I came here with a very clear idea of who Kurt was, and now I know I was entirely wrong. I thought he'd given up on me, that he'd replaced me with the hockey boys."

"What on earth gave you that impression?"

"There's not a single photograph of me in his house. Not a single…memento."

"Ah." She nodded with complete understanding. "Darling, I've just unlocked your dad's office this morning. Take some time alone and have a look around."

"Yes, I will." She hesitated. "I'm almost scared of what I'll find."

"It's only good, sweet girl. I can promise you that." She squeezed Phinny's hand. "I made coffee, so pour yourself a mug and go on in."

"I've got chores to do."

"You've done a wonderful job in my absence, and I thank you for that, but I'm back now. Go on."

"Are you sure?" But even as she said it, she felt the pull, the need to get into that office.

"Positive."

As Phinny started back to the house, Tina called, "I've turned on his computer, so I could catch up on some things for him. Open up his email account, dear. There's a folder with your name, and while he might give me the stink-eye for doing this, I think it's time you got the answers you're looking for."

Chapter Fifteen

HER STOMACH WRENCHED. PART OF HER WANTED TO stay ignorant because she needed to keep her idea of her mum intact. Until the broken engagement, they'd never gone a day without talking to each other. Shopping, lunches, volunteering…*I was her mini me.*

But every day here on the ranch, she learned something that fractured, chipped, and distorted that idea. She feared stepping into the office would shatter it entirely.

But she had to do it. *I have to.*

In the kitchen, she poured herself coffee. Her hand shook as she stirred the sugar and cream. She had no idea what she might find, but as she made her way across the living room, she heard Declan on the phone in the business office. She wanted to ask him to come with her, but that wasn't the kind of relationship he wanted.

No, she had to do this alone.

Drawing a fortifying sip of her creamy coffee, she opened the door and was immediately hit with a familiar scent. One, she'd long forgotten.

It's my dad.

It was earthy, spicy, like an expensive, exotic tea, and it sent her back to childhood. To sitting on his lap while they looked at the big globe in the corner of the office. She remembered hiding her face in his neck when they'd go into town and people would want to chat, ask for his autograph, or take a picture with him.

He'd keep his hand firmly on her back, holding her close, making her feel safe.

Associating Kurt with comfort? It rocked her world. She blew out a tight breath and entered his private realm. His business office was all gleaming bookcases and fancy furniture. But this one…was homey. So homey, it had framed artwork hanging on the dark-paneled walls clearly made by a child.

It took a moment to make sense of what she was seeing, but the paintings were done…

By me.

What? He'd framed them?

Taking a closer look at one, she had a vague memory of sitting outside by the pool under a big umbrella. Up on her knees, she'd swirled a paintbrush in a glass jar. She'd watched as the paint slowly dissipated into the clear water, turning it pink.

Framed photographs covered the desk. Picking up one of her and her dad, she blinked back tears until she could see it clearly. But she couldn't.

Because her heart shattered.

Right then and there.

And it hurt worse than anything she'd ever experienced.

Tears streamed down her face, and she collapsed onto

his leather chair. It hurt worse than anything because now she knew he'd loved her.

Her presence in this room was so real, she swung the chair around half-expecting to find her art supplies still on the credenza. But, no, there wasn't a trace of them. Instead, she found a small dish filled with gray river stones.

It jarred loose another memory of looking down at her feet covered in cold, rushing water. The smooth, slippery rocks she stood on were gray, dark orange, black, and white. Her dad wasn't in the tiny slice of a memory, but he might've been fishing right nearby.

She couldn't believe he'd cherished his time with her enough to hold onto the river rocks she'd collected twenty-some years ago.

Next to the bowl, she picked up a slap bracelet. It plucked a chord in her chest, and the vibration went careening through her. Oh, this she remembered well. They'd entered a store. She could feel her little hand engulfed his big, calloused one. While he'd been talking to someone, Phinny had watched three girls with long blond hair standing in front of a display of brightly colored bracelets. Their mom kept saying, "Just one. You each get *one*."

The girls had slapped the bracelets onto their wrists, squealing when they did it to each other. Her dad had dropped to a crouch and asked if she wanted one. She hadn't particularly. That funny feeling in her chest was because she'd wanted to be part of the trio. She'd been an only child. Oh, man, she'd forgotten just how acutely she'd longed for a sibling, a companion.

So, she'd said, "Yes, please."

"Go ahead and choose one."

She'd joined the girls, but they'd ignored her, continuing to slap bracelets on each other's wrists and laugh. She'd chosen the bright red one with white hearts— but she'd only worn it a few times. She'd forgotten all about it.

But her dad hadn't.

Hang on a second. If he'd cared so much about her that he'd saved everything, then why the hell had he let her go so easily? So what if she'd thrown a tantrum that summer? Why hadn't he come to see her? *Something's not adding up.*

Tina had told her to check his email account, that she'd get her answers there. Quickly, she turned the chair back around and jostled the mouse. As the screen came to life, she noticed pressed flowers under the glass that protected the desk. She couldn't help the smile that burst from her heart.

"Let's go pick flowers."

Holding hands, she and her dad had tromped through fields of wildflowers, picking a few and sticking them in a glass on the kitchen table. Once, she'd been eating, and she'd noticed a little black bug crawling on a petal. She'd flipped out. Screaming, begging her dad to kill it.

Instead, he'd let the beetle crawl over his finger. It waddled like someone late for work on High Street, dodging in and out of pedestrian traffic. She'd calmed down, laughed, and asked if she could hold it.

Wow. The block of ice in the shape of Kurt melted, and affection flooded her.

He was a good man.

A really good man.

"Hey." Declan leaned into the room.

From the way she jolted, he probably thought he'd

caught her doing something bad. "Tina left it open for me. She told me to come in here."

"I know. I talked to her." He quickly scanned the room, his eyes widening when he saw the paintings on the wall and the photos on the desk. "I just wanted to make sure you're okay. I'll leave you to it." Just like that, he was gone.

"I'm not." Her heart thundered. *Please come back. Do this with me.*

A second passed, two, three…and then he reappeared in the doorway. He watched her with concern.

She didn't want to freak him out with her messy emotions, but she needed his strength and comfort now more than she'd ever need another favor. "Will you stay with me?"

"Yeah, of course." He walked right up the desk, lingering as if waiting to see where she wanted him.

"Bring a chair over." She clicked on the email icon. "Tina wants me to look at a folder he kept."

He couldn't fit his long legs between the chair and the desk, so he angled it.

Let me just sit on your lap. "We should switch seats. My legs are shorter." And then maybe in the exchange, she could accidentally fall onto him, and he'd have no choice but to hug her.

He waved the idea away. "What's in it?"

"I don't know. We're about to find out." With her brain revving, it was hard to scroll through the list. Scanning alphabetically, she didn't see her name.

Declan pointed. "There."

My Phinny. She drew in a sharp breath. A tremor rocked through her body at the sweet endearment. She opened the folder.

It contained one single email.

From her mum.

He started to get up. "I'll let you read this alone."

She grabbed his arm. "No, please. Don't leave me." She didn't care anymore about being a hot mess. She just needed him.

"Hey, it's okay. I'm right here." And then he stood, giving her a chin nod. *Get up.*

He took her seat, cupped her hips, and guided her ass right onto his lap. *Oh, this man.*

He sees me.

He gets me.

And he's okay with everything about me.

And it gave her the courage to read her mum's letter.

You're being selfish. Can't you see that? I know you mean well but can't you see the cost of these visits to her? She's inconsolable knowing she has to leave her home and her mummy to fly five thousand miles just to stay on that godforsaken ranch where there's nothing to do and no familiar faces. She's had enough upheaval in her life, moving from Boston to Wyoming to London. Children crave routine. They need stability in order to thrive.

She doesn't want to fish and hike and all those dirty boy things that push her so completely out of her element. By insisting on your custodial rights, you're making her miss out on what every child truly wants and deserves: a family. Andrew and I can give her that. Please, Kurt, think about the future. The older she gets, the more settled she'll become in her activities. She'll want to go on holiday with her friends, and she'll grow to resent having to visit a father who lives across the world that she only sees once or twice a year.

Do you really want her to spend one holiday with you, and the next with us? In the end, I truly believe this will ruin our precious little girl, and I beg you to let her go so I can give her the kind of healthy, stable home life that will turn her into the good, strong woman I know you want her to be.

If you truly love her, you'll give her the home and the stability she deserves.

Phinny couldn't move. She could barely get her lungs to pull in a breath.

Long after reading her mum's letter, she remained still. If not for the warmth of Declan's body, she might shatter like glass on a hot stove. Her spine was so rigid, it would snap if she shifted. Emotion boiled inside her body, foam rising, ready to spill over.

And then he slid his arms through hers, wrapped them around her waist and set his chin on her shoulder. "It's okay. You can break all over me."

It wasn't the words as much as the tone. For this big, gruff man to use that gentle voice, a tone that said, *I can take whatever you can't carry*, it just undid her.

A sob burst free, and then she was crying. Drawing her knees up, she turned in the circle of his arms, setting her hands on his shoulders and her cheek on his chest. A world of hurt engulfed her, and he held her, one hand slowly, lightly stroking her back. He didn't shush her, didn't tense up. He just let her fall to pieces.

But through the sorrow rose two overwhelming emotions. She swiped the tears off her face. "He's gone."

"Yeah, he is."

She sat up. "No, I mean, he's *gone*. And I'll never know him."

One hand cupped her ass to keep her from falling, and the other rested on the side of her thigh.

"My dad was a good man." She gestured around the room. "He loved me. He wanted me. And I pushed him away."

He tipped her chin. "Nah. You were just a kid. Your mom did it." He held her gaze, not betraying a hint of emotion. Just fact.

She had to finally accept the truth about the mother she'd loved and trusted. "*She's* the narcissist. Not Kurt."

"Well, I obviously don't know her, but I don't think she is."

She waited, desperate for him to make sense of her mum's selfish actions.

"I'm not a parent, so I don't know, but I went out with a single mom once, and her biggest issue was sharing her kids with her ex. When she didn't have them for Christmas, she was devastated."

Her mind was too cloudy to fully grasp what he was saying. "Yes, I understand that, but to keep me from my dad. To ask him to walk away. God, I needed him. Didn't she understand my self-esteem hinged on believing my father didn't want me? Didn't love me?"

"It seems like she thought you were young enough that you'd get what you needed from Andrew. Like I said, I don't know your mom, and I'm in no way justifying her actions, but in trying to understand where she was coming from…she was a single mom, she'd met someone wanted to make a family with, and she didn't want to share you with someone who lived so far away. It might've been different if Kurt had lived in the same neighborhood."

"Honestly, I can't even be angry with her right now

because I'm just so devastated that I missed out on knowing him. All my life I waited for him to reach out to me. To send a card, a letter, anything that said he missed me. Wanted me. But I'm an adult now, and I wished I'd made the effort. I hate myself for not doing that." She got off his lap and wandered to the window.

Heart saturated with grief and loss, she crossed her arms over her chest. "And now, I'll never have the chance."

Declan's coaching session had run a little long, so when he looked for Phinny and didn't see her in the stands, he got worried and pulled out his phone. As he typed out a text, kids skated by, and coaches barked instructions. Now that he'd stopped moving, the cold hit his cheeks and fingers.

Declan: **Where did you go?**

"I'm right here." She stood at the side of the rink with a smile bright enough to melt the ice. "You ready to go?"

Unreasonably happy to see her, he skated to the wall. "Yeah. Sorry it went so long."

"Are you kidding me? I asked if I could come with you for a reason."

The tip of her nose was red, and he wanted to kiss her until she warmed up all over. "Because you're dying to get out here and skate?" He always wanted to touch her.

"Uh, no. Because you're the best one out there."

"Not even close. There are six pros on the ice right now. That guy I just coached? He was the lead scorer last season."

"I don't care about stats. Take it from someone who knows nothing about hockey, you're the hottest guy out there."

"*Oh*. We're talking about those kind of stats."

"Right. The ones that matter. Cutest butt, broadest shoulders. If there was a Stanley Cup for the sexiest skater and most confident player, you'd be drinking from it right now."

He grinned. "Huh. I should talk to someone about that. See what I can do." Grabbing her hands, he brought them to his mouth and blew on them. "I think it's time."

"Time for what?"

"For you to get out on the ice. Hard for you to judge without having skated before."

"Oh, no, no. I'm not…there are clinics going on." She tried to yank her hands out of his grasp. "Also, the festival's tomorrow, and I want to help Tina—"

"She doesn't need our help." He tightened his hold. "She's been running it for twenty years, and she's got all the help she needs." Holding her hand in a firm grip, he skated off the ice. "Come on. This'll be fun."

"Uh, no. It'll be a shitshow."

Hearing that word in her posh British accent was adorable. He held her hand while he walked her over to the rental desk. "You've been hanging around the hands too much."

"What does that mean?"

"Have you ever used the word shitshow before?"

She laughed. "No, but what a great word."

Once there, he looked down at her feet. "Kelly, can we get size…?"

Phinny wrenched her hand free. "That's okay. Seriously, the kids are still working. No skates for me."

Kelly—Jaime's cousin who was paying her own way through college by taking odd jobs—set her arms on the counter and hiked herself over it to get a look at Phinny's feet. "Size seven?"

"How did you know?" Phinny asked.

Her green eyes glittered with mischief. "Because handing out skates is what I do for a living. Be right back."

Phinny glanced up at him. "This is a really bad idea."

"Why?"

"Because I'll land on my butt."

"I'm fairly invested in that butt, and I would never let anything happen to it."

Desire flared in her eyes. *Good.* He didn't want to skirt around the truth anymore. No more games.

"No?" She seemed to search his eyes, looking for a conversation he wouldn't have at an ice skating rink.

"If I promise to protect your ass, will you give it a try? I won't let you get hurt."

A slow smile bloomed across her features. "I believe you." Those luscious lips curved up into a smile drew him inexorably to the softness of her mouth—

Skates clunked on the counter. "Here you go." The laughter in Kelly's voice told him she knew exactly what she'd just interrupted. "Have fun."

"Thanks." He tapped the counter. "Hey, how's it going with Ezra?"

That killed her smile. "It's not. It's not going anywhere. We broke up because he's a lying, cheating, horndog asshole. I hate hockey players."

"I'm sorry to hear that." He could see the pain etched into the lines around her eyes. "And I'm sorry he wasn't man enough to break up with you so he could pursue his other interests."

"And by *him* pursing other interests, did you mean his penis?"

"They're one and the same." He leaned toward her. "But just so you know, it's not about hockey players. I've played all my life, and I've never cheated. It's a character issue."

Kelly grew serious. "How am I supposed to know if a guy's going to cheat?"

"You can't always know, but you've got to give a guy a fighting chance. What's the good in painting everyone with the same brush?"

Kelly's shoulders relaxed. "Yeah, you're right. Now get out of here before I tell you all my sad stories."

Just as he turned to leave, Phinny said, "I know you don't know me, but can I tell you what my friends and I used to say to each other?"

"Sure." Kelly sounded wary.

"Instead of becoming bitter, be fabulous."

"I don't feel all that fabulous," Kelly said.

"I'm sure, but after a breakup, we'd go shopping, get a new outfit, or change our hair or make-up, whatever it took to feel great about ourselves. It's hard to get there on your own, so make your friends a powerful posse of badassery."

Kelly cracked a grin. "Powerful posse of badassery. I like that. If I had the money, I'd get my hair done." She glanced at her fingernails. "Or a manicure."

"That's just what my friends used to do, but it's not about spending money. It's about doing something that makes you feel fierce."

"I'm totally going to do that. Thank you."

Declan held Phinny's hand as they headed to the bleachers. "I like that advice."

"It works, too. It doesn't stop you from being sad, but it helps you put one foot in front of the other until you've gotten over a break-up." They sat on a bench, so she could put on her skates. "How do you know her?" As she kicked off her sneakers, she tipped her head toward the counter.

"That's my friend's cousin. I've known her since she was a kid."

"Did you ever date her?"

"Kelly? No. She's Jaime's cousin."

"So what?"

He really didn't want to talk about this. "I don't date women in my circle."

She quit tying her laces to sit up and say, "Circle?"

"You know, sisters of friends or women I work with." He wanted to be on the ice with her. Well, really, he wanted an excuse to hold her hand.

"What does that even mean? Isn't that how we find people to date? From the people in our world?"

"Not me."

She slid her foot into the other skate. "So, basically, what you're saying is you don't date women you're going to bump into after you bang them."

"Something like that."

She peeked at him through a curtain of shiny, silky hair. "Doesn't that get old? Banging women you barely know?"

"Yeah, I guess it does." He wasn't a game player, and he wouldn't start now. But they did live under the same roof, and she had enough on her plate. She didn't need the awkwardness of having some guy want more from her than she wanted from him. Phinny was looking for fun. On the other hand, he didn't see the point in pretending. "To be fair…" Going for it, he looked right into her eyes. "That was before I met you." His stomach dropped like an elevator plunging several floors. "Before I knew the difference." Without waiting to see her reaction, he dropped to a knee and tied her laces.

Whatever. It had to be said. He couldn't hide it, and he'd just have to live with the fall-out. Whatever it was. Finished, he stood and reached for her hand.

When he pulled her up, she nearly crashed into his chest. "Hello."

He couldn't help laughing but that whiff of her sweet scent, her creamy, smooth complexion, and those luscious pink lips got his body humming. She didn't seem uncomfortable with his admission, so maybe it was all right. "Come on." He led her to the ice.

Clutching his hand, the other arm stretched out for balance, she wobbled.

"I'm pretty sure you think it's going to be much worse than it is." Stepping behind her, he angled her shoulders so she could see the youngest kids. "That group right there? They're six years old."

"Yes, languages and athletics come naturally to children."

As he stepped onto the ice, he held both her hands and skated backwards, towing her along. She watched her feet. "Look at me."

When her gaze swung up, he didn't see fear about skating. "I'm putting all my trust in you."

He saw a tender heart. And the protective man in him heard her real meaning and took it seriously. "I got you." *It scares the shit out of me, but I'm here. I'm in it.* Even if it only lasted the eight remaining days she was in town, he knew he had to be with her. "Look at you. You're doing great." Slowly, he led her around the rink.

She relaxed a little. "You like me."

"I do."

"I like you, too." She was shy, bold, fresh, and dirty all at once.

And he loved it. Loved everything about her.

She grew concerned. "The truth is…I've been lying to you."

He faltered. "What do you mean?"

"Well, I thought you only wanted a hookup, so I made up the idea of you doing me a favor so you wouldn't freak out. I didn't want to scare you away." She gazed unseeing over his shoulder. "It's just that I've had more…" She glanced around at the kids and coaches and then tugged on his hands, pulling him right up to her chest. "Fun with you than with anyone I've ever been with." She lowered her voice. "And with all my drama and messy emotions, I don't want you to think I'm a stage-five clinger."

"I can see where you're coming from. And if you were any other woman, you'd be right on the money. But it's you, and I don't think there's anything you could do to make me lose interest."

"Declan." Her eyes went all dreamy. "You're…" Blinking furiously, she shut her mouth. When she pulled her hands away to wipe under her eyes, she lost her balance, and her arms pinwheeled.

It looked like she might go down, so he caught her around the waist and hauled her up to him. "I'm here for your messy emotions, I'm here for your smile…I'm just here, okay?"

She nodded, her cheeks glowing dark pink.

Before he gave into his impulses and kissed her, he let her go. "Now, give it a try on your own."

Once again, she flailed, both arms flapping, and she nearly lost her balance.

And once again, he grabbed her. "You realize you're

269

letting fear get the best of you, right? You're scared of the ice, but you've got this. You're coordinated and athletic."

"How do you know that?"

"Because you've got awards for dressage."

"True, but I'm not sure my seat on a horse translates to standing upright on blades."

"It's all about confidence. You're so sure you're going to fall on your ass, you'll make it happen. Now, come on. You can do this."

"Maybe I just want to keep holding your hand. Did you ever think about that?"

He didn't even bother fighting the smile. "Fine." Instead of skating backwards, he pulled her arm through his.

They made it about two feet before she closed her eyes and inhaled. "Why do you always smell so good?"

"Uh, I shower daily?" He nudged her. "You might want to skate with your eyes open."

"It's not that. There's something about you. Maybe it's just all those pheromones."

"Pheromones?"

"You're very…masculine."

"Unless you want me to carry you off the ice like a caveman and fuck you in the Jeep, we'd better focus on skating." When her eyes flared with desire, he chuckled. "Okay, here's what we're going to do. Pretend your right foot's on a scooter. Now, use your left foot to scoot." He let go of her.

Forehead creased in concentration, she made a slow, deliberate attempt to follow his instructions. "Oh, my God. It's working." Awkwardly, she hitched forward. And then she did it again. She blessed him with one of those big, bright smiles. "You're very nice, you know."

"Less talking, more skating."

"No, I'm serious. You come off all gruff, like you can't be bothered with anything or anyone, but it's not true. You're very loyal. So loyal you dropped out of school to take care of Sam. You're so loyal to Kurt, you're willing to lose your job."

"Look at you. You're skating." He probably did come off gruff, but it was better than looking like a little boy whose crush just checked the Yes box in answer to whether she liked him. He didn't think he'd ever met anyone who made him feel as good about himself as Phinny. "You're doing great."

"Oh, please. I look like a dog scooching on grass." But she kept trying, pushing ahead. "It really was an amazing thing you did for Sam. I was talking to Tina this morning in the garden, and she said you had offers from NHL teams. You'd have been a number one draft pick. You gave up a lot to be there for him."

"He gave up a lot for me."

"She said a bunch of coaches offered to get him round-the-clock nurses so you could finish school and play for them, but you refused."

"Like I gave a shit about hockey or advanced economics when my grandpa was *dying*."

Phinny's feature went soft as melted butter. "You said it."

"Said what?"

"Grandpa. You didn't really call him Sam, did you?"

He shook his head. "Come on. Switch feet. Now, your left foot's on the scooter, and your right's doing the work of pushing you along."

"Calling him Sam gives you distance, so it doesn't hurt as much." She pointed two fingers at his eyes, then turned them to her own. "I see you." After a few attempts to push forward, she managed to even glide. "You're a good coach. You make things very clear."

"Declan, man." Steve LaRoue, one of the Renegades, came to a hard stop in front of them, shaving off a layer of ice. He grinned at Phinny and clapped Declan on the shoulder. "Do you have any time in the next few weeks? We've got our best players on left D and somehow, we still allow more zone entries on that side. Me and Charlie are already here, but our second stringers can come out whenever you have time to work with us."

"I already know what's wrong. Charlie needs a better pivot to get back on dumped pucks quicker. It'll buy you guys an extra half-second."

Steve grinned. "Yeah?"

"I watched you guys play this morning for the kids."

He gave him an approving nod. "So, can you fit us in?"

"Sure. The rink's closed this weekend for the Fourth of July, so how about next week?"

"I appreciate it, man. I'll get your digits from Jaime to confirm." Steve gave Phinny a nod before skating off. Her dazzling smile must've hit him between the horns because he tipped back, then nearly tripped over his own skates trying to turn around and get back to his group of kids.

She didn't even seem to notice. "Have you heard back from the general manager yet?"

"No, but they've already made their decision."

"Are you sure?"

"No." He still held out some hope they'd give him leniency in this situation. "But it's a critical time for coaching, and they're not even sending me tapes or including me in video conferences. They've shut me out."

"How do you feel about that?"

"I'm disappointed. But it's one of those things I can't control. I'm here. I'm committed to seeing this through." He shrugged. *It is what it is.*

"Well, if the Renegades' players are coming to you instead of their own coaches…it just seems like they might want to hire you." She gazed up at him. "Are all of Kurt's hockey boys as good as you?"

"Yes, but there's a reason. Most of the guys we hung out with fell away over the years. Broken bones, concussions…and it wasn't that they lost interest in what we were doing. It was because they couldn't keep up. Eventually, it was just the four of us, and we kept pushing ourselves, looking for bigger and more dangerous challenges." He smiled. "Good times."

"Those experiences…I imagine they made you closer than normal friendships. You must miss them so much. What if they all said they'd own the team? Would you do it then?"

He hadn't even contemplated that question since Booker had bailed on them, and it wouldn't make sense for Cole to quit while he was killing it. "Since it's not possible, I can't really answer that."

"Are you sure?" Phinny teased. "Because I saw that light in your eyes when I threw the idea out there."

"And here I thought I'd perfected the art of the blank expression."

"Oh, you did all right. Maybe I just pay more attention to you than most people."

"Yeah? Why's that?"

"Because I want to know more about you. I'm like a hamster, and you feed me these tiny, little pellets of information. I want more. I want the whole enchilada."

She pushed away from him. "In any event, it's time to go." She did the scooter-skate move until she stepped off the ice.

"Hey, you're just getting the hang of it." When they sat on the bench, he said, "What's the rush?"

Eyes sultry, she leaned in close, and her tongue peeked out to lick her bottom lip. He thought for sure she'd kiss him, but at the last second, she bypassed his mouth and whispered, "You know that caveman you were talking about?"

"Yeah?"

"I've got a favor to ask him."

Chapter Sixteen

Without windows and a roof, sex in the rink's parking lot wasn't possible, so Declan hauled ass home. But he wasn't going to make it. Not when she kept squeezing his thigh, sliding her hand between his legs, and licking his earlobe.

When she rubbed his cock, he jerked the wheel and pulled off the highway. *That's it.* He knew this dirt road. It went straight toward the mountain. Thank God for four-wheel drive and eleven inches of ground clearance. Out here, they'd be remote enough that no one would interrupt them.

Stopping under a canopy of quaking aspen, he unbuckled his seatbelt and reached for her. Without hesitation, she was in his arms, climbing over the gearshift and straddling him. Their mouths attached, their tongues explored, and their hands stroked, gripped, and squeezed.

He tried to unbutton her shirt, but he shook too badly. This hunger…it consumed him. He wanted all of her at once—his cock in her slick, tight channel, her tits filling his palms, and her tongue tangling with his.

He'd never felt this before, this imperative to fuse with someone. These emotions were too big to be contained in his body, and he felt like he was busting out of his skin.

She ripped his jeans open, her hand slipping under the waistband of his boxer briefs, and when she got a hold of his cock, he yanked his mouth away from hers and let out a shout. He'd never been so sensitive, so ready to come from just kissing and touching.

He closed his eyes—he didn't want to see her expression as he fell apart like this, as he struggled to breathe, his hips punching up as she stroked him. He tried to bat her hand away. "Stop."

"No." She reached into her big purse and pulled out a tiny silver tube of hand lotion. Squirting a dab onto her palm, she rubbed it all over him.

Shit. Fuck. "If you don't stop, I'm gonna come." That scent—it was hers. Sweet, fresh, lightly floral…a surge of desire barreled through him.

"Do it. I want you to come all over my hand. Let me watch." Using more lotion, she tightened her grip and then settled back, eyes hot with lust. Her shirt hung open, exposing the pink lace of her bra.

"Phinny."

Her tits jiggled and bounced as she jerked him off. "Yeah?"

"Fuck." His eyes rolled back in his head. Vaguely, he was aware of sunshine filtering through branches, the pine-scented air, and the creak of the leather seat as he shifted all over it, but his orgasm was gathering strength, threatening to tear him wide open, and he had no choice but to succumb. Every muscle in his body clenched down tightly before releasing in an explosive climax that had him shouting.

When he opened his eyes, he found her staring at the hot bursts of semen jetting out of him, and it was such a turn-on, her feminine hand holding him, her jaw slack, her chest rising and falling rapidly, that another wave rippled through him. Hips bucking, his head slammed back. "Jesus, Phinny."

With a gleam in her eyes, she let go. "That was the hottest thing I've ever seen."

Dead. He was dead. As he struggled to catch his breath, she reached into her big, black bag and pulled out a little container of tissue. She cleaned up her hand and his stomach, tossing the refuse on the floorboard.

And then, she gave him a seductive grin and finished unbuttoning her shirt. Shrugging it off, she threw it and her bra onto the passenger seat.

"There's more to this favor of yours?" He pretended to sound put-out.

"I mean…" She eyed his cock. "Only if you're up for it." As it hardened and lengthened, a greedy look filled her eyes. She shifted back to her seat and kicked off her sneakers. "I don't have a condom."

Shit. "Me neither."

She gave him a cautious look. "I haven't been with anybody in almost a year, and I'm on the pill. I'm…good."

"I haven't been with anybody since my physical in May. I'm good, too."

She bit her bottom lip, eyebrows lifting. *We're doing this?*

Need spiked through him. "Fuck, Phinny. I've never gone bare. Ever."

Reaching for the bar beneath his seat, he slid it back as far as it could go. Even though he'd just come, he knew once he got inside her, he wouldn't last. He wanted to control himself. Wanted to rein it in. For her, this was all just fun. It was exciting. For him…he was just so fucking into her. And he knew she'd never stay here. She'd never be happy living on a ranch in Wyoming. He knew that.

As he yanked down his jeans, she shed her shorts and panties. Sunlight turned her blond hair golden, and her blue eyes sparkled. *Look at her. She belongs in the world she grew up in.* Sure, she was pissed at her parents. Her mom, in particular. But she hadn't even been away from home a year. That wasn't long enough to fully detach. In Phinny's heart, she was a Crutchley. Without a doubt, she'd go back to that life.

He'd take what he could get. He wasn't a fool. He knew how lucky he was to have this time with her. But… when she left…

It would gut him.

Why the fuck was he thinking like that? It wasn't like him to go into something half-assed, expecting defeat. It would be stupid to hold back, certain she'd leave him, instead of trying to win her heart. Because…what if she stayed?

Imagine waking up to Phinny every day of my life.

Imagine living with that smile.

Imagine getting to be the one she turns to for…everything.

Fuck. Yes.

It was almost too good to be true.

He supposed the real test would be what she did with the ranch if she won. If she sold it, then yeah, she'd be on the next plane. If she didn't…maybe they'd have a chance.

Unbothered by heavy thoughts, she climbed onto his lap. The space was awkward, but he kept a grip on her thigh, so it wouldn't bang into the gear shift. Watching her raise up on her knees and sink slowly down on him might've been the hottest thing he'd ever seen in his life.

He stuttered out an exhalation because Jesus, she was hot, slick, and so tight his body exploded in chill bumps. Squeezing her ass cheek, he gave it a swat to make her move.

Grinning, she swayed her hips to get him all the way inside. She set her hands on the back of his seat and started rocking on him. Tight, slow motions, like she was enjoying the hell out of every slide of his cock inside her. "You feel so good."

Tell me about it. He had no words. He was mesmerized by her scent, her hair, the sexy rocking of her hips. Totally under her spell, his presence of mind got snatched away. When she grew restless, he knew she couldn't get enough traction in the tight space, so he cupped her ass and did the work for her. Lifting her, he slammed her down in rhythm with the thrust of his hips. He made sure to drag her over his pubic bone to give her that extra stimulation on her clit.

"God, Declan. I feel…"

"Yeah? What do you feel?"

"I just want you so much. So, so, so much."

"Me, too, my golden girl. Me, too."

Her eyes flared at the term of affection, and her fingers went into his hair. "I'm your golden girl."

"You shine so bright. Your eyes, your smile. It's like you've got sunshine inside your heart."

She looked like she might cry, but in a good way. The best way. "I can't believe…" But her mouth closed when he rocked her even harder and faster, and soon she was crying out, her back arching, her face turned up to the sky.

With her hands covering her breasts, fingers pinching her nipples, this magnificent woman was about to come all over his cock. And he was going to get her there. He needed to fuck her into a rip-roaring climax that scared the birds from the trees.

Her tits bounced in front of his face, and she made these strangled cries and guttural grunts, and it was all just so perfect. She was perfect.

"Grind on me. Use me."

It took her a few tries to catch her rhythm, but with every slam, she ground her clit on him. Her cries turned frantic.

"Yeah." He lost his ability to control the situation. "Fuck." He was too far gone, beyond reason, far past self-control, and he just kept working her on his cock.

She went rigid, her back arched, her tits on display to the forest, and then she writhed and twisted all over him. "*Declan.*" She shouted it, one hand shoving the hair out of her eyes.

His orgasm stole his breath, his thoughts, and his vision. It catapulted him into euphoria. Moments later, breathless, sated, he reentered the world and found her slumped against his chest, sighing contentedly.

And for the first time in his life, he knew true and total happiness.

The shuttle dropped them off at the fairgrounds. As she took it all in, Declan came up behind her, setting a hand on her hip. A shiver ran through her.

Is this real life? Declan Cadell's acting like my boyfriend.

She covered his hand with hers. God, she just liked him so much.

"What should we start with?" He said it quietly, and when she leaned back against him, his arm encircled her waist.

As long as she could be with him, she didn't care what they did. But he wanted an answer, so she had to make a decision. On one side, hundreds of vendors sold jewelry, art, soaps, and all kinds of crafts in a sea of white tents, and on the other, curls of smoke wafted from grills and the scent of cotton candy and hot dogs filled the air. She wanted to be everywhere at once.

"I wish I'd listened to you." He'd told her not to eat breakfast, but she'd gotten a whiff of Tina's homemade bread and she'd had to have a slice. Which had led to a second slice. And since she'd been listening to the woman's stories about her life on the ranch, she'd wound up eating a pile of scrambled eggs with salsa and cheddar cheese. "I've never had anything as good as Tina's food."

"That's because everything is grown on the property. But we can come back. Let's walk around first."

"Okay." Right then, someone passed by with a churro, and the smell of fried, sugary dough made her mouth water.

He cracked a grin. "How about we grab some sustenance for our walk? We can share one of those."

"Yes." She towed him over to the kiosk. "God, it smells good." She reached into her purse for her wallet, but he stepped in front of her and handed over a ten-dollar bill.

She still couldn't believe they were together. What in the world did this incredibly competent, successful, elite athlete see in her, a woman who'd lived a life of such privilege she had a total of about five basic life skills?

There was just something about him. Everywhere they want, people stared. And it wasn't just his hard, round ass in those worn jeans or his muscular physique accentuated so beautifully in a white T-shirt. It was his confidence. The vibe he gave off that he didn't need anybody or anything. He was impenetrable.

Except to me.

He lets me in.

It was crazy to think when she'd first arrived, she couldn't wait to get out of here. Three weeks ago, she'd been working in a diner and living in Kentish Town. Lonely, broke, and scared out of her mind. She hadn't seen a path forward.

And now? She had one week left in Calamity, and she never wanted to leave.

Not that she could stay. Other than a massive crush on a gorgeous hockey player, she had nothing here. While she'd like to preserve her dad's legacy, she was in no position to run a cattle ranch.

"Here you go." Declan handed her the churro.

She bit into the crunchy pastry, the sugar and fried flour invading all her senses. "It's delicious. Absolutely smashing." She lifted it to him, but he shook his head. She rubbed his belly. "No, you're right. You must absolutely hold off on that dad bod until you've got six kids." She laughed at his horrified expression. "What? Let me guess, you're never getting married and you're not having kids?"

"No, I never said that."

"You should've seen your expression."

"I'm not against having a family." He took her hand as they headed down a long aisle of vendor tables. "I never dated anyone I wanted to see more than once or twice. It just wasn't something I ever thought about."

"I know exactly what you mean. When Cameron proposed, it shouldn't have come as a surprise. But the idea of being married, having babies…it was just so…" She let her imagination go there, to a kitchen table surrounded by her ex and their two well-groomed children. She shuddered. "I told him I wasn't ready, that I hadn't accomplished anything yet." But now that she was with Declan, she knew it was a lie. "But I just didn't want to marry *him*. The truth is, I don't have a burning need to be wildly successful. I never have." And for some reason she didn't understand, she could only see that here, away from home.

"What's your burning need?"

She gazed up at him, the answer so clear it popped out. "To believe in myself."

"And what needs to happen for you to get there?"

"Ha. You're not going to like my answer."

"Try me." He picked off the top of her churro and popped it into his mouth.

"Fine." The idea was only just forming, but it was so real and true, it flooded her with affection for him. "Just being with you. That's it right there. You make me feel good about myself." The moment the words came out, she could see they were misshapen. "No, that's not right. You make me see myself in a new light. It's not like my parents tell me I'm dumb or useless. It's more that they don't expect anything of me. And you…you seem to like me just for who I am. It's almost like I…I don't know…*delight* you." She stuttered out a laugh as if it would give her cover from exposing herself to him like that. But he didn't get weird about it. Which made her feel like she had it right. She really did delight him. "And I guess it gives me room to…well, believe in myself."

"I like that." His voice got tight. "A lot."

"Yeah, well, it's true." Each booth they passed had impressive art, jewelry, textiles…even large metal sculptures. "Are all these local artists?"

"No. They come from all over the world."

"Really? But Calamity's such a small town."

"Right, but a lot of celebrities and billionaires live here. Not just because of the world-class skiing and the Tetons, but because they're left alone."

"Oh, look. Homemade perfumes and lotions." She made a beeline for the stunning antique atomizers. "What do you have here?" she asked the artisan.

The woman turned around, her cheeks flushed from the heat. "Hello." With her sleek mahogany hair and regal bearing, she was gorgeous and sophisticated. She pulled a sample from a basket. "This is Belle Starr. It's created from the lyantha flower." Her accent seemed a mix of French and English. "Would you like to try it?"

"I'd love to. Thank you." Spritzing her wrist, Phinny inhaled. "I've never smelled anything so wonderful in my life." Bins of gorgeously wrapped bars of soap, glass jars of lotion, and various other toiletries lined both sides of the tent. "I want one of everything."

"I'm so happy to hear that. Thank you."

"Do you live here in town?" Phinny asked.

"Yes, I do."

"You know, I sell a few locally-grown products at a farm stand I run, and if you'd like, I'd be happy to give your products some shelf space. We'd split the profits. I'm only in town one more week, but if you make up some business cards to go with it, it might give you some additional exposure. Honestly, you're really onto something here. It's the loveliest scent ever."

Before the woman could answer, an extremely well-built man entered from a flap at the back of the tent. He had a baby strapped to his broad chest and a little girl snugged to his hip. "Makes sense the loveliest woman would create the loveliest scent." He kissed the woman's cheek. Then, he noticed Declan, and that rugged face cracked into a grin. "Heard you were in town. What kind of trouble you getting' into these days?"

"Not nearly enough."

"Same, man. Same. But that's what happens when you take on the ball and chain." He gave his wife an adoring look.

"He was the last of four brothers to get married," the parfumier said. "He only put a ring on my finger because he didn't want to be left out." She held up her diamond.

Grinning, the man stuck out his hand. "Brodie Bowie, and this is my bride, Rosie."

"So nice to meet you both. I'm Seraphina Crutchley, but please call me Phinny." A bell rang in the center of her chest. For the first time in her life, her last name didn't sound right. Worse, it didn't *feel* right.

She loved the man who'd raised her. She did. *But Kurt's my dad.*

And I'm a Grevers.

"Good to meet you." Brodie grew solemn. "I'm sorry for your loss. Kurt was a good man."

"Thank you," she said. "Did you know him well?"

"I didn't, no. But he was one of the investors for Owl Hoot. It's the original Calamity settlement that my brothers and I turned into a living museum. He had a great respect for history."

"So, I'm learning. I'm going to the Reliquary Museum to see what they've got on the Grevers family."

The rightness of her impromptu decision made her break into a smile. "I've got a lot to learn about my family."

"You are?" Declan seemed happily surprised.

She nodded, and when their gazes locked it was like sunshine pouring down on her, warming her all the way down to her bones.

The daughter on Brodie's hip cupped her little hand and whispered in his ear. "All right, I promised my little princess one of those." He zeroed in on Phinny's churro.

"Never thought I'd see the day, man," Declan said with a smile. "The Bowie brothers, married with kids."

"Please, Daddy?" His little girl kissed his cheek. "I'm so hungry."

"What can I tell you?" Brodie wore a huge grin. "It's torture. Pure torture."

Rosie playfully swatted him. "Go feed your child before she starves to death."

Brodie started out of the tent. "Save yourself," he called over his shoulder. "Stay single."

Rosie laughed, then turned back to them. "I would love to sell some of my products at your farm stand. Thank you for the offer." After they exchanged contact information, another group entered the tent. "Please excuse me." She headed off to greet them.

"They're an adorable family." Phinny sniffed a bar of soap.

"You like it?"

"I love it." But she couldn't afford it. "Let's see what else I can stock in my budding little store." She looped her finger through his belt buckle and dragged him out of the tent. "This is so much fun." The next stall over sold gorgeously crafted furniture. "Are you kidding me?" She ran a hand across the glossy finish. Intricate inlaid designs told stories. "I've never seen anything like it."

Behind a card table stood a tall, white-haired older gentleman in threadbare jeans and boots so worn they had a hole in the toe. Phinny waited for him to finish his transaction with an older couple. Once they left the tent, he pressed a red Sold sticker to a dresser.

"Your work is stunning."

The man gave her grunt of acknowledgment.

He seemed rude, but he might just be shy. "Do you sell in stores?"

"Nope."

Okay, so, not shy then. Just crotchety. Well, money was obviously tight for him. It was hard to earn a living as a creator, but if there was one thing Phinny was good at, it was her people skills. Maybe she could help him make some connections. "Have you tried?"

Instead of answering, he wove through the crush of furniture and headed out the flap at the back of the tent.

She glanced around. "He's trying to move too much product in one day." She checked to see if Declan agreed. "Plus, with that attitude, he'd be better off in his garage making furniture and letting someone else sell for him."

"Maybe he doesn't care if he sells."

"He wouldn't be here if he didn't need the money."

The white flap lifted, and the man backed into the booth hauling a credenza. His muscles strained, and the T-shirt pulled tight across his shoulders. Declan raced forward. "Let me help you with that."

But the man shook his head and carried the table to the front.

Phinny took in the beautifully depicted scene of a cabin in the mountains, a man sitting around a campfire, and the massive forest surrounding him. "This is astonishing craftsmanship. You're so talented." She smiled. "Hello, I'm Phinny, and this is Declan."

"Lachlan." He disappeared back through the flap.

She smoothed a hand across an exquisite depiction of an elk crossing a river. "His work is too good to go unnoticed, and he clearly can't sell it himself. We should help him."

"Not sure how. We don't have connections in the furniture world. Besides, you're only here another week."

"True, but he obviously needs income. I should ask Glori to come have a look at this stuff. Or…" She gazed up at him. "What if we put together a pop-up store for him in town?"

"And by we, you mean you?"

"I'm not a businesswoman by any means, but I think I can pull together a venue, make some flyers, and at least try to get him some customers." For the first time in days, she thought of the Lumley Foundation. They hadn't gotten back to her, and she didn't know what that meant. Were they so horrified by her suggestion that they'd dismissed it outright?

Her future might be up in the air, but she knew she'd rather be running the auction than serving pie and mash in the diner. *Why did I think it was a good idea to study the Classics?*

"Hey." Declan touched her arm. "What're you thinking?"

"That I want people to discover Lachlan's work. I'm positive if we can just get some exposure, all the fancy shops will ask to stock his furniture. They just need to know it exists."

"So, pitch it to him."

"Yeah?" She got up on her toes and kissed his cheek.

"What was that for?"

Because I'm falling in love with you. But she'd never tell him. It wasn't like that with them. Not when she was leaving in a week. So, she told him another, equally important truth.

"For believing in me." And that gave her the confidence to believe in herself.

The very next morning, Declan drove her into town so she could meet with the Cooters. On her lap, she had a tin of cookies she and Tina had baked because Phinny hadn't wanted to just show up and ask for something. She wanted to give, too.

Surely, one of the seniors would know a realtor or property owner who'd help secure an empty store willing to rent out its space for the holiday weekend.

But just as he found a parking spot not far from the diner, her mum called. "Do you mind if I take this? I'll keep it short, but she's been ringing for a few days, and I've been too angry to speak to her."

"What's different now?"

Good question. "I guess having this project has taken my mind off her betrayal."

"Sure." He cut the engine and pulled his phone out of the cup holder. "Go ahead."

She accepted the video-call. "Hey, Mum."

"Where on earth have you been? I've been trying to…" Her mum's expression flattened. "Oh, dear."

"What? What's the matter?" Without even thinking, she quickly smoothed down her hair.

"Have you just woken up?" her mum asked. "Isn't it

eleven in the morning there?"

"It is, and no, I've been up for hours. I've actually been quite busy."

"Doing what?"

Her mum's challenging tone had Declan looking over.

"Every day, I'm getting more products to sell at the farm stand. People are actually approaching me. Plus, we've got the festival at the ranch tomorrow, and I'm helping a talented furniture maker get some traction in the area."

"How are you helping him?" Her mum sounded skeptical.

While it was a fair question, it still hurt. "I'm organizing a pop-up store for him. In fact, I'm in town right now looking for a space. It's got to be huge because the man's got quite an inventory. He's great at making furniture but not so good at selling it." Anticipation rushed through her. She hoped she could pull this off. She would love to set Lachlan up for the rest of his life, so he no longer had to live hand-to-mouth.

Declan reached for her thigh and gave it a squeeze. The simple touch reminded her not to let her mum steal her confidence. "We're just parking now, so I'll speak to you later. I just didn't want you to worry about me."

"Darling…" Her mum let out an exasperated huff.

"What?"

"I'm worried about you." Her mum waved her hand as if she had no words to describe the state of her daughter's appearance.

In the box at the top of the screen, Phinny took in her wild hair. It wasn't even the wind so much as the fact that she hadn't blown it out in…well, she couldn't remember when.

"I suppose it's too late to ship you hair products."

Was it really *that* bad?

"How about I send you to Los Angeles for a spa weekend? You can get a facial and a manicure. We can get some moisture into that hair."

"I don't have time to go to a spa, and my hair's not dry. I just haven't straightened it."

"Well, at least put on some mascara. Do you want me to put some money in your account so you can buy lipstick?"

"I asked you for a loan to get me through this month so I could *eat*, and you refused. But now, when you see I'm not wearing make-up, you want to send me to a spa? Do you hear the absurdity of that?"

"Even at the diner, you had enough pride to put your best foot forward. Now, in that godforsaken Cowtown, you've let yourself go. You've completely given up. I blame Kurt. What he's put you through is humiliating. And if the land weren't worth so much, I'd tell you to walk away. Your pride, your self-esteem, is worth more than that."

"You're worried about my self-esteem?" *Uh oh.* For days now, Phinny had suppressed her anger not only because she'd been busy, but because she'd been happy. She had the rest of her life to be in London and angry with her parents. She'd wanted to preserve her time in this lovely bubble. But her mum had uncorked her, and it was on. "Did my confidence concern you when you let me believe my entire life that my own father didn't want me? Was my confidence your priority when you trained me to be a good girl so Andrew would love me? Because if you really give it some thought, those are serious self-esteem killers right there."

"I don't know what you're going on about. We lived

five thousand miles away, and Kurt's priority was hockey. As for Andrew, of course I wanted you to be a good girl. That's what parents do. We raise our children to be well-behaved."

"Bullshit." The word shot out of her mouth, and her mum recoiled as if she'd been slapped. Phinny didn't care. "Stop it. Stop lying to me. You told me my father couldn't be bothered with his family, that he was so caught up in his fame and glory as a hockey player that he had no time for us. But it's not true."

"Oh, really? And you know this because you've been there for three weeks and talked to people who see him as some sort of local hero because of his celebrity? Well, let me tell you something. I was his wife. The mother of his child."

She shouldn't have this conversation parked at the curb in front of a yoga studio and a museum, but she couldn't stop. "Guess what, Mum? I saw the last email you sent him. He kept it." If she'd had one shred of faith left in her mum, one ounce of hope that the letter had been taken out of context, her mum's stricken expression scorched it to ashes.

They'd been so close all her life—well, until her parents had cut her off—that she didn't want to see her mum in this new light. Her chest tightened, and she blinked back tears. "My dad loved me. He wanted me. You should see his office. It's practically a shrine to his only child. And I can't forgive you for convincing *him* to let me go and *me* that he wasn't a good man. I love Andrew, and I appreciate the way he made me feel like a daughter, but can you imagine how it made me feel to think my own father didn't want me?" No amount of blinking could hold back the tears that spilled onto her cheeks. "But he did. He wanted me. He kept my slap bracelet." She went hot and itchy. "He kept my drawings and my river stones." The rumbling beneath her skin gave way to a total collapse of her heart. Sorrow gushed out, spreading everywhere, making her body heavy with it. "Mummy, how could you do such a cruel thing?"

"I was trying to give you a family. A real father. And I did exactly that." Her mum's voice was shaky. "You don't know what it was like. He was gone from September through April. That's eight months out of the year. And in the four months he wasn't playing, he was off at meetings and watching tape and working out. *He* was always the priority. Always. You and I never were. And after I moved to England, he had even less time with us."

"Do you hear yourself? *You* moved to England. *You're* the reason he had less time with us."

"I knew no one in the States. I was a single mother—"

"God, Mum, stop. I know the whole story. I know he was willing to give up hockey for you."

Her mum's features froze.

"He did everything he could to make you happy." She pulled in a shaky breath. "Even letting me go. What you did to us—"

"Oh, I see. Now you're on his side? The two of you are ganging up against me?"

"He's dead, Mum. The threat's gone. You stole my chance to know my own father." Her breath hitched. It hurt too much. And then Declan was there, prying open her fist, clasping their fingers, and kissing the back of her hand. Knowing he was there gave her the courage to finish the conversation. "Mum, I know what you did. I know all of it now."

Chapter Seventeen

Fear gripped her mum's features.

"You and Andrew would never have gone to Disneyland on your own. You certainly wouldn't have honeymooned there. You manipulated the situation so I would throw a fit and refuse to go visit my father."

Even while the color drained from her face, her mum still held her chin up. "You think I'm evil. You think I had some selfish, ulterior motive. But I know what it's like to have a father not want to know me. I know what it's like to ride a bike past his house and see his other children playing on the lawn. That's a pain I wanted to spare you. I didn't want you to go through life waiting for Kurt to call, for a birthday present that never came. I didn't want you to know what it felt like to have two different bedrooms, to leave your friends behind so you could spend the holiday with a father you barely knew and a stepmother who didn't want you around."

Sorrow bled into her anger, diluting it. For the first time, Phinny understood why her mum had merged them completely into Andrew's family. Why she'd barely known her maternal grandparents.

"You can hate me all you want, but Kurt was never going to give you the kind of family Andrew did. If you'd kept up those summers with him, you'd have spent more time with a nanny than your own father. I did what I had to do because you were my world. I wanted your happiness."

"I believe you were doing what you thought was best for me, and I appreciate the family you gave me. But I can't forgive you for all the years I believed my dad didn't love me. I can't forgive you for it because he's gone now, and I'll never have the chance to know him. Now, I have to go. I have work to do."

"Well, wait a moment before you ring off. I'm calling about the auction." Her mum looked anxious and flustered. "We've got our first meeting about the ball this Wednesday. Would you like me to speak with Helena about hiring you?"

Oh, now she offered to help? "I wish you'd done it when I'd asked you, but now I don't want your help."

"Why? Have you heard from her?"

An idea sprang to life. "No, but my life doesn't hinge on that job anymore." The sun burned the top of her thigh, and as utterly frightening as it was to have such big thoughts, nothing had ever felt more right.

"What does that mean?"

"It means I've got an idea for a business." Saying the words out loud had her pulse racing.

"What business?"

"I'm going to start a store selling locally-sourced products."

"In Kentish Town?" Her mum appeared completely baffled.

"No, in Calamity."

"You can't stay in Calamity. You must come back here. To London. To your family."

Phinny didn't dare look at Declan. She wasn't ready to see his reaction, to know if he liked the idea of her staying or was freaking out about his summer fling latching onto him like a barnacle. "I can do whatever I want. And that includes going into town without make-up and straightening my hair. I'm free here, Mum. I don't have to dance around to make sure my new daddy loves me. It's quite liberating." With her thumb, she disconnected. She'd never spoken to her mum like that. And in the ten months she'd been waiting tables, wondering what path to take next, she'd never once considered launching a business.

As people walked by and windchimes from the yoga studio tinkled, Phinny sat still, letting it all sink in.

She'd told her mother off.

She'd announced her intentions of starting a business.

Whoa. She let out a shaky breath. Slowly, her body cooled down.

"You okay?" That voice. Rough and deep and so full of concern.

She looked down at their joined hands. "Honestly? It feels like a wild roller coaster ride just came to a jolting stop."

"You sure told her what's-what." His teasing tone made her smile.

"I sure did." She unbuckled and swung her jittery legs out of the Jeep.

Meeting her on the sidewalk, he pointed to a funky-looking building next to the yoga studio. "That's the Reliquary Museum."

Covered in street and animal crossing signs, the building was small, the glass so old it seemed to be melting. *So, this is it.* "It's not what I expected at all. It's very cool. They've got wonky hours, so I called and talked to the curator. She's sending someone to meet me here next Monday after the festival."

He caught her hand and towed her into the alley. Sandwiched between two old brick buildings, the air was cooler, and he pushed her up against the wall.

She threaded her hands through his silky hair. "Hi." His cock pressed against her stomach. "You seem happy to see me."

"I'm always happy to see you." He thumbed her bottom lip. "I've seen this mouth wrapped around my cock, remember?"

"Declan." She glanced in either direction to make sure no one was around. "Tell me more."

"Listening to you talk to your mom…"

"Made you hot?"

"Made me like you even more."

"Even more? How much did you like me before?"

"A whole fuck of a lot. After everything you've found out these past three weeks, you could've gone off on her. You could've ripped her a new asshole. But you didn't. You spoke your truth, but you didn't try to hurt her. You're a good person, Seraphina Crutchley. And I'm so damn glad you're going to stay here."

Relief nearly took out her knees. "I wasn't sure what you'd think."

"If there's one thing you can be sure of, it's that I want to be with you." He brushed the hair off her shoulders.

"But what…" Her pulse spiked, and her palms went clammy. "Forgetting about the competition, what would that look like?" The possibility of a real relationship with him was as thrilling as it was terrifying.

"I'd take my share of the Renegades, and you'd open that business."

"The one I told my mum about?"

"Yeah, it's a great idea. Weren't you serious?"

"I am. I think it's brilliant, but I'm not a businesswoman."

"You'd have help. You know that, right? Glori, the Cooters…me. But even if you decide not to do it, I still want you. I want us." He kissed her, and she gave him everything he asked for. Her mouth, her tongue, her fingers fisting in his hair. She hitched up a leg, and he caught it under her thigh. Grinding against him, she gave him everything.

Both of them breathing harshly, she pulled her mouth away. She played with the hair at the back of his neck, and he chased her mouth. But she didn't give it to him. "Declan, I have another favor to ask."

"Anything." His hand squeezed her ass.

"I want us, too. But if we do this, if I stay, you can't… Declan, don't break my heart."

Don't break my heart.

Are you fucking kidding me?

She had no idea how bad he had it for her. No idea. He'd have to work on that. Show her, tell her, whatever it took for her to understand how much he lo—

He choked on his ice water. The Cooter next to him patted his back. "You okay there, son?"

He could only nod and snatch a napkin out of the dispenser to wipe his chin. When he finished, he found a little girl standing on the banquette of her family's booth, staring at him. He could almost hear her thoughts. *You want her to stick around? Then, tell her how you feel.*

Man up.

He'd never said those three words to anyone in his life. He'd loved Sam. He'd loved Kurt. But he'd never told either of them. He'd always figured his actions spoke for him.

Anxiety wound him up, and he tossed the napkin onto the table. Unfinished pie, a half-eaten sandwich, cups of coffee gone cold…the people who'd been sitting here had left, drawn to Phinny. She'd managed to charm an entire community of seniors in the diner.

But he was still stuck in the alley. *I want you. I want us.*

Don't break my heart.

Picking up a spoon, he tapped it on the table until the man next to him put his gnarled hand over his.

"You got someplace else you want to be?"

Declan glanced over to find Phinny deep in conversation with a couple of people. "No, sir." He set the spoon down. She slayed him with her bright, blue eyes and thick, glossy hair, with that smile that lit him up inside.

If anyone needed to worry about his heart…*it's me*. He was the one who had all these feelings for a woman who had no business staying in Wyoming. Even after the phone call with her mom, he still couldn't imagine her choosing a life here.

Right now, it's interesting. It's different. It was especially fun since she'd found a summer romance to get her through a really tough emotional time. But…come on. She'd miss her parents, her luxuries, her balls and auctions and limos and…the whole London scene that couldn't be found in Wyoming.

His phone vibrated, and he pulled it out of his pocket. Not recognizing the number, he was about to let it go to voicemail, but the area code tripped a wire in his brain. Sliding out of the booth, he answered the call as he headed out of the restaurant. "Declan Cadell."

"Declan. This is James O'Brien. GM of the Bombers."

The *Bombers*? They had the most talented roster in the NHL. "Hey. How's it going?"

"Good, good. I'll get right to the point. We heard what happened, and we'd like you to join our team as an assistant coach."

Holy shit. The top team in the league wants me to coach for them? Cupping the back of his head, he slowly turned in a circle.

But wait…what happened?

"I don't know if you've already got something lined up, but we'd like to fly you out here as soon as possible. You interested?"

If I've already got something lined up? What the hell does that mean?

But he knew, didn't he?

The Comets let me go. They hadn't even bothered to tell him. He couldn't believe it.

Fuckers.

Shit. I lost my job. He'd expected it, so it shouldn't hit so hard. And it was less that they didn't have the decency to tell him and more that he liked this gig. Liked the guys.

"Sure, I'm interested." Of course, he wanted to coach the two-time defending Stanley Cup champions.

But as he glanced through the plate glass window, his gaze landed on Phinny, and he knew things had changed. For the first time in his life, he wanted something more than hockey. He wanted her.

"What's your schedule look like?" the GM asked. "I believe you're in Wyoming right now, right?"

"How'd you know?"

"Our goalie's brother is Carl, the wingman of the Renegades. So, we've heard about the coaching you've done for the guys this summer."

"Got it." He stood there a moment, pretty blown away that the Bombers wanted him, but then he saw Phinny throw her head back and laugh, and his focus shifted. If she gave up her life in London to move here, how the hell could he take a job in another state?

Don't break my heart.

He couldn't. Right then, he understood there was nothing to talk about. Now that he knew what it felt like to have her in his life, there wasn't a single temptation that could convince him to walk away from the best thing that had ever happened to him. "James, I appreciate the interest, but I'm going to have to pass."

"We figured you wouldn't leave unless you already lined up something." He sounded disappointed.

"Yeah, but I very much appreciate the offer."

"Well, if anything changes, let me know. You've got my number."

When he disconnected, he found Phinny standing beside him. "Are you okay?"

He pocketed his phone. "Yeah, everything's good."

"Did you get bad news or good? It was hard to tell."

He couldn't help smiling. No one had ever paid such close attention to him. "Both. I lost my job and got a job offer."

Her eyes went wide with concern.

He touched her arm. "I turned it down." *You can trust me.* He drew her close and brought his mouth right next to her ear. "Do you honestly think I'd walk away from a woman like you?"

Her hands went to his waist, her fingers digging in. "Just so it's clear, what kind of woman are we talking about? One that satisfies your sexual appetites?" She pulled back to look him in the eyes. "Or is it my egg-collecting skills?"

He burst out laughing. "It's because of your ass, and the way it fits in my hands." He loved the mischief in her eyes. "But I have other reasons."

"I'm listening."

"It's the way you light up a room." He cupped the face he wanted to look at for the rest of his life. "And my heart." His thumb brushed her cheek. "I would give up everything just to be with you."

"Declan." She got up on her toes and kissed him. It started out sweet and slow, a gesture of affection, but it quickly heated up.

Because her familiar scent surrounded him, and her breasts pressed against him, and the soft, slick, heat of her mouth fired him up.

"Get a room."

They pulled apart to see the elderly man who'd been seated next to Declan shove a baseball cap on his head and take off down the street.

Laughing, she grabbed his hand and headed for the Jeep.

"So, how'd it go in there?" He dug into his pocket for the keys.

"It was just like you said. One of the Cooters is in property development. He's in the middle of an ugly divorce. Ugh." She tipped her head back. "That sounds terrible, doesn't it? Me being excited when he's going through hell?"

"No, it's fine. So, what did he say?"

"They're trying to sell off their holdings, but in the meantime, they're renting the vacant ones out. Anyhow, they've got this fantastic warehouse in a strip mall right near where I bought my clothes. It actually used to be a furniture store, and he said he'd let me use it for the pop-up."

"Sounds perfect."

"It is, but now I have to get Lachlan to agree to do it."

"I thought he already did."

"Well, he grunted something that I chose to take as a yes."

"Wait, you're going to all this effort, and you don't even know if he's going to do it?"

"He *needs* to do it." After climbing into the Jeep, she pulled out her phone. "Now, I just have to convince him that I can pull this off."

After dinner, Declan set the last glass in the dishwasher and dried his hands on a kitchen towel. Beside him, Tina wiped down the counter. She'd seemed preoccupied all night. "How can I help with the festival tomorrow?"

"You just come and enjoy it." Tina rinsed out the sponge. "I've got this thing running like a well-oiled machine."

Something was on her mind, and as much as he wanted to find Phinny, it didn't seem right to leave when Tina was troubled. "You miss him?"

She swung around to him, one hand going to her heart. "Oh." Sadness tightened the skin around her mouth. "More than I can say. This place feels so empty without him. He might not have talked much, but his presence filled it up." Reaching for a dish towel, she folded it in half, then in half again. "So…the contest's coming up. You ready for it?"

"I am." Three and a half weeks ago, he hadn't questioned who'd win. But Phinny had come to care about this place, and she'd learned everything she could. He wasn't so sure anymore.

What he didn't know was what she'd do if she won.

She unfolded the towel, smoothing her palm on it like an iron. "Do you know what you might do with the ranch? It's a full-time job. You can't be doing hockey if you're going to run this place."

Now that he knew what worried her, he could do his part to ease her fears. "I won't give up hockey, but I promise to keep this ranch going just as Kurt intended."

She looked right at him. "And if Phinny wins?"

That's the part I can't control. "She's got a business idea that's based in Calamity."

Tina looked hopeful.

"But I don't know if she'll keep this place. I think she cares enough about it at this point that she won't sell to a developer, though. She'll wait until she finds someone who wants to continue Kurt's work."

"She needs money." Tina's voice lowered to a hush. "She looks rich, but she doesn't spend a dime. She tucks the money she makes at the farm stand into a jar in her room, and she never eats out or buys anything. Not even a T-shirt from Bazoo's."

She might be correct, but it wasn't his place to discuss Phinny's financial situation. "She's got a big heart, and no matter what happens, I can't see her putting everyone out of work and turning her family's land into a subdivision."

"I hope you're right." Shoulders tight with worry, Tina tossed the dish towel in the washing machine. "I'm heading out now. I'll see you in the morning."

"Tina?"

The woman stopped with her hand on the doorknob.

"I stayed here for a reason. I gave up my job to make sure this ranch doesn't fall into the wrong hands. If I have anything to say about it, your life won't change."

She gave him a sad smile. "Well, it's changed all right. I didn't want to come back here, didn't want to be on the ranch without him. But I hear what you're saying, and I appreciate it. Every one of us can get another job, but it's Kurt we want to work for. It's his vision and memory we want to honor. 'Night." She headed out the back door to make her way to her cottage.

As he turned out the lights and crossed the living room, Tina's concerns weighed heavily on him. If he had any say, things would go exactly as she wanted. But certain things were out of his control. Like what Phinny would do when offered seven-hundred-million-dollars.

Just before he flicked off the lamp, he took in the row of framed photographs on the mantle. For the first time, he understood why Kurt didn't have a photograph of his daughter on display. Every time he'd looked at her, it had to have cut him to the bone.

Because life without Phinny...*damn*. He never wanted

to go back to the emotionally flat existence he'd had before he'd met her.

Heading up the stairs, he knew he could ask about her plans—pretty much thought about doing it every single day, just to put the problem to rest—but it wouldn't be fair. It felt too…manipulative. He had to keep their relationship separate from the inheritance.

Would it impact him if she sold Kurt's legacy? Hell, yeah. He'd have a hard time with it, no doubt. But he didn't know if he could end things. He was too into her.

He just didn't know.

Anticipation firing him up, he hurried down the hallway toward her open door. When he got there, he stood in the threshold just taking her in. Silver moonlight spilled across the bed, accentuating her breasts in the flimsy tank top. She was the prettiest woman he'd ever seen, and his heart couldn't take it. It beat so forcefully it hurt.

She watched him, a little unsure. "You all right?"

As he came closer, he lost the ability to speak, to think. All he could do was stare.

She reached for his hand. Hers was so delicate, so gentle. "What're you thinking?"

"That you're perfect." In every way.

And that's when he had his answer. He laid down beside her, putting their joined hands over his heart where the truth beat into his bloodstream. Even if she decided to sell the ranch, he would still want to be with her. There was no other choice.

She rolled onto her side, placing her head on his chest. "You're being weird."

He couldn't say anything, not when the muscle in his throat had tightened into a hard knot.

Reaching under his T-shirt, her warm hand glided up his stomach. Her fingernails made slow circles on his skin. "I've been thinking about the business, and I'm going to pitch it to Glori, see if she'll back me. Since my products are local, my only real start-up costs will be furniture and a few months' rent. I mean, given the response I get from just a table on the side of the road, I can't imagine it'll be long before I'm paying my own way. I just don't think it'll take long to pay her back."

He didn't know why, but he was hyper aware of every sound, from the steady hum of air conditioning to the rustle of her legs under the blanket. If he never had more than this—the gentle stroking of her fingers, the heat of her body, and the soothing tone of her voice—he would die a happy man.

"I was also thinking about the job offer you got, and I hate that you'd give up the one thing you've always wanted. But then I remembered what you'd said about starting a training camp here, and I'm wondering if owning the team and building the training camp would make you happy." She lifted up on an elbow. "I just want to be sure you follow the right path for you. Not me. Not Kurt. *You.*"

"There's only one path that's right for me." Cupping her shoulder, he tipped her onto her back. "And it brought me here. To your bed."

She pushed his hair back behind his ears. "I love the way you look at me. You make me feel beautiful and sexy. You make me feel like I'm the most amazing person you've ever known."

"Because you are. All of those things." He kissed her. The first brush of their lips sent a current of electricity through him. He toppled into her sweet, fresh scent and her sexy little sigh that sounded almost like relief. Needing more, he licked along the seam, and when their tongues collided, he burst into flames.

She was his ignition source. No one else had the power to fire him up the way she did. Braced on his arms, he lowered himself, desperate to feel the curves of her body, to feel her hands smooth down his back and cup his ass.

He loved the way her legs wrapped around him, and her hips ground against his cock, as if she couldn't get enough. "I want you." He left a trail of kisses on the smooth column of her neck, the gentle curve of her collarbone, and then he gently bit her nipple through the thin cotton of her tank top. Sitting back on his heels, he grabbed a fistful of cotton and yanked his T-shirt off. She took the momentary break to shed her clothes, too, and the second she lay back down, his hands covered her breasts, his thumbs caressing the beaded points. She shifted restlessly beneath him, her eyes burning with desire.

He sucked her nipple into his mouth, swirling his tongue and flicking.

"God, Declan."

Every time he was with her, it got better. He slipped inside this sexy space of warm bodies, gripping hands, and an arousal so intense it swept him under. Kissing a path down her stomach, he parted her thighs and licked into her hot, wet pussy.

Her back arched, and he lifted her legs over his shoulders, tilting her ass. When his tongue grazed her clit, she cried out, her hips twisting. Fueled by her gasps and moans, he worked harder to drive her relentlessly closer to release.

Pleasuring her turned him way the fuck on. He

wanted to be the source of her happiness. He wanted her smiles, her hands, her attention—he wanted all of it.

He wanted to consume her.

A bright streak of fear crossed through him, yanking him out of the moment. He broke out in a sweat, his heart beating so fast he grew disoriented.

"Hey." Her voice reached through the panic, and she tugged on his shoulders. "Come here."

He reared up and over her, going back in for a kiss so he wouldn't hear the voice that made him lose control. And then he grabbed his cock, pushing inside her tight, slick core, and when she sighed like she'd touched nirvana, he groaned.

"I want you." *Yes, that's it.* Reducing his feelings to sex settled him down. As he drove into her, a sizzling heat streaked from his cock to his heart to the top of his head. His hips snapped, and he thrust hard, sinking deep, all the way to the hilt.

"Oh, God." Her hands went to his ass, cupping, squeezing, pulling him deeper.

He drove into her, completely lost in everything that was Phinny. Every cell in his body went hot, vital, and tension wound him up so tightly he knew his orgasm would wreck him. Sliding a hand under her ass, he fucked her at just the right angle to scrape across her clit. She set her feet on the mattress, arched her hips, and held herself right where she needed him most.

He'd never felt more connected to another human being in his life. And as she cried out, her head tipping back, the roar of his climax ripped through him. He shouted, fusing their hips together, his punching, hers writhing. One shockwave after another ripped through him, and he never wanted it to end. Finally, he shuddered, and when he collapsed beside her, it took several moments before he came back into his body.

She lay still beside him, her chest rising and falling. He wanted to roll onto his side, tuck his face into her neck, glide his hand up her belly and cup her perfect, plump breast. He wanted to feel her arms come around him, holding him.

But he didn't. Because his blood pressure soared. He shot up. "I'm going to uh…"

She didn't say a word. Just watched him, waiting to see what he'd do, how he'd finish his sentence. But his mind went blank, and his skin prickled like it was covered in a rash. He rolled off the bed, wanting to walk away, but he couldn't. He was locked in her orbit.

Look at her. Her tousled hair, swollen lips, and plump breasts. She leveled a gentle smile at him, and he practically heard the whisper of her thoughts. *It's okay.*

She held out her hand.

He should go.

But if he wanted her to stay, if he wanted to keep her, then he needed to be brave.

He needed to tell her the truth.

And if he couldn't do that—if it was too soon—then he at least needed to let her know that he was all-in. That he wanted her.

No, that she could trust him not to break her heart.

He climbed back into bed, and she snuggled up against him.

And then he stared at the ceiling.

Letting the truth pump into his bloodstream, carry to every corner of his body and soul.

I love her.
I'm in love this woman.

Chapter Eighteen

PHINNY LOVED THE SEPIA-TONED PHOTOGRAPHS IN her dad's albums, but the Wild West Festival made her feel like she'd actually gone back in time. Mitch, dressed as a sheriff, and Tina, wearing a bustle dress and bonnet, had transformed the ranch so completely, she could almost believe the blacksmith working outside the barn teaching people how to make a horseshoe was one of the original Grevers brothers. And that the woman churning butter right nearby was his wife.

A pair of horses clopped along, leading an antique buggy loaded with visitors, and the scent of grilled meat, fresh hay, and sage filled the air.

Tina was right. Everything ran like a well-oiled machine to the point that she and Declan weren't needed at all. They'd spent the morning in town watching the parade, and tonight they'd watch the fireworks at the lake.

Sitting on a wooden fence, the sun warming the top of her head, she watched guests hurry over to grab a good viewing spot at the corral in time for the next barrel race.

Had she ever been this happy? This truly content?

No, she hadn't. She'd spent her whole life trying to be a good daughter so Andrew would love her—no, wait, that wasn't it. *God.* How had she not seen it before now?

It was so he wouldn't leave her like Kurt had.

Of course. And it had impacted every area of her life. Look how hard she'd worked to keep her friends, being the life of the party, constantly coming up with fun ideas. *No wonder I'm so good at glad-handing for auction items.* She lived to make everyone happy. To win them over.

It wasn't like that in Calamity. Here, she could be herself. She didn't even have to try, and people liked her.

Declan made his way over, handing her a cup of pink lemonade. "*Now*, you can have some."

She laughed, taking it from him, but her smile faded at the way he looked at her. His gaze caressed her as gently and lovingly as if it had been his hand.

His grin broke soft and gentle. "Look at you."

"What do you mean?" She took a sip, letting the cold, tart liquid slide down her throat. "Am I a mess?"

"Do you care?"

She grinned. "Not really."

"Good because I don't think I've ever seen you look prettier than right this minute."

The compliment rolled through her in rich, luxurious waves. Being around him put her in a constant state of excitement. She felt like a teenager with her first crush.

"You hungry?" he asked. "Want a burger?"

Enveloped in the happiness of just being with him, she shook her head. Something had changed for them last night. After they'd made love, he'd flipped out. For a moment there, she'd thought he'd pull a runner. That this amazing relationship would end right then and there because she wanted more than he could give.

But when she'd seen true fear in his eyes, all the stories he'd told her had come together to form a picture. Kurt had accused Declan of never finishing anything, and now she understood why. He'd lost his parents, his grandfather, and now Kurt, his father-figure.

All the people he'd loved had left him. She couldn't even imagine how hard it would be to open yourself to love again after that much loss.

But he hadn't run. He'd come back to bed. He'd spent the night with her.

And it gave her so much hope for their future together.

Lifting a lock of hair, he tucked it behind her ear. "What're you thinking?"

"How happy I am to be with you. Three weeks ago, I felt like I'd been dropped onto another planet. This was all so foreign to me."

"And now?"

And now I love you. She did. It was too soon, so she wouldn't say it, but she knew it was true. "I mean, look at it." She took in the mountain ranges, the acres of alfalfa and scrubby meadowlands, and the magnificent house. "It's rough, it's rugged, it's as far from London as you can get, and yet I feel so…peaceful here."

"Are you thinking you'll keep the ranch?"

He might as well have tossed a cup of lemonade in her face. "Declan, no. I can't do that." *Can I?* "Look, I get it now. I know what this land meant to Kurt, but I can't own a cattle ranch. Come on, I would run this place into the ground."

"It practically runs itself."

"You know that's not true. Mitch walked me through everything the other day. I did my due diligence, and what

I saw scared the crap out of me. Initially, sure, I'd just follow what he's laid out. But pretty soon, I'll be at the helm of all this." She made a sweeping motion around her. "I don't even know how to drive a car. There's no way I can run an operation this size. Besides, that money…it's lifechanging. And not just for me. Think of all the good it can do."

"This land has endured and will endure long after the money's been spent."

She hopped off the fence, spilling the lemonade. "Is this going to affect us? Is it going to change your feelings for me?" Honestly, she hadn't even considered that. She'd been caught up in this whirlwind of falling in love for the first time.

His gaze dropped to the dirt. "I don't know."

Stung, she stepped back. She didn't want to lose him, but she also didn't like the idea that their relationship hinged on a decision as important as this. "I have to make the choice that's right for me."

"I know that." His gaze swung up. "I do. That's why I haven't asked before."

Last night, he'd been scared. Now, it was her turn. Look what they were both giving up to be together—and after only knowing each other a little over three weeks. Was the sacrifice worth it? In the long run, would he come to regret giving up coaching for her?

Staying here meant giving up the auction, and that would shut a door. If things didn't work out and she had to go back to London, she might never get back into the world of privilege she'd always known.

He's the worst person I could fall in love with.

And I'm the worst person he could fall in love with. Especially, if I sell this land that means so much to him.

"God, Declan. What do we do? Should we end it right now? Wait until after the contest to see—"

He hauled her to him, cutting off the rest of her sentence with his mouth over hers. He kissed her. Right there in front of families and ranch hands, in front of artisans and barrel riders. He kissed her with an urgency that left her breathless and weak-kneed.

Clutching his T-shirt, she gave into the passion of his kiss. Until he pulled away. This time, as she gazed into his eyes, she didn't see a trace of fear. She saw resolve.

"The money, the ranch…none of it holds a candle to what I feel for you. What I need from you."

"What do you need?" She was so rattled, she could only whisper.

"Just you. More than coaching, more than honoring Kurt's legacy, I need to be with you." He cupped her face with his big hand, the look in his eyes earnest and searching. "I'm sorry. I never should've asked about the land. I won't let it come between us."

"But it will. The contest is this Friday. One of us is going to win." *And then what?*

"Look, I don't play hockey hoping I'll score. Wondering whether I'll win. I play it knowing I'm going to kick ass. I'm in this relationship, Phinny. And I hope you are, too."

She was. Of course, she was.

But there were too many emotions involved. In the long run, he'd resent her for selling the land. For him, it meant honoring Kurt. For her, it was survival. Her stomach still churned when she remembered standing outside her apartment, the key no longer fitting in the lock. She'd had nowhere to go. If Verity hadn't let her sleep on her couch for a few nights, she would have literally been homeless.

She'd had no money. No real-world skills. Verity had a fiancé and hadn't wanted her to stay more than few nights, so she'd had to find another friend who'd let her stay over. *You wouldn't believe how quickly you can go through friends.* When she'd finally gotten the job at the diner, she'd moved into a boarding house.

She'd eaten during her shifts, and she would never forget the day she'd packed someone's leftover dinner into a take-away container while Phoebe, the manager, watched her with horror and pity. She'd felt like a feral cat.

No, I'm sorry. I'm selling the ranch. Not only was she unequipped to run it, but she needed financial independence.

She only hoped Declan would understand.

Declan held the door open and watched as Phinny breezed into the Reliquary Museum and came to a comical stop. "Whoa."

Yeah, the place was very cool. Mounted animal heads hung on the walls and display cases held artifacts. The historic house was stuffed with memorabilia going back hundreds of years.

Touching the bullet hole on a nickel-plated cash register from 1909, she turned to him with an awed grin. "We've got loads of portraits and family jewels at Andrew's country estate, but the Wild West was a whole other world, wasn't it?"

He could only nod. Since he'd never loved anyone before, he still hadn't quite gotten over the enormity of it.

He didn't know how he'd gotten so lucky. *Why would a woman this full of life and love and joy want to be with me?*

"Hello." A woman about their age came around a corner carrying a mug. "Oh. You must be Phinny." She reached her hand out. "I'm Waverly."

"Thank you so much for meeting with us."

"Declan." He shook her hand. "We appreciate your time."

"I know I've been pushy," Phinny said. "But the competition's tomorrow, and we've run out of time."

"Oh, it's my pleasure. My grandmother's the curator, but she's out of town for the month." She grinned. "Believe it or not, she met a surfer on a dating app, and she went to Hawaii to watch him compete. So, she asked me to help her out." Her brow furrowed. "But wait a sec…aren't you two competing against each other?"

"We are, but we both want what's best for my dad's land," Phinny said.

That might've been the first time she'd referred to Kurt as her dad. Maybe she was more invested than she realized.

"So, is your grandmother the only curator?" Phinny asked.

"Oh, no. She gets interns from the university and other volunteers, but people move on. There's not a lot of funding for this little place."

"That surprises me." Phinny's gaze wandered the room. "It's amazing."

"It is, but there are several museums in Jackson County, and this one doesn't compare. It's sort of a pet project of some of the families who've lived here for generations. Basically, everything you see comes from their attics. Speaking of which, let me show you to the Grevers' room."

Something passed through Phinny. He only knew because he had his hand on her hip and felt the slight tremor of energy. Pressing her hands together, she didn't immediately follow the curator. "I don't know why I'm so nervous."

"Maybe because, over the last four weeks, you've come to see them as your family."

"Yes, you're right about that." She reached for his hand. "I'm so glad you're here with me."

"There's nowhere else I want to be."

She grinned. "I never imagined hearing words like that coming out of your mouth."

"They never have." *Until you.*

Together, they walked down a hall to a large room at the back of the house. He'd been here before, of course, but it never lost its magic. Because every single thing in this room was used by Kurt's family members.

"Originally, this museum was nothing more than a one-room shack. It's one of the oldest settlements in Jackson Hole." Waverly stepped aside to let them deeper into the room. "Over generations, they added on."

Slowly taking it all in, Phinny moved toward a glass case against the wall. "It's a map."

"So, picture this," Waverly said. "The five brothers standing around, talking about the land they'd acquired. At this point, they'd walked every square inch, named every butte, mountain, river, and stream. One of them grabs a stick and starts drawing in the dirt. The others join in until together, they map it all out. It was a good, useful tool, so Joshua Grevers drew it onto animal skin with charcoal. And then a few years later, it was transferred onto paper."

"I can totally picture that. Thank you for making it so

vivid." Phinny reached for a rifle, her gaze landing on a bronze plate that read *Mariah Grevers 1892*. A sideboard against the wall held random artifacts, and she looked to Waverly, asking permission.

"You're welcome to touch anything that's not behind a glass frame or locked inside a display case."

"How old is this?" Phinny held up the object.

"It's from around 1900. That's a sad iron. Sad's the old English word for solid." Waverly headed for the door. "All right, well, if you have any questions, just holler. I'll be right down the hall."

Phinny's expression had him moving closer to her. "Hey, you okay?" He could read the mix of emotions duking it out inside his golden girl—awe, sorrow, confusion—and his fingers sifted through the silky hair cascading down her back.

"I'm touching something my great great grandmother used. Right here. In this room."

"Yes." He knew exactly how she felt, even though none of it was his family's.

"I just can't believe it. I mean, I'm touching history." She looked around. "They ate dinner on that table. I can imagine my great great grandmother nursing a baby in that rocking chair. I'm just…overwhelmed." She lifted her gaze to him. "This is my family."

"Yeah, it is." The jolt of anxiety he got surprised him. Because he wanted her to win. To keep the ranch. It was *her* legacy. So where had that shock of fear come from?

Well, fuck. He guessed it meant more to him than he'd realized.

He supposed all he could do was play to win.

Phinny stood backstage at the Music Box, her stomach in knots. She couldn't believe a month had passed since she'd watched Harrison Goodman address the "hockey boys" in his office instead of her.

As Kurt's only child, she'd assumed he'd leave her something meaningful. She hadn't known what. She hadn't really cared. It had been a terrible, confusing time, and at that point, she'd only wanted a glimpse. Peering into the window of his life, getting a sense of him, of what he was thinking—*about me*—would've been enough.

Now, she was ravenous for more. She wanted to dig around her dad's attic and gorge on history. She wanted to meet more of the quirky, eccentric people of Calamity. She could picture herself in her new store making a cup of tea for someone who'd come in to show her a craft they'd never really told anyone about but wondered if Phinny would like to sell. She wanted to become part of this community.

But mostly, she wanted more of the man standing beside her. The man she'd fallen completely, wildly in love with. "This is it." She looked to Declan to find him calm and collected. She gently elbowed him in the stomach. "Your confidence is annoying."

Chuckling, he gave her shoulder a squeeze. "You got this."

"How are you so sure of yourself?"

"Because either outcome is fine with me."

"What does that even mean? One of us wins the ranch, and the other walks away with nothing."

He pressed a sweet kiss on her mouth. "Not true. Either way, I walk away with you." And then he lifted the thick velvet curtain and stepped out onto the stage.

That man held her heart in the palm of his hand.

"You're just trying to throw me off, aren't you?" She followed him out there. "Turn me into a wobbly pudding so I can't think straight."

He just grinned and took his place behind one of three podiums.

She found hers, as well, but wasn't quite as ready as he was to get started. Sure, she'd learned a lot about her dad, she didn't feel she *knew* him. Though he remained a larger-than-life figure, at least she'd come to love the man she'd barely known. And it meant everything to her to honor him tonight by getting all the answers correct.

Declan mouthed, *Kick some ass.*

I will, she mouthed back. Her heart was so full. Maybe she was crazy, but she couldn't help thinking of Declan as her dad's greatest gift to her.

With microphone in hand, Harrison turned around to them. "Are we ready?"

"Yes, sir," Declan said.

"I am." Phinny discreetly wiped her palms on her dress.

The lawyer gave them a nod and turned to face the good number of people who had turned out. "Thank you for coming to the Kurt Grevers Trivia Contest. I know it might seem odd that he arranged this event, but if you knew him at all, you know he had a reason for everything he did. He was a thoughtful man. He was kind and caring, and I believe his intentions were good. Okay, let's get started." He picked up a stack of index cards and tapped them on the desktop. "We have a total of ten questions. You'll both write your answers on your electronic pad, and they'll appear on the screen behind us. There's no timer, so feel free to take as long as you need."

Picking up their styluses, they both nodded,

"Question number one." The lawyer read the top card. "What year did the Grevers brothers sign the deeds to their land?"

Whew. Easy one. She wrote *1864* and knew Declan had done the same.

"Correct." The lawyer cleared his throat. "Number two. Draw a family tree from the brothers to the present. Whoever gets the greatest number of family members correct wins."

Oh. That one flipped the switch on her anxiety. She'd memorized a lot of names and dates but piecing together the entire lineage would be tricky. *Calm down. It'll come to you.* In her mind, she flipped through the pages of the photo albums.

Tuning out the audience, the attorney, and Declan, she brainstormed as many names as she could. Then, she ordered them along a timeline to the best of her ability.

It only struck her when she'd finished that the entire room had watched her writing and erasing dozens of times. She looked over to see Declan waiting patiently for her. She glanced at the board. He'd created a neat and concise tree.

Her heart sank. She'd been so preoccupied with getting it right, she hadn't considered the format. She hadn't made a tree.

Shit. Dammit.

That was stupid.

After the lawyer examined both of their answers, he looked right at her. "You are both correct."

Oh, thank God. Relief barreling through her, she let out a gust of breath.

She remembered what Declan had said to her at the skating rink the other day. *It's all about confidence. You're so sure you're going to fall on your ass, you'll make it happen.*

He was absolutely right. She had to remember that.

"Question number three. What stopped the fire of 1894 from destroying the Grevers' land?"

Immediately, an image came to mind. In the museum yesterday, she'd seen a photograph of scorched earth. She'd meant to ask Waverly about it on their way out but had gotten distracted.

Dammit. She wished she hadn't forgotten.

Would Declan know this one? She glanced over to find him writing furiously.

Of course, he did.

Okay, well, think. She wanted to say the community got together, but if the fire threatened the entire ranch, no number of buckets could douse it. And they didn't have emergency vehicles back then. In her mind's eye, she went back to the photograph, to the museum label, to try and identify a date. Had it been winter? Summer? But she hadn't paid enough attention to it.

Time ticked by, and she got hot around her ears. A rustling sound in the audience drew her attention. *Screen it out.* She closed her eyes, took herself back to the cool of the museum, and let her mind wander across the image hanging on the wall. Blackened tree stumps, grey sky, the earth nearly black…

Because it was wet. Saturated.

Flooded.

Finally, she wrote down her answer. *It rained.*

But wait a minute. What year did he say the fire took place? 1894? Excitement blasted through her. Mitch had burst into the house last week, angry about some fence a neighbor had built on Grevers' land. *Yes.*

She deleted and wrote *The great storm of 1894.*

Nailed it. Apparently, it was the greatest amount of rainfall in recorded history in the area, and it changed the course of the Moose River. Since the deeds stated they owned land to the river, the Grevers had gained a thousand acres. It had also created a feud between her family and the Wilsons that endured to this day.

She hoped it had also doused the fire.

Phinny waited, anxious to see if she'd gotten it right.

A moment later, the attorney spoke into the microphone. "You're both correct."

Happiness rocketed through her. If her dad was watching, she'd like to think she'd made him proud.

Thank you for making me stay here, Dad. Thank you for making me learn my roots, my history.

I only wish I could've learned it from you.

Tears blurred her vision. *I love you, Daddy.*

Lowering her head, she closed her eyes and could've sworn she felt a hand on her back, the ghost of fingers scratching the way she'd always liked. Her skin broke out into chill bumps.

He's here.

He heard me.

And somehow, it set it all to rest. All the years of hurt, rejection…the frustration of not having answers…settled, giving her peace.

"Question number four. How many people on the family tree you just made couldn't make a go of it in Calamity and left to find their fortune elsewhere and never came back?"

I have no idea. That was the one answer she'd never gotten. *What do I do?*

You calm down. You think.

You can't let your dad down.

She'd read everything, poured over photo albums, scoured the museum, but there'd been no mention of someone who'd left to start a dry-cleaning business or become a horse trainer in Kentucky. She'd hadn't seen anything about people who'd left.

But, of course, Declan was already writing down his answer.

Out of nowhere, she was struck with the realization that it was Declan's confidence that meant she was safe with him. She didn't need to worry about him breaking her heart because he knew his own mind. And when he wanted something, he went after it.

And he wants me.

Love surged through her, but she had to force her mind back on the contest. She would just have to make her best guess based on the conversations she'd had with the Cooters, Declan, Tina, Leddy, Glori, and Mitch. She wrote *15.*

"You are both incorrect. The correct answer is zero. No one left the ranch to find a better life. Every Grevers stayed and worked on the land."

"But where is everyone then? Why am I the last one?" Mortification pinched the back of her neck, flooding her with a stinging sensation. She could feel the eyes of everyone in the room on her.

"Not everyone married." The lawyer didn't hesitate to answer. "And not every married couple had children. But no one left." Harrison watched her for a moment, waiting for her to give him the okay to proceed.

When they both got the next three questions correct, Phinny worried the contest would end in a tie. Had her dad planned for something like that? Would they keep going until someone won?

"Question number nine. Name three Grevers who made an impact on the town."

Easy. She quickly answered.

Colt Grevers, one of the five brothers, became the first county sheriff and was responsible for driving outlaws out of the valley.

Abigail Grevers opened the first schoolhouse.

Clara Grevers became a nurse and married a doctor. The two of them birthed every baby in the county for sixty years.

She set down her stylus.

"You're both correct."

She smiled and lifted her eyebrows to Declan. *Look at us go*. He grinned right back.

"And now, our final question. At the moment, you're tied, so if one of you answers correctly and the other does not, the contest ends. Otherwise, I have tiebreaker questions."

They both gave nods of acknowledgment.

"All right, then." The lawyer stared at the index card for a moment before looking first at Declan, then at her. "What did Kurt value most in the world?"

Declan immediately wrote down his answer.

But it wasn't that simple for her. Because while her dad prized the land, he loved it because generations of his ancestors had worked on it, fought on it, and scrabbled to make a living. Clara Grevers left Calamity to get her nursing degree, but she came back to practice in this community.

So, was it the land? Or the family?

Which did her dad value more?

The answer drifted across her skin like a caress. A warmth settled over her, and she just knew. She wrote her answer, then set her stylus down.

Her pulse beat wildly. Her skin went hot at the same time her blood turned cold. If she was wrong…she would just die. Taking shallow breaths, muscles clenched so tightly she ached, she kept her gaze on her desk and waited.

"You are correct," the lawyer said.

Phinny twisted around to read the board.

Declan had written *The ranch.*

She had written *Me.*

So, which was the correct answer?

Everything she'd learned over the past month all funneled down into one truth: my dad loved me.

If she got the answer wrong, then she'd only heard what she'd wanted to hear.

And that meant…he hadn't asked her to stay for a month because he wanted her to know how much he'd missed her. It would mean he'd wanted her to learn about the land so that she wouldn't sell it. So that she'd keep it in the family.

And she didn't think she could come back from that. Not after finally believing he'd not only loved her, but he'd wanted her. That losing her had crushed him.

She almost didn't want to hear the answer. She wanted to walk off the stage and—

"Seraphina Crutchley is the winner."

Emotion erupted, and she lowered her head so no one could see the great, howling sorrow consume her.

Not a moment later, Declan's arms were around her.

"Hey. Are you okay?" He tipped her chin. "Look at me. I need to know what you're feeling."

And she did. She gazed into those concerned eyes and said, "He loved me."

"Yeah, sweetheart. He did."

"He loved me, and he's gone. I'll never know him."

"You know him." His arms tightened. "You *know* him. He made sure of that."

She cried so hard her knees gave out, but Declan caught her. Next thing she knew, she was in his arms, and he was moving. Slipping behind the curtain, he set her down backstage, letting her cry for all she'd lost.

But also, for all she'd gained.

Her dad had truly loved her. He'd wanted her in his life.

And he'd given her Declan, her forever love.

Chapter Nineteen

Joy radiated out of her, and Declan wanted to mainline it. As they waited in Harrison's office, happiness burbled over, and he couldn't help pressing a kiss to her cheek.

As if it were the most natural thing in the world, she threw her arms around his neck. "He wanted me."

"Of course, he did, golden girl." *Who wouldn't?*

She leaned back. "For a minute there, I swear to God, I didn't know which of us had the right answer. I only knew if it was you, I'd be devastated. It just felt like this whole journey to learn about my dad was really to learn that he loved me. And if I was wrong about it…if all he cared about was finding the right steward for his ranch…" She shook her head.

"That's just not the Kurt I knew."

"And now…God." She got up and stepped away from her chair. "Now, I own a *ranch*." Hands on her pinkened cheeks, she whipped back around to him. "Declan, I can't do this. It's not just that I don't know anything about cattle or water rights or feed. It's that I'm not a businesswoman. I'm not the right person for this."

"Kurt believed you were. But he made sure you didn't have to do this alone. He hired the best staff, and he prepared them. He practically wrote a book on every detail of running his operation. So, you have a staff and…you have me." He watched her carefully. "We're in this together."

Relief slackened her shoulders. "You're right. You're absolutely right."

"*But* that's the beauty of his gift. Turns out, it was never about the land. We were wrong about that. It was about making sure you knew he loved you. And now that he's done that, you're free to do whatever you want. Sure, this ranch meant a lot to him, but you meant more. And he wants you to be happy. So, you can sell this place, and he'd be fine with it. Or keep it. It's your choice."

"Sell it? Are you freaking kidding me? This land that's been in my family for generations? Are you out of your mind? I'm not selling a single acre."

Her conviction knocked the breath out of his lungs. *She's not leaving.* She was staying in Calamity, and she was staying with him. He leapt out of his chair and lifted her off the floor, swinging her around.

The door opened, and Harrison walked in. "Oh." He laughed. "I see we're celebrating. Wish I'd thought to bring champagne." He headed behind the desk and dropped into his black leather chair.

After setting her down, they both took their seats, their hands joined on her armrest.

"Well, I'm glad that's over." The lawyer smiled. "You both did an outstanding job. Kurt would be proud of you. Especially…" His eyes clouded with emotion. "Let's just say he's a happy man right now. There's not much more he wanted than for you to understand how he felt about you. Okay." He cleared his throat. "Let's get down to business. Because nothing was ever simple with Kurt…" The attorney waved a document at them. "There's a second codicil. He's offering the winner a choice between the ranch and a cash inheritance."

"What?" She cut a look to Declan. *Did you know about this?*

Hell, no. Declan was surprised, too.

"Phinny, you can either own the Gongshow Ranch or take a lump sum of twenty-five-million dollars." Harrison peered at her over his glasses. "To be clear, the ranch comes with working capital, as well, but that's only to be used for operations." His gaze shifted to Declan. "And whichever she doesn't choose goes to you."

"Wow." She got up. "Wow, wow, wow. Five seconds ago, everything was so perfect, and now…I don't even know what to say." She dragged her fingers through her hair. "I have to work this out. I'm nowhere near the right person to take over for Kurt, but then again, if I give you the land, you won't have the money to start the training camp, so—"

Declan shook his head. "No. Take me out of the equation."

"What? No, it's something we should talk about." He saw the plea in her eyes. *Talk to me.*

But something hardened in him, and he didn't know why. All he knew was she had to make this decision on her own.

As she paced to the window, Declan noticed the attorney's strange expression, and it made him realize he'd turned cold. He didn't mean to do that. It was an automatic thing for him. But he couldn't behave like that if he had a hope in hell of staying with her. He had to communicate. If they were a couple, they had to make decisions together.

But his legs felt like sandbags, and he couldn't get up. He couldn't even look at her.

His heart beat painfully. He almost didn't want to hear her decision. He'd rather stay in tortured limbo than hear a choice that might destroy the only true happiness he'd ever known.

Because from the very start, he'd believed once she had the money, she'd leave. And as close as they'd become, as much as he trusted her feelings for him, his gut told him she just didn't belong here.

She'd been thrown into a strange situation, forced to stay, and Phinny wasn't the type to whine or feel sorry for herself. She was an optimist. She had a cheerful nature. Like her parents cutting her off, she'd made the best of this situation.

And if it came with an accommodating roommate who liked to give her orgasms, then all the better. But he wasn't a good enough reason to stay in Wyoming. Not only were they too different, but this place would get boring fast. Eventually, she'd go back to her posh life in London, marry someone from her world, and live her mom's life of philanthropy, travel, and social events.

The walls closed in, and his clothes grew tight, itchy. He wanted to get out of this office. Change. Get back out on the ice. Hockey, he understood. Skating fast and hard cleared his thoughts, wiped his emotions.

"Okay." She faced them with a smile that radiated confidence.

In a game, right before he got slammed into the

boards, his body girded for the hit. It was doing that right then—as it heated up, his knuckles turning white where he gripped the armrest—right before she said the words that would seal his fate.

Choose the land.

Choose me.

For fuck's sake, Phinny, choose us.

"I'm going to take the money. And give Declan the ranch."

Phinny had expected him to be thrilled—he got the land that meant so much to him—but on the drive home, Declan was quiet. Contemplative.

The funny thing was that it hadn't been a hard choice at all. Once she'd calmed down from the shock of it all, she'd known exactly how it needed to go.

Or at least she thought she had. "Hey, did I make the wrong choice?"

He pulled up to the gate and waited for it to swing open. "There was no wrong choice. So, what're you going to do with the money?"

"Never eat ramen again?"

He didn't even smile. Just tightened his grip on the steering wheel.

"I'd like to start that business."

He nodded, hitting the accelerator and driving through.

"I know I don't have experience, but like you said, I can hire an attorney and an accountant." She didn't even know what she needed. *That's how ignorant I am.* "I'll talk to Glori. She'll help me come up with a game plan."

Not all the RVs had left yet, and a group of people sat on picnic tables laughing and telling stories. Adorably, the two women with the loom still wore their costumes.

"Declan? You don't seem happy."

He reached for her hand. "Sorry. It's been a hell of a month, and this was an outcome I hadn't anticipated."

"No, me neither. But can you at least tell me what you're thinking?"

"Owning Kurt's ranch is a big responsibility."

Oh, God. What if she'd misunderstood? *He's a hockey player. What if the last thing in the world he wants is to run a ranch?* "Did I get this all wrong?" Maybe he'd only wanted the land to keep her from selling it. Wasn't that why he'd worked with her this whole time? So she could learn about her history and ultimately win? He'd wanted *her* to keep up her dad's research and everything that went into creating a model of future ranching and farming technology. "Have I just burdened you?"

"Not at all. I'm honored to continue this for him."

"Then what's wrong?" She lifted a knee onto her seat and turned toward him. "Please tell me."

"Nothing. I'm just looking forward to telling everyone they're not losing their jobs. It's all good."

"Yes, that's good, but I'm not so sure we are. You've pulled away."

In the driveway, he cut the engine but didn't get out. "That's fair. It's just…you've got a lot of money now."

"Yeah. So?" *That's a good thing, right? Oh, wait. Of course.* He had the land but not the funds. He needed to borrow some of it. "How much do you think you'll need for the training center?" She didn't think the investment would earn out anytime soon, but she'd help him however she could. "I'd like a nest egg of ten million dollars or so that I never touch, but I'd be happy to help however I can."

"What? No. I don't want your money. I don't ever… that's not what I've been thinking about." He leaned over and kissed her on the mouth. "I'm sorry. I've been in my own head." He blew out a slow breath. "Instead of asking you, I've been making assumptions about your next move. I know you've had a good time out here, but it's not home. It's not the lifestyle you're used to. And you're never going to find that here."

"Oh, I get it. So, what you're saying is I'm rich now, I can call up Verity and the girls and see if they want to hang out. I can hire a cook and a driver and spend my days shopping. God, Declan. Is that really how you see me?"

"No. Of course not." He almost sounded offended.

"Then what?" But she didn't give him a chance to answer. She was too worked up. "My thought process was that we're in this together. That's what you said, right? *We're in this together.* So, I thought about our highest values. For you, it's roots. For me, it's financial security." Okay, you know what? Nothing she said would convince him she'd changed, so she'd have to go with actions.

Pulling out her phone, she searched her recent calls. She hadn't told him yet—things had been crazy between the festival and the contest—but she'd gotten the job. Mrs. Lumley had left a voicemail two days ago saying they could offer her a small stipend. She hadn't responded.

Well, I'm doing it now.

"Who're you calling?" he asked.

Holding up a finger for him to wait, she found Mrs. Lumley's number in her recent calls and tapped the screen. One ring, two…

As certain as she was about her decision, she got that twist in her stomach for letting down the woman who'd always been so intimidating and important.

"Phinny, darling," Mrs. Lumley said. "How are you, dear?"

"I'm doing well, thank you." She watched Declan's expression. "I'm sorry for not returning your call sooner, but it's been quite hectic out here."

"Of course. We are feeling a bit pinched on the timing, though."

"Yes, I know, and I apologize for that. I want to thank you for the job offer."

His elbows locked, and his arms went ramrod straight.

"But I'm afraid I have to pass. You know the foundation means the world to me, but I've decided to stay in the States. I'm going to start a business here."

"I don't understand." Mrs. Lumley's tone turned frosty. "Didn't you ask me for this job?"

"Yes." The joy went right out of her, and she shifted away from Declan. "And I'm so sorry, but my circumstances have changed." *Ugh.* Now, she felt like an asshole.

"I went out on a limb for you because of your family and because of what you once meant to my son, so I must say I'm extremely disappointed to grant you this favor only to have you reject it."

"I'm so sorry. I feel awful about it."

"Particularly since the planning committee has already begun its work, and you were one of our key members. I'm seeing a pattern of carelessness from you, and I'm quite sure I don't like it. Goodbye." The line went dead.

Phinny sat in the car, the sun burning her thighs, a bee darting around her head. An eerie sense of dread churned through her. She'd wanted to prove to Declan that he could trust his heart with her.

Instead, she'd antagonized one of the most powerful women in the United Kingdom.

"I'm guessing that didn't go well."

"No. She's angry. I mean, after all she went through to get me a salary…"

"Doesn't she run the foundation?"

"Of course."

"So, how much work did she have to do? A few conversations?"

"She had to present it to the board. You have to be careful what you put up for a vote. Everyone has their own agendas." It would be embarrassing for her. That was the real issue.

"You can take the job, you know."

That snapped her out of it. "No, Declan, I can't. My life has changed, and I live here now. I called her in front of you to prove that I'm staying here. Nothing could make me go back to my old life. *Nothing.*"

"Okay, then."

She didn't like when he got all emotionless like that. She hated when she couldn't read him. "I thought you'd be happy." Because it meant he'd shut down.

"I am." He got out of the Jeep. "I'm just not sure it's as simple as you'd like it to be."

"What does that mean?" But he was already heading to the house. She stayed put for a moment, an uneasy feeling creeping up her spine. She knew she'd made the right decision. She wouldn't change it for anything.

But he was right. It wouldn't be that simple.

There would be a consequence. She just didn't know what.

. . .

Phinny had a lot riding on today. It was just a pop-up store, but she'd arranged every detail herself. She was pretty damn proud of herself for securing a last-minute and affordable building large enough to house Lachlan's entire collection of furniture.

She hadn't had time to submit an announcement in local newspapers, but she did post on as many Calamity and Jackson social media sites as she could find. She'd put up flyers and, most importantly, she'd asked the Cooters to spread the word.

Given that she was starting her own business in town, and she'd really put her name out there, today had to be a success.

As they turned into the parking lot, she saw the moving truck. She'd offered to pay for it, but Lachlan had just hung up on her. "He's here." They'd come early to make sure the space was clean and aired out. "I hope he brought some guys to help him unload."

"Well, I'm here. I can help."

Excitement had her unbuckling even before Declan parked. "He's going to make serious bank today." But more importantly, she hoped he'd launch a business that would support him the rest of his life. No one should be financially insecure at Lachlan's age.

Declan turned into a spot in front of the entrance. "You want me to help him unload or get started sweeping?"

"Let's take a look at the space first."

Right then, Lachlan strode out of the store. He didn't look pleased.

Jumping out of the Jeep, she hurried over. "Hey. We're

here. If it's a mess in there, don't worry. The owner didn't have time to bring in a clean-up crew, so Declan and I brought our own supplies."

Lachlan narrowed his eyes against the early morning sun. "It's not happening."

"What do you mean?"

"They're setting up for a volleyball tournament in there." His gruff voice sounded annoyed.

Dread sliced through her, opening a vein of self-doubt. "No, no. They probably *had* a tournament. They're taking it down now. We've got the building today and tomorrow." She could not have gotten this wrong. She just couldn't have. Something as simple as the date? She pulled up the email with the attached contract and quickly scrolled through it. *Oh, thank God.* "No, see?" She tapped the screen to show him. "We're good. It's ours."

"Don't know what to tell you." He moved past her, pulling his keys out of his pocket.

"Wait, where are you going?"

"Home."

"No. Hang on, please. Let me talk to them." She was already on the move. "I'll get it all sorted. Give me five minutes." She dashed into the building to find a hive of activity. Someone was unrolling tape for court lines while others assembled nets and poles. "Excuse me," she asked a woman with a clipboard. "Hello. I'm Phinny Crutchley, and I've rented this space for a furniture pop-up store."

"Okay. Well, we're setting up for a two-day tournament."

Her heart pounded, but she didn't betray the slightest concern. "We've somehow got our wires crossed." She held up her phone to show the contract. "See, we've rented it for today and tomorrow."

Now, the woman looked concerned. "So did we." Holding her clipboard to the side of her mouth, she shouted, "Clayton."

A man jogged over. "What's up?" He gave her a nod. "Hey."

"Hello. There seems to be a misunderstanding." For the third time, she held up her phone. "I've rented the space this weekend."

The smile faded. "That's not possible." He read the contract dates. "Okay, hang on. Let me check." He pulled out his phone and tapped away. His brow creased as he transferred his gaze back to hers. "Huh. Looks like we booked the same dates."

"How is this possible?" the woman asked. "Check the address. Maybe one of us is at the wrong strip mall."

Phinny searched her recent calls. "Let me call Dale." The man who'd rented the place to her said it had been empty for nearly a year. As the phone rang, she headed outside to make sure Lachlan hadn't left. She found him talking to Declan and another guy in the shade of the overhang. It was the large man she'd met in the perfumer's tent, the one with two children. *Brodie.*

"I'm heading out," Lachlan said.

"Oh, please don't do that. I'm calling the property owner right now. I'll take care of it."

Ignoring her, the older man headed for his truck.

This can't be happening. It had all seemed so simple. She'd been sure she could pull this off.

Fortunately, Dale answered right away. "Hello?"

"Hey, it's Phinny."

"Oh, hey. Everything okay?"

"No. We're at the store, but there's a group setting up for a volleyball tournament."

"What? How's that possible?"

"I don't know, but they showed me their contract, and it's for the same location and same dates."

"Dammit. Hang on. Let me check the calendar."

Lachlan drove the truck to the end of the lot, before backing into a space and turning around. Frantic, Phinny reached for Declan. "Please tell him not to leave. I'm going to take care of everything."

"Yeah, you don't really tell Lachlan anything," Brodie said.

"What does that mean? He needs this."

"You ever met a bison?" Brodie smiled. "That's my uncle."

Declan's eyebrows shot up. "Lachlan's your uncle?"

She felt so relieved to hear he had a family, especially Brodie and Rosie who both looked like good, kind people.

"Phinny?" Dale came back on the line. "Listen, it looks like my ex-wife rented the place out to the volleyball people. We have an electronic calendar, so she could see I'd already reserved the place, but she went ahead and deleted it so she could book this tournament."

"What? Why would she do that?"

"Because she's trying to stick it to me. Look, I'm really sorry about this."

"This makes no sense. I *paid* you for it." She paced a few steps away from the men. "You can't do this. This man…he needs this pop-up. You can't do this to him." She lowered her voice. "He has no money. He's trying to build a career here."

"What?" Brodie asked Declan. "What's she talking about?"

"Phinny." Declan touched her shoulder to get her attention.

But she was listening to Dale. "If the club's already in the store, there's nothing I can do. My ex fucked us all over. What's new?"

"Okay, but there has to be another location. He rented a huge truck for his furniture. We can go somewhere else. You said you own a lot of property."

"Yeah, I do, but most of it's fully rented, which is why I can't sell them and cut myself off from my ex. I'm sorry, Phinny. There's nothing I can do. I'll refund you right now." He disconnected.

"I can't believe this." She turned to the men. "I'll find you a new space right now. I promise. This is not over."

"Nah, don't worry about it." Brodie didn't seem the least bit bothered by the whole mess. "Besides, the signs lead people here. I'm not sure they'll be interested in going to a second location."

"But we could try. We can't just bail on him. He paid for rental trucks." Frazzled, she was losing her cool.

"Phinny." Speaking gently but pointedly, Declan held her gaze with a powerful reassurance. "Lachlan's okay."

Brodie looked between them, clearly confused. "I don't know what my uncle told you to make you think he's hurting financially—"

"No, he never said anything. But he was…well…" She couldn't tell him that the condition of the man's boots and threadbare jeans made it obvious. "He drove customers away." How did she get her point across? "Some steady sales could bring him a little more…security."

"My uncle's practically a hermit," Brodie said. "He's got a nice place of his own, but he prefers his cabin in the woods. He doesn't need to sell his furniture."

"Oh, okay. I'm sorry for assuming…"

"Nah, you tried to do a good thing for him." Brodie

waved Lachlan off before turning back to her. "Okay, I'm going to head out. Thank you for trying." He got into his SUV.

Phinny stood there, defeated and embarrassed. "I can't believe this. How in the world did this happen?"

He wrapped an arm around her, kissing her cheek. "You did nothing wrong." Then, he started back toward the Jeep. "Let's get out of here."

She followed, and it felt like she was sleepwalking. Nothing made sense. "What a disaster."

They got in the car and buckled up. "Look, this isn't on you. You didn't mess anything up. And no one's pissed. Brodie thinks it's nice that you tried to do this for his uncle."

"He made it sound like Lachlan doesn't need the money, so they must think I'm ridiculous."

"He wouldn't have gone to all this trouble if he didn't need your help. I get the impression he makes furniture but doesn't bother selling it. And I think you've got a new client to add to your locally-sourced products. You can have a section of your shop with his smaller pieces."

"If you knew his nephew, how did you not know Lachlan? It's a small town."

"I went to school with the Bowie brothers, but I didn't know them well. I was into hockey hardcore at that point, and they were training for the Olympics. I had no idea they were related to Lachlan. He's one of those legends in town. You'll never see him during tourist season, but when he does show up somewhere, everyone notices."

"How did he make his wealth then?"

"I don't know about him, but Brodie's dad—I'm guessing Lachlan's brother—was a venture capitalist. They're well-off."

"And by well-off, do you mean comfortable?"

"I mean billionaires."

The man was a *billionaire?* And she'd… "Oh, God." She lowered her head into her hands. "Kill me. Kill me right now. I made such a fool of myself."

"I can promise you no one thinks you're anything but kind and generous."

No matter what anyone said, no matter that Dale and his ex were vengeful and messing with each other, the only thing the Bowie family would remember was that Seraphina Crutchley had screwed up royally. That their uncle had gone to the exhausting work of loading an entire moving van full of heavy furniture only to discover the space had been double-booked.

Word would spread fast of her incompetence.

How could she ask people to sell their goods in her shop now?

Chapter Twenty

Her phone vibrated and danced on the nightstand, startling her awake.

Not wanting to disturb Declan, she grabbed it and quietly padded out of the room. Seeing her stepfather's name on the screen—coming so soon after bailing on Mrs. Lumley—had her heart racing. "Hey, Drewsy." She tried for light and airy.

"Seraphina."

Oh, crap. His clipped tone had her shriveling like plastic to a flame.

"I've just got off the phone with Reginald Lumley."

She should've told her parents. Nothing was worse than being blindsided. "I'm so sorry about that." Even though she was a grown woman who stood by her decision, she hated upsetting her stepfather. "I know it's an awful situation, but my circumstances have changed. I had no choice."

"Darling, this is simply not done. You asked our friends for a paid position, and they gave it to you. I don't need to tell you this is a *family* foundation. The *family* runs it. They don't have salaried positions because their sole purpose is to raise money for women and children."

Well, of course they did have some executives on their payroll, but she understood what he meant. The Crutchleys were considered family. "I know, and I feel terrible about it, but I've got news, Andrew. I'm going to stay here."

"So, you won the contest?" Diverted, he went into business-mode.

Thankfully. "I did."

"That's wonderful." He chuckled, sounding relieved. "Well done. I'll just ring him back and tell him you don't need the salary after all. All right then, your mum and I will cover your bills until we sell the property. In the meantime, we'll fly out there in the next day or two and help you prepare it for sale. Once it's in the hands of a realtor, we can manage the rest from here. I'll phone Reginald right now."

Anxiety ripped through her body like a bullet. "No. Don't do that. I'm not selling the ranch, and I'm not going back to London. Andrew, I'm staying in Calamity."

"What are you going on about? Of course, you're selling. What are you going to do with a cattle ranch in the States?"

I've given it away. But the idea of telling him made her sick to her stomach. He would never understand. "I've met someone, and I'm really happy here. I'm staying in Calamity and living on my dad's ranch."

"Your *dad's* ranch? He's your dad now, is he?"

"No, it's not like that." Flustered, she sat down at the top of the stairs. "You raised me, and no one can replace you in my life. But I've learned that Kurt wanted me."

"You've learned this from a dead man?"

"Well, yes, I've seen his office and read…his correspondence." She switched the phone to her other hand, swiping the clammy palm on her T-shirt. "I'm just saying I see things more clearly now."

He blew out a breath of exasperation. "We've done you a terrible disservice by sheltering you the way we have. Now listen to me, this man you've apparently fallen for is playing you. Anyone from that area knows the value of the property. He wants to get his hands on the money."

"*What?* I'm not stupid. I'm not…Andrew, he's the man I competed against."

"You see? He didn't win the land, so he'll get it by seducing you."

"He's not…that's not what happened. We fell in love with each other." Of course, Declan had never said the words. But it would come. She was sure of it. He just had a hard time opening up. "The first time I met him was in the lawyer's office. The moment he learned about the contest, he offered to walk away. He said he wouldn't interfere with my birthright. The only reason he stayed for the competition was so I *wouldn't* sell it."

"You must sell the land. It's not even a question. Your life is here with us. With your family. You're twenty-five years old. What if you get pregnant with this man? Do you really want to raise a family five thousand miles away? That would break your mother's heart."

She wasn't really speaking to her mum at the moment, so that wasn't exactly a selling point.

"It would surely break mine."

Oh, Drewsy. Affection eased the knot in her gut. "That's not something we need to worry about. Trust me, I'm not looking that far into the future. I'm not ready to have a child." In many ways, she felt like her life had just begun. Like she'd emerged from a cocoon and could see the world through fresh eyes. "Look, I know this is big news. It's huge for me, too, but—"

"Listen to me. I know how it is to get swept away by a new love, but you must look at the bigger picture. You must consider your future. If you don't sell the land…how will you support yourself? Phinny, I won't be able to loan you money. I can't support you."

Her back straightened. "I don't need your money. After I won, I learned there was a second codicil. The winner could choose between the land and a cash inheritance. I gave Declan the land, and I took the money. And I haven't asked you for a dime since you cut me off, so I don't know why you think I'd start now. In any event, I can't take the job because I'm staying here, and I'm going to start my own business."

"What business? What scheme has this cowboy led you into?" She'd never heard him so distraught. "Seraphina, you must come home straight away. Is it too late to change your mind about the will?" He'd grown agitated in a way she'd never heard before. "Forget coming home, I'll catch a flight first thing in the morning."

"It's too late. I've signed the papers."

"What have you done? I don't know how much you inherited, but it's clear this man's going to help you blow through it. Is the business your new friend's idea? Did he ask for a loan to buy feed and a new tractor?"

Blow through my money. The very idea sent her reeling. That would never happen. "No, it's my idea. I'm going to start a shop for locally-sourced products. No one's done it here yet, and it's a really good idea."

"Perhaps for someone who has experience and business sense. You know nothing about running a store. It's not like a swap meet, where you set an old belt and a worn pair of shoes on a table and hope some tosser comes along and buys it. Businesses are complicated. Honestly, I don't know what to do with you right now."

Obviously, she had no experience. That point had been driven home when she'd messed up Lachlan's pop-up store. Imagine if she used some of her inheritance to buy a building or some inventory—and then it went sideways? What potential did she have to earn it back? The only income she'd ever made came from tips at a diner.

"Look, you've come into a large sum of money. You've no experience managing it. I'm going to insist you come home and take the job with the foundation."

"No, I'm not going to do that. I live here now, and I don't need the money anymore. Andrew, I've got twenty-five million dollars."

"We all have twenty-five million dollars." By his tone, she could tell his cheeks had turned a mottled red. "We have more than that. That's why we run foundations and give as much as we do. Why on earth do you think your mother works so tirelessly with her philanthropies? *From whom much is given, much is expected.* We raised you with that belief, and I won't let one month in America change that."

"That's not what's happening. You're not listening to me. Andrew, I've fallen in love. Not just with a man but with my life here, and I want to see it through. I want to live on this ranch in this amazing town. I want to meet people and find out what curious and interesting things they do in their spare time. I love the idea of selling products they thought were just a hobby, of giving them an income, and sharing their passions with others in the community." *Yes.* Everything she'd said restored her confidence *and* her spirit.

"Enough." His voice cracked. "You are *required* to take this job. If you don't, it will reflect on us, and it will have real impact on our memberships, invitations, and business. You're either inside the circle, or you're outside, and the Crutchley family's been in it for four hundred years."

She understood what he was saying. The Lumleys had an exclusive contract with Andrew's linen-supply business. Plus, she'd already turned down Cameron's proposal. Walking away from the foundation after coming into a sizable inheritance would make her family look horrifyingly bad. But she couldn't lose the beautiful life she'd just created. She wouldn't. "I'm sorry for any inconvenience I've caused you and my mum. I love you both very much, and I would never want to hurt you." She took in a shaky breath. "But I'm not going to take the job."

Andrew went quiet, and it killed her. Every second that ticked past accelerated her heartbeat. A cold bead of perspiration trickled down her back.

"I didn't want to tell you this, but I see I must." He stopped speaking, the only sound coming from his labored breaths. "I've suffered some financial setbacks in the past few years. Between the market crash and a few bad investments, I'm in a precarious situation. Losing the Lumley contracts would devastate this family."

"Oh, God." She'd had no idea.

"You mustn't tell your mother. She's not to know. But it's imperative that you ring Mrs. Lumley back and take this job. I cannot sustain the loss of their business. Do you understand?"

"Yes. Of course."

"We would have to sell our home and the country estate that's been in my family for generations. Think about the impact on your mum. You remember how your friends turned their backs on you? The same thing will happen to your mother, only it will be so much worse. She'll be cast out of society. Do you want that for her?"

"No." Reeling as though she'd been struck by a lorry, her voice was barely a whisper. Of course, she had no choice in the matter. She couldn't possibly let her parents suffer like that. "I'll do it this year, and then I'm moving out here to be with Declan."

"That's perfectly fine. And when you're home, we'll meet with Frederick to set up a portfolio, so you'll never have to worry about money again. We'll even open a Fun Money account so you can play with these business ideas of yours."

Fun money. God, how little he thought of her. She couldn't bear talking to him one more minute. "I'll call Mrs. Lumley now."

Disconnecting, she lowered her head in her hands and closed her eyes. The world wavered like a boat at sea.

Of course, she would do what was right for her family. Between the debacle with Cameron and now the job, she was the one who'd jeopardized the relationship. She had to save them.

She just hoped like the hell it didn't cost her the love of her life.

Declan stood in the bunkhouse addressing Kurt's staff. "I'm sure everyone knows by now that Phinny won the trivia contest, but there was another codicil to the will, and I wanted to let you know that *I've* inherited the ranch."

The room went perfectly quiet. And then a moment later, a chair scraped back on the concrete floor and Tina got up, making her way to him, arms open. "That's real good news." She hugged him. "Real good."

Mitch clapped him on the back. "Guess I'll reserve my thoughts until I hear what your plans are."

Tina waved him off. "You know what this place means to him."

"Need to hear it." Mitch gestured to the others. "We all do."

"That's fair." He was damn glad he could give them the answer they all hoped for. "Kurt had time before he passed to write up very clear instructions for his vision, including the research he was investing in, so he's made it easy for me to take over exactly how he intended. And in order to implement that, I don't have a choice but to keep all of you. Otherwise, I might've gone with better-looking people."

A few people burst out laughing.

"Probably even some hockey players since I understand what they're talking about."

They were all cracking up, and he knew it was more relief than humor. It felt good. Everything felt good. The ranch stayed intact, and he got Phinny. He didn't know how or why a woman like that wanted his moody ass, but she did. He was pissed at himself for underestimating her, thinking she'd want to go back to her fancy world when anyone could see how happy she was here. How she'd come into her own.

"What about hockey?" Mitch asked. "Are you here full-time or are you going back to Pittsburgh?"

"I've got part ownership of the Renegades, so I'm staying right here." It sucked, giving up his shot at coaching an NHL team. But Phinny had given up running the auction, so he could do the same. Because he loved her. Loved her harder and deeper than anything.

Phinny was his heart. Hockey was a career.

Time to finish up and let them get back to work. "In any event, I'll be around, learning as much as I can, but I'm not going to get in anyone's way. Kurt trusted all of you to do your jobs, and thanks to your efforts, this place is one of the most profitable ranches in the west."

"In the whole country," someone shouted.

"In the fucking world."

He chuckled. "True, true. All right, that's it. Until there's a reason to change something, it's going to be business as usual. Including those bonuses he gives you guys."

And right there—that's what cleared all their expressions. Knowing they could afford to do the work they loved seemed to seal the deal. As they all headed outside and back to work, Mitch and Tina caught up with him.

"I think it all worked out the way it should," Tina said.

"I don't know about that. I'm not a Grevers, and I know he'd rather have kept it in the family. But it's better than selling the place."

She tipped her head in confusion. "Don't you know? You were his family. He loved all you boys, but you were like a son to him. Take it from someone who knew Kurt for over two decades, he's resting in peace now that he knows this place is in your hands."

Letting the two of them head for the house without

him, Declan hung back. He took a moment to let her words sink in. As he closed his eyes, a breeze ruffled his hair, and his skin prickled with awareness. For one vivid, startling moment, he could see Kurt in his mind's eye, as clearly as if he were standing right in front of him. He even got a whiff of his distinctive scent—that hint of pine and woodsmoke, of a man who lived outdoors.

Weirdest thing of all? Kurt was giving him one of those rare smiles that made him feel like he'd done something good and meaningful. And for the first time in years, Declan felt like he was in the right place. Like all the pieces had come together in just the way they were meant to be.

"I won't let you down."

"Won't let who down?" Phinny's voice snapped him out of his thoughts.

The vision had been so real, he hadn't realized he'd said it out loud. Laughing, he wrapped his arms around her. "Kurt. I just talked to the staff and told them their jobs were safe, that I'd keep things going just as their boss intended."

"You're the boss now." When his smile faltered, she said, "That's scary, I know." She slipped her hands under his shirt and ran them up his chest. "Better you than me." She gave him a teasing smile that quickly faded. "Hey, I need to talk to you."

"Sure. I have to meet with Hank, but I've got a few minutes. What's up?"

Staff continued to trickle out of the bunkhouse, and she tugged on his arm. "Let's go inside." She reached for his hand. "You're meeting with the lawyer tomorrow, right? About the team ownership?"

Something seemed off with her. He wasn't used to

seeing that troubled furrow on her forehead. "Yep." He brought their hands to his mouth and kissed the back of hers. Just from being near her, everything in him expanded, opened, making more room for the crazy emotion roiling through him. He stepped ahead of her and opened the door.

Once inside, she turned to him. "Are you happy with your decision? To quit coaching and own a team?"

So, that's what's worrying her. It was time to tell her.

Fear squeezed his heart, but he pushed through it. They'd both made sacrifices to be together. He had to do this. He had to step over that invisible line he'd drawn to keep himself…what? Safe? To keep his heart protected?

Too late. If she left him, he'd be devastated. She'd broken through, and he wouldn't have it any other way. There was no one else in the world like this woman.

My woman.

Swooping her off her feet and into his arms, he carried her into the living room.

"Declan." Legs dangling, hands clasped around his neck, she laughed. "What're you doing?"

He turned around, dropped onto the couch, and positioned her on his lap. "I—" His throat closed up. Lowering his forehead to hers, he breathed in her sweet scent, let it work its magic. It wove through him, calming him, giving him strength. He breathed until he was ready to be the fearless man she deserved. "You asked me if I'm happy with my decision. I'm happy with you. Phinny." He sucked in a sharp breath. "I love you."

Her eyes flared, then glistened.

"I've always been grateful for my life. Sam was good to me, and I grew up with a great group of friends. And even if hockey didn't work out the way I'd expected, I was grateful to have a career on the ice. Turns out I'm not only good at coaching, I like it. But happy?" He shook his head. "I only understood what the word meant when I met you. I love you, Phinny. So, when you ask me if I'm happy with my decision, the answer's yes. I'm happy with my decision because I get to be with you."

Her pained expression made him wonder what he was doing wrong. Except…maybe he'd made it sound like he was giving up something to be with her. "Forget my career. That means nothing in the scheme of things. Phinny, all I want is to be with you. I want to wake up with you every morning. I want to see your smile and hear your laugh. I'm happy, Phinny. I'm happy with *you*."

She pulled out of his hold and climbed off his lap to sit beside him. Knees drawn to her chest, arms hugging them, she'd curled into a ball.

Oh, fuck. A chill gripped his spine. She looked sick with remorse. "What? Just say it." If she told him this had been nothing but a fun time for her, that she'd gotten carried away with all the strange newness here, he'd be the biggest fool on the planet. "What's wrong? Did something happen?"

"Declan, I took the job."

His body went hard. "What job?" He needed her to spell it out.

"With the Lumley Foundation. I had to."

"Okay." The strangest sensation crept over him. He could actually feel himself shutting down. *Don't do that. Listen to her.* "What happened?"

"Andrew called. He told me he's in a bad financial situation. If the Lumleys cancel his contracts, he'll have to sell his assets. That means our home, the country house…everything."

"So, he wants your money?"

"No, but he needs me to take the job I asked for, so the Lumleys don't turn against us. Declan, they have the power to ruin him."

Every now and then, he had a dream where he jumped off a cliff, only to realize he'd forgotten his parachute. *That's what this feels like.*

Snatching a throw pillow, she held it on her lap. "My mum would be penniless. She'll lose all her friends. Her entire world."

"Okay." The ground came up fast, and he braced for impact.

"I can't do that to them. As much as I don't want to go back, I can't just walk away and leave my parents twisting in the wind. You understand, right?"

He thought he was nodding. He was trying to move his head. But he couldn't be sure.

"And so, I told him I'd come back and do the job this one last time, but after that, I'm moving here permanently. I don't want…" She reached for him. "Declan, I love you, too. Everything you said, it's exactly what I feel. You make me so happy, and it'll only be until next May. You can come visit me, and of course, I'll come here. I'll spend lots of time here."

Oddly, the impact never came. Instead of landing, he…floated. He looked where her hand connected with his arm and marveled at the fact that he didn't feel it.

"I mean, I really only need to be in London for meetings and…well, I mean, there's lots of events. That's where I chat people up and find out what they have to offer. Ugh. Forget it. That's not the point." She straddled his lap and cupped his jaw. "Declan, I love you. I love you so much, and I want to be with you. I want to stay here, but I have to do the right thing." She grabbed his hand and put it on her thigh. "Why are you not talking to me? Why are you just sitting there? I'm not breaking up with you. We won't be long distance for long. The ball's in May, but really, once I get the items lined up, most of my job's over. From then on, I can work from here."

He gave himself an internal shake. "Right." He got up, taking her with him, and set her down. "Look, I get it." He didn't know why he'd spaced out like that. "It's no big deal. You can't do anything to jeopardize your stepfather's livelihood." He started off.

"No, don't do that. Don't walk away from me."

"I have to meet with Hank. I told you."

"Forget that right now. This is our first speedbump, and we have to get through it. Every couple has disagreements."

"We're not fighting. I get it." He understood that she was still under the thumb of her parents. And once she got back to London, they'd suck her back into her fancy lifestyle with balls and galas and powerful men proposing to her. They had that kind of power over her. Obviously.

I guarantee she won't be pining for a cattle ranch in Wyoming.

It wasn't like he hadn't anticipated this. He might've hoped for a different outcome, but it was always going to end with her leaving.

"So, we're okay?" Her tone was firm, her eyes pleading. "We're going to do long distance?"

"No." Jesus, the way she flinched, as though he'd yanked the carpet out from under her feet, was almost enough to make him change his mind. He didn't want to hurt her. Then again, the kindest thing he could do was tell the truth. Rip the Band-Aid off. "That's not going to work."

"What won't work?"

"Long distance. I've got a ranch to run. A team to own. Plus, with you in London, there's a seven-hour time difference. When you have time to talk, I'll be going to work. I'm just being realistic."

"No, you're not. You're acting like a robot right now." Her eyes had gone wild, and she grabbed his wrist, giving him a shake. "You just said you loved me. You don't bail at the first sign of trouble. God, Declan. We'll be like any normal couple. We'll both work and still be together." Her features wrenched in anxiety, and he could only guess he looked dull because that's how he felt inside.

He wasn't the most self-aware guy on the planet. He could admit that. But he did know one thing about himself. He couldn't wait around and hope that Phinny would come back to him.

And just like that, he came back into his body, felt the rightness of his world again. "I do love you. And maybe if we'd had more time together, it could've grown deep enough to weather a hit as big as this one. But we've only known each other four weeks." Everything he said made sense. "Play time's over. Now, we go back to regular programming." And yet…nothing was sticking. It was like he was hovering over the moment instead of living it. His thoughts drifted in his mind like dandelion fluff.

"Declan." Her face went red, her tone shrill. "Stop it. We're not breaking up. This is not my fault. It's not my choice."

He'd do just about anything to take that hysterical look out of her eyes.

But in that moment, he had nothing to give.

"Hank's waiting." And then, he walked out of the room.

Hair in her eyes, perspiration beading over her lip, Phinny sat on top of the suitcase, jamming her butt down, trying to force the zipper to move. But it wouldn't budge.

Something else had to go. She'd already taken out the shorts and trainers, but she couldn't part with the Wild Billy T-shirt, the boots, or the pink cowboy hat. Toppling onto the mattress, she pulled off her ballet flats. She'd have to wear the damn boots and hat on the plane. Her mum would have a fit when she saw her, but she didn't care.

She didn't care about much of anything. Yesterday, after Declan had dumped her, she'd gone to bed, curled into the fetal position, and bawled her eyes out. Despair had sucked her in, and she hadn't been able to find her way out for hours.

Until it struck her that she'd have to see him in the morning. With her bloodshot, puffy eyes, chapped lips, and snotty nose, she'd get to watch him make his smoothie as if he hadn't carved her heart out with a spoon.

Nope. Not going to happen. So, she'd called for a car, taken a shower, and packed. In twenty minutes, she'd leave this place she'd come to love.

What choice did she have? She had to take the job, and Declan wouldn't do long distance.

God, she hated him. Hated him so much. For being a coward. For being stubborn.

For not loving me enough to fight for me.

Hot tears streaked down her cheeks, leaving her skin, her heart, her soul, blistered and raw. *Just go. Get out of here*. Shoving her feet back into the flats, she flipped the top of the suitcase open and tossed out the top layer of clothing. Out went the stupid boots she'd never wear in London, out went the hat already misshapen from being forced into her luggage.

Just fuck it. Without her new clothes, the bag easily zipped up. As she took one last look around the bedroom, sorrow sank its claws into her heart. For the first time in her life, she'd known true, genuine, happiness, and now… the asshole hockey boy had ripped it from her.

It was still dark—not even five in the morning—but she wanted to be gone before he woke up. She had just enough time to feed Tigger his stupid egg.

God, she would miss him. She would miss the chickens. And Tina. And Hank.

Dammit. Why did Declan have to be such a jerk? Each step took her further from her source of happiness and closer to the life she dreaded going back to. By the time she reached Declan's closed door, she'd worked herself into a tizzy. She stood there, listening. She wanted to beg him to change his mind. She wanted to tell him he could fuck right off, that this was her dad's ranch, and she could stay on it if she wanted to.

But she couldn't because she'd given it to him.

Anger rose like a banshee, the shriek in her head so loud, she was sure the whole world could hear it. He got to stay in her house, carry on without her like she'd never existed. He hadn't said goodbye. Or cried or shouted or even looked sad.

He hadn't felt anything at all.

That's not okay. She flung the door open, ready to rip into him but found him curled up in bed, facing away from her. Unmoving. Covers pulled up to his ears.

It was like turning the burner off on the stove, all the boiling anger went flat. Her heart ached for this man. Because under the scruff and tats, the hard muscles honed by ruthless discipline and exercise, hid a man who'd faced losses so staggering, he'd stopping feeling anything.

Until me. Leaving her suitcase in the hallway, she stepped into the room. "I love you, you butthead. I love you more than I ever thought possible. I didn't even know I could feel this much love."

A prickle of awareness hit the back of her neck. Her body went into high alert, and she didn't know why. Until she noticed his reflection in the window he faced. His eyes were open. He was listening.

"And you love me, too." His total lack of response was killing her. "But I'm not talking to the man I love right now. I'm talking to the little boy who's standing at the mailbox waiting for his parents to come home." *God.* The image was so powerful, she went weak. "You're paralyzed by fear. Your parents, Sam, Kurt…even your friends disappeared in the blink of an eye. I get it, I do. You have no control over when the people you love will be taken from you. *I* might be taken from you, too. And so, you play dead inside. But you're not dead, Declan. I know that because I've felt your passion, your love, your happiness, your joy. And it's because of *me*. I make you feel all those things, and because of that, everything's changed. You're never going to be dead inside again because I live there. And I've got bad news for you, hockey boy. Now, it's going to be more painful to live without me than to take the risk of loving me. Love is risky. *Life* is risky. It's that way for all of us. But I'm worth the risk, Declan." She stood there, not even hoping for a response. Just letting it all sink in.

I love him.

I want to spend my life with him.
I'm worth the risk.
I'm worth it.

"But it's something you'll have to figure out on your own. And here's the good news. When you do, I'll be waiting for you. *That's* how strong our love is." And then, she quietly closed the door, grabbed the handle of her suitcase, and headed down the stairs.

Chapter Twenty-One

With the puck in the curve of his stick, Declan tore across the ice. Cold air blowing through his mask, his body hot underneath all the padding, he slammed into the Renegades' defenseman, skimmed around a pack of enforcers, and sailed toward the net. He cocked his arms back and fired.

Chest pumping, adrenaline spiking, it took a minute for him to register the applause and whistles. He pulled off his helmet to find the parents in the bleachers giving him a standing ovation.

Ozinkski skated past. "Remind me again why you're not playing?"

"I ran out of guys to beat."

The first line defender threw his head back and laughed. But Declan *had* gone a little nuts there. He'd meant to show a technique, but somehow, he'd gotten a wild hair up his ass, and he'd wound up taking off with the puck.

Yeah, it wasn't a wild hair. It was Phinny. She'd been

gone three weeks, and he missed her so damn much. And he couldn't stop thinking about what she'd said.

Now, everything's changed.

You're never going to be dead inside again because I live there.

She was right. Now that he knew what it felt like to have her in his life, there was no going back. There was just the constant ache of missing her.

And hating himself for hurting her.

The night he'd callously broken up with her, he'd heard her crying. He'd tried to stay away, tried to meet Jaime at a bar in town, but he couldn't do it. He'd wound up standing outside her door and listening to her sob so hard she was gasping for breath.

And what had he done? Instead of pulling her into his arms, instead of fixing the damage he'd caused, he'd walked away.

It felt like a puck had slammed him right in the chest, blowing a chunk of his heart out.

Knowing he had to calm the fuck down, he skated off the ice and nearly collided into Glori.

She carried a stack of boxes. "For a second there, I thought you were Kurt."

He set his stick down so he could relieve her of them. "Are these the granola bars?"

"Yep. I only made five hundred because I'm retired, and I'm not going back to work." She smiled at him. "I'm *not.*"

"Uh huh. Sure." He knew she was teasing, but he couldn't get into it. Because he'd hurt the woman he loved. He'd done the right thing—they wouldn't have lasted. He'd just handled it terribly.

"I heard your girlfriend went back to England with a satchel stuffed with twenties."

"She did." He didn't like what her tone implied. "She's got a job there that she couldn't bail on."

"So, she's not coming back?"

He shrugged. Now that she'd been back in her element for three weeks, her bank account loaded, was she wondering how she ever could've thought she'd be happy as a clerk in a store in Wyoming?

That's *how strong our love is.*

No, he knew her better than that. She was waiting for him to pull his head out of his ass.

Glori set her hands on her hips. "I'm surprised. After everything she learned about her dad and her family, I thought for sure she'd want to keep the ranch."

"She did. She just thought…" *Whatever.* He didn't need to rehash the story.

"She thought what?" She folded her arms across her chest. "I'd like to know her logic."

She thought we'd be together. That we'd live there… happily ever after. "From the time I was a kid, I wanted to build a training facility for hockey players. Like in Canada where local families sponsor the players in junior hockey? I wanted to do that on Kurt's land."

"I remember. Didn't you ask him about it after Sam died?"

He nodded. "He said I never finished anything so why would he think I'd follow through with that?"

"Huh. Maybe that's because you never found anything worth finishing. Maybe jobs aren't as important to you as family or roots. Maybe Kurt knew that." She searched his features. "Sounds like Phinny did, too."

Fuck. He really didn't need to talk about this. He'd

made peace with his decision. "Maybe, but long distance doesn't work."

"Who says?"

"I do, okay? I'm going to own a damn NHL team and run Kurt's ranch. When do you think I have time to fly to London and hang out with her? Even if she came for a visit, I wouldn't get to see her once the season started. You know what it's like. You dated Kurt for years."

She arched a brow and folded her arms across her chest.

"Look, it doesn't matter. You know as well as I do that she doesn't belong here. And now with all that money…" Except, of course, she'd been happy here without make-up and spa days. She'd never cared that her clothes came from a big box store. "She grew up with extreme wealth. It's what she's used to. And she was only in Calamity a month. It's not her real life." *Come on. Anyone can see that.*

"Sure, when I first met her, I had the impression she was a socialite, but she worked her tail off here. And she seemed gung-ho about that store of hers. I think maybe you've got it backwards."

"What do you mean?"

"You think she can't wait to get back to the balls and butlers and the shopping sprees at Harrod's, but maybe she's had a lifetime of that and coming here showed her that none of it made her happy."

She was right, and it made his heart beat out of control. "Yeah, maybe. But we're too different. Pretty soon, she'll forget all about us."

I'll be waiting for you. That's *how strong our love is.*

He grew restless, anxious, and wanted to get back out on the ice.

"Well, if she does, that's your fault."

He shot her a look. *What?*

"She wanted to stay here. She wanted to be with you. So, if she forgets about her dream of opening a store here, that's because you pushed her to find something else." Glori watched him for a moment with a thoughtful expression. "But I guess it's a moot point since you obviously don't love her enough."

"I fucking love her." *Shit.* His outburst drew the attention of the people sitting near them in the stands. Loving her had never been the issue. It was knowing she wasn't meant for this world.

She broke into a satisfied smile. "I know." But then, she grew serious. "Look, it's not too difficult to figure out that it feels safer to walk away before you get hurt. But when you look ahead to a future without her, do you see yourself ever finding this kind of happiness again?"

"No." *Of course not.*

"Then, what are you doing? Quit hiding behind excuses." She grabbed the boxes back. "Get your ass on a plane and go get your woman."

Declan entered the attorney's office, ready to sign the papers assigning him part ownership of the Renegades. He hadn't heard from Cole or Booker, so he had no idea if they'd changed their minds. He couldn't see how they would—not with their careers so hot.

"Go on in," the receptionist said.

"Thank you."

Jaime was already seated, his knee jackhammering. "Hey, man."

"Hey." Declan greeted his friend before turning to shake the lawyer's hand.

"Great. We're all here." Harrison smiled. "Okay, let's get started."

"I guess we're not waiting for Cole and Booker?" Declan glanced at the door.

"They're not coming." Jaime sat up. "It's just us."

The lawyer held up a document. "I received this notarized letter from Booker relinquishing his interest in the team. And since Kurt specifically stated the rights can't be sold or transferred that would mean the three remaining parties each own one-third of the team. But Cole emailed to say he's giving up his share, so the team will be co-owned by the two of you. That is, if you both want it." The lawyer addressed Declan.

"I do. I want it." He'd made peace with not coaching. It was all right. He was fine.

The lawyer pulled out two sets of identical contracts and lay them in front of each man. "You'll just need to sign—"

"Hang on." Jaime lunged for the pen. "Let me sign first."

"Take it easy, man." Declan chuckled. "It's not like the first person to sign has a bigger say in decision-making."

"I know, dumbass. But I need to be the owner first." The tip of his pen scratched as Jaime hastily marked his initials where indicated. "Okay. Now, I can make you an offer."

"You're not buying me out, rich boy." Declan shook his head.

"He just said two seconds ago that's not possible." His friend tapped the contract. "The will forbids trading, selling, or transferring ownership." With a shit-eating grin, he said, "How would you like to be the coach of the Renegades?"

What? Is this real? "I would like that very fucking much." Excitement rumbled under his skin, little sparks that triggered a chain reaction until his entire body was buzzing. "But how is that possible? They have a coach."

"He had all these ideas for the team, but none of them ever panned out. He's aggressive and keeps changing the line-up, and he won't give them the time to work together to develop the chemistry they need. After hanging out with you this summer, the guys decided they like your vision. They like the way you talk to them. They like you." Jaime smacked his shoulder. "They want you."

"Even after I raged on the ice the other day?"

"Especially after that. You know hockey from the inside out. They want you."

Well, damn. Of course, he wanted to coach the Renegades. "What does this mean for ownership, though? Do I have to give up my share?" Because no matter how much he wanted to coach the Renegades, he still felt that stubborn pull to honor Kurt's wishes. His mentor had never steered him wrong, and he almost felt like there was a plan in all this that he didn't feel right messing with.

"Well, that's the next order of business." The lawyer sat back in his chair. "Instead of relinquishing your rights, I can make you all silent partners. Jaime would make all the decisions. You, Booker, and Cole would have no say and no involvement in meetings. We could either give it an end-date, or we can leave it open."

"Kurt wanted us back together." Declan wanted that, too. And not because he was alone in the world, but because he missed his friends. "That works for me." He jerked his thumb to Jaime. "The way this guy blows through coaches, I'll need a fallback plan anyway."

They both laughed, and Declan knew Jamie was as

relieved as he was. Neither had wanted Cole and Booker out of the picture, so leaving the door open felt good.

"All right, then." The lawyer leaned forward and gathered the two sets of documents. "Let me get some new contracts worked up. Jaime will own the team, and the three of you will be silent partners."

Declan should be elated. He should be flying high. Not only did he get to coach, but he got to lead Kurt's team. The one Kurt bought for them.

But the only person he wanted to share the news with lived in London. Because he'd pushed her away. And for what? He'd thought she was under her parents' thumb, but what had he just said about honoring Kurt? *And he wasn't even my dad.*

Taking the job at the foundation meant Phinny was a good, loyal person. It should give him comfort that she'd have her family's back.

That she wouldn't leave him.

Just as she'd told him. "I think I fucked up."

Jaime shot him a look. "You *don't* want to coach?"

"No, I do. I meant about something else. People are always telling me I'm a badass on the ice."

"You are. You're the most confident, focused player I know. You're fearless."

"But I'm a coward in the ways that matter." *Oh, fuck.* Like uncorking a bottle of champagne, something popped inside his chest, and all the love he'd tried so hard to hold back came gushing out.

Everything Phinny had said was true.

Whatever he'd been doing to protect his heart…it didn't work anymore. Now that he knew happiness, passion, and love, there was no going back.

He knew what it meant to live his dream—he'd just

gotten the job as an NHL coach. Phinny should get to live hers. Whether it was running the auction or opening a store, she needed his support and encouragement. And if it meant they lived apart for a while, so what?

When Harrison walked back into the room, Declan stood up. "Hey, you knew all of Kurt's business associates and friends, right?"

"I do. What did you need?"

"I've got to make things right with my girl, and I'm going to need some help."

She'd waited for him long enough.

If Phinny didn't relax her facial muscles and kick off her pointy-toed high heels, she was going to lose it. She also wouldn't mind stripping off the shapewear that made it difficult to draw a full breath, but one didn't do such things on a receiving line at the gala celebrating the end of Cowes Week.

Bored, she took in the massive crystal chandeliers, the marble parquet floor, and the catering staff moving through the room with pewter trays of appetizers and bubbly champagne. Feet screaming in pain, she kicked off a pump and flexed her toes.

Her mum discreetly nudged her, forcing Phinny to slap the smile back on and curtsey in front of Lady Kent.

"Lovely to see you, Phinny, dear." The woman smiled warmly. "We must speak about the auction. Come and find me later, and I'll make some introductions."

"Thank you. That would be wonderful." It was, after all, Phinny's job to finagle as many items as possible out of the extremely wealthy guests.

For so many years, she'd lived for these events. But now, she could see what she'd loved was the time with her mum, as they got their hair and make-up done together and sorted through the dresses, shoes, and clutches the stylist brought them. She knew that because for one blissful month she'd gotten to experience an entirely different kind of life. One that included hot sex and stunning mountain ranges, Jeep rides with the top down and full-bellied laughter.

She missed Declan so much. Missed everything about her life on the ranch, even mucking the stalls. She'd never have imagined how good it would feel to make her own food and clean her own messes—to be fully engaged in her life.

And, frankly, she didn't want to pry a vacation home out of rich people. She didn't want to flatter and smile and work the room. She wanted to make sure Tigger didn't steal her hens' eggs. She wanted to see if the pumpkins she'd planted had grown. And she very much wanted to work at her farm stand and chat with the people who stopped to see what she was selling.

And that was the difference. She was good at chatting and socializing because she liked getting to know people. She wanted to sell Carl's honey because it brought his work to a wider audience and because she liked *him*. With her customers, she wasn't pretending to be nice or gracious. She wasn't trying to get something from them.

"What's the matter with you tonight?" her mum whispered harshly.

"I don't want to be here." The words slipped right out of her mouth.

Her mum shot her a look. Unfortunately, so did the Duke of Kent. She could've sworn the sides of his mouth tipped up. She curtseyed for him, noting there were only a few more people, and then it would be time to work the room. She had a list of potential donors to seek out.

After the duke passed by, her mum whispered, "Pull yourself together. This is your job."

"I know. I guess I just don't want this life anymore."

"We're not discussing it here."

But she'd reached her breaking point. The receiving line was nearly done anyway, so she left and made her way into the ballroom. The scent of warm dough and roasted meat sailed by, and Phinny's mouth watered. "May I?" she asked the formally dressed waiter. She took one and bit into the gruyere, sage, and prosciutto wrapped in a flaky, twisted crust. *Delicious*. She hadn't taken a napkin, so she licked her lips to catch the crumbs that stuck to her lipstick.

Only after swallowing did she notice her mum standing beside her with a horrified expression. "You're not on a farm, Seraphina. What's next, licking your fingers?"

Slowly, Phinny slid one into her mouth, hollowing her cheeks as she sucked.

"Is everything all right?" Andrew asked as he joined them. "Why've you left the receiving line? And why are you licking your fingers?"

She was being childish instead of truthful. It was time to own it. "I didn't think it was possible to change so completely in just a month, but…it is. I did." She gave them an apologetic smile. "Mum, Andrew, I'm sorry, but I can't do this anymore. I'm exhausted. All the rules, the formalities, the endless dressing up…and for what? What's the point?"

Andrew sighed. "The *point* is lifelong friendships and business relationships."

"The Honorable Judge and Mrs. Colin Reading," the announcer called.

What had she told Declan? Now that he knew what love and happiness felt like, there was no going back? Well, the same applied to her. She simply couldn't do it anymore. "I love you both. So much. But I've spent my whole life trying to be everything you've wanted me to be, and it just doesn't make me happy."

"What are you saying?" Her mum looked genuinely concerned.

When another waiter passed by, Phinny grabbed a crab cake and popped it into her mouth. "Mm. Thank you."

"Perhaps, now is not the time for this conversation." Andrew gave a meaningful lift of his eyebrows. Just over his shoulder, the Lumleys were holding court with the mayor of London.

"I just told you I'm not happy, and if you'd really heard me, you wouldn't care about what other people think. But it's not your fault. It's mine. I'm the one who's been smiling and wearing pretty bows in my hair when all I've ever wanted is for you to love me for who I am."

"Of course, I love you, Phinny. You must know that."

"I know that you love the sides of myself I show you because I work so hard for your approval."

"Where is this coming from?" His broad shoulders stiffened.

"I would rather give you my inheritance than work for people who would kick you out of their social circle just because I didn't marry their son. Or seek revenge by pulling their contracts."

"Miss Thelonia Birtwistle," the announcer called.

Her parents stood there with owlish eyes, obviously

having no idea what to make of her. But she'd never been more clear-headed in her entire life. "Honestly, if something as basic as declining a job offer is enough to cut you out of your business and social circles, what kind of relationships are they? Should you really have to try so hard to live by all these horrid rules? You run a successful business, so why not find new contacts? Anything so you don't have to live the rest of your lives compromising your dignity…your *happiness* like this." But a deeper truth popped out, spreading slowly through her like warm, sweet caramel. "Mum, I know you didn't like Calamity, but I love it, and do you want to know why?" She said it with the first genuine sense of peace in the three weeks since she'd been home. "I like who I am there. And I don't have to be a doctor or a lawyer to feel I have value. Sure, I'm good at pulling together auction items, but what I really excel at is just being me."

Oh, yes. A fizzy warmth spread through her. *That's it right there.*

It's enough just to be me.

"Phinny, darling…" Her mum looked to Andrew as though seeking understanding. "We never pushed her into medicine or law?"

Using the tip of her left shoe, Phinny lowered the strap of her right one and stepped out of it. *Ah, freedom.* She did the same with the other. Standing four and a half inches lower, she smiled. "No, you didn't. You didn't encourage me to be or do anything. And I guess the message I got was that I had no talent or skills. And because you made me dance so hard for Andrew, I wound up losing myself completely." Her mum was distraught, and Andrew was preoccupied with money and survival and only wanted her to do her job—something she understood only too well—

so she needed to leave before she made a scene in front of his friends and colleagues. "But it's all right. I've found myself now." She patted her mum's arm as if to say *You needn't worry.* "I'm going to talk to Mrs. Lumley. Actually, I'll tell you first." She reached for both of their hands. "Mummy, Drewzy, I'm going to give my notice. I miss Declan and my hens and Leddy and Glori and all my new friends, and I really want to open up my store because while I might not be a businesswoman, I have so many people who want to help me in Calamity."

"You promised you'd do it this year." She'd never seen Andrew lose his composure, but the elegant man was sweating. "You know the cost to me."

"I do, and I won't leave until they've found my replacement. And, really, how hard can it be? It's just putting together auction items." Shoving her feet back into her pumps, she wrapped her arms around her stepfather and whispered in his ear. "I can't see Mr. Lumley going to the trouble of finding a new linen supplier just because my plans changed, but if he does, I'll help you in any way I can. Just say the word and I'll transfer money into your account. I won't let you lose anything." When she started to pull away, his arms tightened.

"I fear I'm losing *you.*"

She breathed in his expensive aftershave and the hint of cigar clinging to his tuxedo jacket. "No, that will never happen. You're my Drewsy. But we'll talk about it more later." She kissed his cheek and stepped away, heading for the coat room, and fueled by the anticipation of her newfound freedom.

"Ambassador Cartwright and his guest, Mr. Declan Cadell," the announcer called.

What? The thrill of hearing his name struck her heart like a bolt of lightning. *He can't possibly be* here. She spun around to find the love of her life standing in the receiving line. He wore the ridiculous cowboy hat she'd bought him and a *tuxedo*. She hadn't even known he owned one.

As he shook hands with Mrs. Lumley, he glanced over his shoulder, and their gazes collided.

Joy exploded in her chest. Phinny ran. She took off across the marble floor, unintentionally bashing into Sir Edmond's shoulder. "Sorry. So sorry." But she kept going, and when they finally met, she threw herself into his arms. She heard a rip of fabric, but she didn't care. "Declan." She turned her face into his neck. "Oh, my God. I can't believe you're here."

He didn't say a word, but she felt his body go hot, and his hands fist in her dress.

Pulling back, she cupped his beloved face in her hands. "Am I dreaming? Are you real?" Her heart thundered, and she could barely catch her breath.

"I'm here." His jaw snapped shut, and he swallowed. "Phinny, I'm sorry." He had a wild look in his eyes, an intensity that grabbed her, screening out every other person in the room. "I love you, and the worst thing I've ever done is hurt you. I hate that you spent even one minute thinking I didn't want you, that you aren't perfect, that I don't support you in everything you want to do in life." He looked down at his black dress shoes. Then, taking in a breath, his gaze swung back to her. "I was no different from your parents, cutting you off because you didn't do what I wanted."

"Oh, no. No, no, no. Your motivations were totally different. It's not the same thing."

"The end result is. Phinny, you don't have to choose

between me and your dreams. You don't have to live where I live. If you love doing the auction, then we'll have homes in London and Calamity. The last three weeks have been the worst in my life, and I never want to live without you again. I want to support your dreams. I want to be by your side for everything—"

She sealed his mouth with hers. Only a quick, hard kiss, because she felt so desperate, so overwhelmed, she knew she'd surely strip out of her clothes just to feel his warm, hard body pressed against hers. "I missed you." All those sleepless nights, the ache deep in her bones... "I thought I would die without you."

"You never have to be without me." His voice sounded savage. "I want to be good for you. I want to be the best thing that ever happened to you." With a finger, he tipped her chin, and their mouths met, starved for each other, desperate to close the cold, barren gap between them.

A man cleared his voice, and Declan slowed the kiss, cooled the ardor, until he gave her one last, sweet press of his lips.

A tuxedo coat went around her shoulders, and she gazed up at the tall, silver-haired fox standing beside them. Only then did she become aware of the airiness she'd felt on her behind. Recalling the rip, her eyelids fluttered closed. "Thank God I wore underpants."

With his arm around her in a possessive grip, Declan said, "Phinny, this is Wesley Cartwright. He's—"

"The United States Ambassador to the Court of St. James." Clearly impressed, her stepfather joined them. He shook the man's hand. "Andrew Crutchley, and my wife Lady Lucinda Crutchley."

Her mum stood beside him, glee in her eyes. "I'm delighted to see you again."

"I'm delighted to be here." The man spoke with an American accent. He smiled warmly at Phinny. "I couldn't be happier to meet you. You might not know this"—his gaze cut momentarily to her mother—"but I'm your godfather. Kurt and I met in college and played hockey together. Your father was like a brother to me, and I know he'd be happy that for some reason you've agreed to hang out with this young troublemaker. A man he entrusted his land and his hockey team with."

A framed photograph appeared in her mind's eye. "Oh, yes. I saw pictures of you in his house. Weren't you the best man in his wedding?"

"I was. And next time I'm in London, I'll be sure to visit you."

She gazed up at Declan. "Actually, I'm moving to the States."

His hand squeezed hers. "But what about your job here?"

She didn't want to discuss it in front of the ambassador, but Andrew stepped in and said, "The wonderful news is that my wife will be taking over Phinny's job at the foundation." He gave Phinny a warm smile. "So, she's free to go wherever will make her happy."

Her heart squeezed with affection. *Thank you, Drewsy. Thank you so much.*

Her mum maintained a perfectly believable smile. "I could never do as good a job as my daughter, but I will give it my all."

She took a step back. "Mum, Andrew, this is Declan. He's one of the hockey players Kurt mentored, and the love of my life."

Declan pumped her stepdad's hand. "Very glad to meet you." He nodded to her mum. "Mrs. Crutchley. I'm sorry for intruding on the gala, but I wanted to introduce you both to the ambassador."

"That's right," the tall, broad-shouldered man said. "I understand you supply linens to the Lumley Hotel chain?"

"We do." Andrew grew enlivened.

"Well, I don't know if your services extend to the United States, but I know of a high-end chain opening three hundred resorts next year in North America, and I don't believe they've secured contracts just yet." He clapped Declan on the shoulder. "But before we talk business, why don't we let these kids go? I'm sure Phinny and Declan have some catching up to do."

"We do. Mr. and Mrs. Crutchley, it was great to meet you. And thank you for letting me steal your daughter away." Declan tugged on her hand. "Let's get out of here." But as they took off, she winced, and he stopped. "What's wrong?"

"Nothing. It's just these shoes. It's no matter. Let's just go."

He led her right out the front door and down the steps.

"Oh, the ambassador's coat." She started to pull it off.

His big hands came to rest on her shoulders. "Trust me, he doesn't care about it. Besides, I think enough people got to see that fine peach of an ass for one night." When she winced again, he dashed off to the rental car waiting in front of the valet stand and pulled a pair of pink cowboy boots out of the backseat. Crouching before her, he peeled off each glittery high heel and replaced them with her nicely worn-in boots.

She was so in love with this man she could hardly contain it. "I can't believe you brought these." She took her heels from him and tossed them into the bushes. And then, she was back in his arms. "I don't understand any of this. How do you know an ambassador?"

"I had to make things right with you, and that meant a hell of a lot more than saying I'm sorry. Or that I love you, and I miss you, and I can't live without you."

"Oh, trust me. That would've done the trick."

He gave her a grin that melted her panties right off. "I want you to be happy, to live your dreams, and I figured the only way to do that is to be free of obligations. Which meant I had to find a way to help your family, so I talked to Harrison, and he introduced me to your godfather."

"Well, aren't you the overachiever? You nailed it. You've made my stepfather a very happy and financially-secure man." She tugged on his lapels. "And what do I get out of all of this?"

"You get anything your big heart desires."

"Anything?"

He stood there, so powerful and strong. Confident and real. "Anything."

She believed him. "Oh, where do I begin? Let's see." She ticked off her fingers. "I want to open a store in Calamity. I want to wear a costume in next year's Wild West Festival. Hm, what else…"

"Nothing comes to mind, huh?"

She went all sultry. "Well, there's one thing."

"Name it."

She looked into those hazel eyes and felt his love pouring into her, filling her soul all the way to bursting. "I want your kisses. Every day for the rest of my life. I want your arms wrapped around me all night, every night. I want to ride in the Jeep with you all over Teton County and watch sunrises and sunsets and everything in between, and I want…" She crooked a finger, and he leaned in close to her mouth. "I want to make love to you any time I want. Is there room in your life for all that?"

He smiled, eyes shining. "There's room for everything you are, and as long as I get to be by your side, I'll be a happy man. So, go after your dreams, golden girl, whatever that means, wherever that takes you."

"All roads lead to you, Declan Cadell. You're the love of my life. Now take me home, hockey boy."

Epilogue

PHINNY DIDN'T KNOW WHY DECLAN HAD ADDED another shoot-out to the schedule. It was nearly dusk, and the last shuttle of the day would be leaving in ten minutes, clearing out the last remaining visitors at the Wild West Festival. It seemed unnecessary, but she went along with it.

She was having a blast, so why not? "You ever try'n steal from me again, and I'll put a bullet right through your head." In her pink cowboy boots and a fringed vest, she aimed her toy gun at the group of three costumed actors.

And, honestly, Declan in chaps, a black Stetson, and a holster slung low around his hips was *hot.*

With his hands up, the youngest of the hockey kids Declan was mentoring said, "Yes, ma'am."

The other one had grown out a handlebar mustache for the occasion. "We're real sorry, ma'am."

And then Declan went totally off-script and darted over to Hank. He snatched the Stetson right off his head and hoisted it in the air, like he'd pulled off a hat trick.

"What'd I tell you?" Phinny knew she sounded

ridiculous trying to pull off a Texas gunslinger with her British accent, but she was having the time of her life. "Put the hat down, you thievin' hound."

"Come on, boys. Run." Leading the way, Declan made a run for it, and she pulled the trigger three times. *Bang bang bang.* The other two dropped to the ground and played dead. Declan, though…she didn't know what was up with him. He held his arms open wide and made a slow spin, drawing out his death in a way that had the small audience cracking up. He landed on his back, legs shaking, arms waggling.

She was laughing too hard to figure out why he wasn't dying like he was supposed to, so she made her way over and straddled his body, pointing the gun at him. "Don't make me keel you dead."

"Do it." Rearing up, he grabbed her wrist and pulled her down to her knees. "Put me out of my misery."

What in the world? "I'm tryin', but you jes won't die." She couldn't stop laughing.

"Can't. Not until you fulfill my last dying wish."

Oh, my God. He was being ridiculous. She glanced to the crowd, her gaze falling on her parents who watched with delight. "All right, cowboy. What's your last dying wish?"

"To win your heart."

This man. "You already done that." She stroked his cheek with the back of her hand. "Done a real good job of it, too."

"I need you to prove it." Giving her a devilish grin, he yanked her again, and she collapsed onto his chest. "Reach into my pocket, pretty lady."

"This is a family show, cowboy." But she obliged, pulling a hard, velvet box out of his jeans. A *ring* box. Her heart nearly exploded, and she jerked upright. "*Declan.*" Overcome, she got to her feet and bent over, covering her mouth with her hands. "Oh, my God. Oh, my God. Are you serious?" He gave her the panty-melting grin she'd never get enough of. "Oh, my *God.*"

In one smooth move, he got up and planted a knee in the dirt. "Seraphina Crutchley, I'm crazy in love with you. All I want is to wake up to your beautiful face, make babies with you, and be right by your side for every step of this beautiful journey we're on together. You make me happy. You make me whole. Please put me out of my misery and marry me."

"Yes, yes, yes. A thousand times yes." As she reached for him, he got up and kissed her. Then, he slid the stunning diamond and sapphire engagement ring on her finger. She threw herself into his arms, and he held her so tightly he lifted her off her feet. "I love you. I love you so much."

"Ew." The voice of Declan's hockey boy broke through their romantic haze. "That's gross."

The crowd broke out in laughter.

"You never said there'd be kissing." Disgusted, the boy got up, dusted off his jeans, and stomped off.

Laughing, Declan pulled her into his arms, tipping her chin. Turning his back on the lingering crowd, he said, "You gonna marry me?"

"Oh, yeah. I'm gonna marry you, and I'm never gonna let you go."

"Well, then, you're one lucky woman."

Deliriously happy, she arched a brow.

But he just grinned at her challenging expression. "Since I love nothing more than seeing you smile, I'm going to make sure I put one on your face every day for the rest of our lives."

"Oh, I like that. And since *I* love nothing more than lying in your arms, I'm never going to get out of…no, wait. That's not the same thing. We'll have to get out of bed *sometime.*"

He laughed. "Come on. Let's celebrate." As the last shuttle of the day pulled out, he led her to the barn.

"You know, I can think of way more romantic places for us to celebrate than a *farm building.*"

"There are many ways to celebrate, but you just keep those dirty thoughts on the back burner. We'll get to them later. For now…" He opened the door, and she realized she was completely wrong. The entire place was lit up with fairy lights draping from the walls, bouquets of flowers decorating café tables, and a buffet table loaded with baskets and platters of food.

He'd turned it into the *perfect* place for a celebration. "What have you done?"

He wrapped an arm around her, pulling her close where she always wanted to be. "Everyone wanted to celebrate with us."

"How did 'everyone' know?"

"Well, it started with me asking Glori for advice on rings. Then, I went to the jewelry store and ran into Rosie and Brodie…word spread, and they all wanted to be here for us."

She couldn't believe how many people had shown up. "Everyone's here." Her parents, Jaime, Leddy and Carl, Glori, the Bowie brothers and their wives and children… all the local artisans who sold their goods in her store. "The whole town." She fell into his warm, strong embrace. "I love you so much. I can't believe you did all this."

"Oh, honestly, you two are inseparable." Her mum tapped Declan's arm. "You might want to get your boys under control." Her gaze swept to the top floor of the barn where the hockey boys were tossing hay at each other, dust and sticks floating to the ground.

"Dammit." He kissed her cheek. "Be right back."

Once he left, her mum said, "Congratulations, my love. I don't think I've ever seen you as happy as you are here."

It had taken several months for her mum to be able to drop her own defenses and accept the damage she'd done. Only after a couple of heart-to-heart talks was Phinny able to begin the process of forgiving her.

And now that Andrew had a contract with an American hotel chain, her parents came to visit several times a year. Her mum had begun doing some interior design consulting. She was good at it, and the pro bono work she'd done for the chain had led to paying jobs. Her mum seemed well and truly satisfied in a way she never had before. It seemed finding your good work did that for a person.

"Did you help him with all this?" Phinny took in the people laughing and candle wicks flickering.

"He'd already done most of it. And I must say, I was quite impressed. I'd expected hockey stick chandeliers and puck garlands, but he apparently has better taste than I'd imagined." Her mum smiled to let her know she was teasing.

Knowing her parents and future husband got along meant the world to her.

"Darling, do you see the woman chatting at the table behind me? The one with the colorful scarf?"

Phinny looked. "Oh, yes, that's Waverly. I met her at the Reliquary Museum last year."

"Poor dear lost her husband at such a young age, and she's turned to baking. She even took a pastry course in Paris. She brought the most delectable desserts for the party. You must try one. And I think you should consider selling them in your store."

"Pastries?"

"Fresh, gourmet pastries. And we'll get you a coffee machine so you can make espressos and tea."

"I love that idea. I'll talk to her. Thanks, Mum."

"Let me make you a plate. They're divine."

As her mum headed to the buffet table, Phinny stood back and took it all in. It had taken some time to forgive her mum, but now that she had, they had a good relationship because it was authentic. *I'm authentic.* When she'd moved out here, she'd stopped dancing for her parents, and they'd had to meet her on her terms. They'd fallen in love with Calamity and the Gongshow Ranch.

And her fiancé.

She watched Declan join in the hay-throwing fight, her heart so full of love she thought it might burst. He caught her watching and mouthed, *I love you, golden girl.*

Her whole body went electric. *I love you more, hockey boy.*

Thank you for reading THE DEEPER I FALL! You're going to love LOVE ME LIKE YOU DO, the next book in the Calamity Falls series about the hottest hockey player in the NHL and the single mom of three little girls living in his house. This larger-than-life party boy never imagined he'd spend his nights learning how to braid hair on YouTube tutorials! You're going to swoon as you watch him find the family he's never had!

Do you subscribe to my newsletter? Get on that right now because I've got an EXCLUSIVE novella for my readers in 2022! You'll get 2 chapters a month of this super sexy, fun romance! #rockstarromance #whenyourcelebritycrushbecomesyourboyfriend #teenidol

Need more Calamity Falls, where the people are wild at heart?

KEEP ON LOVING YOU
WE BELONG TOGETHER
THE VERY THOUGHT OF YOU
JUST THE WAY YOU ARE
IT WAS ALWAYS YOU
CAN'T HELP FALING IN LOVE
COME AWAY WITH ME
WHOLE LOTTA LOVE
YOU'RE STILL THE ONE
THE DEEPER I FALL
LOVE ME LIKE YOU DO

Have you read the Rock Star Romance series? Come meet the sexy rockers of Blue Fire:

YOU REALLY GOT ME
I WANT YOU TO WANT ME
TAKE ME HOME TONIGHT
MORE THAN A FEELING

Look for LOVE ME LIKE YOU DO in September 2022! Grab a FREE copy of PLANES, TRAINS, AND HEAD OVER HEELS. And come hang out with me on Facebook, Twitter, Instagram, Goodreads, and Pinterest or in my private reader group.

Do you love second chance romances?
How about an elite athlete who's only ever loved one woman? Check out the first book in the Calamity Falls series, Keep On Loving You!

Excerpt of Keep On Loving You

HER SENSES FILLED WITH THE SCENT OF LAUNDRY detergent, Calliope Bell leaned against the washing machine as she read the comments from Traci Allen's Instagram page.

You rat bastard. There is no excuse. You hear me? None. I don't care if you miss the Pope's wedding, you don't abandon your girlfriend when she needs you. Fin Bowie, you suck!

Oh, my God, you left your girlfriend alone in a hospital in a foreign country??? How heartless can you be? You are the worst boyfriend, Fin Bowie!

He totally is. Fin Bowie's seriously the worst boyfriend ever. I can't even.

Ha! Fin Bowie = world's worst boyfriend!

#worldsworstboyfriend

Callie couldn't believe it. What had Fin *done*?

A bark of laughter jerked her attention out the mudroom window to the rehearsal dinner going on in her parent's backyard. The lowering sun glanced off silver bolo ties, gold bangles, and belt buckles. She should be out there with her brother and his bride, but these comments… so many women advancing on Fin with pitchforks in their hands.

As much as she wanted to revel in his just-rewards, she knew how horrifying this kind of attention would be to him. He wanted to be a known as a champion like his older brothers—not some social media celebrity.

Well, he'd brought it on himself. Since breaking up with her six years ago, he'd gone off the rails. At first, seeing him party with so many women had gutted her. Scooped out her heart and rendered her a puddle of goo. So, she'd blocked him. It had been the only way to get on with her life.

On some level, she'd understood. Until the breakup, he'd only ever been with her. Of course he'd go hog-wild with other women. He was a passionate, wild man.

Only this time he'd messed with the wrong woman.

Her thumb flicked the bottom of the screen, unleashing a whole new wave of comments.

Who leaves their girlfriend alone in a foreign country? Kick that dog to the curb, Traci. Sending you healing vibes. #worldsworstboyfriend

Something about this whole thing was off, though. As far as she could tell, Traci Allen, the famous snowboarder, had posted a screenshot of a text Fin had sent her. Callie scrolled back up to read it again.

Thanks for a great time. ☺ **Gotta jet. Talk soon**.

But Traci hadn't explained it. She'd just left an ambiguous comment.

When you're in the hospital and Fin Bowie sends you this.

Traci's whole life was documented on her Instagram page, so if she and Fin had been romantically involved, wouldn't there be pictures of him? Callie couldn't see a single one. And Traci had only mentioned his name once, when she'd talked about going on one of his backcountry trips.

So how had that one post turned Fin into the World's Worst Boyfriend?

Callie reread the initial responses. In the beginning, her fans had asked questions. When Traci hadn't responded, they'd begun to speculate. And those assumptions had turned into a story: Fin had dumped his girlfriend to catch a flight back to the States so he could go to his friend's wedding. Within a matter of hours, he'd begun trending.

And the hashtag was *everywhere*.

"Oh." Her mom tossed an armful of damp kitchen towels into the washing machine. "What're you doing in here?" She looked at the phone in Callie's hands. Hope enlivened her tired features. "The fellowship?"

A hot flush of shame had Callie pressing the phone to her stomach. Between finals and graduation, she hadn't been in touch with her family, so they didn't know her plans. "No, the interview isn't until August twenty-fifth."

"Oh." Her mom's expression turned curious. "So, is it about a job?"

"No." Because why else would she be holed up in the laundry room at her brother's rehearsal dinner when she was only in town for three days? "Actually, I've decided to just work part-time at the diner and the bar. Julian's parents invited me to hang out with them this summer so they can introduce me to the movers and shakers of the Manhattan art world. It would take me a decade to make the kind of connections they have."

"Makes sense." Pushing her long, gray-streaked hair off her face, her mom nodded to the phone. "So, what's got you so enthralled that you'd leave your handsome boyfriend alone with a bunch of strangers?"

The arrow hit right in the center of her conscience. Reflexively, she glanced out the window, searching for him. "Is he okay?" Since they'd only been dating six months, she hadn't brought him home yet. Julian didn't know a single person in Calamity Falls.

"Oh, come on. He's Prince Charming. Nothing but gracious and kind."

She wanted to be proud of her well-mannered boyfriend, but there was something slightly off in her mom's tone.

Her mom made a *gimme* motion with her fingers, and Callie turned the phone around.

One glance, and her mom got it. "Ah. How many comments are we up to now?"

Callie couldn't have been more grateful for a mom who never judged her. "Ten thousand."

Her mom's eyes widened. "Wow." She rested her hip against the dryer and folded her arms across her stomach. "I don't know. I'm having a hard time believing Fin could abandon his girlfriend in a foreign hospital."

Callie gaped at her mother. "Are you kidding me?"

"Oh, stop it. It's not the same thing. He's not seventeen anymore, and you weren't hospitalized."

"Mom, he bailed on me three hours before we were supposed to leave for the airport." *To be with his brother.* Just like he'd abandoned Traci for Ryder's wedding. Fin and Callie's brother might not be related by blood, but the bond went as deep.

Amazing how six years later the crap she'd buried could rise like steam and give her hot flashes. *I thought I was done with this.*

Her mom adjusted the belt of her peach-colored dress. "Does it make you feel better knowing it wasn't you? It's just who he is?"

"No." Nothing would ever make her feel better about how Fin had ended their relationship. The shock of it still moved inside her body, a live thing trapped and scrabbling against the walls. "Because you're right. Something's not right about it. Other than posting the screen shot, Traci's been off social media. Her fans are making assumptions."

"Then why are you so interested in reading the comments?"

"Because it's happening to *Fin.* That's pretty crazy, right? That my ex has turned into a meme?"

"Well, he's a Bowie. They're celebrities."

"Yeah, in the world of extreme sports." While trophies and awards motivated—*validated*—his brothers, Fin was a true artist. He trained and hit the slopes to push himself, his body, and to breach the limits of his capabilities. Being known as a scoundrel would strike at the very core of his identity. "He doesn't want this kind of attention."

Her mom's gaze flicked outside, clearly anxious to get back out there. "Oh, I don't know. A man with his own website can't be too worried about attention."

Fin probably only ran it to prove to his brothers he wasn't just playing around out there. That he was as serious an athlete as they were.

Like she knew anything about him anymore. She hadn't talked to him in six years.

But she'd have to talk to him today, wouldn't she? The minute she left this room, he'd come for her like a heat-seeking missile. Her skin crackled with anticipation.

"Come on, let's go." Her mom started for the door but hesitated when Callie didn't follow.

"I'll be right behind you. I just…" *You what?* She wasn't ready. "I need to take a quick look at my emails."

Her mom watched her for a moment before letting out a harsh breath. "He's the best man, Callie. You've had a lot of time to prepare for this."

"I'm not…" She didn't want her mom to see her as the drama queen teenager she'd once been. "Look, I haven't seen him in a long time. It's just…it's going to be uncomfortable."

"Isn't that why you brought your boyfriend with you?"

Normally, she loved that her mom pulled no punches. Tonight, though, a little pretending wouldn't hurt. "God, Mom." She stuttered out an uncomfortable laugh. "I wanted you guys to meet him." But her bluster collapsed under her mom's unrelenting stare. "I mean, obviously, on some level…" *Oh, just say it.* "Yes, okay? That's one of the reasons I brought him."

"There you go. Find your shield and stand behind him."

Oh, ouch. All at once she could see her mom's attitude was anything but casual. "Why are you angry at me? So, I need a few minutes to myself. It's not easy for me to be around him."

"Yes, Callie, I get that. We all get that. But it's been six years. And if you'd just talk to him, you wouldn't have to keep avoiding him." Her mom blew out a frustrated breath. "Don't you *want* to move on?"

The words stung. *Move on?* She'd done exactly that. With her undergrad and graduate degrees from NYU, she'd made her dream of living in New York City a reality. A few years from now, she'd—hopefully—become a museum curator.

She wanted to say, *Look at me.* There was none of the old Callie left. How could her mom not see that? "Are you kidding me? I have completely moved on. I'm a few months away from working at the MoCA. I have the best boyfriend in the world." Who couldn't be more different from Fin. "He and his parents have been wonderful to me. I love my life." And, frankly, it hurt that her mom couldn't see it.

"Yes, you've done a bang-up job of reinventing yourself. Congratulations. But I don't know how you think you can start a new relationship when you haven't closed out of the last one. You've got the degrees and clothes and bank account of an adult, so now act like one. Go out there and talk to Fin. Face the terrible decisions you both made so you can move on."

Frustration and anger got her blood pumping. "I'm not an adult because I won't talk to my ex-boyfriend? *There's nothing to talk about.* He made his decision, and I made mine not to put up with his crap anymore." It wasn't like her mom could relate. She'd married her high school sweetheart. "Mom, he's never going to change. This meme proves that. He's always going to put his brothers before anyone else." *Before me.* "Moving on means accepting Fin for who he is and not trying to change him. *That's closure.*"

"Then why are you hiding in the laundry room at your brother's rehearsal dinner?"

"Ellen?" The caterer leaned in. "We're about to pass out the champagne. You want to give the heads-up to anyone giving toasts?"

"Sure." Her mom nodded warmly, and then turned back to Callie. "Put your phone away and be here for your brother, okay?"

Callie ran her fingers over the heavy, jeweled bracelet Julian had given her for graduation. "Of course." Heart pounding, she followed her mom out the back door. As she crossed the scarred wooden deck, she dropped her phone into her clutch, accepting that her mom was right.

Callie had lost touch with her brother; she barely even knew his bride. She wanted to get to know her four-year-old nephew and spend time with her parents without the constant worry that Fin might show up. It was time to put the past to rest and just…be home.

Stepping off the deck, she thought of Julian's mother, the way she so fluidly and elegantly worked a room. *Yes. Be Mrs. Reyes.* She'd simply act like she was at an art gallery opening, and Fin was just someone in the room.

Well, someone she'd had sex with. A lot. In pretty raunchy ways. *Oh, Lord.*

Stop it.

Think about the meme. Because if Fin had bailed on Traci like that, then he hadn't changed. And that emboldened her. Because it meant he could never hurt her again.

She'd never give him the chance.

When she stepped onto the grass, she put her weight

on her toes to keep her sharp heels from sinking into the dirt. She scanned the yard. The moment her gaze landed on Julian, the pressure on her chest lifted.

Urbane, polished, and charming, her boyfriend stood out among the other guests in their Western-wear and more casual attire. In his custom-made Brioni suit and crisp, white dress shirt, his hair slicked back off his handsome face, Julian looked like a model for a watch ad.

Callie made a bee-line for him. Weaving through round tables covered in white linens, she noticed the pink and lavender flower centerpieces with flickering candles were the only nod to décor. But with the Grand Tetons as a backdrop, what else did they need? The striking sight never grew old, especially now when twilight cast purple and peach shadows over the starkly rugged peaks.

With a smile in place, she glided past familiar faces. A jolt of anxiety zinged through her when she saw a wall of muscle blocking her boyfriend. Two of Fin's brothers reached for champagne flutes on a wicker tray. *Crap*. The heel of her five-inch stiletto sank into the grass, breaking her stride. A cold sting of embarrassment shot through her, but she quickly corrected. Perspiration sprang out on her forehead. She stopped herself from patting it away so she didn't mess up her foundation.

Fortunately, they'd moved on by the time she got there, revealing Julian's companion.

Megan. Ugh. Obviously, she'd known her friend would be at the wedding. She just would've preferred if their first reunion in years didn't take place in front of her boyfriend. No one understood her better, though, so she had to hope her friend got why she'd fallen out of touch. "Megan. It's so good to see you."

But when she leaned in for a hug, her friend's arms remained at her sides. "Hey." She didn't even smile.

Heat raced up Callie's neck, enflaming her cheeks. Trying to cover for her embarrassment, she placed a hand on Julian's biceps and channeled his mother. "I see you've met Megan."

"Yes, I have." Julian gave a gracious nod to her old friend. "We've been chatting about her yoga studio."

"Well, it was nice to meet you." But Megan's flat tone said otherwise, and she turned to go.

Underneath the shock of her friend's blatant rejection ran the horrifying awareness that Callie had earned it.

How in the world had she assumed Megan would understand what she'd gone through when Callie had never told her? "Megan, I—"

Her friend stopped and turned to her with a challenging expression.

Did she really want to have this conversation in front of Julian? Later tonight, she'd pull her aside and they could talk. But for now…For now, Callie needed to keep it together. "It's great to see you. So, you teach yoga? Where?"

When Megan didn't immediately respond, Julian said, "Here. In Calamity."

"That's great." But she couldn't hide her surprise. Megan had always wanted to be in theater.

"I keep trying to get Calliope to use my yogi, but she refuses," Julian said.

Having grown up with obscene wealth, Julian had no understanding of her financial situation. Not only couldn't Callie afford yoga classes, but she wasn't about to sponge off her boyfriend. *Crashing at his place is bad enough.*

"*Calliope*?" Megan seemed surprised to hear Julian use her full name. No one did that.

"Yes." Julian beamed a proud smile and wrapped an arm around her, tucking her in against him. His expensive cologne overwhelmed the scents of sage and mountain air. "Calliope and I met in the graduate program at NYU." He gave her an adoring smile. "I fell in love with her the moment I saw her."

Gratitude flooded her. She loved his unwavering devotion. But she had to fix things with Megan, so she reached for her friend's forearm. "Hey, can we talk later? I'd love to catch up with you."

A server appeared, offering them a tray of flutes.

"Ah, perfect." Julian lifted two glasses and handed one to Megan and the other to Callie. He took a third one for himself before thanking the server. "I'm so pleased to meet Calliope's friends and family. How long have you two known each other?"

"We met in elementary school." Callie hadn't told him anything about her past, so now wasn't the time to reveal that she'd had no real friends until Megan. An introvert, she'd kept mostly to herself. Well, until she and Fin had gotten together—and then the whole world had split open. "She was my closest friend."

Megan's attention roamed the crowd, barely acknowledging her.

She'd try another tactic. "Do you remember that time we—"

"What's with the hair, wild thing?" The all-too familiar voice cracked through her like a thunderclap.

It might have been a while since she'd heard it, but her body responded like a rosebud starved for sunlight. Every cell bloomed and strained in his direction.

Her stomach lurched, and she did *not* want to turn around. She didn't want to look at him. With fight or flight kicking in, it took every bit of strength she had not to run like he'd just tossed a lit match at her feet and set her on fire.

"Hey, Fin," Megan said.

Brushing Callie's arm as he reached across the small circle they made, Fin met Megan in the middle for a hug. His scent—that hint of sage and clean clothes, the essence of *Fin*—swirled around her, filling her senses and sending her crashing back in time. She had a matter of seconds to pull herself together and treat him like an acquaintance. Julian didn't know about him, so she needed to just be *normal*, but turbulence scrambled her system, and her mind went blank.

And that pissed her off. She'd prepared for this moment. Hell, she'd rehearsed it. But living it, having him right *here*, she just...*dammit*. No matter how many nights she'd lain awake scripting this interaction, she couldn't control her body's reaction.

Come on. She gave herself an internal shake. *He's just a guy.*

But when he pulled back, he turned his full attention on her and...*Oh, my God.*

For the first time in years, she looked Fin Bowie, in all his six feet two inches of rock-hard muscle, in the eyes. A tremble started from deep within, rising in velocity until her composure shook like a tree in a violent storm. The last time she'd seen him, he'd been a boy. A gorgeous, untamed, mischievous boy who'd kept her on edge for most of her life. His wild, free spirit made him impossible to nail down.

But the boy she'd loved so fiercely had nothing on the

man who stood before her. With his overgrown dark hair and bright blue eyes, he was a shock of rugged, raw power next to her lean, elegant boyfriend.

Of course he'd worn jeans to a rehearsal dinner, the white button down shirt the only nod to the dressy occasion. Not like Julian's pressed shirt, though. No, Fin's looked like he'd swiped it off a pile of discarded clothes on the floor on his way out of the shower. He'd shoved the sleeves up to his elbows, exposing tanned, muscular forearms.

Julian would have carefully folded the cuff until it fell just below the elbow. And he would've spent a minute adjusting it in front of a mirror.

Fin didn't own a mirror.

"Fin." The way he tilted his head in confusion made her think she sounded more stuck-up than pleasant. *Snap out of it right now.* But she couldn't—not when he looked at her as if he could see straight through her make-up and fancy clothes, right down to the trembling heart of her.

He reached for a lock of her hair and tugged it. "You iron it?"

Julian, always well-mannered, stepped back to include the new addition in the conversation. "Her hair?"

Fin tugged it again. "It's brown."

"That's her natural color." Julian's smile remained fixed despite the crinkle on his brow. He reached out his hand. "Julian Reyes."

"Fin Bowie." Fin shifted his beer bottle to his other hand so they could shake, and Callie caught the moment Fin noticed the slight sheen on Julian's manicured fingernails.

Too quickly, Fin let go and turned his attention back to her. He didn't move closer, but somehow she felt crowded by him. The entire backyard and all its guests faded away until it was just the two of them. She could smell the mountain air on his skin. He was sun-warmed meadows and bracing snow-covered summits. He was tangled sheets and calloused hands. Bone-melting kisses and thrilling gropes in public places.

He was abject heartbreak.

"Liked it platinum." Fin's deep, rough voice sounded like it might crack from the heavy emotion it carried.

"Platinum?" Julian spluttered. "When have you ever colored your hair?"

"Are you serious?" Megan laughed. "How long have you known her?"

"Two years." Julian gave Callie an assessing look.

She squeezed his hand. *Later.* "We should probably find our seats."

"She used to dye it a new color every semester." Megan had a gleam in her eyes. "That was her thing."

"I would've liked to have seen that," Julian said.

Gracious words, but she knew better. She'd have been invisible to Julian back then. He thought people who wore gauges and piercings and dyed their hair pink were compensating for a lack of authentic creativity. They showed the world how funky they were because they lacked the guts to actually create something.

"Come on." Callie pulled on his arm. "It's time for toasts." She shot Fin a look. *Thanks for starting this.*

But instead of his usual challenging response, he just looked baffled.

"Actually, I'd love to know what she was like back then," Julian said.

"She was a total tomboy," Megan said. "She got into more trouble than—"

"I don't know what a *tomboy* is," Fin said. "But if you're trying to say Callie could run faster and stomp landings and kick our asses up to Dead Man's summit, then, yeah, she was a badass." He turned fully to Julian. "You're from the east coast. You grow up making snowmen?"

"I might have made one." Julian offered a guarded smile.

"Yeah, well, my brothers and I didn't make snow *men*. We made snow targets. We'd build a row of snow mounds with holes in the middle. Big hole for the first one, smaller hole for each one down the line, until the last one had a hole the size of a small skillet. We've got pretty good aim, but this one?" He tipped his chin toward Callie. "She was the only one of us that got a snowball through the smallest one."

The tinkle of silver tapping glass cut the hum of conversation. Everyone turned to the head table where her brother stood. "Could you all please take your seats? We're about to start the toasts."

The crowd around them started moving, but Fin's compelling gaze kept them rooted. "Tomboy?" He shrugged. "I only know that Callie was confident, strong. Fearless. Everything a woman should be."

Her heart clenched painfully that he'd come to her defense like that, but it only took a moment to see that he wasn't defending her at all. His gaze held no warmth.

He was just telling the truth. *That's how he sees me.*

Pressure weighed on her chest—loss, regret, frustration, and pain. So much pain.

Megan gave Fin a challenging look. "Oh, cut it out. You know exactly what I mean. It's not an insult. It's who she was. She didn't care about make-up or clothes. She didn't even brush her hair half the time."

A slow, delicious smile kicked up the corner of Fin's mouth. "Wild thing."

Jesus. Julian knew nothing about her past. He didn't need to hear her old nickname or see the way Fin looked at her—like they'd just stumbled out of a closet with their hair mussed and her panties balled up in his pocket.

"I'm going to find our seats." Callie got one step away when she heard Fin say, "Know how I became an extreme athlete?"

"I didn't know you were an athlete, but I'd like to hear the story," Julian said.

"*Fin.*" Callie gestured to the table where her brother stood waiting for the guests to settle. "Aren't you making a toast?"

"This won't take long." He turned back to Julian. "We were snowboarding. Me and my brothers and Callie. Right there." He lifted his beer bottle to the Tetons. "We wound up on this spine we'd never been on before, and we were all just flying. Time of our lives. Well, this one"—he pointed the bottle toward Callie—"flew off the edge of a cliff. Jesus, it was like..." His thumb rubbed his lower lip. "I thought I'd lost her. No way could anyone survive a fall like that. And it all happened so fast, it wasn't like we could do anything to save her. One minute we're tearing down the mountain, the next....she was gone. I wanted to jump off right after her, but Will, my brother, grabbed me." He gestured with both arms what a bear hug would look like from behind. "I stood there watching her sail— free falling—sure she was going to hit a rock and crumple into a broken heap. But you know what she did?"

She doubted anyone would notice the unease beneath

Julian's fixed smile. He listened with rapt attention, yet the undercurrent of *what the hell* pulsed through him. He looked like he'd blinked and opened his eyes to find himself surrounded by Oompa Loompas.

But whose fault was that? She hadn't told him any of this.

"What?" Julian's tone was bright, interested.

"She landed it. She fuckin' landed it. Never seen anything like it."

Callie remembered the moment vividly. She *had* been in freefall. The world had gone silent, a blur of colors: white, bright blue, green. A strange stillness had settled over her, her entire being on heightened alert. The earth had come up fast, mostly rock, but a patch of glistening white called to her and she'd leaned in that direction. She hadn't prayed or screamed or anything. Just remained perfectly still and focused.

And when she'd landed on deep, powdery snow, her bones rattling, her teeth clacking, she'd felt a heady sense of elation.

But the best moment came later when she'd come to a stop, heart flopping in her chest like a live fish on a dock. She'd looked up to see the stunned faces of all four Bowie brothers. At that point, the older ones had already made a name for themselves in snowboarding and skiing competitions in the state. They were big, brawny, fearless athletes. All of them had stood there gobsmacked.

But it was Fin's expression—the awe, the pride—that stuck with her. She'd never doubted Fin's love. He'd always been hers. But in that moment, he'd given her something else: a profound sense of confidence.

"And on that note," Megan said. "I'm going to sit down." She took off through the crowd.

The moment she left, Julian said, "So, piecing things together here, you two dated?"

"Ah, I wouldn't call it *dating*." Fin's tone conjured tangled sheets and sweaty bodies, deep, sensuous kisses, and fists full of hair.

The shock of it had Julian's eyes going wide.

Oh, dammit all to hell. Heat spread through her limbs, and perspiration prickled under her arms. *What have you done?*

She was an idiot not to have filled him in on her past. But, honestly, while they'd known each other for two years, they'd only been dating six months. As friends, they'd talked about their classes, dinner plans, and gallery openings. So, when they'd started going out, they'd been long past those getting-to-know-you conversations.

Thinking back, though, she realized he'd never asked. He'd known she was from Wyoming, had briefly and occasionally chatted with her parents on FaceTime, but he'd never asked about her exes or old friends or anything. He'd never wondered what she'd been like before he'd met her.

After the party, she'd answer all his questions. "Fin and I dated in high school."

Julian gave a broad smile. "And, more importantly, you *snowboard*?"

A couple of times over the years, he'd invited her on ski trips with his family, but she'd always declined. Even if she could afford to ski in Aspen, she couldn't give up a week's pay to go on vacation. "Well, we live in the mountains. Everyone here does."

Okay, enough chitchat. She'd embarrassed Julian, and she had to make it right. Grabbing her boyfriend's hand, she forced a tight smile. "It was wonderful catching up with you." Before turning away, though, she caught the disappointment in Fin's eyes.

Wow, this was not going how she'd expected at all. She'd pictured giving Fin a cocky eat-your-heart-out smile when he saw how well she'd turned out. She'd never imagined he'd look at her like *that*. She led Julian to their table, unused to his body being so stiff and unyielding.

With a hand holding his suitcoat closed, he leaned across the table and shook hands with their tablemates. Then, he held a chair out for her. Tucking in close, he said, "I would've appreciated a little warning."

"I know. I'm sorry."

"Callie, sweetheart." A stout woman approached with her arms open wide.

Callie popped back up and leaned into her aunt's embrace. "Hi, Aunt Muriel."

She smelled of cough drops and bacon from the canapés. "It's been too long. How's my favorite girl?"

Her uncle pried her loose and hugged her so hard her feet lifted off the grass. Her heel slipped out of her shoe, so when he set her back down she had to reach for Julian's arm to steady herself.

"I didn't recognize you." The elderly man clamped his big paws on her shoulders. "Your aunt said, Oh, there's our Callie, and I said, Where?" He gave a hearty laugh and then turned his attention to Julian. "Isn't she a stunner? She used to—"

Oh, God, no. No more stories. "Uncle John, Aunt Muriel, I'd like you to meet my boyfriend, Julian Reyes. Julian, this is my Aunt Muriel and Uncle John."

Her handsome, polished boyfriend gave her uncle a firm handshake. "Wonderful to meet you. I'm so pleased to finally meet Calliope's family."

"We're so proud of her," Aunt Muriel said. "*Two* college degrees. And just look at her. Sweetheart, you take my breath away. I can see that New York City's everything you wanted it to be." She pressed hand over her heart. "We've missed you so much. I'm sorry we didn't make it for your graduation."

"Oh, no, don't worry. It's not the same thing for graduate school."

"How's the job hunt, angel?" Her aunt looked concerned.

She'd mentioned the competitive job market when she'd come home over Christmas, but she'd failed to fill her family in when she'd settled on a plan, and that made her feel pretty lousy. "I'm starting with a fellowship, actually. In the art world, it's the best way to get the job I'm looking for. Julian and I have both applied to the Museum of Contemporary Art." With his parents on the board, the fellowship was a sure-thing. She gave Julian a conspiratorial look, but he kept his smile fixed on her relatives.

Whoa. She'd really hurt him.

"Did you apply to any fellowships out West?" her aunt asked.

Before she could answer her uncle jumped in. "Can't remember a time our Callie didn't talk about moving to New York City and being an artist."

Her aunt let out a *Ha!* "*I* can't remember a time she didn't race in twenty minutes late, her jeans filthy, her hair wind-blown, and out of breath from whatever mischief she'd just gotten into."

"Mischief, huh?" Resentment edged into Julian's tone.

"Oh, this girl." Her uncle smiled with pure delight. "She's always been a handful."

"She and those Bowies." Laughing, Aunt Muriel shook her head. "My goodness, they were rabble-rousers. But look at her now. I hardly recognize her." She smoothed a hand down Callie's stick-straight hair. "You look gorgeous, honey."

A tingle at the back of her neck had her glancing over to the head table. With his gaze on her, Fin lifted his champagne flute.

"We should take our seats." Aunt Muriel gave her a big smile. "We'll catch up later."

Fin didn't have to say a word for the guests to quiet down. All eyes on him, he pointed to a table on the far left. "Lloyd, I speak for the entire wedding party when I say thank you for grooming."

Laughter rippled across the lawn, and a man shouted, "Naomi gave him a cut and a shave this morning. I sent a picture into the Calamity Falls Press."

After the laughter died down, Fin's finger shifted to somewhere in the middle of the lawn. "Miss Sandy, I owe you one. If you hadn't sent me home from school that day in third grade, I might've wound up looking just like Lloyd. Or a Yeti. So, thank you."

Callie found it hard to join the laughter at that one. Fin's dad only had five rules for his boys, and the first was that they couldn't leave anyone behind. But his older brothers didn't want to be held back by their youngest sibling, so they'd sneak out in the morning or while he napped or did homework.

And it drove Fin *wild*. So, he'd set his alarm to wake up early and wait for the sound of their footsteps in the hallway. That meant most mornings in grade school he'd shown up in whatever filthy clothes he'd worn the day before. Until Miss Sandy had sent him home to get cleaned up, forcing their dad to do something about it.

"All right." Fin's tone quelled the chatter. "Let's get these toasts done so we can dig into the wonderful meal provided by the Bell family."

The guests clapped, and someone called, "Woo hoo." Her brother had his arm stretched along the back of his bride's chair. Everyone watched Fin, but when he didn't immediately speak, a strange tension gripped the crowd. Either he hadn't prepared anything, or he'd forgotten what he wanted to say because he looked down at his place setting and tugged on his scruff.

Until he looked abruptly at her, and awareness flashed across her skin.

Something in his expression told her he was about to blow her world wide open.

About the Author

Award-winning author Erika Kelly writes sexy and emotional small town romance. Married to the love of her life and raising four children, she lives in the southwest, drinks a lot of tea, and is always waiting for her cats to get off her keyboard.

https://www.erikakellybooks.com/

Printed in Great Britain
by Amazon

17075160R00246